Unanimo

TERRY P

"There is no end to the wacky wonders . . .
no fantasies as consistently, inventively
mad . . . wild and wonderful!"
Isaac Asimov's Science Fiction Magazine

"Simply the best humorous writer
of the twentieth century."
Oxford Times

"Pratchett's Monty Python-like plots are
almost impossible to describe. His talent for
characterization and dialogue and his
pop-culture allusions steal the show."
Chicago Tribune

"Trying to summarize the plot of a Pratchett
novel is like describing *Hamlet* as a play
about a troubled guy with an Oedipus complex
and a murderous uncle."
Barbara Mertz

"Pratchett has now moved beyond the limits
of humorous fantasy, and should be recognized
as one of the more significant contemporary
English language satirists."
Publishers Weekly

"Think J.R.R. Tolkien with a sharper,
more satiric edge."
Houston Chronicle

"Discworld takes the classic fantasy universe
through its logical, and comic, evolution."
Cleveland Plain Dealer

By Terry Pratchett

The Dark Side of the Sun
Strata
Good Omens (with Neil Gaiman)
The Long Earth (with Stephen Baxter)
The Long War (with Stephen Baxter)

For Young Adults
The Carpet People
The Bromeliad Trilogy: *Truckers • Diggers • Wings*
The Johnny Maxwell Trilogy: *Only You Can Save Mankind*
Johnny and the Dead • Johnny and the Bomb
The Unadulterated Cat (illustrated by Gray Jollife)
Nation

The Discworld® Books
The Color of Magic • The Light Fantastic • Equal Rites
Mort • Sourcery • Wyrd Sisters • Pyramids
Guards! Guards! • Eric (with Josh Kirby) *• Moving Pictures*
Reaper Man • Witches Abroad • Small Gods
Lords and Ladies • Men at Arms • Soul Music • Feet of Clay
Interesting Times • Maskerade • Hogfather • Jingo
The Last Continent • Carpe Jugulum
The Fifth Elephant • The Truth • Thief of Time
Night Watch • Monstrous Regiment • Going Postal
Thud! • Where's My Cow? (illustrated by Melvyn Grant)
Making Money • Unseen Academicals • Snuff

The Last Hero (illustrated by Paul Kidby)
The Art of Discworld (illustrated by Paul Kidby)
The Streets of Ankh-Morpork (with Stephen Briggs)
The Discworld Companion (with Stephen Briggs)
The Discworld Mapp (with Stephen Briggs)
The Wit and Wisdom of Discworld (with Stephen Briggs)
The Discworld Graphic Novels:
The Color of Magic • The Light Fantastic

For Young Adults
The Amazing Maurice and His Educated Rodents
The Wee Free Men • A Hat Full of Sky
Wintersmith • I Shall Wear Midnight
The Illustrated Wee Free Men (illustrated by Stephen Player)

ATTENTION: ORGANIZATIONS AND CORPORATIONS
HarperCollins books may be purchased for educational, business,
or sales promotional use. For information, please e-mail the Special
Markets Department at SPsales@harpercollins.com.

Terry Pratchett

Maskerade

A Novel of Discworld®

HARPER

An Imprint of HarperCollinsPublishers

This is a work of fiction. Names, characters, places, and incidents are products of the author's imagination or are used fictitiously and are not to be construed as real. Any resemblance to actual events, locales, organizations, or persons, living or dead, is entirely coincidental.

HARPER

An Imprint of HarperCollins*Publishers*
10 East 53rd Street
New York, New York 10022-5299

Copyright © 1995 by Terry and Lyn Pratchett
Terry Pratchett® and Discworld® are registered trademarks.
ISBN 978-0-06-227552-3

All rights reserved. No part of this book may be used or reproduced in any manner whatsoever without written permission, except in the case of brief quotations embodied in critical articles and reviews. For information address Harper paperbacks, an Imprint of HarperCollins Publishers.

First Harper premium printing: February 2014
First HarperTorch mass market printing: August 2000
First HarperCollins mass market printing: November 1998
First HarperCollins hardcover printing: October 1997

HarperCollins ® and Harper ® are registered trademarks of Harper-Collins Publishers.

Printed in the United States of America

Visit Harper paperbacks on the World Wide Web at
www.harpercollins.com

10 9 8 7 6

If you purchased this book without a cover, you should be aware that this book is stolen property. It was reported as "unsold and destroyed" to the publisher, and neither the author nor the publisher has received any payment for this "stripped book."

*My thanks to the people who showed me
that opera was stranger than I could imagine.
I can best repay their kindness
by not mentioning their names here.*

The wind howled. The storm crackled on the mountains. Lightning prodded the crags like an old man trying to get an elusive blackberry pip out of his false teeth.

Among the hissing furze bushes a fire blazed, the flames driven this way and that by the gusts.

An eldritch voice shrieked: "When shall we . . . two . . . meet again?"

Thunder rolled.

A rather more ordinary voice said: "What'd you go and shout that for? You made me drop my toast in the fire."

Nanny Ogg sat down again.

"Sorry, Esme. I was just doing it for . . . you know . . . old time's sake . . . Doesn't roll off the tongue, though."

"I'd just got it nice and brown, too."

"Sorry."

"Anyway, you didn't have to shout."

"Sorry."

"I mean, I ain't deaf. You could've just asked me in a normal voice. And I'd have said, 'Next Wednesday.'"

"Sorry, Esme."

1

"Just you cut me another slice."

Nanny Ogg nodded, and turned her head. "Magrat, cut Granny ano . . . oh. Mind wandering there for a minute. I'll do it myself, shall I?"

"Hah!" said Granny Weatherwax, staring into the fire.

There was no sound for a while but the roar of the wind and the sound of Nanny Ogg cutting bread, which she did with about as much efficiency as a man trying to chainsaw a mattress.

"I thought it'd cheer you up, coming up here," she said after a while.

"Really." It wasn't a question.

"Take you out of yourself, sort of thing . . ." Nanny went on, watching her friend carefully.

"Mm?" said Granny, still staring moodily at the fire.

Oh dear, thought Nanny. I shouldn't've said *that*.

The point was . . . well, the point was that Nanny Ogg was worried. Very worried. She wasn't at all sure that her friend wasn't . . . well . . . going . . . well, sort of . . . in a manner of speaking . . . well . . . black . . .

She knew it happened, with the really powerful ones. And Granny Weatherwax was pretty damn powerful. She was probably an even more accomplished witch now than the infamous Black Aliss, and everyone knew what had happened to *her* at the finish. Pushed into her own stove by a couple of kids, and everyone said it was a damn good thing, even if it took a whole week to clean the oven.

But Aliss, up until that terrible day, had terrorized the Ramtops. She'd become so good at magic that there wasn't room in her head for anything else.

They said weapons couldn't pierce her. Swords bounced off her skin. They said you could hear her mad laughter a mile off, and of course, while mad laughter was always part of a witch's stock-in-trade in necessary circumstances, this was *insane* mad laughter, the worst kind. And she turned people into gingerbread and had a house made of frogs. It had been very nasty, toward the end. It always was, when a witch went bad.

Sometimes, of course, they didn't go bad. They just went . . . somewhere.

Granny's intellect needed something to *do*. She did not take kindly to boredom. She'd take to her bed instead and send her mind out Borrowing, inside the head of some forest creature, listening with its ears, seeing with its eyes. That was all very well for general purposes, but she was too good at it. She could stay away longer than anyone Nanny Ogg had ever heard of.

One day, almost certainly, she wouldn't bother to come back . . . and this was the worst time of the year, with the geese honking and rushing across the sky every night, and the autumn air crisp and inviting. There was something terribly tempting about that.

Nanny Ogg reckoned she knew what the cause of the problem was.

She coughed.

"Saw Magrat the other day," she ventured, looking sidelong at Granny.

There was no reaction.

"She's looking well. Queening suits her."

"Hmm?"

Nanny groaned inwardly. If Granny couldn't even

be bothered to make a nasty remark, then she was *really* missing Magrat.

Nanny Ogg had never believed it at the start, but Magrat Garlick, wet as a sponge though she was half the time, had been dead right about one thing.

Three was a natural number for witches.

And they'd lost one. Well, not lost, exactly. Magrat was queen now, and queens were hard to mislay. But . . . that meant that there were only two of them instead of three.

When you had three, you had one to run around getting people to make up when there'd been a row. Magrat had been good for that. Without Magrat, Nanny Ogg and Granny Weatherwax got on one another's nerves. With her, all three had been able to get on the nerves of absolutely everyone else in the whole world, which had been a lot more fun.

And there was no having Magrat back . . . at least, to be precise about it, there was no having Magrat back *yet*.

Because, while three was a good number for witches . . . it had to be the *right* sort of three. The right sort of . . . *types*.

Nanny Ogg found herself embarrassed even to think about this, and this was unusual because embarrassment normally came as naturally to Nanny as altruism comes to a cat.

As a witch, she naturally didn't believe in any occult nonsense of any sort. But there were one or two truths down below the bedrock of the soul which had to be faced, and right in among them was this business of, well, of the maiden, the mother and the . . . other one.

There. She'd put words around it.

Of course, it was nothing but an old superstition and belonged to the unenlightened days when "maiden" or "mother" or . . . the other one . . . encompassed every woman over the age of twelve or so, except maybe for nine months of her life. These days, any girl bright enough to count and sensible enough to take Nanny's advice could put off being at least one of them for quite some time.

Even so . . . it was an *old* superstition—older than books, older than writing—and beliefs like that were heavy weights on the rubber sheet of human experience, tending to pull people into their orbit.

And Magrat had been married for three months. That ought to mean she was out of the first category. At least—Nanny twitched her train of thought on to a branch line—she *probably* was. Oh, *surely.* Young Verence had sent off for a helpful manual. It had pictures in it, and numbered parts. Nanny knew this because she had sneaked into the royal bedroom while visiting one day, and had spent an instructive ten minutes drawing mustaches and spectacles on some of the figures. Surely even Magrat and Verence could hardly fail to . . . No, they must have worked it out, even though Nanny had heard that Verence had been seen inquiring of people where he might buy a couple of false mustaches. It'd not be long before Magrat was eligible for the second category, even if they were both slow readers.

Of course, Granny Weatherwax made a great play of her independence and self-reliance. But the point about that kind of stuff was that you needed someone around to be proudly independent and self-reliant *at*. People who didn't need people needed people around to know that they were the kind of people who didn't need people.

It was like hermits. There was no point freezing your nadgers off on top of some mountain while communing with the Infinite unless you could rely on a lot of impressionable young women to come along occasionally and say "Gosh."

They needed to be three again. Things got exciting, when there were three of you. There were rows, and adventures, and things for Granny to get angry about, and she was only happy when she was angry. In fact, it seemed to Nanny, she was only Granny Weatherwax when she was angry.

Yes. They needed to be three.

Or else . . . it was going to be gray wings in the night, or the clang of the oven door . . .

The manuscript fell apart as soon as Mr. Goatberger picked it up.

It wasn't even on proper paper. It had been written on old sugar bags, and the backs of envelopes, and bits of out-of-date calendar.

He grunted, and grabbed a handful of the musty pages to throw them on the fire.

A word caught his eye.

He read it, and his eye was dragged to the end of the sentence.

Then he read to the end of the page, doubling back a few times because he hadn't quite believed what he'd just read.

He turned the page. And then he turned back.

And then he read on. At one point he took a ruler out of his drawer and looked at it thoughtfully.

He opened his drinks cabinet. The bottle tinkled cheerfully on the edge of the glass as he tried to pour himself a drink.

Then he stared out of the window at the Opera House on the other side of the road. A small figure was brushing the steps.

And then he said, "Oh, my."

Finally he went to the door and said, "Could you come in here, Mr. Cropper?"

His chief printer entered, clutching a sheaf of proofs. "We're going to have to get Mr. Cripslock to engrave page II again," he said mournfully. "He's spelled 'famine' with seven letters—"

"Read this," said Goatberger.

"I was just off to lunch—"

"Read this."

"Guild agreement says—"

"Read this and see if you still have an appetite."

Mr. Cropper sat down with bad grace and glanced at the first page.

Then he turned to the second page.

After a while he opened the desk drawer and pulled out a ruler, which he looked at thoughtfully.

"You've just read about Bananana Soup Surprise?" said Goatberger.

"Yes!"

"You wait till you get to Spotted Dick."

"Well, my old granny used to make Spotted Dick—"

"Not to this recipe," said Goatberger, with absolute certainty.

Cropper fumbled through the pages. "Blimey! Do you think any of this stuff works?"

"Who cares? Go down to the Guild right now and hire all the engravers that're free. Preferably elderly ones."

"But I've still got the Grune, June, August and Spune predictions for next year's Almanac to—"

"Forget them. Use some old ones."

"People'll notice."

"They've never noticed before," said Mr. Goatberger. "You know the drill. Astounding Rains of Curry in Klatch, Amazing Death of the Seriph of Ee, Plague of Wasps in Howondaland. This is a lot more important."

He stared unseeing out of the window again.

"*Considerably* more important."

And he dreamed the dream of all those who publish books, which was to have so much gold in your pockets that you would have to employ two people just to hold your trousers up.

The huge, be-columned, gargoyle-haunted face of Ankh-Morpork's Opera House was there, in front of Agnes Nitt.

She stopped. At least, *most* of Agnes stopped. There was a lot of Agnes. It took some time for outlying regions to come to rest.

Well, this was it. At last. She could go in, or she could go away. It was what they called a life choice. She'd never had one of those before.

Finally, after standing still for long enough for a pigeon to consider the perching possibilities of her huge and rather sad black floppy hat, she climbed the steps.

A man was theoretically sweeping them. What he was in *fact* doing was moving the dirt around with a broom, to give it a change of scenery and a chance to make new friends. He was dressed in a long coat that was slightly too small for him, and had a black beret perched incongruously on spiky black hair.

"Excuse me," said Agnes.

The effect was electric. He turned around, tangled one foot with the other, and collapsed onto his broom.

Agnes's hand flew to her mouth, and then she reached down.

"Oh, I'm so sorry!"

The hand had that clammy feel that makes a holder think longingly of soap. He pulled it away quickly, pushed his greasy hair out of his eyes and gave her a terrified smile; he had what Nanny Ogg called an underdone face, its features rubbery and pale.

"No trouble miss!"

"Are you all right?"

He scrambled up, got the broom somehow tangled between his knees, and sat down again sharply.

"Er . . . shall I hold the broom?" said Agnes helpfully.

She pulled it out of the tangle. He got up again, after a couple of false starts.

"Do you work for the Opera House?" said Agnes.

"Yes miss!"

"Er, can you tell me where I have to go for the auditions?"

He looked around wildly. "Stage door!" he said. "I'll show you!" The words came out in a rush, as if he had to line them up and fire them all in one go before they had time to wander off.

He snatched the broom out of her hands and set off down the steps and toward the corner of the building. He had a unique stride: it looked as though his body were being dragged forward and his legs had to flail around underneath it, landing wherever they could find room. It wasn't so much a walk as a collapse, indefinitely postponed.

His erratic footsteps led toward a door in the side wall. Agnes followed them in.

Just inside was a sort of shed, with one open wall and a counter positioned so that someone standing there could watch the door. The person behind it must have been a human being because walruses don't wear coats. The strange man had disappeared somewhere in the gloom beyond.

Agnes looked around desperately.

"Yes, miss?" said the walrus man. It really was an *impressive* mustache, which had sapped all the growth from the rest of its owner.

"Er . . . I'm here for the . . . the auditions," said Agnes. "I saw a notice that said you were auditioning—"

She gave a helpless little smile. The doorkeeper's face proclaimed that it had seen and been unimpressed by more desperate smiles than even Agnes could have eaten hot dinners. He produced a clipboard and a stub of pencil.

"You got to sign here," he said.

"Who was that . . . person who came in with me?"

The mustache moved, suggesting a smile was buried somewhere below. "Everyone knows our Walter Plinge."

This seemed to be all the information that was likely to be imparted.

Agnes gripped the pencil.

The most important question was: what should she call herself? Her name had many sterling qualities, no doubt, but it didn't exactly roll off the tongue. It snapped off the palate and clicked between the teeth, but it didn't roll off the tongue.

The trouble was, she couldn't think of one with great rotational capabilities.

Catherine, possibly.

Or . . . Perdita. She could go back to trying Perdita. She'd been embarrassed out of using that name in Lancre. It was a mysterious name, hinting of darkness and intrigue and, incidentally, of someone who was quite thin. She'd even given herself a middle initial—X—which stood for "someone who has a cool and exciting middle initial."

It hadn't worked. Lancre people were depressingly resistant to cool. She had just been known as "that Agnes who calls herself Perditax."

She'd never *dared* tell anyone that she'd like her *full* name to be Perdita X Dream. They just wouldn't *understand*. They'd say things like: if you think that's the right name for you, why have you still got two shelves full of soft toys?

Well, here she could start afresh. She was good. She knew she was good.

Probably no hope for the Dream, though.

She was probably stuck with the Nitt.

* * *

Nanny Ogg usually went to bed early. After all, she was an old lady. Sometimes she went to bed as early as six A.M.

Her breath puffed in the air as she walked through the woods. Her boots crunched on the leaves. The wind had died away, leaving the sky wide and clear and open for the first frost of the season, a petal-nipping, fruit-withering little scorcher that showed you why they called Nature a mother . . .

A third witch, she thought.

Three witches could sort of . . . spread the load.

Maiden, mother and . . . crone. There.

The trouble was that Granny Weatherwax combined all three in one. She was a maiden, as far as Nanny knew, and she was at least in the right age-bracket for a crone; and, as for the third, well . . . cross Granny Weatherwax on a bad day and you'd be like a blossom in the frost.

There was bound to be a candidate for the vacancy, though. There were several young girls in Lancre who were just about the right age.

Trouble was, the young men of Lancre knew it too. Nanny wandered the summer hayfields regularly, and had a sharp if compassionate eye and damn good over-the-horizon hearing. Violet Frottidge was walking out with young Deviousness Carter, or at least doing something within ninety degrees of walking out. Bonnie Quarney had been gathering nuts in May with William Simple, and it was only because she'd thought ahead and taken a little advice from Nanny that she wouldn't be bearing fruit in February. And pretty soon now young Mildred

Tinker's mother would have a quiet word with Mildred Tinker's father, and *he'd* have a word with his friend Thatcher and *he'd* have a word with his son Hob, and then there'd be a wedding, all done in a properly civilized way except for maybe a black eye or two.* No doubt about it, thought Nanny with a misty-eyed smile: innocence, in a hot Lancre summer, was that state in which innocence is lost.

And then a name rose out of the throng. Oh, yes. *Her.* Why hadn't she thought of *her?* But you didn't, of course. Whenever you thought about the young girls of Lancre, you didn't remember her. And then you said, "Oh, yes, her too, of course. O' course, she's got a wonderful personality. And good hair, of course."

She was bright, and talented. In many ways. Her voice, for one thing. That was her power, finding its way out. And of course she also had a wonderful personality, so there'd be not much chance of her being . . . disqualified . . .

Well, that was settled, then. Another witch to bully and impress would set Granny up a treat, and Agnes would be bound to thank her eventually.

Nanny Ogg was relieved. You needed at least three witches for a coven. Two witches was just an argument.

She opened the door of her cottage and climbed the stairs to bed.

Her cat, the tom Greebo, was spread out on the eiderdown like a puddle of gray fur. He didn't even

---

*The people of Lancre thought that marriage was a very serious step that ought to be done properly, so they practiced quite a lot.

awake as Nanny lifted him up bodily so that, nightdress-clad, she could slide between the sheets.

Just to keep bad dreams at bay, she took a swig out of a bottle that smelled of apples and happy brain-death. Then she pummeled her pillow, thought "Her . . . yes," and drifted off to sleep.

Presently Greebo awoke, stretched, yawned and hopped silently to the floor. Then the most vicious and cunning a pile of fur that ever had the intelligence to sit on a bird table with its mouth open and a piece of toast balanced on its nose vanished through the open window.

A few minutes later, the cockerel in the garden next door stuck up his head to greet the bright new day and died instantly in mid- "doodle-doo."

There was a huge darkness in front of Agnes while, at the same time, she was half-blinded by the light. Just below the edge of the stage, giant flat candles floated in a long trough of water, producing a strong yellow glare quite unlike the oil lamps of home. Beyond the light, the auditorium waited like the mouth of a very big and extremely hungry animal.

From somewhere on the far side of the lights a voice said, "When you're ready, miss."

It wasn't a particularly unfriendly voice. It just wanted her to get on with it, sing her piece, and go.

"I've, er, got this song, it's a—"

"You've given your music to Miss Proudlet?"

"Er, there isn't an accompaniment actually, it—"

"Oh, it's a *folk* song, is it?"

There was a whispering in the darkness, and some-one laughed quietly.

"Off you go then . . . Perdita, right?"

Agnes launched into the Hedgehog Song, and knew by about word seven that it had been the wrong choice. You needed a tavern, with people leering and thumping their mugs on the table. This big brilliant emptiness just sucked at it and made her voice hesitant and shrill.

She stopped at the end of verse three. She could feel the blush starting somewhere around her knees. It'd take some time to get to her face, because it had a lot of skin to cover, but by then it'd be strawberry pink.

She could hear whispering. Words like "timbre" emerged from the susurration and then, she wasn't surprised to hear, came "impressive build." She did, she knew, have an impressive build. So did the Opera House. She didn't have to feel good about it.

The voice spoke up.

"You haven't had much training, have you, dear?"

"No." Which was true. Lancre's only other singer of note was Nanny Ogg, whose attitude to songs was purely ballistic. You just pointed your voice at the end of the verse and went for it.

Whisper, whisper.

"Sing us a few scales, dear."

The blush was at chest-height now, thundering across the rolling acres . . .

"Scales?"

Whisper. Muffled laugh.

"Do–Re–Mi? You know, dear? Starting low? La–la–lah?"

"Oh. Yes."

As the armies of embarrassment stormed her

neckline, Agnes pitched her voice as low as she could and went for it.

She concentrated on the notes, working her way stolidly upward from sea-level to mountaintop, and took no notice at the start when a chair vibrated across the stage or, at the end, when a glass broke somewhere and several bats fell out of the roof.

There was silence from the big emptiness, except for the thud of another bat and, far above, a gentle tinkle of glass.

"Is . . . is that your full range, lass?"

People were clustering in the wings and staring at her.

"No."

"No?"

"If I go any higher people faint," said Agnes. "And if I go lower everyone says it makes them feel uncomfortable."

Whisper, whisper. Whisper, *whisper*, whisper.

"And, er, any other—?"

"I can sing with myself in thirds. Nanny Ogg says not everyone can do that."

"Sorry?"

"Like . . . Do–Mi. At the same time."

Whisper, whisper.

"Show us, lass."

"♪♫ *Laaaaaa*♪ ♫"

The people at the side of the stage were talking excitedly.

Whisper, whisper.

The voice from the darkness said: "Now, your voice projection—"

"Oh, I can do *that*," snapped Agnes. She was getting rather fed up. "Where would you like it projected?"

"I'm sorry? We're talking about—"

Agnes ground her teeth. She *was* good. And she'd show them . . .

"To here?"

"Or there?"

"Or here?"

It wasn't that much of a trick, she thought. It could be very impressive if you put the words in the mouth of a nearby dummy, like some of the traveling showmen did, but you couldn't pitch it far away and still manage to fool a whole audience.

Now that she was accustomed to the gloom she could just make out people turning around in their seats, bewildered.

"What's your name again, dear?" The voice, which had at one point shown traces of condescension, had a distinct beaten-up sound.

"Ag— Per . . . Perdita," said Agnes. "Perdita Nitt. Perdita X . . . Nitt."

"We may have to do something about the Nitt, dear."

Granny Weatherwax's door opened by itself.

Jarge Weaver hesitated. Of course, she *were* a witch. People'd told him this sort of thing happened.

He didn't like it. But he didn't like his back, either, especially when his back didn't like him. It came to something when your vertebrae ganged up on you.

He eased himself forward, grimacing, balancing himself on two sticks.

The witch was sitting in a rocking chair, facing away from the door.

Jarge hesitated.

"Come on in, Jarge Weaver," said Granny Weatherwax, "and let me give you something for that back of yours."

The shock made him try to stand upright, and *this* made something white-hot explode somewhere in the region of his belt.

Granny Weatherwax rolled her eyes, and sighed. "Can you sit down?" she said.

"No, miss. I can fall over on a chair, though."

Granny produced a small black bottle from an apron pocket and shook it vigorously. Jarge's eyes widened.

"You got that all ready for me?" he said.

"Yes," said Granny truthfully. She'd long ago been resigned to the fact that people expected a bottle of something funny-colored and sticky. It wasn't the medicine that did the trick, though. It was, in a way, the spoon.

"This is a mixture of rare herbs and suchlike," she said. "Including sucrose and akwa."

"My word," said Jarge, impressed.

"Take a swig now."

He obeyed. It tasted faintly of licorice.

"You got to take another swig last thing at night," Granny went on. "An' then walk three times round a chestnut tree."

". . . three times round a chestnut tree . . ."

"An' . . . an' put a pine board under your mattress. Got to be pine from a twenty-year-old tree, mind."

". . . twenty-year-old tree . . ." said Jarge. He felt he should make a contribution. "So's the knots in me back end up in the pine?" he hazarded.

Granny was impressed. It was an outrageously ingenious bit of folk hokum worth remembering for another occasion.

"You got it exactly right," she said.

"And that's it?"

"You wanted more?"

"I . . . thought there were dancin' and chantin' and stuff."

"Did that before you got here," said Granny.

"My word. Yes. Er . . . about payin' . . ."

"Oh, I don't want payin'," said Granny. "'S bad luck, taking money."

"Oh. Right." Jarge brightened up.

"But maybe . . . if your wife's got any old clothes, p'raps; I'm a size twelve, black for preference, or bakes the odd cake, no plums, they gives me wind, or got a bit of old mead put by, could be, or p'raps you'll be killing a hog about now, best back's my favorite, maybe some ham, a few pig knuckles . . . anything you can spare, really. No obligation. I wouldn't go around puttin' anyone under obligation, just 'cos I'm a witch. Everyone all right in your house, are they? Blessed with good health, I hope?"

She watched this sink in.

"And now let me help you out of the door," she added.

Weaver was never quite certain about what happened next. Granny, usually so sure on her feet, seemed to trip over one of his sticks as she went through the door, and fell backward, holding his shoulders, and somehow her knee came up and hit a spot on his backbone as she twisted sideways, and there was a *click*—

"Aargh!"

"Sorry!"

"Me back! Me *back*!"

Still, Jarge reasoned later, she was an old woman. And she might be getting clumsy and she'd always been daft, but she made good potions. They worked damn fast, too. He was carrying his sticks by the time he got home.

Granny watched him go, shaking her head.

People were so *blind*, she reflected. They preferred to believe in gibberish rather than chiropracty.

Of course, it was just as well this was so. She'd much rather they went "oo" when she seemed to know who was approaching her cottage than work out that it conveniently overlooked a bend in the track, and as for the door latch and the trick with the length of black thread . . .*

But what had she done? She'd just tricked a rather dim old man.

She'd faced wizards, monsters and elves . . . and now she was feeling pleased with herself because she'd fooled Jarge Weaver, a man who'd twice failed to become Village Idiot through being overqualified.

It was the slippery slope. Next thing it'd be cack-

---

*Not that she sat looking out of the window. She'd been watching the fire when she picked up the approach of Jarge Weaver. But that wasn't the *point*.

ling and gibbering and luring children into the oven.
And it wasn't as if she even *liked* children.

For years Granny Weatherwax had been contented
enough with the challenge that village witchcraft
could offer. And then she'd been forced to go traveling, and she'd seen a bit of the world, and it had
made her itchy—especially at this time of the year,
when the geese were flying overhead and the first
frost had mugged innocent leaves in the deeper val-
leys.

She looked around at the kitchen. It needed sweeping. The washing-up needed doing. The walls had
grown grubby. There seemed to be so much to do
that she couldn't bring herself to do any of it.

There was a honking far above, and a ragged V of
geese sped over the clearing.

They were heading for warmer weather in places
Granny Weatherwax had only heard about.

It was tempting.

The selection committee sat around the table in
the office of Mr. Seldom Bucket, the Opera House's
new owner. He'd been joined by Salzella, the musical director, and Dr. Undershaft, the chorus master.

"And so," said Mr. Bucket, "we come to . . . let's
see . . . yes, Christine . . . Marvelous stage presence,
eh? Good figure, too." He winked at Dr. Undershaft.

"Yes. Very pretty," said Dr. Undershaft flatly.
"Can't sing, though."

"What you artistic types don't realize is this is
the Century of the Fruitbat," said Bucket. "Opera is
a production, not just a lot of songs."

"So you say. But . . ."

"The idea that a soprano should be fifteen acres of bosom in a horned helmet belongs to the past, like."

Salzella and Undershaft exchanged glances. So he was going to be *that* kind of owner . . .

"Unfortunately," said Salzella sourly, "the idea that a soprano should have a reasonable singing voice does not belong to the past. She has a good figure, yes. She certainly has a . . . sparkle. But she can't *sing*."

"You can train her, can't you?" said Bucket. "A few years in the chorus . . ."

"Yes, maybe after a few years, if I persevere, she will be merely very bad," said Undershaft.

"Er, gentlemen," said Mr. Bucket. "Ahem. All right. Cards on the table, eh? I'm a simple man, me. No beating about the bush, speak as you find, call a spade a spade—"

"Do give us your forthright views," said Salzella. *Definitely* that kind of owner, he thought. Self-made man proud of his handiwork. Confuses bluffness and honesty with merely being rude. I wouldn't mind betting a dollar that he thinks he can tell a man's character by testing the firmness of his handshake and looking deeply into his eyes.

"I've been through the mill, I have," Bucket began, "and I made myself what I am today—"

Self-raising flour? thought Salzella.

"—but I have to, er, declare a bit of a financial interest. Her dad did, er, in fact, er, lend me a fair whack of money to help me buy this place, and he made a heartfelt fatherly request in regard to his daughter. If I bring it to mind correctly, his exact words, er, were: 'Don't make me have to break your legs.' I don't expect you *artistes* to understand. It's a business thing. The gods help those who help themselves, that's my motto."

Salzella stuck his hands in his waistcoat pockets, leaned back and started to whistle softly.

"I *see*," said Undershaft. "Well, it's not the first time it's happened. Normally it's a ballerina, of course."

"Oh, it's nothing like *that*," said Bucket hurriedly. "It's just that with the money comes this girl Christine. And you have to admit, she does *look* good."

"Oh, very well," said Salzella. "It's your Opera House, I'm sure. And now . . . Perdita . . . ?"

They smiled at one another.

"Perdita!" said Bucket, relieved to get the Christine business over so that he could go back to being bluff and honest again.

"Perdita X," Salzella corrected him.

"What will these girls think of next?"

"I think she will prove an asset," said Undershaft.

"Yes, if we ever do that opera with the elephants."

"But the range . . . what a range she's got . . ."

"Quite. I saw you staring."

"I *meant* her *voice*, Salzella. She will add body to the chorus."

"She *is* a chorus. We could sack everyone else. Ye gods, she can even sing in harmony with herself. But can you see her in a major role?"

"Good grief, no. We'd be a laughingstock."

"Quite so. She seems quite . . . amenable, though."

"Wonderful personality, I thought. And good hair, of course."

* * *

She'd never expected it to be this easy . . .

Agnes listened in a kind of trance while people talked at her about wages (very little), the need for training (a lot), and accommodation (members of the chorus lived in the Opera House itself, up near the roof).

And then, more or less, she was forgotten about. She stood and watched at the side of the stage while a group of ballet hopefuls were put through their delicate paces.

"You do have an amazing voice," said someone behind her.

She turned. As Nanny Ogg had once remarked, it was an education seeing Agnes turn around. She was light enough on her feet but the inertia of outlying parts meant that bits of Agnes were still trying to work out which way to face for some time afterward.

The girl who had spoken to her was slightly built, even by ordinary standards, and had gone to some pains to make herself look even thinner. She had long blond hair and the happy smile of someone who is aware that she is thin and has long blond hair.

"My name's Christine!" she said. "Isn't this exciting?!"

And she had the type of voice that can exclaim a question. It seemed to have an excited little squeak permanently screwed to it.

"Er, yes," said Agnes.

"I've been waiting for this day for *years*!"

Agnes had been waiting for it for about twenty-four hours, ever since she'd seen the notice outside the Opera House. But she'd be danged if she'd say that.

"Where did you train?!" said Christine. "I spent three years with Mme. Venturi at the Quirm Conservatory!"

"Um. I was . . ." Agnes hesitated, trying out the upcoming sentence in her head. ". . . I trained with . . . Dame Ogg. But she hasn't got a conservatory, because it's hard to get the glass up the mountain."

Christine didn't appear to want to question this. Anything she found too difficult to understand, she ignored.

"The money in the chorus isn't very good, is it?!" she said.

"No." It was less than you'd get for scrubbing floors. The reason was that, when you advertised a dirty floor, hundreds of hopefuls didn't turn up.

"But it's what I've always wanted to do! Besides, there's the status!"

"Yes, I expect there is."

"I've been to look at the rooms we get! They're very poky! What room have you been given?!"

Agnes looked down blankly at the key she had been handed, along with many sharp instructions about *no men* and an unpleasant not-that-*you*-need-telling expression on the chorus mistress's face.

"Oh . . . I7."

Christine clapped her hands. "Oh, goody!!"

"Pardon?"

"I'm *so* glad!! You're next to me!!"

Agnes was taken aback. She'd always been resigned to being the last to be picked in the great team game of Life.

"Well . . . yes, I suppose so . . ." she said.

"You're so lucky!! You've got such a majestic figure for opera!! And such marvelous hair, the way you pile it up like that!! Black suits you, by the way!!"

Majestic, thought Agnes. It was a word that would never, ever have occurred to her. And she'd always steered away from white because in white she looked like a washing-line on a windy day.

She followed Christine.

It occurred to Agnes, as she trudged after the girl en route to her new lodgings, that if you spent much time in the same room as Christine you'd need to open a window to stop from drowning in punctuation.

From somewhere at the back of the stage, quite unheeded, someone watched them go.

People were generally glad to see Nanny Ogg. She was good at making them feel at home in their own home.

But she *was* a witch, and therefore also expert at arriving just after cakes were baked or sausages were made. Nanny Ogg generally traveled with a string bag stuffed up one knee-length knicker leg—in case, as she put it, someone wants to give me something.

"So, Mrs. Nitt," she observed, around about the third cake and fourth cup of tea, "how's that daughter of yours? Agnes it is to whom I refer."

"Oh, didn't you hear, Mrs. Ogg? She's gone off to Ankh-Morpork to be a singer."

Nanny Ogg's heart sank.

"That's nice," she said. "She has a good singing

voice, I remember. Of course, I gave her a few tips. I used to hear her singing in the woods."

"It's the air here," said Mrs. Nitt. "She's always had such a good chest."

"Yes, indeed. Noted for it. So . . . er . . . she's not here, then?"

"You know our Agnes. She never says much. I think she thought it was a bit dull."

"Dull? Lancre?" said Nanny Ogg.

"That's what I said," said Mrs. Nitt. "I said we get some lovely sunsets up here. And there's the fair every Soul Cake Tuesday, regular."

Nanny Ogg thought about Agnes. You needed quite large thoughts to fit all of Agnes in.

Lancre had always bred strong, capable women. A Lancre farmer needed a wife who'd think nothing of beating a wolf to death with her apron when she went out to get some firewood. And, while kissing initially seemed to have more charms than cookery, a stolid Lancre lad looking for a bride would bear in mind his father's advice that kisses eventually lost their fire but cookery tended to get even better over the years, and direct his courting to those families that clearly showed a tradition of enjoying their food.

Agnes was, Nanny considered, quite good-looking in an expansive kind of way; she was a fine figure of typical young Lancre womanhood. This meant she was approximately two womanhoods from anywhere else.

Nanny also recalled her as being rather thoughtful and shy, as if trying to reduce the amount of world she took up.

But she had shown signs of craft ability. That was only to be expected. There was nothing like that *not fitting in* feeling to stimulate the old magical nerves; that was why Esme was so good at it. In Agnes's case this had manifested itself in a tendency to wear soppy black lace gloves and pale makeup and call herself Perdita plus an initial from the arse of the alphabet, but Nanny had assumed that would soon burn off when she got some serious witchcraft under her rather strained belt.

She should have paid more attention to the thing about music. Power found its way out by all sorts of routes . . .

Music and magic had a lot in common. They were only two letters apart, for one thing. And you couldn't do both.

Damn. Nanny had rather been counting on the girl.

"She used to send off to Ankh-Morpork for music," said Mrs. Nitt. "See?"

She handed Nanny several piles of papers.

Nanny leafed through them. Song sheets were common enough in the Ramtops, and a singsong in the parlor was considered the third best thing to do on long dark evenings. But Nanny could see this wasn't ordinary music. It was far too crowded for that.

"*Cosi fan Hita,*" she read. "*Die Meistersinger von Scrote.*"

"That's foreign," said Mrs. Nitt proudly.

"It certainly is," said Nanny.

Mrs. Nitt was looking expectantly at her.

"What?" said Nanny, and then, "Oh."

Mrs. Nitt's eyes flickered to her emptied teacup and back again.

Nanny Ogg sighed and laid the music aside. Occasionally she saw Granny Weatherwax's point. Sometimes people expected too little of witches.

"Yes, indeedy," she said, trying to smile. "Let us see what destiny in the form of these dried-up bits of leaf has in store for us, eh?"

She set her features in a suitable occult expression and looked down into the cup.

Which, a second later, smashed into fragments when it hit the floor.

It was a small room. In fact it was half a small room, since a thin wall had been built across it. Junior members of the chorus ranked rather lower in the opera than apprentice scene shifters.

There was room for a bed, a wardrobe, a dressing-table and, quite out of place, a huge mirror, as big as the door.

"Impressive, isn't it?!" said Christine. "They tried to take it out but it's built into the wall, apparently!! I'm sure it will be very useful!!"

Agnes said nothing. Her own half-room, the other half of this one, didn't have a mirror. She was glad of that. She did not regard mirrors as naturally friendly. It wasn't just the images they showed her. There was something . . . *worrying* . . . about mirrors. She'd always felt that. They seemed to be looking at her. Agnes hated being looked at.

Christine stepped into the small space in the middle of the floor and twirled. There was something very enjoyable about watching her. It was the sparkle,

Agnes thought. Something about Christine suggested sequins.

"Isn't this nice?!" she said.

Not liking Christine would be like not liking small fluffy animals. And Christine was just like a small fluffy animal. A rabbit, perhaps. It was certainly impossible for her to get a whole idea into her head in one go. She had to nibble it into manageable bits.

Agnes glanced at the mirror again. Her reflection stared at her. She could have done with some time to herself right now. Everything had happened so quickly. And this place made her uneasy. Everything would feel a lot better if she could just have some time to herself.

Christine stopped twirling. "Are you all right?!"

Agnes nodded.

"Do *tell* me about yourself!!"

"Er . . . well . . ." Agnes was gratified, despite herself. "I'm from somewhere up in the mountains you've probably never heard of . . ."

She stopped. A light had gone off in Christine's head, and Agnes realized that the question had been asked not because Christine in any way wanted to know the answer but for something to say. She went on: ". . . and my father is the Emperor of Klatch and my mother is a small tray of raspberry puddings."

"That's interesting!" said Christine, who was looking at the mirror. "Do you think my hair looks right?!"

What Agnes would have said, if Christine had been capable of listening to anything for more than a couple of seconds, was:

She'd woken up one morning with the horrible realization that she'd been saddled with a lovely personality. It was as simple as that. Oh, and very good hair.

It wasn't so much the personality, it was the "but" that people always added when they talked about it. *But she's got a lovely personality*, they said. It was the lack of choice that rankled. No one had asked her, before she was born, whether she wanted a lovely personality or whether she'd prefer, say, a miserable personality but a body that could take size nine in dresses. Instead, people would take pains to tell her that beauty was only skin-deep, as if a man ever fell for an attractive pair of kidneys.

She could feel a future trying to land on her.

She'd caught herself saying "poot!" and "dang!" when she wanted to swear, and using pink writing paper.

She'd got a reputation for being calm and capable in a crisis.

Next thing she knew she'd be making shortbread and apple pies as good as her mother's, and then there'd be no hope for her.

So she'd introduced Perdita. She'd heard somewhere that inside every fat woman was a thin woman trying to get out,* so she'd named her Perdita. She was a good repository for all those thoughts that Agnes couldn't think on account of her wonderful personality. Perdita would use black writing paper if she could get away with it, and would be beautifully

---

*Or, at least, dying for chocolate.

pale instead of embarrassingly flushed. Perdita wanted to be an interestingly lost soul in plum-colored lipstick. Just occasionally, though, Agnes thought Perdita was as dumb as she was.

Was the only alternative the witches? She'd felt their interest in her, in a way she couldn't exactly identify. It was of a piece with knowing when someone was watching you, although she had, in fact, occasionally seen Nanny Ogg watching her in a critical kind of fashion, like someone inspecting a secondhand horse.

She knew she *did* have some talent. Sometimes she knew things that were going to happen, although always in a sufficiently confused way that the knowledge was totally useless until afterward. And there was her voice. She was aware it wasn't quite natural. She'd always enjoyed singing and, somehow, her voice had just done everything she'd wanted it to do.

But she'd seen the ways the witches lived. Oh, Nanny Ogg was all right—quite a nice old baggage really. But the others were weird, lying crosswise on the world instead of nicely parallel to it like everyone else . . . old Mother Dismass who could see into the past and the future but was totally blind in the present, and Millie Hopwood over in Slice, who stuttered and had runny ears, and as for Granny Weatherwax . . .

Oh, *yes*. Finest job in the world? Being a sour old woman with no friends?

They were always looking for weird people like themselves.

Well, they could look in vain for Agnes Nitt.

Fed up with living in Lancre, and fed up with the

witches, and above all fed up with being Agnes Nitt, she'd . . . escaped.

Nanny Ogg didn't look built for running, but she covered the ground deceptively fast, her great heavy boots kicking up shoals of leaves.

There was a trumpeting overhead. Another skein of geese passed across the sky, so fast in pursuit of the summer that their wings were hardly moving in the ballistic rush.

Granny Weatherwax's cottage looked deserted. It had, Nanny felt, a particularly empty feel.

She scurried around to the back door and burst through, pounded up the stairs, saw the gaunt figure on the bed, reached an instant conclusion, grabbed the pitcher of water from its place on the marble washstand, ran forward . . .

A hand shot up and grabbed her wrist.

"I *was* having a *nap*," said Granny, opening her eyes. "Gytha, I swear I could feel you comin' half a mile away—"

"We got to make a cup of tea quick!" gasped Nanny, almost sagging with relief.

Granny Weatherwax was more than bright enough not to ask questions.

But you couldn't hurry a good cup of tea. Nanny Ogg jiggled from one foot to the other while the fire was pumped up, the small frogs fished out of the water bucket, the water boiled, the dried leaves allowed to seep.

"I ain't saying nothing," said Nanny, sitting down at last. "Just pour a cup, that's all."

On the whole, witches despised fortune-telling

from tea-leaves. Tea leaves are not uniquely fortunate in knowing what the future holds. They are really just something for the eyes to rest on while the mind does the work. Practically anything would do. The scum on a puddle, the skin on a custard . . . anything. Nanny Ogg could see the future in the froth on a beer mug. It invariably showed that she was going to enjoy a refreshing drink which she almost certainly was not going to pay for.

"You recall young Agnes Nitt?" said Nanny as Granny Weatherwax tried to find the milk.

Granny hesitated.

"Agnes who calls herself Perditax?"

"Perdita X," said Nanny. She at least respected anyone's right to recreate themselves.

Granny shrugged. "Fat girl. Big hair. Walks with her feet turned out. Sings to herself in the woods. Good voice. Reads books. Says 'poot!' instead of swearing. Blushes when anyone looks at her. Wears black lace gloves with the fingers cut out."

"You remember we once talked about maybe how possibly she might be . . . suitable."

"Oh, there's a twist in the soul there, you're right," said Granny. "But . . . it's an unfortunate name."

"Her father's name was Terminal," said Nanny Ogg reflectively. "There were three sons: Primal, Medial and Terminal. I'm afraid the family's always had a problem with education."

"I *meant* Agnes," said Granny. "Always puts me in mind of carpet fluff, that name."

"Prob'ly that's why she called herself Perdita," said Nanny.

"Worse."

"Got her fixed in your mind?" said Nanny.

"Yes, I suppose so."

"Good. Now look at them tea leaves."

Granny looked down.

There was no particular drama, perhaps because of the way Nanny had built up expectations. But Granny did hiss between her teeth.

"Well, now. There's a thing," she said.

"See it? See it?"

"Yep."

"Like . . . a skull?"

"Yep."

"And them eyes? I nearly pi — I was pretty damn surprised by them eyes, I can tell you."

Granny carefully replaced the cup.

"Her mam showed me her letters home," said Nanny. "I brung 'em with me. It's worrying, Esme. She could be facing something bad. She's a Lancre girl. One of ours. Nothing's too much trouble when it's one of your own, I always say."

"Tea leaves can't tell the future," said Granny quietly. "Everyone knows that."

"Tea leaves don't know."

"Well, who'd be so daft as to tell anything to a bunch of dried leaves?"

Nanny Ogg looked down at Agnes's letters home. They were written in the careful rounded script of someone who'd been taught to write as a child by copying letters on a slate, and had never written enough as an adult to change their style. The person writing them had also very conscientiously drawn faint pencil lines on the paper before writing.

Dear Mam, I hope this finds you as it leaves me. Here I am in Ankh-Morpork and everything is all right, I have not been ravished yet!! I am staying at 4 Treacle Mine Road, it is alright and . . .

Granny tried another.

Dear Mum, I hope you are well. Everything is fine but, the money runs away like water here. I am doing some singing in taverns but I am not making much so I went to see the Guild of Seamstresses about getting a sewing job and I took along some stitching to show them and you'd be <u>amazed</u>, that's all I can say . . .

And another . . .

Dear Mother, Some good news at last. Next week they're holding auditions at the Opera House . . .

"What's opera?" said Granny Weatherwax.

"It's like theater, with singing," said Nanny Ogg.

"Hah! *Theater*," said Granny darkly.

"Our Nev told me about it. It's all singing in foreign languages, he said. He couldn't understand any of it."

Granny put down the letters.

"Yes, but your Nev can't understand a lot of things. What was he doing at this opera theater, anyway?"

"Nicking the lead off the roof." Nanny said this quite happily. It wasn't theft if an Ogg was doing it.

"Can't tell much from the letters, except that she's picking up an education," said Granny. "But it's a long way to—"

There was a hesitant knock on the door. It was Shawn Ogg, Nanny's youngest son and Lancre's entire civil and public service. Currently he had his postman's badge on; the Lancre postal service consisted of taking the mailbag off the nail where the coach left it and delivering it to the outlying homesteads when he had a moment, although many citizens were in the habit of going down to the sack and rummaging until they found some mail they liked.

He touched his helmet respectfully at Granny Weatherwax.

"Got a lot of letters, mum," he said to Nanny Ogg. "Er. They're all addressed to, er, well . . . er . . . you'd better have a look, mum."

Nanny Ogg took the proffered bundle.

" 'The Lancre Witch,' " she said aloud.

"That'd be me, then," said Granny Weatherwax firmly, and took the letters.

"Ah. Well, I'd better be going . . ." said Nanny, backing toward the door.

"Can't imagine why people'd be writing to me," said Granny, slitting an envelope. "Still, I suppose news gets around." She focused on the words.

" 'Dear Witch,' " she read, " 'I would just like to say how much I appreciated the Famous Carrot and Oyster Pie recipe. My husband—' "

Nanny Ogg made it halfway down the path before her boots became, suddenly, too heavy to lift.

"Gytha Ogg, you come back here right now!"

Agnes tried again. She didn't really know anyone in Ankh-Morpork and she did need someone to talk to, even if they didn't listen.

"I suppose mainly I came because of the witches," she said.

Christine turned, her eyes wide with fascination. So was her mouth. It was like looking at a rather pretty bowling ball.

"Witches?!" she breathed.

"Oh, yes," said Agnes wearily. Yes. People were always fascinated by the idea of witches. They should try living around them, she thought.

"Do they do spells and ride around on broomsticks?!"

"Oh, yes."

"No wonder you ran away!"

"What? Oh . . . no . . . it's not like that. I mean, they're not *bad*. It's much . . . worse than that."

"Worse than bad?!"

"They think they know what's best for everybody."

Christine's forehead wrinkled, as it tended to when she was contemplating a problem more complex than "What is your name?"

"That doesn't sound very ba—"

"They . . . mess people around. They think that just because they're right that's the same as good! It's not even as though they do any *real* magic. It's all fooling people and being clever! They think they can do what they like!"

The force of the words knocked even Christine back. "Oh, dear!! Did they want you to do something?!"

"They want me to *be* something. But I'm not going to!"

Christine stared at her. And then, automatically, forgot everything she'd just heard.

"Come on," she said, "let's have a look around!!"

Nanny Ogg balanced on a chair and took down an oblong wrapped in paper.

Granny watched sternly with her arms folded.

"Thing is," Nanny babbled, under the laser glare, "my late husband, I remember him once sayin' to me, after dinner, he said, 'You know, mother, it'd be a real shame if all the stuff you know just passed away when *you* did. Why don't you write some of it down?' So I scribbled the odd one, when I had a moment, and then I thought it'd be nice to have it all properly done so I sent it off to the Almanac people in Ankh-Morpork and they hardly charged me anything and a little while ago they sent me this, I think it's a very good job, it's amazing how they get all the letters so neat—"

"You done a *book*," said Granny.

"Only cookery," said Nanny Ogg meekly, as one might plead a first offense.

"What do you know about it? You hardly ever do any cooking," said Granny.

"I do specialities," said Nanny.

Granny looked at the offending volume.

"*The Joye of Snacks*," she read out loud. "'Bye A Lancre Witch.' Hah! Why dint you put your own name on it, eh? Books've got to have a name on 'em so's everyone knows who's guilty."

"It's my *gnome de plum*," said Nanny. "Mr. Goatberger the Almanac man said it'd make it sound more mysterious."

Granny cast her gimlet gaze to the bottom of the crowded cover, where it said, in very small lettering, "CXXviith Printyng. More Than Twenty Thoufand Solde! One half dollar."

"You sent them some money to get it all printed?" she said.

"Only a couple of dollars," said Nanny. "Damn good job they made of it, too. And then they sent the money back afterward, only they got it wrong and sent three dollars extra."

Granny Weatherwax was grudgingly literate but keenly numerate. She assumed that anything written down was probably a lie, and that applied to numbers, too. Numbers were used only by people who wanted to put one over on you.

Her lips moved silently as she thought about numbers.

"Oh," she said, quietly. "And that was it, was it? You never wrote to him again?"

"Not on your life. Three dollars, mind. I dint want him saying he wanted 'em back."

"I can see that," said Granny, still dwelling in the world of numbers. She wondered how much it cost to do a book. It couldn't be a lot: they had sort of printing mills to do the actual work.

"After all, there's a lot you can do with three dollars," said Nanny.

"Right enough," said Granny. "You ain't got a pencil about you, have you? You being a literary type and all?"

"I got a slate," said Nanny.

"Pass it over, then."

"I bin keeping it by me in case I wake up in the night and I get an idea for a recipe, see," said Nanny.

"Good," said Granny vaguely. The slate pencil squeaked across the gray tablet. *The paper must cost something. And you'd probably have to tip someone a couple of pennies to sell it . . .* Angular figures danced from column to column.

"I'll make another cup of tea, shall I?" said Nanny, relieved that the conversation appeared to be coming to a peaceful end.

"Hmm?" said Granny. She stared at the result and drew two lines under it. "But you enjoyed it, did you?" she called out. "The writin'?"

Nanny Ogg poked her head around the scullery door. "Oh, yes. The money dint matter," she said.

"You've never been very good at numbers, have you?" said Granny. Now she drew a circle around the final figure.

"Oh, you know me, Esme," said Nanny cheerfully. "I couldn't subtract a fart from a plate of beans."

"That's good, 'cos I reckon this Master Goatberger owes you a bit more than you got, if there's any justice in the world," said Granny.

"Money ain't everything, Esme. What I say is, if you've got your health—"

"I reckon, if there's any justice, it's about four or five thousand dollars," said Granny quietly.

There was a crash from the scullery.

"So it's a good job the money don't matter," Granny Weatherwax went on. "It'd be a terrible thing otherwise. All that money, matterin'."

Nanny Ogg's white face appeared around the edge of the door. "He never!"

"Could be a bit more," said Granny.

"It never!"

"You just adds up and divides and that."

Nanny Ogg stared in horrified fascination at her own fingers.

"But that's a—" She stopped. The only word she could think of was "fortune" and that wasn't adequate. Witches didn't operate in a cash economy. The whole of the Ramtops, by and large, got by without the complications of capital. *Fifty* dollars was a fortune. A hundred dollars was a, was a, was . . . well, it was *two* fortunes, that was what it was.

"It's a lot of money," she said weakly. "What couldn't I do with money like that?"

"Dunno," said Granny Weatherwax. "What did you do with the three dollars?"

"Got it in a tin up the chimney," said Nanny Ogg.

Granny nodded approvingly. This was the kind of good fiscal practice she liked to see.

"Beats me why people'd fall over themselves to read a cookery book, though," she added. "I mean, it's not the sort of thing that—"

The room fell silent. Nanny Ogg shuffled her boots.

Granny said, in a voice laden with a suspicion that

was all the worse because it wasn't yet quite sure what it was suspicious of: "It *is* a cookery book, isn't it?"

"Oh, yes," said Nanny hurriedly, avoiding Granny's gaze. "Yes. Recipes and that. Yes."

Granny glared at her. "*Just* recipes?"

"Yes. Oh, yes. Yes. And some . . . cookery anecdotes, yes."

Granny went on glaring.

Nanny gave in.

"Er . . . look under Famous Carrot and Oyster Pie," she said. "Page 25."

Granny turned the pages. Her lips moved silently. Then: "I *see*. Anything else?"

"Er . . . Cinnamon and Marshmallow Fingers . . . page 17 . . ."

Granny looked it up.

"And?"

"Er . . . Celery Astonishment . . . page 10."

Granny looked *that* up, too.

"Can't say it astonished *me*," she said. "And . . . ?"

"Er . . . well, more or less all of Humorous Puddings and Cake Decoration. That's all of Chapter Six. I done illustrations for that."

Granny turned to Chapter Six. She had to turn the book around a couple of times.

"What one you looking at?" said Nanny Ogg, because an author is always keen to get feedback.

"Strawberry Wobbler," said Granny.

"Ah. That one always gets a laugh."

It did not appear to be obtaining one from Granny. She carefully closed the book.

"Gytha," she said, "this is *me* askin' you this. Is there any page in this book, is there any single recipe, which does not in some way relate to . . . goings-on?"

Nanny Ogg, her face red as her apples, seemed to give this some lengthy consideration.

"Porridge," she said, eventually.

"Really?"

"Yes. Er. No, I tell a lie, it's got my special honey mixture in it."

Granny turned a page.

"What about this one? Maids of Honor?"

"*Weeelll*, they starts *out* as Maids of Honor," said Nanny, fidgeting with her feet, "but they ends up Tarts."

Granny looked at the front cover again. *The Joye of Snacks.*

"An' you actually set out to—"

"It just sort of turned out that way, really."

Granny Weatherwax was not a jouster in the lists of love but, as an intelligent onlooker, she knew how the game was played. No wonder the book had sold like hot cakes. Half the recipes told you how to make them. It was surprising the pages hadn't singed.

And it was by "A Lancre Witch." The world was, Granny Weatherwax modestly admitted, well aware of who *the* witch of Lancre was; *viz*, it was her.

"Gytha Ogg," she said.

"Yes, Esme?"

"Gytha Ogg, you look me in the eye."

"Sorry, Esme."

" 'A Lancre Witch,' it says here."

"I never thought, Esme."

"So you'll go and see Mr. Goatberger and have

this stopped, right? I don't want people lookin' at me and thinkin' about the Banana Soup Surprise. I don't even *believe* the Banana Soup Surprise. And I ain't relishin' going down the street and hearin' people makin' cracks about bananas."

"Yes, Esme."

"And I'll come with you to make sure you do."

"Yes, Esme."

"And we'll talk to the man about your money."

"Yes, Esme."

"And we might just drop in on young Agnes to make sure she's all right."

"Yes, Esme."

"But we'll do it diplomatic like. We don't want people thinkin' we're pokin' our noses in."

"Yes, Esme."

"No one could say I interfere where I'm not wanted. You won't find anyone callin' *me* a busybody."

"Yes, Esme."

"That was, 'Yes, Esme, you won't find anyone callin' *you* a busybody,' was it?"

"Oh, yes, Esme."

"You sure about that?"

"Yes, Esme."

"Good."

Granny looked out at the dull gray sky and the dying leaves and felt, amazingly enough, her sap rising. A day ago the future had looked aching and desolate, and now it looked full of surprises and terror and bad things happening to people . . .

If she had anything to do with it, anyway.

In the scullery, Nanny Ogg grinned to herself.

* * *

Agnes had known a little bit about the theater. A traveling company came to Lancre sometimes. Their stage was about twice the size of a door, and "backstage" consisted of a bit of sacking behind which was usually a man trying to change trousers and wigs at the same time and another man, dressed as a king, having a surreptitious smoke.

The Opera House was almost as big as the Patrician's palace, and far more palatial. It covered three acres. There was stabling for twenty horses and two elephants in the cellar; Agnes spent some time there, because the elephants were reassuringly larger than her.

There were rooms behind the stage so big that entire sets were stored there. There was a whole ballet school somewhere in the building. Some of the girls were on stage now, ugly in woolly jumpers, going through a routine.

The inside of the Opera House—at least, the backstage inside—put Agnes strongly in mind of the clock her brother had taken apart to find the tick. It was hardly a building. It was more like a machine. Sets and curtains and ropes hung in the darkness like dreadful things in a forgotten cellar. The stage was only a small part of the place, a little rectangle of light in a huge, complicated darkness full of significant machinery . . .

A piece of dust floated down from the blackness high above. She brushed it off.

"I thought I heard someone up there," she said.

"It's probably the Ghost!!" said Christine. "We've got one, you know! Oh, I said *we*!! Isn't this exciting?!"

"A man with his face covered by a white mask," said Agnes.

"Oh?! You've heard about him, then?!"

"What? Who?"

"The Ghost!!"

Blast, thought Agnes. It was always ready to catch her out. Just when she thought she'd put all that behind her. She'd know things without quite knowing why. It upset people. It certainly upset her.

"Oh, I . . . suppose someone must have told me . . ." she mumbled.

"He moves around the Opera House invisibly, they say!! One moment he'll be in the Gods, next moment he'll be backstage somewhere!! No one knows how he does it!!"

"Really?"

"They say he watches every performance!! That's why they never sell tickets for Box Eight, didn't you know?!"

"Box Eight?" said Agnes. "What's a Box?"

"Boxes! You know? That's where you get the best people?! Look, I shall show you!"

Christine marched to the front of the stage and waved a hand grandly at the empty auditorium.

"The Boxes!" she said. "Over there! And right up there, the Gods!"

Her voice bounced back from the distant wall.

"Aren't the best people in the Gods? It sounds—"

"Oh, no! The best people will be in Boxes! Or possibly in the Stalls!"

Agnes pointed.

"Who's down there? They must get a good view—"

"Don't be silly!! That's the Pit!! That's for the musicians!!"

"Well, that makes sense, anyway. Er. Which one's Box Eight?"

"I don't know! But they say if ever they sell seats in Box Eight there'll be a dreadful tragedy!! Isn't that romantic?!"

For some reason Agnes's practical eye was drawn to the huge chandelier that hung over the auditorium like a fantastic sea monster. Its thick rope disappeared into the darkness near the ceiling.

The glass chimes tinkled.

Another flare of that certain power which Agnes did her best to suppress at every turn flashed a treacherous image across her mind.

"That looks like an accident waiting to happen if ever I saw one," she mumbled.

"I'm sure it's *perfectly* safe!!" trilled Christine. "I'm *sure* they wouldn't allow—"

A chord rolled out, shaking the stage. The chandelier tinkled, and more dust came down.

"What was that?" said Agnes.

"It was the organ!! It's so big it's behind the stage!! Come on, let's go and see!!"

Other members of the staff were hurrying toward the organ. There was an overturned bucket nearby, and a spreading pool of green paint.

A carpenter reached past Agnes and picked up an envelope that was lying on the organ seat.

"It's for the boss," he said.

"When it's *my* mail, the postman usually just knocks," said a ballerina, and giggled.

Agnes looked up. Ropes swung lazily in the musty

darkness. For a moment she thought she saw a flash of white, and then it was gone.

There was a shape, just visible, tangled in the ropes.

Something wet and sticky dripped down and splashed on the keyboard.

People were already screaming when Agnes reached past, dipped her finger in the growing puddle, and sniffed.

"It's blood!" said the carpenter.

"It's blood, isn't it?" said a musician.

"Blood!!" screamed Christine. "Blood!!"

It was Agnes's terrible fate to keep her head in a crisis. She sniffed her finger again.

"It's turpentine," said Agnes. "Er. Sorry. Is that wrong?"

Up in the tangle of ropes, the figure moaned.

"Shouldn't we get him down?" she added.

Cando Cutoff was a humble woodcutter. He wasn't humble *because* he was a woodcutter. He would still have been quite humble if he'd owned five logging mills. He was just naturally humble.

And he was unpretentiously stacking some logs at the point where the Lancre road met the main mountain road when he saw a farm cart rumble to a halt and unload two elderly ladies in black. Both carried a broomstick in one hand and a sack in the other.

They were arguing. It was not a raised-voice argument, but a chronic wrangle that had clearly been going on for some time and was set in for the rest of the decade.

"It's all very well for you, but it's *my* three dollars so I don't see why I can't say how we go."

"I likes flying."

"And I'm telling you it's too draughty on broom-sticks this time of year, Esme. The breeze gets into places I wouldn't dream of talking about."

"Really? Can't imagine where those'd be, then."

"Oh, Esme!"

"Don't 'Oh, Esme' me. It weren't *me* that come up with the Amusing Wedding Trifle with the Special Sponge Fingers."

"Anyway, Greebo don't like it on the broomstick. He's got a delicate stomach."

Cutoff noticed that one of the sacks was moving in a lazy way.

"Gytha, I've seen him eat half a skunk, so don't tell me about his delicate stomach," said Granny, who disliked cats on principle. "Anyway . . . he's been do-ing It again."

Nanny Ogg waved her hands airily.

"Oh, he only does It sometimes, when he's really in a corner," she said.

"He did It in ole Mrs. Grope's henhouse last week. She went in to see what all the ruckus was, and he did It right in front of her. She had to have a lie-down."

"He was probably more frightened than she was," said Nanny defensively.

"That's what comes of getting strange ideas in for-eign parts," said Granny. "Now you've got a cat who— Yes, what is it?"

Cutoff had meekly approached them and was hov-ering in the kind of half-crouch of someone trying to be noticed while also not wanting to intrude.

"Are you ladies waiting for the stagecoach?"

"Yes," said the taller of the ladies.

"Um, I'm afraid the next coach doesn't stop here. It doesn't stop until Creel Springs."

They gave him a couple of polite stares.

"Thank you," said the tall one. She turned to her companion.

"It gave her a nasty shock, anyway. I dread to think what he'll learn *this* time."

"He pines when I'm gone. He won't take food from anyone else."

"Only 'cos they try to poison him, and no wonder."

Cutoff shook his head sadly and wandered back to his log pile.

The coach turned up five minutes later, coming around the corner at speed. It drew level with the women—

—and stopped. That is, the horses tried to stand still and the wheels locked.

It wasn't so much a skid as a spin, and the whole thing gradually came to rest about fifty yards down the road, with the driver in a tree.

The women strolled toward it, still arguing.

One of them poked the driver with her broomstick. "Two tickets to Ankh-Morpork, please."

He landed in the road.

"What do you mean, two tickets to Ankh-Morpork? The coach doesn't stop here!"

"Looks stopped to *me*."

"Did you *do* something?"

"What, us?"

"Listen, lady, even if I *was* stopping here the tickets are forty damn dollars each!"

"Oh."

"Why've you got broomsticks?" shouted the driver. "Are you witches?"

"Yes. Have you got any special low terms for witches?"

"Yeah, how about 'meddling, interfering old baggages'?"

Cutoff felt that he must have missed part of the conversation, because the next exchange went like this:

"What was that again, young man?"

"Two complimentary tickets to Ankh-Morpork, ma'am. No problem."

"Inside seats, mind. No traveling on the top."

"Certainly, ma'am. Excuse me while I just kneel in the dirt so's you can step up, ma'am."

Cutoff nodded happily to himself as the coach pulled away again. It was nice to see that good manners and courtesy were still alive.

With great difficulty and much shouting and untangling of ropes far above, the figure was lowered to the stage.

He was soaked in paint and turpentine. The swelling audience of off-duty staff and rehearsal truants crowded in around him.

Agnes knelt down, loosened his collar and tried to unwind the rope that had caught around arm and neck.

"Does anyone know him?" she said.

"It's Tommy Cripps," said a musician. "He paints scenery."

Tommy moaned, and opened his eyes.

"I saw him!" he muttered. "It was horrible!"

"Saw what?" said Agnes. And then she had a sudden feeling that she'd intruded on some private conversation. Around her there was a babble of voices.

"Giselle said she saw him last week!"

"He's here!"

"It's happening again!"

"Are we all *doomed*?!" squeaked Christine.

Tommy Cripps gripped Agnes's arm.

"He's got a face like death!"

"Who?"

"The Ghost!"

"What gho—?"

"It's white bone! He has no nose!"

A couple of ballet dancers fainted, but carefully, so as not to get their clothes dirty.

"Then how does he—" Agnes began.

"I saw him too!"

On cue, the company turned.

An elderly man advanced across the stage. He wore an ancient opera hat and carried a sack over one shoulder, while his spare hand made the needlessly expansive gestures of someone who has got hold of some direful information and can't wait to freeze all nearby spines. The sack must have contained something alive, because it was bouncing around.

"I saw him! Ooooooh yes! Wi' his great black cloak and his white face with no eyes but only two holes where eyes should be! Ooohhhh! And—"

"He had a mask on?" said Agnes.

The old man paused and shot her the dark look reserved for all those who insist on injecting a note of sanity when things are getting interestingly ghastly.

"And he had no nose!" he went on, ignoring her.

"I just *said* that," muttered Tommy Cripps, in a rather annoyed voice. "I told them that. They already know that."

"If he had no nose, how did he sme—" Agnes began, but no one was listening to her.

"Did you mention about the eyes?" said the old man.

"I was just getting round to the eyes," snapped Tommy. "Yes, he had eyes like—"

"*Are* we talking about some kind of mask here?" said Agnes.

Now everyone was giving her that kind of look UFOlogists get when they suddenly say, "Hey, if you shade your eyes you can see it is just a flock of geese after all."

The man with the sack coughed and regrouped. "Like great holes, they were—" he began, but it was clear that it had all been spoiled for him. "Great holes," he said sourly. "That's what I saw. And no nose, I might add, thank you so very much."

"It's the Ghost again!" said a scene-shifter.

"He jumped out from behind the organ," said Tommy Cripps. "Next thing I knew, there was a rope around my neck and I was upside-down!"

The company looked at the man with the sack, in case he could trump this.

"Great big black holes," he managed, sticking to what he knew.

"All right, everyone, what's going on here?"

An imposing figure strode out of the wings. He had flowing black hair, carefully brushed to give it a carefree alfresco look, but the face underneath was the face of an organizer. He nodded at the old man with the sack.

"What are you staring at, Mr. Pounder?" he said.

The old man looked down. "I knows what I saw, Mr. Salzella," he said. "I see *lots* o' things, I do."

"As much as is visible through the bottom of a bottle, I have no doubt, you old reprobate. What happened to Tommy?"

"It was the Ghost!" said Tommy, delighted to have center-stage again. "He swooped out at me, Mr. Salzella! I think my leg is broken," he added quickly, in the voice of one who is suddenly aware of the time-off opportunities of the situation.

Agnes expected the newcomer to say something like "Ghosts? There's no such thing." He had the kind of *face* that said that.

Instead, he said, "Back again, is he? Where did he go?"

"Didn't see, Mr. Salzella. He just swooped off again!"

"Some of you help Tommy down to the canteen," said Salzella. "And someone else fetch a doctor—"

"His leg isn't broken," said Agnes. "But that's a nasty rope burn on his neck and he's filled his own ear with paint."

"What do you know about it, miss?" said Tommy. A paint-filled ear didn't sound as though it had the possibilities of a broken leg.

"I've . . . er . . . had some training," said Agnes, and then added quickly, "It's a nasty burn, though, and of course there may be some delayed shock."

"Brandy is very good for that, isn't it?" said Tommy.

"Perhaps you could try forcing some between my lips?"

"Thank you, Perdita. The rest of you, go back to what you were doing," said Salzella.

"Big dark holes," said Mr. Pounder. "Big ones."

"Yes, thank you, Mr. Pounder. Help Ron with Mr. Cripps, will you? Perdita, you come here. And you, Christine."

The two girls stood before the director of music.

"Did *you* see anything?" said Salzella.

"I saw a great creature with great flapping wings and great big holes where his eyes should be!!" said Christine.

"I'm afraid I just saw something white up in the ceiling," said Agnes. "Sorry."

She blushed, aware of how useless that sounded. Perdita would have seen a mysterious cloaked figure or something . . . something *interesting* . . .

Salzella smiled at her. "You mean you just see things that are really there?" he said. "I can see you haven't been with the opera for long, dear. But I may say I'm pleased to have a level-headed person around here for once—"

"Oh, *no*!" screamed someone.

"It's the Ghost!!" shrieked Christine, automatically.

"Er. It's the young man behind the organ," said Agnes. "Sorry."

"Observant as well as level-headed," said Salzella. "Whereas I can see that you, Christine, will fit right in here. What's the matter, André?"

A fair-haired young man peered around the organ pipes.

"Someone's been smashing things, Mr. Salzella," he said mournfully. "The pallet springs and the back-falls and everything. Completely ruined. I'm sure I won't be able to get a tune out of it. And it's *price-less*."

Salzella sighed. "All right. I'll tell *Mister* Bucket," he said. "Thank you, everyone."

He gave Agnes a gloomy nod, and strode off.

"You shouldn't ort to do that to people," said Nanny Ogg in a vague sort of way, as the coach began to get up speed.

She looked around with a wide, friendly grin at the now rather disheveled occupants of the coach.

"Morning," she said, delving into the sack. "I'm Gytha Ogg, I've got fifteen children, this is my friend Esme Weatherwax, we're going to Ankh-Morpork, would anyone like an egg sandwich? I've brung plenty. The cat's been sleepin' on them but they're fine, look, they bend back all right. No? Please yourself, I'm sure. Let's see what else we've got . . . ah, has anybody got an opener for a bottle of beer?"

A man in the corner indicated that he might have such a thing.

"Fine," said Nanny Ogg. "Anyone got something to drink a bottle of beer out of?"

Another man nodded hopefully.

"Good," said Nanny Ogg. "Now, has anybody got a bottle of beer?"

Granny, for once not the center of attention as all horrified eyes were on Nanny and her sack, surveyed the other occupants of the coach.

The express stage went right over the Ramtops

and all the way through the patchwork of little countries beyond. If it cost forty dollars just from Lancre, then it must have cost these people a lot more. What sort of folk spent the best part of two months' wages just to travel fast and uncomfortably?

The thin man who sat clutching his bag was probably a spy, she decided. The fat man who'd volunteered the glass looked as if he sold things; he had the unpleasant complexion of someone who'd hit too many bottles but missed too many meals.

They were huddled together on their seat because the rest of it was occupied by a man of almost wizardly proportions. He didn't appear to have woken up when the coach stopped. There was a handkerchief over his face. He was snoring with the regularity of a geyser, and looked as though the only worries he might have in the world were a tendency for small objects to gravitate toward him, and the occasional tide.

Nanny Ogg continued to rummage around in her bag and, as was the case when she was preoccupied, her mouth had wired itself to her eyeballs without her brain intervening.

She was used to traveling by broomstick. Long-distance ground travel was a novelty to her, so she'd prepared with some care.

". . . lessee now . . . book of puzzles for long journeys . . . cushion . . . foot powder . . . mosquito trap . . . phrase book . . . bag to be sick into . . . oh dear . . ."

The audience, which against all probability had managed to squeeze itself farther away from Nanny during the litany, waited with horrified interest.

"What?" said Granny.

"How often d'you reckon this coach stops?"

"What's the matter?"

"I should've gone before we left. Sorry. It's the jolting. Anyone know if there's a privy on this thing?" she added brightly.

"Er," said the probable spy, "we generally wait until the next stop, or—" He stopped. He had been about to add "there's always the window," which was a manly option on the bumpier rural stretches, but he stopped himself in the horrible apprehension that this ghastly old woman might seriously consider the possibility.

"There's Ohulan just a bit further on the road," said Granny, who was trying to doze. "You just wait."

"This coach doesn't stop at Ohulan," said the spy helpfully.

Granny Weatherwax raised her head.

"Up until now, that is," said the spy.

Mr. Bucket was sitting in his office trying to make sense of the Opera House's books.

They didn't make *any* kind of sense. He reckoned he was as good as the next man at reading a balance sheet, but these were to bookkeeping what grit was to clockwork.

Seldom Bucket had always enjoyed opera. He didn't understand it and never had, but he didn't understand the ocean either and he enjoyed that, too. He'd looked upon the purchase as, well, something to do, a sort of working retirement. The offer had been too good to pass up. Things had been getting pretty tough in the wholesale cheese-and-milk-derivatives business, and he'd been looking forward to the quieter climes of the world of art.

The previous owners had put on some good operas. It was only a shame that their genius hadn't run to bookkeeping as well. Money seemed to have been taken out of the accounts when anyone needed it. The financial-record system largely consisted of notes on torn bits of paper saying: "I've taken $30 to pay Q. See you Monday. R." Who was R? Who was Q? What was the money for? You wouldn't get away with this sort of thing in the world of cheese.

He looked up as the door opened.

"Ah, Salzella," he said. "Thank you for coming. You don't know who Q is, by any chance?"

"No, Mr. Bucket."

"Or R?"

"I'm afraid not." Salzella pulled up a chair.

"It's taken me all morning, but I've worked out we pay more than fifteen hundred dollars a year for ballet shoes," said Bucket, waving a piece of paper in the air.

Salzella nodded. "Yes, they do rather go through them at the toes."

"I mean, it's ridiculous! I've still got a pair of boots belonging to my father!"

"But ballet shoes, sir, are rather more like foot gloves," Salzella explained.

"You're telling me! They cost seven dollars a pair and they last hardly any time at all! A few performances! There must be some way we can make a saving . . . ?"

Salzella gave his new employer a long, cool stare.

"Possibly we could ask the girls to spend more time in the air?" he said. "A few extra *grands jetés*?"

Bucket looked puzzled. "Would that work?" he said suspiciously.

"Well, their feet wouldn't be on the ground for so long, would they?" said Salzella, in the tones of one who knows for a fact that he's much more intelligent than anyone else in the room.

"Good point. Good point. Have a word with the ballet mistress, will you?"

"Of course. I am sure she will welcome the suggestion. You may well have halved costs at a stroke."

Bucket beamed.

"Which is perhaps just as well," said Salzella. "There is, in fact, another matter that I've come to see you about . . ."

"Yes?"

"It is to do with the organ we had."

"Had? What do you mean, *had*?" said Bucket, adding, "You're going to tell me something expensive, are you? What have we got now?"

"A lot of pipes and some keyboards," said Salzella. "Everything else has been smashed."

"Smashed? Who by?"

Salzella leaned back. He was not a man to whom amusement came easily, but he realized that he was rather enjoying this.

"Tell me," he said, "when Mr. Pnigeus and Mr. Cavaille sold you this Opera House, did they mention anything . . . supernatural?"

Bucket scratched his head. "Well . . . yes. After I'd signed and paid. It was a bit of a joke. They said: 'Oh, and by the way, people say there's some man in evening dress who haunts the place, haha, ridiculous, isn't it, these theatrical people, like children really, haha, but you may find it keeps them happy if you always keep Box Eight free on first nights, haha.' I remember that quite well. Handing over thirty thousand dollars concentrates the memory a bit. And then they rode off. Quite a fast carriage, now I come to think about it."

"Ah," said Salzella, and he almost smiled. "Well, now that the ink is dry, I wonder if I might fill you in on the fine detail . . ."

Birds sang. The wind rattled the dried seed heads of moorland flowers.

Granny Weatherwax poked in the ditches to see if there were any interesting herbs hereabouts.

High over the hills, a buzzard screamed and wheeled.

The coach stood by the side of the road, despite the fact that it should have been speeding along at least twenty miles away.

At last Granny grew bored, and sidled toward a clump of gorse bushes.

"How're you doing, Gytha?"

"Fine, fine," said a muffled voice.

"Only I reckon the coach driver is getting a bit impatient."

"You can't hurry Nature," said Nanny Ogg.

"Well, don't blame me. *You* was the one who said it was too draughty on the broomsticks."

"You make yourself useful, Esme Weatherwax," said the voice from the bushes, "by obligin' me and findin' any dock or burdock plants that might happen to be around out there, thank you very much."

"Herbs? What're you plannin' with them?"

"I'm plannin' to say, 'Thank goodness, big leaves, just what I need.'"

Some distance from the bushes where Nanny Ogg was communing with Nature there was, placid under the autumn sky, a lake.

In the reeds, a swan was dying. Or was due to die.

There was, however, an unforeseen snag.

Death sat down on the bank.

Now LOOK, he said, I KNOW HOW IT IS SUPPOSED TO GO. SWANS SING JUST ONCE, BEAUTIFULLY, BEFORE THEY DIE. THAT'S WHERE THE WORD "SWANSONG" ORIGINATES. IT IS VERY MOVING. NOW, LET US TRY THIS AGAIN . . .

He produced a tuning fork from the shadowy recesses of his robe and twanged it on the side of his scythe.

THERE'S YOUR NOTE . . .

"Uh-uh," said the swan, shaking its head.

WHY MAKE IT DIFFICULT?

"I like it here," said the swan.

THAT HAS NOTHING TO DO WITH IT.

"Did you know I can break a man's arm with a blow of my wing?"

HOW ABOUT IF I GET YOU STARTED? DO YOU KNOW "MOONLIGHT BAY"?

"That's no more than a barbershop ditty! I happen to be a swan!"

"LITTLE BROWN JUG"? Death cleared his throat. HA HA HA, HEE HEE HEE, LITTLE—

"That's a song?" The swan hissed angrily and swayed from one crabbed foot to the other. "I don't know who you are, sirrah, but where *I* come from we've got better taste in music."

REALLY? WOULD YOU CARE TO SHOW ME AN EX-AMPLE?

"Uh-uh!"

DAMN.

"Thought you'd got me there, didn't you," said the swan. "Thought you'd tricked me, eh? Thought I might unthinkingly give you a couple of bars of the Pedlar's Song from LOHEN-SHAAK, eh?"

I DON'T KNOW THAT ONE.

The swan took a deep, labored breath.

"That's the one that goes 'SCHNEIDE MEINEN EIGENEN HALS—'"

THANK *YOU*, said Death. The scythe moved.

"Bugger!"

A moment later the swan stepped out of its body and ruffled fresh but slightly transparent wings.

"Now what?" it said.

THAT'S UP TO YOU. IT'S ALWAYS UP TO YOU.

Mr. Bucket leaned back in his creaky leather chair with his eyes shut until his director of music had finished.

"So," Bucket said. "Let me see if I've got this right. There's this Ghost. Every time anyone loses a hammer in this place, it's been stolen by the Ghost. Every time someone cracks a note, it's because of the Ghost. But *also*, every time someone *finds* a lost object, it's because of the Ghost. Every time someone has a very good scene, it must be because of the

Ghost. He sort of comes with the building, like the rats. Every so often someone sees him, but not for long because he comes and goes like a . . . well, a Ghost. Apparently we let him use Box Eight for *free* on every first-night performance. And you say people *like* him?"

" 'Like' isn't quite the right word," said Salzella. "It would be more correct to say that . . . well, it's pure superstition, of course, but they think he's lucky. *Thought* he was, anyway."

And you wouldn't understand a thing about that, would you, you coarse little cheesemonger, he added to himself. *Cheese is cheese. Milk goes rotten naturally. You don't have to make it happen by having several hundred people wound up until their nerves go twang . . .*

"Lucky," said Bucket flatly.

"Luck is very important," said Salzella, in a voice in which pained patience floated like ice cubes. "I imagine that temperament is not an important factor in the cheese business?"

"We rely on rennet," said Bucket.

Salzella sighed. "Anyway, the company feel that the Ghost is . . . lucky. He used to send people little notes of encouragement. After a really good performance, sopranos would find a box of chocolates in their dressing room, that sort of thing. And dead flowers, for some reason."

"*Dead* flowers?"

"Well, not flowers at all, as such. Just a bouquet of dead rose-stems with no roses on them. It's something of a trademark of his. It's considered lucky."

"Dead flowers are lucky?"

"Possibly. Live flowers, certainly, are terribly bad

luck on stage. Some singers won't even have them in their dressing room. So . . . dead flowers are safe, you might say. Odd, but safe. And it didn't worry people because everyone thought the Ghost was on their side. At least, they did. Until about six months ago."

Mr. Bucket shut his eyes again. "Tell me," he said.

"There have been . . . accidents."

"What kind of accidents?"

"The kind of accidents that you prefer to call . . . accidents."

Mr. Bucket's eyes stayed closed. "Like . . . the time when Reg Plenty and Fred Chiswell were working late one night up on the curdling vats and it turned out Reg had been seeing Fred's wife and somehow"—Bucket swallowed—"somehow he must have tripped, Fred said, and fallen—"

"I am not familiar with the gentlemen concerned but . . . *that* kind of accident. Yes."

Bucket sighed. "That was some of the finest Farmhouse Nutty we ever made."

"Do you want me to tell you about *our* accidents?"

"I'm sure you're going to."

"A seamstress stitched herself to the wall. A deputy stage manager was found stabbed with a prop sword. Oh, and you wouldn't like me to tell you what happened to the man who worked the trapdoor. And all the lead mysteriously disappeared from the roof, although personally I don't think that was the work of the Ghost."

"And everyone . . . calls these . . . accidents?"

"Well, you wanted to sell your cheese, didn't you? I can't imagine anything that would depress the house like news that dead bodies are dropping like flies out of the flies."

He took an envelope out of his pocket and placed it on the table.

"The Ghost likes to leave little messages," he said. "There was one by the organ. A scenery painter spotted him and . . . nearly had an accident."

Bucket sniffed the envelope. It reeked of turpentine.

The letter inside was on a sheet of the Opera House's own note paper. In neat, copperplate writing, it said:

Ahahahahaha! Ahahahaha! Aahahaha!
BEWARE!!!!!

Yrs sincerely
The Opera Ghost

"What sort of person," said Salzella patiently, "sits down and *writes* a maniacal laugh? And all those exclamation marks, you notice? Five? A sure sign of someone who wears his underpants on his head. Opera can do that to a man. Look, at least let's search the building. The cellars go on forever. I'll need a boat—"

"A *boat*? In the *cellar*?"

"Oh. Didn't they tell you about the subbasement?"

Bucket smiled the bright, crazed smile of a man who was nearing double exclamation marks himself.

"No," he said. "They didn't tell me about the subbasement. They were too busy not telling me that someone goes around killing the company. I don't recall anyone saying 'Oh, by the way, people are dying a lot, and incidentally there's a touch of rising damp—'"

"They're flooded."

"Oh, good!" said Bucket. "What with? Buckets of blood?"

"Didn't you have a look?"

"They said the cellars were fine!"

"And you believed them?"

"Well, there was rather a lot of champagne . . ."

Salzella sighed.

Bucket took offense at the sigh. "I happen to pride myself that I am a good judge of character," he said. "Look a man deeply in the eye and give him a firm handshake and you know everything about him."

"Yes, indeed," said Salzella.

"Oh, blast . . . Señor Enrico Basilica will be here the day after tomorrow. Do you think something might happen to him?"

"Oh, not much. Cut throat, perhaps."

"What? You think so?"

"How should I know?"

"What do you want me to do? Close the place? As far as I can see it doesn't make any money as it is! Why hasn't anyone told the Watch?"

"That would be *worse*," said Salzella. "Big trolls in rusty chain mail tramping everywhere, getting in everyone's way and asking stupid questions. They'd close us down."

Bucket swallowed. "Oh, we can't have that," he said. "Can't have them . . . putting everyone on edge."

Salzella sat back. He seemed to relax a little. "On edge? Mr. Bucket," he said, "this is *opera*. *Everyone* is *always* on edge. Have you ever heard of a catastrophe curve, Mr. Bucket?"

Seldom Bucket did his best. "Well, I know there's a dreadful bend in the road up by—"

"A catastrophe curve, Mr. Bucket, is what opera runs along. Opera happens because a large number of things amazingly fail to go wrong, Mr. Bucket. It works because of hatred and love and nerves. All the time. This isn't cheese. This is opera. If you wanted a quiet retirement, Mr. Bucket, you shouldn't have bought the Opera House. You should have done something peaceful, like alligator dentistry."

Nanny Ogg was easily bored. But, on the other hand, she was also easy to amuse.

"Certainly an interestin' way to travel," she said. "You do get to see places."

"Yes," said Granny. "Every five miles, it seems to me."

"Can't think what's got into me."

"I shouldn't think the horses have managed to get faster'n a walk all morning."

They were, by now, alone except for the huge snoring man. The other two had got out and joined the travelers on top.

The main cause of this was Greebo. With a cat's unerring instinct for people who dislike cats he'd leapt heavily into their laps and given them the "young masser back on de ole plantation" treatment. And he'd treadled them into submission and then settled down and gone to sleep, claws gripping not sufficiently to draw blood but definitely to suggest that this was an option should the person move or breathe.

And then, when he was sure they were resigned to the situation, he'd started to smell.

No one knew where it came from. It was not associated with any known orifice. It was just that, after five minutes' doze, the air above Greebo had a penetrating smell of fermented carpets.

He was now trying it out on the very large man. It wasn't working. At last Greebo had found a stomach too big for him. Also, the continuing going up and down was beginning to make him feel ill.

The snores reverberated around the coach.

"Wouldn't like to come between *him* and his pudding," said Nanny Ogg.

Granny was staring out of the window. At least, her face was turned that way, but her eyes were focused on infinity.

"Gytha?"

"Yes, Esme?"

"Mind if I ask you a question?"

"You don't normally ask if I mind," said Nanny.

"Doesn't it ever get you down, the way people don't think properly?"

Oh-oh, thought Nanny. I reckon I got her out just in time. Thank goodness for literature.

"How d'you mean?" she said.

"I means the way they distracts themselves."

"Can't say I ever really thought about it, Esme."

"Like . . . s'pose I was to say to you, Gytha Ogg, your house is on fire, what's the first thing you'd try to take out?"

Nanny bit her lip. "This is one of them personality questions, ain't it?" she said.

"That's right."

"Like, you try to guess what I'm like by what I say . . ."

"Gytha Ogg, I've known you all my life, I *knows* what you're like. I don't need to guess. But answer me, all the same."

"I reckon I'd take Greebo."

Granny nodded.

" 'Cos that shows I've got a warm and considerate nature," Nanny went on.

"No, it shows you're the kind of person who tries to work out what the right answer's supposed to be," said Granny. "Untrustworthy. That was a witch's answer if ever I heard one. Devious."

Nanny looked proud.

The snores changed to a *blurt-blurt* noise and the handkerchief quivered.

". . . treacle pudding, with lots of custard . . ."

"Hey, he just said something," said Nanny.

"He talks in his sleep," said Granny Weatherwax. "He's been doing it on and off."

"I never heard him!"

"You were out of the coach."

"Oh."

"At the last stop he was going on about pancakes with lemon," said Granny. "And mashed potatoes with butter."

"Makes me feel hungry just listening to that," said Nanny. "I've got a pork pie in the bag somewhere—"

The snoring stopped abruptly. A hand came up and moved the handkerchief aside. The face beyond was friendly, bearded and small. It gave the witches a shy smile which turned inexorably toward the pork pie.

"Want a slice, mister?" said Nanny. "I've got some mustard here, too."

"Oo, would you, dear lady?" said the man, in a squeaky voice. "Don't know when I last had a pork pie—oh, dear . . ."

He grimaced as if he'd just said something wrong, and then relaxed.

"Got a bottle of beer if you want a drop, too," said Nanny. She was one of those women who enjoy seeing people eat almost as much as eating itself.

"Beer?" said the man. "Beer? You know, they don't let me drink beer. Hah, it's supposed to be the wrong ambience. I'd give *anything* for a pint of beer—"

"Just a 'thank you' would do," said Nanny, passing it over.

"Who's this 'they' to whom you refers?" said Granny.

"'S my fault really," said the man, through a faint spray of pork crumbs. "Got caught up, I suppose . . ."

There was a change in the sounds from outside. The lights of a town were going past and the coach was slowing down.

The man forced the last of the pie into his mouth and washed it down with the dregs of the beer.

"Oo, lovely," he said. Then he leaned back and put the handkerchief over his face.

He raised a corner. "Don't tell anyone I spoke to you," he said, "but you've made a friend of Henry Slugg."

"And what do you do, Henry Slugg?" said Granny, carefully.

"I'm . . . I'm on the stage."

"Yes. We can see," said Nanny Ogg.

"No, I meant—"

The coach stopped. Gravel crunched as people climbed down. The door was pulled open.

Granny saw a crowd of people peering excitedly through the doorway, and reached up automatically to straighten her hat. But several hands reached out for Henry Slugg, who sat up, smiled nervously, and let himself be helped out. Several people also shouted out a name, but it wasn't the name of Henry Slugg.

"Who's Enrico Basilica?" said Nanny Ogg.

"Don't know," said Granny. "Maybe he's the person Mr. Slugg's afraid of."

The coaching inn was a run-down shack, with only two bedrooms for guests. As helpless old ladies traveling alone, the witches got one, simply because all hell would have been let loose if they hadn't.

Mr. Bucket looked pained.

"I may just be a big man in cheese to you," he said, "you may think I'm just some hard-headed businessman who wouldn't know culture if he found it floating in his tea, but I have been a patron of the opera here and elsewhere for many years. I can hum nearly the whole of—"

"I am sure you've *seen* a lot of opera," said Salzella. "But . . . how much do you know about production?"

"I've been behind the scenes in lots of theaters—"

"Oh, *theater*," said Salzella. "Theater doesn't even approach it. Opera isn't theater with singing and dancing. Opera's *opera*. You might think a production like *Lohenshaak* is full of passion, but it's a sandpit of toddlers compared to what goes on behind the scenes. The singers all loathe the sight of one another, the chorus despises the singers, they both hate the orchestra, and everyone fears the conductor; the staff on one prompt side won't talk to the staff on the opposite prompt side, the dancers are all crazed from hunger in any case, and that's only the start of it, because what is really—"

There was a series of knocks at the door. They were painfully irregular, as if the knocker were having to concentrate quite hard.

"Come in, Walter," said Salzella.

Walter Plinge shuffled in, a pail dangling at the end of each arm. "Come to fill your coal scuttle Mr. Bucket!"

Bucket waved a hand vaguely, and turned back to the director of music. "You were saying?"

Salzella stared at Walter as the man carefully piled lumps of coal in the scuttle, one at a time.

"Salzella?"

"What? Oh. I'm sorry . . . what was I saying?"

"Something about it being only the start?"

"What? Oh. Yes. Yes . . . you see, it's fine for actors. There's plenty of parts for old men. Acting's something you can do all your life. You get *better* at it. But when your talent is singing or dancing . . . Time creeps up behind you, all the . . ." He fumbled for a word, and settled lamely for "Time. Time is the poison. You watch backstage one night and you'll see the dancers checking all the time in any mirror they can find for that first little imperfection. You watch the singers. Everyone's on edge, everyone knows that this might be their last perfect night, that tomorrow might be the beginning of the end. That's why everyone worries about luck, you see? All the stuff about live flowers being unlucky, you remember? Well, so's green. And real jewelry worn onstage. And real mirrors on stage. And whistling onstage. And peeking at the audience through the main curtains. And using new makeup on a first night. And knitting onstage, even at rehearsals. A yellow clarinet in the orchestra is very unlucky, don't ask me why. And as for stopping a performance before its proper ending, well, that's worst of all. You might as well sit under a ladder and break mirrors."

Behind Salzella, Walter carefully placed the last lump of coal on the pile in the scuttle and dusted it carefully.

"Good grief," said Bucket, at last. "I thought it was tough in cheese."

He waved a hand at the pile of papers and what passed for the accounts. "I paid thirty thousand for this place," he said. "It's in the center of the city! Prime site! I thought it was hard bargaining!"

"They'd have probably accepted twenty-five."

"And tell me again about Box Eight. You let this Ghost have it?"

"The Ghost considers it is his for every first night, yes."

"How does he get in?"

"No one knows. We've searched and searched for secret entrances . . ."

"He really doesn't pay?"

"No."

"It's worth fifty dollars a night!"

"There will be trouble if you sell it," said Salzella.

"Good grief, Salzella, you're an educated man! How can you sit there so calmly and accept this sort of madness? Some creature in a mask has the run of the place, gets a prime Box all to himself, kills people, and you sit there saying there will be trouble?"

"I told you: the show must go on."

"*Why?* We never said 'the cheese must go on'! What's so special about the show going on?"

Salzella smiled. "As far as I understand it," he said, "the . . . power behind the show, the soul of the show, all the effort that's gone into it, call it what you will . . . it leaks out and spills everywhere. That's why they burble about 'the show must go on.' It *must* go on. But most of the company wouldn't even understand why anyone should ask the question."

Bucket glared at the pile of what passed for the Opera House's financial records.

"They certainly don't understand bookkeeping! Who does the accounts?"

"All of us, really," said Salzella.

"*All* of you?"

"Money gets put in, money gets taken out . . ." said Salzella vaguely. "Is it important?"

Bucket's jaw dropped. "Is it *important*?"

"Because," Salzella went on, smoothly, "opera doesn't make money. Opera never makes money."

"Good grief, man! *Important*? What'd I ever have achieved in the cheese business, I'd like to know, if I'd said that money wasn't important?"

Salzella smiled humorlessly. "There are people out on the stage right now, sir," he said, "who'd say that you would probably have made better cheeses." He sighed, and leaned over the desk. "You see," he said, "cheese *does* make money. And opera *doesn't*. Opera's what you spend money *on*."

"But . . . what do you get out of it?"

"You get opera. You put money in, you see, and opera comes out," said Salzella wearily.

"There's no *profit*?"

"Profit . . . profit," murmured the director of music, scratching his forehead. "No, I don't believe I've come across the word."

"Then how do we manage?"

"We seem to rub along."

Bucket put his head in his hands. "I mean," he muttered, half to himself, "I knew the place wasn't making much, but I thought that was just because it was run badly. We have big audiences! We charge a mint for tickets! Now I'm told that a Ghost runs around killing people and we don't even make any money!"

Salzella beamed. "Ah, *opera*," he said.

Greebo stalked over the inn's rooftops.

Most cats are nervous and ill at ease when taken out of their territory, which is why cat books go on about putting butter on their paws and so on, presumably because constantly skidding into the walls will take the animal's mind off where the walls actually *are*.

But Greebo traveled well, purely because he took it for granted that the whole world was his dirt box.

He dropped heavily onto an outhouse roof and padded toward a small open window.

Greebo also had a cat's approach to possessions,

which was simply that nothing edible had a right to belong to other people.

From the window came a variety of smells which included pork pies and cream. He squeezed through and dropped onto the pantry shelf.

Of course, sometimes he got caught. At least, sometimes he got *discovered* . . .

There *was* cream. He settled down.

He was halfway down the bowl when the door opened.

Greebo's ears flattened. His one good eye sought desperately for an escape route. The window was too high, the person opening the door was wearing a long dress that militated against the old "through the legs" routine and . . . and . . . and . . . *there was no escape* . . .

His claws scrabbled on the floor . . .

Oh no . . . *here it came* . . .

Something flipped in his body's morphogenic field. Here was a problem a cat shape couldn't deal with. Oh, well, we know another one. Sometimes Greebo could be almost . . . human.

Crockery crashed around him. Shelves erupted as his head rose. A bag of flour exploded outward to make room for his broadening shoulders.

The cook stared up at him. Then she looked down. And then up. And then, her gaze dragged as though it were on a winch, down again.

She screamed.

Greebo screamed.

He grabbed desperately at a bowl to cover that part which, as a cat, he never had to worry about exposing.

He screamed again, this time because he'd just poured lukewarm pork dripping all over himself.

His groping fingers found a large copper jelly mold. Clasping it to his groinal areas, he barreled forward and fled out of the pantry and out of the kitchen and out of the dining room and out of the inn and into the night.

The spy, who was dining with the traveling salesman, put down his knife.

"That's something you don't often see," he said.

"What?" said the salesman, who'd had his back to the excitement.

"One of those old copper jelly molds. They're worth quite a lot now. My aunt had a very good one."

The hysterical cook was given a big drink and several members of staff went out into the darkness to investigate.

All they found was a jelly mold, lying forlornly in the yard.

At home Granny Weatherwax slept with open windows and an unlocked door, secure in the knowledge that the Ramtops' various creatures of the night would rather eat their own ears than break in. In dangerously civilized lands, however, she took a different view.

"I really don't think we *need* to shove the bed in front of the door, Esme," said Nanny Ogg, heaving on her end.

"You can't be too careful," said Granny. "Supposing some man started rattlin' the knob in the middle of the night?"

"Not at our time of life," said Nanny sadly.

"Gytha Ogg, you are the most—"

Granny was interrupted by a watery sound. It came from behind the wall and went on for some time.

It stopped, and then started again—a steady splashing that gradually became a trickle. Nanny started to grin.

"Someone fillin' a bath?" said Granny.

". . . or I suppose it could be someone fillin' a bath," Nanny conceded.

There was the sound of a third jug being emptied. Footsteps left the room. A few seconds later a door opened and there was a rather heavier tread, followed after a brief interval by a few splashes and a grunt.

"Yes, a man gettin' into a bath," said Granny. "What're you doin', Gytha?"

"Seein' if there's a knothole in this wood somewhere," said Nanny. "Ah, here's one—"

"Come back here!"

"Sorry, Esme."

And then the singing started. It was a very pleasant tenor voice, given added timbre by the bath itself.

"Show me the way to go home, I'm tired and I want to go to bed—"

"Someone's enjoyin' themselves, anyway," said Nanny.

"—wherever I may roam—"

There was a knock at the distant bathroom door, upon which the singer slipped smoothly into another language:

"—*per via di terra, mare o schiuma*—"

The witches looked at one another.

A muffled voice said, "I've brought you your hot-water bottle, sir."

"Thank you verr' mucha," said the bather, his voice dripping with accent.

Footsteps went away in the distance.

"—*Indicame la strada* . . . to go home." Splash, splash. "Good eeeeevening, frieeeends . . ."

"Well, well, well," said Granny, more or less to herself. "It seems once again that our Mr. Slugg is a secret polyglot."

"Fancy! And you haven't even looked through the knothole," said Nanny.

"Gytha, is there anything in the whole world you can't make sound grubby?"

"Not found it yet, Esme," said Nanny brightly.

"I *meant* that when he mutters in his sleep and sings in his bath he talks just like us, but when he thinks people are listening he comes over all foreign."

"That's probably to throw that Basilica person off the scent," Nanny said.

"Oh, I reckon Mr. Basilica is very close to Henry Slugg," said Granny. "In fact, I reckon that they're one and—"

There was a gentle knock at the door.

"Who's there?" Granny demanded.

"It's me, ma'am. Mr. Slot. This is my tavern."

The witches pushed the bed aside and Granny opened the door a fraction.

"Yes?" she said suspiciously.

"Er . . . the coachman said you were . . . witches?"

"Yes?"

"Maybe you could . . . help us?"

"What's wrong?"

"It's my boy . . ."

Granny opened the door farther and saw the woman standing behind Mr. Slot. One look at her face was enough. There was a bundle in her arms.

Granny stepped back. "Bring him in and let me have a look at him."

She took the baby from the woman, sat down on the room's one chair, and pulled back the blanket. Nanny Ogg peered over her shoulder.

"Hmm," said Granny, after a while. She glanced at Nanny, who gave an almost imperceptible shake of her head.

"There's a curse on this house, that's what it is," said Slot. "My best cow's been taken mortally sick, too."

"Oh? You have a cowshed?" said Granny. "Very good place for a sickroom, a cowshed. It's the warmth. You better show me where it is."

"You want to take the boy down there?"

"Right now."

The man looked at his wife, and shrugged. "Well, I'm sure you know your business best," he said. "It's this way."

He led the witches down some back stairs and across a yard and into the fetid sweet air of the byre. A cow was stretched out on the straw. It rolled an eye madly as they entered, and tried to moo.

Granny took in the scene and stood looking thoughtful for a moment.

Then she said, "This will do."

"What do you need?" said Slot.

"Just peace and quiet."

The man scratched his head. "I thought you did a chant or made up some potion or something," he said.

"Sometimes."

"I mean, I know where there's a toad . . ."

"All I shall require is a candle," said Granny. "A new one, for preference."

"That's all?"

"Yes."

Mr. Slot looked a little put out. Despite his distraction, something about his manner suggested that Granny Weatherwax was possibly not that much of a witch if she didn't want a toad.

"And some matches," said Granny, noting this. "A pack of cards might be useful, too."

"And I'll need three cold lamb chops and exactly two pints of beer," said Nanny Ogg.

The man nodded. This didn't sound too toadlike, but it was better than nothing.

"What'd you ask for that for?" hissed Granny, as the man bustled off. "Can't imagine what good those'd do! Anyway, you already had a big dinner."

"Well, I'm always prepared to go that extra meal. You won't want me around and I'll get bored," said Nanny.

"Did I say I didn't want you around?"

"Well . . . even I can see that boy is in a coma, and the cow has the Red Bugge if I'm any judge. That's bad, too. So I reckon you're planning some . . . direct action."

Granny shrugged.

"Time like that, a witch needs to be alone," said Nanny. "But you just mind what you're doing, Esme Weatherwax."

The child was brought down in a blanket and made as comfortable as possible. The man followed behind his wife with a tray.

"Mrs. Ogg will do her necessary procedures with the tray in her room," said Granny haughtily. "You just leave me in here tonight. And no one is to come in, right? No matter what."

The mother gave a worried curtsy. "But I thought I might look in about midn—"

"No one. Now, off you go."

When they'd been gently but firmly ushered out, Nanny Ogg stuck her head around the door. "What *exactly* are you planning, Esme?"

"You've sat up with the dyin' often enough, Gytha."

"Oh, yes, it's . . ." Nanny's face fell. "Oh, Esme . . . you're not going to . . ."

"Enjoy your supper, Gytha."

Granny closed the door.

She spent some time arranging boxes and barrels so that she had a crude table and something to sit on. The air was warm and smelled of bovine flatulence. Periodically she checked the health of both patients, although there was little enough to check.

In the distance the sounds of the inn gradually subsided. The last one was the clink of the innkeeper's keys as he locked the doors. Granny heard him walk across to the cowshed door and hesitate. Then he went away, and began to climb the stairs.

She waited a little longer and then lit the candle.

Its cheery flame gave the place a warm and comforting glow.

On the plank table she laid out the cards and attempted to play Patience, a game she'd never been able to master.

The candle burned down. She pushed the cards away, and sat watching the flame.

After some immeasurable piece of time the flame flickered. It would have passed unnoticed by anyone who hadn't been concentrating on it for some while.

She took a deep breath and—

"Good morning," said Granny Weatherwax.

GOOD MORNING, said a voice by her ear.

Nanny Ogg had long ago polished off the chops and the beer, but she hadn't got into bed. She lay on it, fully clothed, with her arms behind her head, staring at the dark ceiling.

After a while there was a scratching on the shutters. She got up and opened them.

A huge figure leapt into the room. For a moment the moonlight lit a glistening torso and a mane of black hair. Then the creature dived under the bed.

"Oh, deary deary me," said Nanny.

She waited for a while, and then fished a chop bone off her tray. There was still a bit of meat on it. She lowered it toward the floor.

A hand shot out and grabbed it.

Nanny sat back.

"Poor little man," she said.

It was only on the subject of Greebo that Nanny's otherwise keen sense of reality found itself all twisted. To Nanny Ogg he was merely a larger version of the little fluffy kitten he had once been. To everyone else he was a scarred ball of inventive malignancy.

But now he had to deal with a problem seldom encountered by cats. The witches had, a year ago, turned him into a human, for reasons that had seemed quite necessary at the time. It had taken a lot of effort, and his morphogenic field had reasserted itself after a few hours, much to everyone's relief.

But magic is never as simple as people think. It has to obey certain universal laws. And one is that, no matter how hard a thing is to do, once it *has* been done it'll become a whole lot easier and will therefore be done a lot. A huge mountain might be scaled by strong men only after many centuries of failed attempts, but a few decades later grandmothers will be strolling up it for tea and then wandering back afterward to see where they left their glasses.

In accordance with this law, Greebo's soul had noted that there was one extra option for use in a tight corner (in addition to the usual cat assortment of run, fight, crap or all three together) and that was: Become Human.

It tended to wear off after a short time, most of which he spent searching desperately for a pair of pants.

There were snores from under the bed. Gradually, to Nanny's relief, they turned into a purr.

Then she sat bolt upright. She was some way from the cowshed but . . .

"*He's* here," she said.

Granny breathed out, slowly.

"Come and sit where I can see you. That's good

manners. And let me tell you right now that I ain't at all afraid of you."

The tall, black-robed figure walked across the floor and sat down on a handy barrel, leaning its scythe against the wall. Then it pushed back its hood.

Granny folded her arms and stared calmly at the visitor, meeting his gaze eye-to-socket.

I AM IMPRESSED.

"I have faith."

REALLY? IN WHAT PARTICULAR DEITY?

"Oh, none of *them*."

THEN FAITH IN WHAT?

"Just faith, you know. In general."

Death leaned forward. The candlelight raised new shadows on his skull.

COURAGE IS EASY BY CANDLELIGHT. YOUR FAITH, I SUSPECT, IS IN THE FLAME.

Death grinned.

Granny leaned forward, and blew out the candle. Then she folded her arms again and stared fiercely ahead of her.

After some length of time a voice said, ALL RIGHT, YOU'VE MADE YOUR POINT.

Granny lit a match. Its flare illuminated the skull opposite, which hadn't moved.

"Fair enough," she said, as she relit the candle. "We don't want to be sitting here all night, do we? How many have you come for?"

ONE.

"The cow?"

Death shook his head.

"It could *be* the cow."

NO. THAT WOULD BE CHANGING HISTORY.

"History is about things changing."

No.

Granny sat back.

"Then I challenge you to a game. That's traditional. That's *allowed*."

Death was silent for a moment.

THIS IS TRUE.

"Good."

CHALLENGING ME BY MEANS OF A GAME IS ALLOWABLE.

"Yes."

HOWEVER . . . YOU UNDERSTAND THAT TO WIN ALL YOU MUST GAMBLE ALL?

"Double or quits? Yes, I know."

BUT NOT CHESS.

"Can't abide chess."

OR CRIPPLE MR. ONION. I'VE NEVER BEEN ABLE TO UNDERSTAND THE RULES.

"Very well. How about one hand of poker? Five cards each, no draws? Sudden death, as they say."

Death thought about this, too.

YOU KNOW THIS FAMILY?

"No."

THEN WHY?

"Are we talking or are we playing?"

OH, VERY WELL.

Granny picked up the pack of cards and shuffled it, not looking at her hands, and smiling at Death all the time. She dealt five cards each, and reached down . . .

A bony hand grasped hers.

BUT *FIRST*, MISTRESS WEATHERWAX—WE WILL EXCHANGE CARDS.

He picked up the two piles and transposed them, and then nodded at Granny.

MADAM?

Granny looked at her cards, and threw them down.

FOUR QUEENS. HMM. THAT IS VERY HIGH.

Death looked down at his cards, and then up into Granny's steady, blue-eyed gaze.

Neither moved for some time.

Then Death laid the hand on the table.

I LOSE, he said. ALL I HAVE IS FOUR ONES.

He looked back into Granny's eyes for a moment. There was a blue glow in the depth of his eye-sockets. Maybe, for the merest fraction of a second, barely noticeable even to the closest observation, one winked off.

Granny nodded, and extended a hand.

She prided herself on the ability to judge people by their gaze and their handshake, which in this case was a rather chilly one.

"Take the cow," she said.

IT IS A VALUABLE CREATURE.

"Who knows what the child will become?"

Death stood up, and reached for his scythe.

He said, Ow.

"Ah, yes. I couldn't help noticing," said Granny Weatherwax, as the tension drained out of the atmosphere, "that you seem to be sparing that arm."

OH, YOU KNOW HOW IT IS. REPETITIVE ACTIONS AND SO ON . . .

"It could get serious if you left it."

HOW SERIOUS?

"Want me to have a look?"

WOULD YOU MIND? IT CERTAINLY ACHES ON COLD NIGHTS.

Granny stood up and reached out, but her hands went straight through.

"Look, you're going to have to make yourself a bit more solid if I'm to do anything—"

POSSIBLY A BOTTLE OF SUCKROSE AND AKWA?

"Sugar and water? I expect you *know* that's only for the hard of thinking. Come on, roll up that sleeve. Don't be a big baby. What's the worst I can do to you?"

Granny's hands touched smooth bone. She'd felt worse. At least these had never had flesh on them.

She felt, thought, gripped, twisted . . .

There was a click.

Ow.

"Now try it above the shoulder."

ER. HMM. YES. IT DOES SEEM CONSIDERABLY MORE FREE. YES, INDEED. MY WORD, YES. THANK YOU VERY MUCH.

"If it gives you trouble again, you know where I live."

THANK YOU. THANK YOU VERY MUCH.

"You know where everyone lives. Tuesday mornings is a good time. I'm generally in."

I SHALL REMEMBER. THANK YOU.

"By appointment, in your case. No offense meant."

THANK YOU.

Death walked away. A moment later there was a faint gasp from the cow. That and a slight sagging of the skin were all that apparently marked the transition from living animal to cooling meat.

Granny picked up the baby and laid a hand on its forehead.

"Fever's gone," she said.

MISTRESS WEATHERWAX? said Death from the doorway.

"Yes, sir?"

I HAVE TO KNOW. WHAT WOULD HAVE HAPPENED IF I HAD NOT . . . LOST?

"At the cards, you mean?"

YES. WHAT WOULD YOU HAVE DONE?

Granny laid the baby down carefully on the straw, and smiled.

"Well," she said, "for a start . . . I'd have broken your bloody arm."

Agnes stayed up late, simply because of the novelty. Most people in Lancre, as the saying goes, went to bed with the chickens and got up with the cows.* But she watched the evening's performance, and watched the set being struck afterwards, and watched the actors leave or, in the case of younger chorus members, head off for their lodgings in odd corners of the building. And then there was no one else, except Walter Plinge and his mother sweeping up.

She headed for the staircase. There didn't seem to be a candle anywhere back here, but the few left burning in the auditorium were just enough to give the darkness a few shades.

---

*Er. That is to say, they went to bed at the same time as the chickens went to bed, and got up at the same time as the cows got up. Loosely worded sayings can really cause misunderstandings.

The stairs went up the wall at the rear of the stage, with nothing but a rickety handrail between them and the drop. Besides leading to the attics and storeroom on the upper floors, they were also one route to the fly loft and the other secret platforms where men in flat hats and gray overalls worked the magic of the theater, usually by means of pulleys—

There was a figure on one of the gantries over the stage. Agnes saw it only because it moved slightly. It was kneeling down, looking at something. In the darkness.

She stepped back. The stair creaked.

The figure jerked around. A square of yellow light opened in the darkness, its beam pinning her against the brickwork.

"Who's there?" she said, raising a hand to shade her eyes.

"Who's *that*?" said a voice. And then, after a moment, "Oh. It's . . . Perdita, isn't it?"

The square of light swung toward her as the figure made its way over the stage.

"André?" she said. She felt inclined to back away, if only the brickwork would let her.

And suddenly he was on the stairs, quite an ordinary person, no shadow at all, holding a very large lantern.

"What are you doing here?" said the organist.

"I . . . was just going to bed."

"Oh, yes." He relaxed a little. "Some of you girls have got rooms here. The management thought it was safer than having you going home alone late at night."

"What are you doing up here?" said Agnes, suddenly aware that there was just the two of them.

"I was . . . looking at the place where the Ghost tried to strangle Mr. Cripps," said André.

"Why?"

"I wanted to make certain everything was safe now, of course."

"Didn't the stagehands do that?"

"Oh, you know them. I just thought I'd better make certain."

Agnes looked down at the lantern.

"I've never seen one like that before. How did you make it light up so quickly?"

"Er. It's a dark lantern. There's this flap, you see," he demonstrated, "so you can shut it right down and open it up again . . ."

"That must be very useful when you're looking for the black notes."

"Don't be sarcastic. I just don't want there to be any more trouble. You'll find that *you* start looking around when—"

"*Goodnight*, André."

"Goodnight, then."

She hurried up the rest of the flights and ducked into her bedroom. No one followed her.

When she'd calmed down, which took some time, she undressed in the voluminous tent of her red flannel nightdress and got into bed, resisting any temptation to pull the covers over her head.

She stared at the dark ceiling.

"That's stupid," she thought, eventually. "He was on the stage this morning. *No one* could move that fast . . ."

She never knew whether she actually got some sleep or whether it happened just as she was dozing off, but there was a very faint knock at the door.

"Perdita!?"

Only one person she knew could exclaim a whisper.

Agnes got up and padded over to the door. She opened the door a fraction, just to check, and Christine half-fell into the room.

"What's the matter?"

"I'm frightened!!"

"What of?"

"The mirror!! It's *talking* to me!! Can I sleep in your room?!"

Agnes looked around. It was crowded enough with the two of them standing up in it.

"The mirror's *talking*?"

"Yes!!"

"Are you sure?"

Christine dived into Agnes's bed and pulled the covers over her. "Yes!!" she said, indistinctly.

Agnes stood alone in the darkness.

People always tended to assume that she could cope, as if capability went with mass, like gravity. And merely saying briskly, "Nonsense, mirrors don't talk," would probably not be any help, especially with one half of the dialogue buried beneath the bedclothes.

She felt her way into the next room, stubbing her foot on the bed in the darkness.

There must be a candle in here, somewhere. She felt for the tiny bedside table, hoping to start the reassuring rattle of a matchbox.

A faint glimmer from the midnight city filtered through the window. The mirror seemed to glow.

She sat down on the bed, which creaked ominously under her.

Oh well . . . one bed was as good as another . . .

She was about to lie back when something in the darkness went: . . . *ting*.

It was a tuning fork.

And a voice said: "Christine . . . please attend."

She sat upright, staring at the darkness.

And then realization dawned. No men, they'd said. They'd been very strict about that, as if opera were some kind of religion. It was not a problem in Agnes's case, at least in the way they meant, but for someone like Christine . . . They said love always found a way and, of course, so did a number of associated activities.

Oh, good grief. She felt the blush start. In darkness! What kind of a reaction was that?

Agnes's life unrolled in front of her. It didn't look as though it were going to have many high points. But it did hold years and years of being capable and having a lovely personality. It almost certainly held chocolate rather than sex and, while Agnes was not in a position to make a direct comparison, and regardless of the fact that a bar of chocolate could be made to last all day, it did not seem a very fair exchange.

She felt the same feeling she'd felt back home. Sometimes life reaches that desperate point where the wrong thing to do has to be the right thing to do.

It doesn't matter what direction you go. Sometimes you just have to *go*.

She gripped the bedclothes and replayed in her mind the way her friend spoke. You had to have that little gulp, that breathless tinkle in the tone that people got whose minds played with the fairies half the time. She tried it out in her head, and then delivered it to her vocal cords.

"Yes?! Who's there?!"

"A friend."

Agnes pulled the bedclothes up higher. "In the middle of the *night*?!"

"Night is nothing to me. I belong to the night. And I can help you." It was a pleasant voice. It seemed to be coming from the mirror.

"Help me to do what?!"

"Don't you want to be the best singer in the opera?"

"Oh, Perdita is a *lot* better than me!!"

There was silence for a moment, and then the voice said: "But while I cannot teach her to look and move like you, I can teach you to sing like her."

Agnes stared into the darkness, shock and humiliation rising from her like steam.

"Tomorrow you will sing the part of Iodine. But I will teach you how to sing it *perfectly* . . ."

Next morning the witches had the interior of the coach almost to themselves. News like Greebo gets around. But Henry Slugg was there, if that was indeed his name, sitting next to a very well-dressed, thin little man.

"Well, here we are again, then," said Nanny Ogg.

Henry smiled nervously.

"That was some good singing last night," Nanny went on.

Henry's face set in a good-natured grimace. In his eyes, terror waved a white flag.

"I am afraid Señor Basilica doesn't speak Morporkian, ma'am," said the thin man. "But I will translate for you, if you like."

"What?" said Nanny. "Then how come—*Ow!*"

"Sorry," said Granny Weatherwax. "My elbow must have slipped."

Nanny Ogg rubbed her side. "I was *saying*," she said, "that he was—*Ow!*"

"Dear me, I seem to have done it again," said Granny. "This gentleman was telling us that his friend *doesn't speak our language*, Gytha."

"Eh? But—What? Oh. But—Ah. Really? Oh. All right," said Nanny. "Oh, yes. Eats our pies, though, when—*Ow!*"

"Excuse my friend, it's her time of life. She gets confused," said Granny. "We did enjoy his singing. I Ieard him through the wall."

"You were very fortunate," said the thin man primly. "Sometimes people have to wait years to hear Señor Basilica—"

"—probably waiting for him to finish his dinner—" a voice muttered.

"—in fact, at La Scalda in Genua last month his singing made ten thousand people shed tears."

"—hah, I can do *that*, I don't see there's anything special about *that*—"

Granny's eyes hadn't left Henry "Señor Basilica" Slugg's face. He had the expression of a man whose profound relief was horribly tempered by a dread that it wouldn't last very long.

"Señor Basilica's fame has spread far and wide," said the manager primly.

"—just like Senior Basilica," muttered Nanny. "On other people's pies, I expect. Oh, yes, too posh for us now, just because he's the only man you could find on an atlas—*Ow!*"

"Well, well," said Granny, smiling in a way that everyone except Nanny Ogg would think of as innocent. "It's nice and warm in Genua. I expect Señor Basilica really misses his home. And what do you do, young sir?"

"I am his manager and translator. Er. You have the advantage of me, ma'am."

"Yes, indeed." Granny nodded.

"We have some good singers where we come from, too," said Nanny Ogg, rebelliously.

"Really?" said the manager. "And where do you ladies come from?"

"Lancre."

The man politely endeavored to position Lancre on his mental map of great centers of music. "Do you have a conservatory there?"

"Yes, indeed," said Nanny Ogg stoutly, and then, just to make sure, she added, "You should see the size of my tomatoes."

Granny rolled her eyes. "Gytha, you *haven't* got a conservatory. It's just a big windowsill."

"Yes, but it catches the sun nearly all day—*Ow . . .*"

"I expect Señor Basilica is going to Ankh-Morpork?" said Granny.

"We," said the manager, primly, "have allowed

the Opera House to engage us for the rest of the season—"

His voice faltered. He'd looked up at the luggage rack. "What's *that*?"

Granny glanced up. "Oh, that's Greebo," she said.

"And Mister Basilica's not to eat him," said Nanny.

"What *is* it?"

"He's a cat."

"It's *grinning* at me." The manager shifted uneasily. "And I can smell something," he said.

"'S funny," said Nanny. "I can't smell a *thing*."

There was a change in the sound of the hooves outside, and the coach lurched as it slowed.

"Ah," said the manager awkwardly, "I . . . er . . . I see we're stopping to change horses. It's a, a nice day. I think I may just, er, see if there's room on the seats outside."

He left when the coach stopped. When it started again, a few minutes later, he hadn't come back.

"Well, well," said Granny, as they lurched away again, "it seems there's just you and me, Gytha. And Señor Basilica, who doesn't speak our language. Does he, Mr. Henry Slugg?"

Henry Slugg took out a handkerchief and wiped his forehead. "Ladies! Dear ladies! I beg you, for pity's sake . . ."

"Have you done anything bad, Mr. Slugg?" said Nanny. "Took advantage of women who dint want to be took advantage of? Stole? (Apart from lead on roofs and other stuff people wouldn't miss.) Done any murders of anyone who dint deserve it?"

"No!"

"He tellin' the truth, Esme?"

Henry writhed under Granny Weatherwax's stare. "Yes."

"Oh, well, that's all right, then," said Nanny. "I *understand*. I don't have to pay taxes myself, but I know all about people not wantin' to."

"Oh, it's not that, I assure you," said Henry. "I have people to pay my taxes for me . . ."

"That's a good trick," said Nanny.

"Mr. Slugg's got a different trick," said Granny. "I reckon I know the trick. It's like sugar and water."

Henry waved his hands uncertainly. "It's just that if they knew . . ." he began.

"Everything's better if it comes from a long way away. That's the secret," said Granny.

"It's . . . yes, that's part of it," said Henry. "I mean, no one wants to listen to a Slugg."

"Where're you from, Henry?" said Nanny.

"*Really* from," said Granny.

"I grew up in Rookery Yard in the Shades. They're in Ankh-Morpork," said Henry. "It was a terrible rough place. There were only three ways out. You could sing your way out or you could fight your way out."

"What was the third way?" said Nanny.

"Oh, you could go down that little alleyway into Shamlegger Street and then cut down into Treacle Mine Road," said Henry. "But no one ever amounted to anything who went *that* way."

He sighed. "I made a few coppers singing in taverns and such like," he said, "but when I tried for anything better they said 'What is your name?' and I said 'Henry Slugg' and they'd laugh. I thought of changing my name, but everyone in Ankh-

Morpork knew who I was. And no one wanted to listen to anyone called plain Henry Slugg."

Nanny nodded. "It's like with conjurers," she said. "They're never called Fred Wossname. It's always something like The Great Astoundo, Fresh From the Court of the King of Klatch, and Gladys."

"And everyone takes notice," said Granny, "and are always careful not to ask themselves: if he's come from the King of Klatch, why's he doing card tricks here in Slice, population seven."

"The trick is to make sure that everywhere you go, you are from somewhere else," said Henry. "And then I *was* famous, but . . ."

"You'd got stuck as Enrico," said Granny.

He nodded. "I was only going to do it to make some money. I was going to come back and marry my little Angeline—"

"Who was she?" said Granny.

"Oh, a girl I grew up with," said Henry, vaguely.

"Sharing the same gutter in the back streets of Ankh-Morpork, kind of thing?" said Nanny, in an understanding voice.

"Gutter? In those days you had to put your name down and wait five years for a gutter," said Henry. "We thought people in gutters were *nobs*. We shared a drain. With two other families. And a man who juggled eels."

He sighed. "But I moved on, and then there was always somewhere else to go, and they liked me in Brindisi . . . and . . . and . . ."

He blew his nose on the handkerchief, carefully folded it up, and produced another one from his pocket.

"I don't mind the pasta and the squid," he said. "Well, not much . . . But you can't get a decent pint for love nor money and they put olive oil on everything and tomatoes give me a rash and there isn't what I'd call a good hard cheese in the whole country."

He dabbed at his face with the handkerchief.

"And people are so kind," he said. "I thought I'd get a few beefsteaks when I traveled but, *wherever* I go, they do pasta especially for me. In tomato sauce! Sometimes they fry it! And what they do to the squid . . ." He shuddered. "Then they all grin and watch me eat it. They think I enjoy it! What I'd give for a plate of nice roast mutton with clootie dumplings . . ."

"Why don't you *say*?" said Nanny.

He shrugged. "Enrico Basilica eats pasta," he said. "There's not much I can do about it now."

He sat back. "You're interested in music, Mrs. Ogg?"

Nanny nodded proudly. "I can get a tune out of just about anything if you give me five minutes to study it," she said. "And our Jason can play the violin and our Kev can blow the trombone and all my kids can sing and our Shawn can fart any melody you care to name."

"A very talented family, indeed," said Enrico. He fumbled in a waistcoat pocket and took out two oblongs of cardboard. "So please, ladies, accept these as a small token of gratitude from someone who eats other people's pies. Our little secret, eh?" He winked desperately at Nanny. "They're open tickets for the opera."

"Well, that's amazin'," said Nanny, "because we're going to—*Ow*!"

"Why, thank you very much," said Granny Weatherwax, taking the tickets. "How very gracious of you. We shall be sure to go."

"And if you'll excuse me," said Enrico, "I must catch up on my sleep."

"Don't worry, I shouldn't think it's had time to get far away," said Nanny.

The singer leaned back, pulled the handkerchief over his face and, after a few minutes, began to snore the happy snore of someone who had done his duty and now with any luck wouldn't have to meet these rather disconcerting old women ever again.

"He's well away," said Nanny, after a while. She glanced at the tickets in Granny's hand. "You want to visit the opera?" she said.

Granny stared into space.

"I *said*, do you want to visit the opera?"

Granny looked at the tickets. "What I want don't signify, I suspect," she said.

Nanny Ogg nodded.

Granny Weatherwax was firmly against fiction. Life was hard enough without lies floating around and changing the way people thought. And because the theater was fiction made flesh, she hated the theater most of all. But that was it—*hate* was exactly the right word. Hate is a force of attraction. Hate is just love with its back turned.

She didn't *loathe* the theater, because, had she done so, she would have avoided it completely. Granny now took every opportunity to visit the traveling theater that came to Lancre, and sat bolt upright in

the front row of every performance, staring fiercely.
Even honest Punch and Judy men found her sitting
among the children, snapping things like "'Tain't
so!" and "Is that any way to behave?" As a result,
Lancre was becoming known throughout the Sto
Plains as a really tough gig.

But what she *wanted* wasn't important. Like it or
not, witches are drawn to the edge of things, where
two states collide. They feel the pull of doors, cir-
cumferences, boundaries, gates, mirrors, masks . . .

. . . and stages.

Breakfast was served in the Opera House's refectory
at half-past nine. Actors were not known for their
habit of early rising.

Agnes started to fall forward into her eggs and
bacon, and stopped herself just in time.

"*Good* morning!!"

Christine sat down with a tray on which was,
Agnes was not surprised to see, a plate holding one
stick of celery, one raisin and about a spoonful of
milk. She leaned toward Agnes and her face very
briefly expressed some concern. "Are you all right?!
You look a little peaky!!"

Agnes caught herself in mid-snore.

"I'm fine," she said. "Just a bit tired . . ."

"Oh, good!!" This exchange having exhausted her
higher mental processes, Christine went back to op-
erating on automatic. "Do you like my new dress?!"
she exclaimed. "Isn't it *fetching*?!"

Agnes looked at it. "Yes," she said. "Very . . . white.
Very lacy. Very figure-hugging."

"And do you know what?!"

"No. What?"

"I already have a secret admirer!! Isn't that *thrilling*?! All the great singers have them, you know!!"

"A secret admirer . . ."

"Yes!! This dress!! It arrived at the stage door just now!! Isn't that exciting?!"

"Amazing," said Agnes, glumly. "And it's not as if you've even sung. Er. Who's it from?"

"He didn't say, of course!! It has to be a *secret* admirer!! He'll probably want to send me flowers and drink champagne out of my shoe!!"

"Really?" Agnes made a face. "Do people *do* that?"

"It's traditional!!"

Christine, boiling over with cheerfulness, had some to share . . .

"You do look *very* tired!" she said. Her hand went to her mouth. "Oh!! We swapped rooms, didn't we!! I was *so* silly!! And, d'you know," she added with that look of half-empty cunning that was the nearest she came to guile, "I could have *sworn* I heard singing in the night . . . someone trying scales and things?!"

Agnes had been brought up to tell the truth. She knew she should say: "I'm sorry, I appear to have got your life by mistake. There seems to have been a bit of a confusion . . ."

But, she decided, she'd also been brought up to do what she was told, not to put herself first, to be respectful to her elders and to use no swearword stronger than "poot."

She could borrow a more interesting future. Just for a night or two. She could give it up any time she liked.

"You know, that's funny," she said, "because I'm right next door to you and *I* didn't."

"Oh?! Well, that's all right, then!!"

Agnes stared at the tiny meal on Christine's tray. "Is that *all* you're having for breakfast?"

"Oh, yes! I can just blow up like a balloon, dear!! It's lucky for you, *you* can eat anything!! Don't forget it's practice in half an hour!"

And she skipped off.

She's got a head full of air, Agnes thought. I'm sure she doesn't mean to say anything hurtful.

But, deep inside her, Perdita X Dream thought a rude word.

Mrs. Plinge took her broom out of the cleaning cupboard, and turned.

"Walter!"

Her voice echoed around the empty stage.

"Walter?"

She tapped the broom-handle warily. Walter had a routine. It had taken her years to train him into it. It wasn't like him not to be in the right place at the right time.

She shook her head, and started work. She could see it'd be a mop job later. It would probably be ages before they got rid of the smell of turpentine.

Someone came walking across the stage. They were whistling.

Mrs. Plinge was shocked.

"Mr. Pounder!"

The Opera House's professional rat catcher stopped, and lowered his struggling sack. Mr. Pounder wore an old opera hat to show that he was a cut above your normal rodent operative, and its brim was thick with wax and the old candle ends he used to light his way through the darker cellars.

He'd worked among the rats so long that there was something ratlike about him now. His face seemed to be merely a rearward extension of his nose. His mustache was bristly. His front teeth were prominent. People found themselves looking for his tail.

"What's that, Mrs. Plinge?"

"You know you mustn't whistle onstage! That's terrible bad luck!"

"Ah, well, it's 'cos of *good* luck, Mrs. Plinge. Oh, yes! If you did know what I d'know, you'd be a happy man, too. O' course, in your case you'd be a happy woman, on account of you being a woman. Ah! Some of the things I've seen, Mrs. Plinge!"

"Found gold down there, Mr. Pounder?"

Mrs. Plinge knelt down carefully to scrape away a spot of paint.

Mr. Pounder picked up his sack and continued on his way.

"Could be gold, Mrs. Plinge. Ah. Could very *well* be gold—"

It took a moment for Mrs. Plinge to coax her arthritic knees into letting her stand up and shuffle around.

"Pardon, Mr. Pounder?" she said.

Somewhere in the distance, there was a soft thump as a bundle of sandbags landed gently on the boards.

The stage was big and bare and empty, except for a sack which was scuttling determinedly for freedom.

Mrs. Plinge looked both ways very carefully.

"Mr. Pounder? Are you there?"

It suddenly seemed to her that the stage was even bigger and even more distinctly empty than before.

"Mr. Pounder? Cooo-eee?"

She craned around.

"Hello? Mr. Pounder?"

Something floated down from above and landed beside her.

It was a grubby black hat, with candle ends around the brim.

She looked up.

"Mr. Pounder?" she said.

Mr. Pounder was used to darkness. It held no fears for him. And he'd always prided himself on his night vision. If there was any light at all, any speck, any glimmer of phosphorescent rot, he could make use of it. His candled hat was as much for show as anything else.

His candled hat . . . he'd thought he'd lost it but, it was strange, here it was, still on his head. Yes, indeed. He rubbed his throat thoughtfully. There was something important he couldn't quite remember . . .

It was *very* dark.

SQUEAK?

He looked up.

Standing in the air, at eye-level, was a robed figure about six inches high. A bony nose, with bent gray whiskers, protruded from the hood. Tiny skeletal fingers gripped a very small scythe.

Mr. Pounder nodded thoughtfully to himself. You didn't rise to membership of the Inner Circle of the Guild of Rat Catchers without hearing a few whispered rumors. Rats had their own Death, they said, as well as their own kings, parliaments and nations. No human had ever seen it, though.

Up until now.

He felt honored. He'd won the Golden Mallet for most rats caught every year for the past five years, but he respected them, as a soldier might respect a cunning and valiant enemy.

"Er . . . I'm dead, aren't I . . . ?"

SQUEAK.

Mr. Pounder felt that many eyes were watching him. Many small, shining eyes.

"And . . . what happens now?"

SQUEAK.

The soul of Mr. Pounder looked at his hands. They seemed to be elongating, and getting hairier. He could feel his ears growing, and a certain rather embarrassing elongation happening at the base of his spine. He'd spent most of his life in a single-minded activity in dark places, yet even so . . .

"But I don't *believe* in reincarnation!" he protested.

SQUEAK.

And this, Mr. Pounder understood with absolute rodent clarity, meant: reincarnation believes in *you*.

Mr. Bucket went through his mail very carefully, and finally breathed out when the pile failed to disgorge another letter with the Opera House crest.

He sat back and pulled open his desk drawer for a pen.

There was an envelope there.

He stared at it, and then slowly picked up his paper knife.

Sliiiiit . . .

. . . rustle . . .

I will be obliged if Christine sings the role
of Jodine in "La Triviata" tonight.
The weather continues fine. I trust you are well.

Yrs
The Opera Ghost

"Mr. Salzella! *Mr. Salzella!*"

Bucket pushed back his chair and hurried to the door, opening it just in time to confront a ballerina, who screamed at him.

Since his nerves were already strained, he responded by screaming back at her. This seemed to have the effect that usually a wet flannel or a slap was necessary to achieve. She stopped and gave him an affronted look.

"He's struck again, hasn't he!" moaned Bucket.

"He's here! It's the Ghost!" said the girl, determined to get the line out even though it was not required.

"Yes, yes, I think I *know*," muttered Bucket. "I just hope it wasn't anybody expensive."

He stopped halfway along the corridor and then spun around. The girl cringed away from his wavering finger.

"At least stand on tiptoe!" he shouted. "You probably cost me a dollar just running up here!"

There was a crowd in a huddle on the stage. In the center was that new girl, the fat one, kneeling down and comforting an old woman. Bucket vaguely recognized the latter. She was one of the staff that had come with the Opera House, as much part of the whole thing as the rats or the gargoyles that infested the rooftops.

She was holding something in front of her. "It just fell out of the flies," she said. "His poor hat!"

Bucket looked up. As his eyes grew accustomed to the darkness he made out a shape up among the battens, spinning slowly . . .

"Oh, *dear*," he said. "And I thought he'd written such a *polite* letter . . ."

"Really? Then now read *this* one," said Salzella, coming up behind him.

"Must I?"

"It's addressed to you."

Bucket unfolded the piece of paper.

Hahahaha! Ahahahaha!

Yrs
    The Opera Ghost

PS: Ahahahaha!!!!!

He gave Salzella an agonized look. "Who's the poor fellow up there?"

"Mr. Pounder, the rat catcher. Rope dropped around his neck, other end attached to some sandbags. They went down. He went . . . up."

"I don't understand! Is this man *mad*?"

Salzella put an arm around his shoulders and led him away from the crowd. "Well, now," he said, as kindly as he could. "A man who wears evening dress all the time, lurks in the shadows and occasionally kills people. Then he sends little notes, *writing* maniacal laughter. Five exclamation marks again, I notice. We have to ask ourselves: is this the career of a sane man?"

"But *why* is he doing it?" wailed Bucket.

"That is only a relevant question if he is sane," said Salzella calmly. "He may be doing it because the little yellow pixies tell him to."

"Sane? How can he be sane?" said Bucket. "You were right, you know. The atmosphere in this place'd drive *anyone* crazy. I very well may be the only one here with both feet on the ground!" He turned. His eyes narrowed when he saw a group of chorus girls whispering nervously.

"You girls! Don't just stand there! Let's see you jump up and down!" he rasped. "On one leg!"

He turned back to Salzella. "What was I saying?"

"You were saying," said Salzella, "that you have both feet on the ground. Unlike the *corps de ballet*. And the corpse de Mr. Pounder."

"I think that comment was in rather poor taste," said Bucket coldly.

"My view," said the director of music, "is that we should shut down, get all the able-bodied men together, issue them with torches, go through this place from top to bottom, flush him out, chase him through the city, catch him and beat him to a pulp, and then throw what's left into the river. It's the only way to be sure."

"You *know* we can't afford to shut down," Bucket said. "We seem to make thousands a week but we seem to spend thousands a week, too. I'm sure I don't know where it goes— I thought running this place was just a matter of getting bums on seats, but every time I look up there's a bum spinning gently in the air— What's he going to do next, I ask myself—"

They looked at one another and then, as if pulled by some kind of animal magnetism, their gazes turned and flew out over the auditorium until they found the huge, glittering bulk of the chandelier.

"Oh, no . . ." moaned Bucket. "He wouldn't, would he? That *would* shut us down."

Salzella sighed. "Look, it weighs more than a ton," he said. "The supporting rope is thicker than your arm. The winch is padlocked when it's not in use. It's *safe.*"

They looked at one another.

"I'll have a man guard it every minute there's a performance," said Salzella. "I'll do it personally, if you like."

"And he wants Christine to sing Iodine tonight! She's got a voice like a whistle!"

Salzella raised his eyebrows. "That at least is not a problem, is it?" he said.

"Isn't it? It's a key role!"

Salzella put his arm around the owner's shoulders. "I think perhaps it is time for you to explore a few more little-known corners of the wonderful world that is opera," he said.

The stagecoach rolled to a halt in Sator Square, Ankh-Morpork. The coach agent was waiting impatiently.

"You're fifteen hours late, Mr. Reever!" he shouted.

The coach driver nodded impassively. He laid the reins down, jumped off the box, and inspected the horses. There was a certain woodenness about his movements.

Passengers were grabbing their baggage and hurrying away.

"Well?" said the agent.

"We had a picnic," said the coach driver. His face was gray.

"You stopped for a *picnic*?"

"And a bit of a singsong," said the driver, pulling the horses' feed bags from under the seat.

"You are telling me that you stopped the mail coach for a picnic and a singsong?"

"Oh, and the cat got stuck up a tree." He sucked his hand, and the agent noticed that a handkerchief was tied around it.

A hazy look of recollection clouded the driver's eyes. "And then there were the stories," he said.

"What stories?"

"The little fat one said everyone had to tell a story to help pass the time."

"Yes? Well? I don't see how that could slow you down!"

"You should've heard *her* story. The one about the very tall man and the piano? I was so embarrassed I fell off the coach. I wouldn't use words like that even to my own dear grandmother!"

"And of course," said the agent, who prided himself on his ironic approach, "the word *timetable* never crossed your mind while all this was going on?"

The driver turned to look directly at him for the first time. The agent took a step back. Here was a man who had hang-glided over Hell.

"*You* tell them," said the driver, and walked away.

The agent stared after him, and then walked around to the door.

A small man with a hunted look climbed out, dragging a huge fat man behind him and gabbling urgently in a language the agent didn't understand.

And then the agent was left alone with a coach and horses and an expanding circle of hurrying passengers.

He opened the door and peered inside.

"Good morning, mister," said Nanny Ogg.

He looked, in some puzzlement, from her to Granny Weatherwax.

"Is everything all right, ladies?"

"Very nice journey," said Nanny Ogg, taking his arm. "We shall def'nitly patronize you another time."

"The driver seemed to think there was a problem . . ."

"Problem?" said Granny. "I didn't notice any problems. Did you, Gytha?"

"He could've been a bit quicker fetching the ladder," said Nanny, climbing down. "And I'm sure he muttered something under his breath that time we stopped to admire the view. But I'm prepared to be gracious about it."

"You stopped to admire the *view*?" said the agent. "When?"

"Oh, several times," said Nanny. "No sense in rushing around the whole time, is there? More haste less speed, etcetera. Could you point us in the direction of Elm Street? Only we've lodgings at Mrs. Palm's. Our Nev speaks highly of the place, he says no one ever looked for him there . . ."

The agent stepped back, as people generally did in the face of Nanny's pump-action chatter.

"Elm Street?" he stuttered. "But . . . *respectable* ladies shouldn't go there . . ."

Nanny patted him on the shoulder. "That's good," she said. "That way we won't run into anyone we know."

As Granny walked past the horses they tried to hide behind the coach.

Bucket smiled brightly. There were little beads of sweat around the edges of his face.

"Ah, Perdita," he said. "Do sit down, lass. Er. You are enjoying your time with us so far?"

"Yes, thank you, Mr. Bucket," said Agnes dutifully.

"Good. That's good. Isn't that good, Mr. Salzella? Don't you think that's good, Dr. Undershaft?"

Agnes looked at the three worried faces.

"We're all very pleased," said Mr. Bucket. "And, er, well, we have an *amazing* offer for you which I'm sure will help you to enjoy it *even more*."

Agnes watched the assembled faces. "Yes?" she said guardedly.

"I know you, er, have only been with us hardly any time but we have decided to, er"—Bucket swallowed, and glanced at the other two for moral support—"let you sing the part of Iodine in tonight's production of *La Triviata*."

"Yes?"

"Um. It isn't *the* major role but of course it does include the famous 'Departure' aria . . ."

"Oh. Yes?"

"Er . . . there is, er . . . that is, er . . ." Bucket gave up and looked helplessly at his director of music. "Mr. Salzella?"

Salzella leaned forward. "What in fact we would like you to do . . . Perdita . . . is *sing* the role, indeed, but not, in fact . . . *play* the role."

Agnes listened while they explained. She'd stand in the chorus, just behind Christine. Christine would be told to sing very softly. It had been done dozens of times before, Salzella explained. It was done far more often than the audiences ever realized—when singers had a sore throat, or had completely dried, or had turned up so drunk they could barely stand, or, in one notorious instance many years previously, had died in the interval and subsequently sung their famous aria by means of a broom handle stuck up their back and their jaw operated with a piece of string.

It wasn't immoral. The show had to go on.

The ring of desperately grinning faces watched her.

I could just walk away, she thought. Walk away from these grinning faces and the mysterious Ghost. They couldn't stop me.

But there's nowhere to walk to except back.

"Yes, er, yes," she said. "I'm very . . . er . . . but why do it like this? Couldn't I simply take her place and sing the part?"

The men looked at one another, and then all started talking at once.

"Yes, but you see, Christine is . . . has . . . more stage experience—"

"—technical grasp—"

"—stage presence—"

"—apparent lyrical ability—"

"—fits the costume—"

Agnes looked down at her big hands. She could feel the blush advancing like a barbarian horde, burning everything as it came.

"We would like you, as it were," said Bucket, "to *ghost* the part . . ."

"Ghost?" said Agnes.

"It's a stage term," said Salzella.

"Oh, I see," said Agnes. "Yes. Well, of course. I shall certainly do my best."

"*Jolly* good," said Bucket. "We won't forget this. And I'm certain a very suitable part for you will come along very soon. See Dr. Undershaft this afternoon and he will take you through the role."

"Er. I know it quite well, I think," said Agnes, uncertainly.

"Really? How?"

"I've been . . . taking lessons."

"That *is* good, lass," said Mr. Bucket. "Shows keenness. We're very impressed. But see Dr. Undershaft in any case . . ."

Agnes got up and, still looking down, trooped out.

Undershaft sighed and shook his head.

"Poor child," he said. "Born too late. Opera *used* to be just about voices. You know, I remember the days of the great sopranos. Dame Violetta Gigli, Dame Clarissa Extendo . . . whatever became of them, I sometimes wonder."

"Didn't the climate change?" said Salzella nastily.

"There goes a figure that should prompt a revival of *The Ring of the Nibelungingung*," Undershaft went on. "Now that *was* an opera."

"Three days of gods shouting at one another and twenty minutes of memorable tunes?" said Salzella. "No, thank you very much."

"But can't you hear her singing Hildabrun, leader of the Valkyries?"

"Yes. Oh, yes. But unfortunately I can also hear her singing Nobbo the dwarf and Io, Chief of the Gods."

"Those were the days," said Undershaft sadly, shaking his head. "We had *proper* opera then. I recall when Dame Veritasi stuffed a musician into his own tuba for yawning—"

"Yes, yes, but this is the Century of the Fruitbat," said Salzella, standing up. He glanced at the door again, and shook his head.

"Amazing," he said. "Do you think she knows how fat she is?"

The door of Mrs. Palm's discreet establishment opened at Granny's knock.

The person on the other side was a young woman. Very obviously a young woman. There was no possible way that she could have been mistaken for a young man in any language, especially Braille.

Nanny peered around the young lady's powdered shoulder at the red plush and gilt interior beyond, and then up at Granny Weatherwax's impassive face, and then back at the young lady.

"I'll tan our Nev's hide when I get home," she muttered. "Come away, Esme, you don't want to go in there. It'd take too long to explain—"

"Why, Granny Weatherwax!" said the girl happily. "And who's this?"

Nanny looked up at Granny, whose expression hadn't changed.

"Nanny Ogg," Nanny said eventually. "Yes, I'm Nanny Ogg. Nev's mum," she added darkly. "Yes, indeed. Yes. On account of me bein' a"—the words "respectable widow woman" tried to range themselves in her vocal cords, and shriveled at the sheer enormity of the falsehood, forcing her to settle for "mother to him. Nev. Yes. Nev's mum."

"Hello, Colette," said Granny. "What fascinatin' earrings you are wearing. Is Mrs. Palm at home?"

"She's always at home to *important* visitors," said Colette. "Do come in, everyone will be so pleased to see you again!"

There were cries of welcome as Granny stepped into the scarlet gloom.

"What? You've been here before?" said Nanny, eying the pink flesh and white lace that made up much of the scenery.

"Oh, yes. Mrs. Palm is an old friend. Practic'ly a witch."

"You . . . you do *know* what *kind* of place this is, do you, Esme?" said Nanny Ogg. She felt curiously annoyed. She'd happily give way to Granny's expertise in the worlds of mind and magic, but she felt very strongly that there were some more specialized areas that were definitely Ogg territory, and Granny Weatherwax had no business even to know what they were.

"Oh, yes," said Granny, calmly.

Nanny's patience gave out. "It's a house of ill repute, is what it is!"

"On the contrary," said Granny. "I believe people speak very highly of it."

"You *knew*? And you never told *me*?"

Granny raised an ironic eyebrow. "The lady who invented the Strawberry Wobbler?"

"Well, yes, but—"

"We all live life the best way we can, Gytha. And there's a lot of people who think *witches* are bad."

"Yes, but—"

"Before you criticize someone, Gytha, walk a mile in their shoes," said Granny, with a faint smile.

"In those shoes *she* was wearin', I'd twist my ankle," said Nanny, gritting her teeth. "I'd need a ladder just to get in 'em." It was infuriating, the way Granny tricked you into reading her half of the dialogue. And opened your mind to yourself in unexpected ways.

"And it's a welcoming place and the beds are soft," said Granny.

"Warm, too, I expect," said Nanny Ogg, giving in. "And there's always a friendly light in the window."

"Dear me, Gytha Ogg. I always thought you were unshockable."

"Shockable, no," said Nanny. "Easily surprised, yes."

Dr. Undershaft the chorus master peered at Agnes over the top of his half-moon spectacles.

"The, um, 'Departure' aria, as it is known," he said, "is quite a little masterpiece. Not one of the great operatic highlights, but very memorable nevertheless."

His eyes misted over. "*'Questa maledetta'* sings Iodine, as she tells Peccadillo how hard it is for her to
leave him . . . *'Questa maledetta porta si bloccccccca, Si
blocca comunque diavolo lo faccccc-cio . . . !'* "

He stopped and made great play of cleaning his
glasses with his handkerchief.

"When Gigli sang it, there wasn't a dry eye in the
house," he mumbled. "I was there. It was then that I
decided that I would . . . oh, great days, indeed." He
put his glasses on and blew his nose.

"I'll run through it once," he said, "just so that
you can understand how it is supposed to go. Very
well, André."

The young man who had been drafted to play the
piano in the rehearsal room nodded, and winked surreptitiously at Agnes.

She pretended not to have seen him, and listened
with an expression of acute studiousness as the old
man worked his way through the score.

"And now," he said, "let us see how you manage."

He handed her the score and nodded at the pianist.

Agnes sang the aria, or at least a few bars of it.
André stopped playing and leaned his head against
the piano, trying to stifle a laugh.

"Ahem," said Undershaft.

"Was I doing something wrong?"

"You were singing tenor," said Undershaft, looking sternly at André.

"She was singing in *your* voice, sir!"

"Perhaps you can sing it like, er, Christine would
sing it?"

They started again.

"Kwesta!? Maledetta!! . . ."

Undershaft held up both hands. André's shoulders were shaking with the effort of not laughing.

"Yes, yes. Accurately observed. I dare say you're right. But could we start again and, er, perhaps you would sing it how you think it should be sung?"

Agnes nodded.

They started again . . .

. . . and finished.

Undershaft had sat down, half-turned away. He wouldn't look round to face her.

Agnes stood watching him uncertainly. "Er. Was that all right?" she said.

André the pianist got up slowly and took her hand. "I think we'd better leave him," he said softly, pulling her toward the door.

"Was it that bad?"

"Not . . . exactly."

Undershaft raised his head, but didn't turn it toward her. "More practice on those *R*s, madam, and strive for greater security above the stave," he said hoarsely.

"Yes. Yes, I will."

André led her out into the corridor, shut the door, and then turned to her.

"That was astounding," he said. "Did you ever hear the great Gigli sing?"

"I don't even know who Gigli *is*. What was I singing?"

"You didn't know that either?"

"I don't know what it *means*, no."

André looked down at the score in his hand. "Well,

I'm not much good at the language, but I suppose the opening could be sung something like this:

> *This damn door sticks*
> *This damn door sticks*
> *It sticks no matter what the hell I do*
> *It's marked "Pull" and indeed I am pulling*
> *Perhaps it should be marked "Push"?*

Agnes blinked. "That's *it*?"

"Yes."

"But I thought it was supposed to be very moving and romantic!"

"It *is*," said André. "It *was*. This isn't real life, this is *opera*. It doesn't *matter* what the words mean. It's the feeling that matters. Hasn't anyone told—? Look, I'm in rehearsals for the rest of the afternoon, but perhaps we could meet tomorrow? Perhaps after breakfast?"

Oh, no, thought Agnes. Here it comes. The blush was moving inexorably upward. She wondered if one day it might reach her face and carry on going, so that it ended up as a big pink cloud over her head.

"Er, yes," she said. "Yes. That would be . . . very helpful."

"Now I've got to go." He gave her a weak little smile, and patted her hand. "And . . . I'm really sorry it's happening this way. Because . . . that was astounding."

He went to walk away, and then stopped. "Uh . . . sorry if I frightened you last night," he said.

"What?"

"On the stairs."

"Oh, that. I wasn't frightened."

"You . . . er . . . didn't mention it to anyone, did you? I'd hate people to think I was worrying over nothing."

"Hadn't given it another thought, to tell you the truth. I know you can't be the Ghost, if that's what you're worried about. Eh?"

"Me? The Ghost. Haha!"

"Haha," said Agnes.

"So, er . . . see you tomorrow, then . . ."

"Fine."

Agnes headed back to her room, deep in thought.

Christine was there, looking critically at herself in the mirror. She spun around as Agnes entered; she even *moved* with exclamation marks.

"Oh, Perdita!! Have you heard?! I'm to sing the part of Iodine tonight!! Isn't that *wonderful*?!" She dashed across the room and endeavored to pick Agnes up and hug her, settling eventually for just hugging her.

"And I heard they're already letting you in the chorus!?"

"Yes, indeed."

"Isn't that nice?! I've been practicing all morning with Mr. Salzella. Kesta!? Mallydetta!! Porter see bloker!!" She twirled happily. Invisible sequins filled the air with their shine.

"When I am very famous," she said, "you won't regret having a friend in me!! I shall do my very best to help you!! I am sure you bring me luck!!"

"Yes, indeed," said Agnes, hopelessly.

"Because my dear father told me that one day a dear little pixie would arrive to help me achieve my great ambition, and, do you know, I think that little pixie is *you*!!"

Agnes smiled unhappily. After you'd known Christine for any length of time, you found yourself fighting a desire to look into her ear to see if you could spot daylight coming the other way.

"Er. I thought we had swapped rooms?"

"Oh, *that*!!" said Christine, smiling. "Wasn't I *silly*?! Anyway, I shall need the big mirror now that I am to be a prima donna! You don't mind, do you!?"

"What? Oh. No. No, of course not. Er. If you're sure . . ."

Agnes looked at the mirror, and then at the bed. And then at Christine.

"No," she said, shocked at the enormity of the idea that had just presented itself, delivered from the Perdita of her soul. "I'm sure that will be fine."

Dr. Undershaft blew his nose and tried to tidy himself up.

Well, he didn't have to stand for it. Perhaps the child was somewhat on the heavy side, but Gigli, for example, had once crushed a tenor to death and no one had thought any worse of her for it.

He'd protest to Mr. Bucket.

Dr. Undershaft was a single-minded man. He believed in voices. It didn't *matter* what anyone looked like. He never watched opera with his eyes open. It was the music that mattered, not the acting and certainly not the shape of the singers.

What did it matter what shape she was? Dame Tessitura had a beard you could strike a match on and a nose flattened half across her face, but she was still one of the best basses who ever opened beer bottles with her thumb.

Of course Salzella said that, while everyone accepted that large women of fifty could play thin girls of seventeen, people wouldn't accept that a fat girl of seventeen could do it. He said they'd cheerfully swallow a big lie and choke on a little fib. Salzella said that sort of thing.

Something was going wrong these days. The whole place seemed . . . sick, if a building could be sick. The crowds were still coming, but the money just didn't seem to be there anymore; everything seemed to be so expensive . . . And now they were owned by a *cheese monger*, for heaven's sake, some grubby counter jumper who'd probably want to bring in fancy ideas. What they needed was a businessman, some clerk who could add up columns of figures properly and not interfere. That was the trouble with all the owners he had experienced—they started off thinking of themselves as businessmen, and then suddenly began to think they could make an artistic contribution.

Still, possibly cheese mongers had to add up cheeses. Just so long as this one stayed in his office with the books, and didn't go around acting as though he owned the place just because he happened to own the place . . .

Undershaft blinked. He'd gone the wrong way again. No matter how long you'd been here, this place was a maze. He was behind the stage, in the orchestra's room. Instruments and folding chairs had been stacked everywhere. His foot toppled a beer bottle.

The twang of a string made him look around. Broken instruments littered the floor. There were half a dozen smashed violins. Several oboes had been broken. The trom had been pulled right out of a trombone.

He looked up into someone's face.

"But . . . why are *you*—"

The half-moon spectacles tumbled over and over, and smashed on the boards.

Then the attacker lowered his mask, as smooth and white as the skull of an angel, and stepped forward purposefully . . .

Dr. Undershaft blinked.

There was darkness. A cloaked figure raised its head and looked at him through bony white sockets.

Dr. Undershaft's recent memories were a little confused, but one fact stood out.

"Aha," he said. "Got you! You're the Ghost!"

YOU KNOW, YOU'RE RATHER AMUSINGLY WRONG.

Dr. Undershaft watched another masked figure pick up the body of . . . Dr. Undershaft, and drag it into the shadows.

"Oh, I *see*. I'm dead."

Death nodded.

SUCH WOULD APPEAR TO BE THE CASE.

"That was murder! Does anyone know?"

THE MURDERER. AND YOU, OF COURSE.

"But *him*? How can—?" Undershaft began.

WE MUST GO, said Death.

"But he just killed me! Strangled me with his bare hands!"

YES. CHALK IT UP TO EXPERIENCE.

"You mean I can't do anything about it?"

LEAVE IT TO THE LIVING. GENERALLY SPEAKING, THEY GET UNEASY WHEN THE DECEASED TAKES A CONSTRUCTIVE ROLE IN A MURDER INVESTIGATION. THEY TEND TO LOSE CONCENTRATION.

"You know, you do have a very good bass voice."

THANK YOU.

"Are there going to be . . . choirs and things?"

WOULD YOU LIKE SOME?

Agnes slipped out through the stage door and into the streets of Ankh-Morpork.

She blinked in the light. The air felt slightly prickly, and sharp, and too cold.

What she was about to do was wrong. Very wrong. And all her life she'd done things that were right.

Go on, said Perdita.

In fact, she probably wouldn't even do it. But there was no harm in just asking where there was an herbal shop, so she asked.

And there was no harm in going in, so she went in.

And it certainly wasn't against any kind of law to buy the ingredients she bought. After all, she might get a headache later on, or be unable to sleep.

And it would mean nothing at all to take them back to her room and tuck them under the mattress.

That's right, said Perdita.

In fact, if you averaged out the moral difficulty of what she was proposing over all the little activities she had to undergo in order to do it, it probably wasn't that bad at all, really—

These comforting thoughts were arranging

themselves in her mind as she headed back. She turned a corner and nearly walked into Nanny Ogg and Granny Weatherwax.

She flung herself against the wall and stopped breathing.

They hadn't seen her, although Nanny's foul cat leered at her over its owner's shoulder.

They'd take her back! She just knew they would!

The fact that she was a free agent and her own mistress and quite at liberty to go off to Ankh-Morpork had nothing to do with it. They'd *interfere*. They always did.

She scurried back along the alley and ran as fast as she could to the rear of the Opera House.

The stage-doorkeeper took no notice of her.

Granny and Nanny strolled through the city toward the area known as the Isle of Gods. It wasn't exactly Ankh and it wasn't exactly Morpork, being situated where the river bent so much it almost formed an island. It was where the city kept all those things it occasionally needed but was uneasy about, like the Watch-house, the theaters, the prison and the publishers. It was the place for all those things which might go off bang in unexpected ways.

Greebo ambled along behind them. The air was full of new smells, and he was looking forward to seeing if any of them belonged to anything he could eat, fight or ravish.

Nanny Ogg found herself getting increasingly worried. "This isn't really *us*, Esme," she said.

"Who is it, then?"

"I mean the book was just a bit of fun. No sense in making ourselves unpopular, is there?"

"Can't have witches being done down, Gytha."

"I don't feel done down. I felt fine until you *told* me I was done down," said Nanny, putting her finger on a major sociological point.

"You've been exploited," said Granny firmly.

"No I ain't."

"Yes you have. You're a downtrodden mass."

"No I ain't."

"You've been swindled out of your life savings," said Granny.

"Two dollars?"

"Well, it's all you'd actually *saved*," said Granny, accurately.

"Only 'cos I spent everything else," said Nanny. Other people salted away money for their old age, but Nanny preferred to accumulate memories.

"Well, there you are, then."

"I was putting that by for some new piping for my still up at Copperhead," said Nanny.* "You know how that scumble eats away at the metal—"

"You were putting a little something by for some security and peace of mind in your old age," Granny translated.

---

*Distillation of alcohol was illegal in Lancre. On the other hand, King Verence had long ago given up any idea of stopping a witch doing something she wanted to do, so merely required Nanny Ogg to keep her still somewhere it wasn't obvious. She thoroughly approved of the prohibition, since this gave her an unchallenged market for her own product, known wherever men fell backward into a ditch as "suicider."

"You don't get peace of mind with my scumble," said Nanny happily. "Pieces, yes, but not peace. It's made from the finest apples, you know," she added. "Well, mainly apples."

Granny stopped outside an ornate doorway, and peered at the brass plate affixed thereon.

"This is the place," she said.

They looked at the door.

"I've never been one for front doors," said Nanny, shifting from one foot to the other.

Granny nodded. Witches had a thing about front doors. A brief search located an alleyway which led around the back of the building. Here was a pair of much larger doors, wide open. Several dwarfs were loading bundles of books onto a cart. A rhythmic thumping came from somewhere beyond the doorway.

No one took any notice of the witches as they wandered inside.

Movable type was known in Ankh-Morpork, but if wizards heard about it they moved it where no one could find it. They generally didn't interfere with the running of the city, but when it came to movable type the pointy foot was put down hard. They had never explained why, and people didn't press the issue because you didn't press the issue with wizards, not if you liked yourself the shape you were. They simply worked around the problem, and engraved everything. This took a long time and meant that Ankh-Morpork was, for example, denied the benefit of newspapers, leaving the population to fool themselves as best they could.

A press was thumping gently at one end of the warehouse. Beside it, at long tables, a number of dwarfs and humans were stitching pages together and gluing on the covers.

Nanny took a book off a pile. It was *The Joye of Snacks*.

"Can I help you, ladies?" said a voice. Its tone suggested very clearly that it wasn't anticipating offering any kind of help whatsoever, except out into the street at speed.

"We've come about this book," said Granny.

"I'm Mrs. Ogg," said Nanny Ogg.

The man looked her up and down.

"Oh yes? Can you identify yourself?"

"Certainly. I'd know me anywhere."

"Hah! Well, I happen to know what Gytha Ogg looks like, madam, and she does not look like *you*."

Nanny Ogg opened her mouth to reply, and then said, in the voice of one who has stepped happily into the road and only now remembers about the onrushing coach: ". . . Oh."

"And how do you know what Mrs. Ogg looks like?" said Granny.

"Oh, is that the time? We'd better be going—" said Nanny.

"Because, as a matter of fact, she sent me a picture," said Goatberger, taking out his wallet.

"I'm sure we're not at *all* interested," said Nanny hurriedly, pulling on Granny's arm.

"I'm *extremely* interested," said Granny. She snatched a folded piece of paper out of Goatberger's hands, and peered at it.

"Hah! Yes . . . that's Gytha Ogg all right," she said. "Yes, indeed. I remember when that young artist came to Lancre for the summer."

"I wore my hair longer in those days," muttered Nanny.

"Just as well, considering," said Granny. "I didn't know you had *copies*, though."

"Oh, you know how it is when you're young," said Nanny dreamily. "It was doodle, doodle, doodle all summer long." She awoke from her reverie. "And I still weigh the same now as I did then," she added.

"Except that it's shifted," said Granny, nastily.

She handed the sketch back to Goatberger. "That's her all right," she said. "But it's out by about sixty years and several layers of clothing. This is Gytha Ogg, right here."

"You're telling me *this* came up with Banana Soup Surprise?"

"Did you try it?" said Nanny.

"Mr. Cropper the head printer did, yes."

"Was he surprised?"

"Not half as surprised as Mrs. Cropper."

"It can take people like that," said Nanny. "I think perhaps I overdo the nutmeg."

Goatberger stared at her. Doubt was beginning to assail him. You only had to look at Nanny Ogg grinning back at you to believe she *could* write something like *The Joye of Snacks*.

"Did you really write this?" he said.

"From memory," said Nanny, proudly.

"And now she'd like some money," said Granny.

Mr. Goatberger's face twisted up as though he'd just eaten a lemon and washed it down with vinegar.

"But we gave her the money *back*," he said.

"See?" said Nanny, her face falling. "I told you, Esme—"

"She wants some more," said Granny.

"No, I don't—"

"No, she doesn't!" Goatberger agreed.

"She does," said Granny. "She wants a little bit of money for every book you've sold."

"I don't expect to be treated like royalty," said Nanny.*

"You shut up," said Granny. "I know what you want. We want some money, Mr. Goatberger."

"And what if I won't give it to you?"

Granny glared at him.

"Then we shall go away and think about what to do next," she said.

"That's no idle threat," said Nanny. "There's a lot of people've regretted Esme thinking about what to do next."

"Come back when you've thought, then!" snapped Goatberger. He stormed off. "I don't know, authors wanting to be paid, good grief—"

He disappeared among the stacks of books.

"Er . . . do you think that could have gone better?" said Nanny.

Granny glanced at the table beside them. It was stacked with long sheets of paper. She nudged a dwarf,

---

*Strictly speaking, this means being chased by photographers anxious to get a picture of you with your vest off.

who had been watching the argument with some amusement.

"What're these?" she said.

"They're proofs for the Almanack." He saw her blank expression. "They're sort of a trial run for the book so's we can check that all the spelling mistakes have been left in."

Granny picked it up. "Come, Gytha," she said.

"I don't want trouble, Esme," said Nanny Ogg as she hurried after her. "It's only money."

"It ain't money any more," said Granny. "It's a way of keepin' score."

Mr. Bucket picked up a violin. It was in two pieces, held together by the strings. One of them broke.

"Who'd do something like this?" he said. "Honestly, Salzella . . . what *is* the difference between opera and madness?"

"Is this a trick question?"

"No!"

"Then I'd say: better scenery. Ah . . . I thought so . . ."

Salzella rooted among the destruction, and stood up with a letter in his hand.

"Would you like me to open it?" he said. "It's addressed to you."

Bucket shut his eyes.

"Go on," he said. "Don't bother about the details. Just tell me, how many exclamation marks?"

"Five."

"Oh."

Salzella passed the paper over.

Bucket read:

Dear Bucket

Whoops!
Ahahahahahahahaha ! ! ! ! !

Yrs
The Opera Ghost

"What can we do?" he said. "One moment he writes polite little notes, the next he goes mad on paper!"

"Herr Trubelmacher has got everyone out hunting for new instruments," said Salzella.

"Are violins more expensive than ballet shoes?"

"There are few things in the world more expensive than ballet shoes. Violins happen to be among them," said Salzella.

"Further expense!"

"It seems so, yes."

"But I thought the Ghost *liked* music! Herr Trubelmacher tells me the organ is beyond repair!!!"

He stopped. He was aware that he had exclaimed a little less rationally than a sane man should.

"Oh, well," Bucket continued wearily. "The show must go on, I suppose."

"Yes, indeed," said Salzella.

Bucket shook his head. "How's it all going for tonight?"

"I think it will work, if that's what you mean. Perdita seems to have a very good grasp of the part."

"And Christine?"

"She has an astonishingly good grasp of wearing a dress. Between them, they make one prima donna."

The proud owner of the Opera House got slowly to his feet. "It all seemed so simple," he moaned. "I thought: opera, how hard can it be? Songs. Pretty girls dancing. Nice scenery. Lots of people handing over cash. Got to be better than the cut-throat world of yogurt, I thought. Now everywhere I go there's—"

Something crunched under his shoe. He picked up the remains of a pair of half-moon spectacles.

"These are Dr. Undershaft's, aren't they?" he said. "What're they doing here?"

His eyes met Salzella's steady gaze.

"Oh, *no*," he groaned.

Salzella turned slightly, and stared hard at a big double-bass case leaning against the wall. He raised his eyebrows.

"Oh, *no*," said Bucket, again. "Go on. Open it. My hands have gone all sweaty . . ."

Salzella padded across to the case and grasped the lid. "Ready?"

Bucket nodded, wearily.

The case was flung open.

"Oh, no!"

Salzella craned round to see.

"Ah, yes," he said. "A broken neck, and the body has been kicked in considerably. That'll cost a dollar or two to repair, and no mistake."

"And all the strings are busted! Are double basses more expensive to rebuild than violins?"

"I am afraid that all musical instruments are incredibly expensive to repair, with the possible exception of the triangle," said Salzella. "However, it could have been worse, hmm?"

"What?"

"Well, it *could* have been Dr. Undershaft in there, yes?"

Bucket gaped at him, and then shut his mouth.

"Oh, Yes. Of course. Oh, yes. That would have been worse. Yes. Bit of luck there, I suppose. Yes. Um."

"So that's an opera house, is it?" said Granny. "Looks like someone built a great big box and glued the architecture on afterward."

She coughed, and appeared to be waiting for something.

"Can we have a look around?" said Nanny dutifully, aware that Granny's curiosity was equaled only by her desire not to show it.

"It can't do any harm, I suppose," said Granny, as if granting a big favor. "Seein' as we've nothing else to do right this minute."

The Opera House was, indeed, that most efficiently multifunctional of building designs. It was a cube. But, as Granny had pointed out, the architect had suddenly realized late in the day that there ought to be *some* sort of decoration, and had shoved it on hurriedly, in a riot of friezes, pillars, corybants, and curly bits. Gargoyles had colonized the higher reaches. The effect, seen from the front, was of a huge wall of tortured stone.

Round the back, of course, there was the usual drab mess of windows, pipes and damp stone walls. One of the rules of a certain type of public architecture is that it only happens at the front.

Granny paused under a window. "Someone's singing," she said. "Listen."

"La–la–la–la–la–LAH," trilled someone. "Do–Re–Mi–Fah–So–La–Ti–Do . . ."

"That's opera, right enough," said Granny. "Sounds foreign to me."

Nanny had an unexpected gift for languages; she could be comprehensibly incompetent in a new one within an hour or two. What she spoke was one step away from gibberish but it was authentically *foreign* gibberish. And she knew that Granny Weatherwax, whatever her other qualities, had an even bigger tin ear for languages than she did for music.

"Er. Could be," she said. "There's always a lot going on, I know that. Our Nev said they sometimes do different operations every night."

"How did he find that out?" said Granny.

"Well, there was a lot of lead. That takes some shifting. He said he liked the noisy ones. He could hum along and also no one heard the hammering."

The witches strolled onward.

"Did you notice young Agnes nearly bump into us back there?" said Granny.

"Yes. It was all I could do not to turn around," said Nanny.

"She wasn't very pleased to see us, was she? I practically heard her gasp."

"That's very suspicious, if you ask me," said Nanny. "I mean, she sees two friendly faces from back home, you'd expect her to come runnin' up . . ."

"We're old friends, after all. Old friends of her grandma and her mum, anyway, and that's practic'ly the same."

"Remember those eyes in the teacup?" said Nanny. "She could be under the gaze of some strange occult force! We got to be careful. People can be very tricky when they're in the grip of a strange occult force. Remember Mr. Scruple over in Slice?"

"That wasn't a strange occult force. That was acid stomach."

"Well, it certainly seemed strangely occult for a while. Especially if the windows were shut."

Their perambulation had taken them to the Opera House's stage door.

Granny looked up at a line of posters.

"La Triviata," she read aloud. "*The Ring of the Nibelungingung . . . ?*"

"Well, basically there are two sorts of opera," said Nanny, who also had the true witch's ability to be confidently expert on the basis of no experience whatsoever. "There's your heavy opera, where basically people sing foreign and it goes like 'Oh, oh, oh, I am dyin', oh, I am dyin', oh, oh, oh, that's what I'm doin'," and there's your light opera, where they sing in foreign and it basically goes 'Beer! Beer! Beer! Beer! I like to drink lots of beer!', although sometimes they drink champagne instead. That's basically all of opera, reely."

"What? Either dyin' or drinkin' beer?"

"Basically, yes," said Nanny, contriving to suggest that this was the whole gamut of human experience.

"And that's opera?"

"We-ll . . . there might be *some* other stuff. But mostly it's stout or stabbin'."

Granny was aware of a presence.

She turned.

A figure had emerged from the stage door, carrying a poster, a bucket of glue and a brush.

It was a strange figure, a sort of neat scarecrow in clothes slightly too small for it, although, to be truthful, there were probably no clothes that would have fit that body. The ankles and wrists seemed infinitely extensible and independently guided.

It encountered the two witches standing at the poster board, and stopped politely. They could *see* the sentence marshaling itself behind the unfocused eyes.

"Excuse me ladies! The show must go on!"

The words were all there and they made sense, but each sentence was fired out into the world as a unit.

Granny pulled Nanny to one side.

"Thank you!"

They watched in silence as the man, with great and meticulous care, applied paste to a neat rectangle and then affixed the poster, smoothing every crease methodically.

"What's your name, young man?" said Granny.

"Walter!"

"That's a nice beret you have there."

"My mum bought it for me!"

Walter chased the last air bubble to the edge of the paper and stood back. Then, completely ignoring the witches in his preoccupation with his task, he picked up the paste pot and went back inside.

The witches stared at the new poster in silence.

"Y'know, I wouldn't mind seein' an operation," said Nanny, after a while. "Senior Basilica did give us the tickets."

"Oh, you know me," said Granny. "Can't be having with that sort of thing at all."

Nanny looked sideways at her, and grinned to herself. This was a familiar Weatherwax opening line. It meant: Of course I want to, but you've got to persuade me.

"You're right, o' course," she said. "It's for them folks in all their fine carriages. It's not for the likes of us."

Granny looked hesitant for a moment.

"I expect it's having ideas above our station," Nanny went on. "I expect if we went in they'd say: Be off, you nasty ole crones . . ."

"Oh, they would, would they?"

"I don't expect they want common folk like what we are comin' in with all those smart nobby people," said Nanny.

"Is that a fact? Is that a fact, madam? You just come with me!"

Granny stalked round to the front of the building, where people were already alighting from coaches. She pushed her way up the steps and shouldered through the crowd to the ticket office.

She leaned forward. The man behind the grille leaned back.

"Nasty old crones, eh?" she snapped.

"I beg your pardon—?"

"Not before time! See here, we've got tickets for—" She looked down at the pieces of cardboard, and pulled Nanny Ogg over. "It says here *Stalls*. The cheek of it! Stalls? Us?" She turned back to the ticket man. "See here, Stalls aren't good enough, we want seats in"—she looked up at the board by the ticket window—"the Gods. Yes, that sounds about right."

"I'm sorry? You've got tickets for Stalls seats

and you want to exchange them for seats in the Gods?"

"Yes, and don't you go expecting us to pay any more money!"

"I wasn't going to ask you for—"

"Just as well!" said Granny, smiling triumphantly. She looked approvingly at the new tickets. "Come, Gytha."

"Er, excuse me," said the man as Nanny Ogg turned away, "but what is that on your shoulders?"

"It's . . . a fur collar," said Nanny.

"Excuse *me*, but I just saw it flick its tail."

"Yes. I happen to believe in beauty without cruelty."

Agnes was aware of something happening backstage. Little groups of men were forming, and then breaking up as various individuals hurried away about their mysterious tasks.

Out in front the orchestra was already tuning up. The chorus was filing on to be A Busy Marketplace, in which various jugglers, gypsies, sword swallowers and gaily dressed yokels would be entirely unsurprised at an apparently drunken baritone strolling on to sing an enormous amount of plot at a passing tenor.

She saw Mr. Bucket and Mr. Salzella deep in argument with the stage manager.

"How can we search the entire building? This place is a maze!"

"He might have just wandered off somewhere . . . ?"

"He's as blind as a bat without those glasses."

"But we can't be *certain* something's happened to him."

"Oh, yes? You didn't say that when we opened the double-bass case. You were certain he was going to be inside. Admit it."

"I . . . wasn't expecting just to find a smashed double bass, yes. But I was feeling a bit mithered at that point."

A sword swallower nudged Agnes.

"What?"

"Curtain up in one minute, dear," he said, smearing mustard on his sword.

"Has something happened to Dr. Undershaft?"

"Couldn't say, dear. You wouldn't have any salt, would you?"

" 'Scuse me. 'Scuse me. Sorry. 'Scuse me. Was that your foot? 'Scuse me . . ."

Leaving a trail of annoyed and pained patrons in their wake, the witches trod their way to their seats.

Granny elbowed herself comfortable and then, having in some matters the boredom threshold of a four-year-old, said: "What's happenin' now?"

Nanny's skimpy knowledge of opera didn't come to her aid. So she turned to the lady beside her.

" 'Scuse me, could I borrow your program? Thank you. 'Scuse me, could I borrow your spectacles? So kind."

She spent a few moments in careful study.

"This is the overture," she said. "It's kind of a free sample of what's going to happen. 'S got a summary of the story, too. *La Triviata*."

Her lips moved as she read. Occasionally her brow wrinkled.

"Well, it's quite simple reely," she said, at last. "A

lot of people are in love with one another, there's considerable dressing up as other people and general confusion, there's a cheeky servant, no one really knows who anyone is, a couple of ole dukes go mad, chorus of gypsies, etc. Your basic opera. Someone's prob'ly going to turn out to be someone else's long-lost son or daughter or wife or something."

"Shh!" said a voice behind them.

"Wish we'd brought something to eat," muttered Granny.

"I think I've got some peppermints in my knicker leg."

"Shh!"

"I would like my spectacles back, please."

"Here you are, ma'am. They're not very good, are they?"

Someone tapped Nanny Ogg on the shoulder. "Madam, your fur stole is eating my chocolates!"

And someone tapped Granny Weatherwax on *her* shoulder. "Madam, kindly remove your hat."

Nanny Ogg choked on her peppermint.

Granny Weatherwax turned to the red-faced gentleman behind her. "You do know what a woman in a pointy hat is, don't you?" she said.

"*Yes*, madam. A woman in a pointy hat is sitting in front of me."

Granny gave him a stare. And then, to Nanny's surprise, she removed her hat.

"I do beg your pardon," she said. "I can see I was inadvertently bad-mannered. Pray excuse me."

She turned back to the stage.

Nanny Ogg started breathing again. "You feeling all right, Esme?"

"Never better."

Granny Weatherwax surveyed the auditorium, oblivious to the sounds around her.

"*I assure you, madam, your fur is eating my choco-lates. It's started on the second layer!*"

"*Oh, dear. Show him the little map inside the lid, will you? He's only after the truffles, and you can soon rub the dribble off the others.*"

"*Do you mind being quiet?*"

"*I don't mind, it's this man and his chocolates that's making the noise—*"

A big room, Granny thought. A great big room without windows . . .

There was a tingling in her thumbs.

She looked at the chandelier. The rope disappeared into an alcove in the ceiling.

Her gaze passed along the rows of Boxes. They were all quite crowded. On one, though, the curtains were almost closed, as if someone inside wanted to see out without being seen.

Then Granny looked among the Stalls. The audience was mainly human. Here and there was the hulking shape of a troll, although the troll equivalent of operas usually went on for a couple of years. A few dwarf helmets gleamed, although dwarfs normally weren't interested in anything without dwarfs in. There seemed to be a lot of feathers down there, and here and there the glint of jewelry. Shoulders were being worn bare this season. A lot of attention had been paid to appearances. The people were here to look, not to see.

She closed her eyes.

This was when you started being a witch. It wasn't

when you did headology on daft old men, or mixed up medicines, or stuck up for yourself, or knew one herb from another.

It was when you opened your mind to the world and carefully examined everything it picked up.

She ignored her ears until the sounds of the audience became just a distant buzz.

Or, at least, a distant buzz broken by the voice of Nanny Ogg.

"Says here that Dame Timpani, who sings the part of Quizella, is a diva," said Nanny. "So I reckon this is like a part-time job, then. Prob'ly quite a good idea, on account of you have to be able to hold your breath. Good trainin' for the singin'."

Granny nodded without opening her eyes.

She kept them closed as the opera started. Nanny, who knew when to leave her friend to her own devices, tried to keep quiet but felt impelled to give out a running commentary.

Then she said, "There's Agnes! Hey, that's Agnes!"

"Stop wavin' and sit down," murmured Granny, trying to hold on to her waking dream.

Nanny leaned over the balcony.

"She's dressed up as a gypsy," she said. "And now there's a girl come forward to sing"—she peered at the stolen program—"the famous 'Departure' aria, it says here. Now that's what I call a good voice—"

"That's Agnes singin'," said Granny.

"No, it's this girl Christine."

"Shut your eyes, you daft old woman, and tell me if that isn't Agnes singin'," said Granny.

Nanny Ogg obediently shut her eyes for a

moment, and then opened them again. "It's Agnes singing!"

"Yes."

"But there's that girl with the big smile right out there in front moving her lips and everything!"

"Yes."

Nanny scratched her head. "Something a bit wrong here, Esme. Can't have people stealing our Agnes's voice."

Granny's eyes were still shut. "Tell me if the curtains on that Box down there on the right have moved," she said.

"I just saw them twitch, Esme."

"Ah."

Granny let herself relax again. She sank into the seat as the aria washed over her, and opened her mind once more . . .

Edges, walls, doors . . .

Once a space was enclosed it became a universe of its own. Some things remained trapped in it.

The music passed through one side of her head and out the other, but with it came other things, strands of things, echoes of old screams . . .

She drifted down further, down below the conscious, into the darkness beyond the circle of firelight.

There was fear here. It stalked the place like a great dark animal. It lurked in every corner. It was in the stones. Old terror crouched in the shadows. It was one of the most ancient terrors, the one that meant that no sooner had mankind learned to walk on two legs than it dropped to its knees. It was the terror of impermanence, the knowledge that all this would pass away, that a beautiful voice or a wonderful figure was something whose arrival you couldn't control and whose departure you couldn't delay. It wasn't what she had been looking for, but it was perhaps the sea in which it swam.

She went deeper.

And there it was, roaring through the nighttime of the soul of the place like a deep cold current.

As she drew closer she saw that it was not one thing but two, twisted around one another. She reached out . . .

Trickery. Lies. Deceit. Murder.

"No!"

She blinked.

Everyone had turned to look at her.

Nanny tugged at her dress. "Sit down, Esme!"

Granny stared. The chandelier hung peacefully over the crowded seats.

"They beat him to death!"

"What's that, Esme?"

"And they throw him into the river!"

"Esme!"

"*Sh!*"

"*Madam, will you sit down at once!*"

". . . *and now it's started on the Nougat Whirls!*"

Granny snatched at her hat and did a crabwise run along the row, crushing some of the finest footwear in Ankh-Morpork under her thick Lancre soles.

Nanny hung back reluctantly. She'd quite enjoyed the song, and she wanted to applaud. But her pair of hands wasn't necessary. The audience had exploded as soon as the last note had died away.

Nanny Ogg looked at the stage, and took note of something, and smiled. "Like that, eh?"

"Gytha!"

She sighed. "Coming, Esme. 'Scuse me. 'Scuse me. Sorry. 'Scuse me . . ."

Granny Weatherwax was out in the red plush corridor, leaning with her forehead against the wall.

"This is a bad one, Gytha," she muttered. "It's all twisted up. I ain't at all sure I can make it happen right. The poor soul . . ."

She straightened up. "Look at me, Gytha, will you?"

Gytha obediently opened her eyes wide. She winced a little as a fragment of Granny Weatherwax's consciousness crept behind her eyes.

Granny put her hat on, tucking in the occasional errant wisp of gray hair and then taking, one by one, the eight hat pins and ramming them home with the same frowning deliberation with which a mercenary might check his weapons.

"All right," she said at last.

Nanny Ogg relaxed. "It's not that I mind, Esme," she said, "but I wish you'd use a mirror."

"Waste of money," said Granny.

Now fully armored, she strode off along the corridor.

"Glad to see you didn't lose your temper with the man who went on about your hat," said Nanny, running along behind.

"No point. He's going to be dead tomorrow."

"Oh, dear. What of?"

"Run over by a cart, I think."

"Why didn't you tell him?"

"I could be wrong."

Granny reached the stairs and thundered down them.

"Where're we going?"

"I want to see who's behind those curtains."

The applause, distant but still thunderous, filled the stairwell.

"They certainly like Agnes's voice," said Nanny.

"Yes. I hopes we're in time."

"Oh, bugger!"

"What?"

"I left Greebo up there!"

"Well, he likes meeting new people. Good grief, this place is a *maze*."

Granny stepped out into a curved corridor, rather plusher than the one they had left. There was a series of doors along it.

"Ah. Now, then . . ."

She walked along the row, counting, and then tried a handle.

"Can I help you, ladies?"

They turned. A little old woman had come up softly behind them, carrying a tray of drinks.

Granny smiled at her. Nanny Ogg smiled at the tray.

"We were just wondering," said Granny, "which person in these Boxes likes to sit with the curtains nearly shut?"

The tray began to shake.

"Here, shall I hold that for you?" said Nanny. "You'll spill something if you're not careful."

"What do you know about Box Eight?" said the old lady.

"Ah. Box Eight," said Granny. "That'd be the one, yes. That's this one over here, isn't it . . . ?"

"No, please . . ."

Granny strode forward and grasped the handle.

The door was locked.

The tray was thrust into Nanny's welcoming hands. "Well, thank you, I don't mind if I do . . ." she said.

The woman pulled at Granny's arm. "Don't! It'll bring terrible bad luck!"

Granny thrust out her hand. "The key, madam!" Behind her, Nanny inspected a glass of champagne.

"Don't make him angry! It's bad enough as it is!" The woman was clearly terrified.

"Iron," said Granny, rattling the handle. "Can't magic iron . . ."

"Here," said Nanny, stepping forward a little unsteadily. "Give me one of your hat pins. Our Nev's taught me all kindsa tricks . . ."

Granny's hand rose to her hat, and then she looked at Mrs. Plinge's lined face. She lowered her hand.

"No," she said. "No, I reckon we'll leave it for now . . ."

"I don't know what's happening . . ." sobbed Mrs. Plinge. "It never used to be like this . . ."

"Have a good blow," said Nanny, handing her a grubby handkerchief and patting her kindly on the back.

". . . there was none of this killing people . . . he just wanted somewhere to watch the opera . . . it made him feel better . . ."

"Who's this we're talking about?" said Granny.

Nanny Ogg gave her a warning look over the top

of the old woman's head. There were some things best left to Nanny.

". . . he'd unlock it for an hour every Friday for me to tidy up and there was always his little note saying thank you or apologizing for the chocolates down the seat . . . and where was the harm in it, that's what I'd like to know . . ."

"Have another good blow," said Nanny.

". . . and now there's people dropping like flies out of the flies . . . they say it's him, but I know he never meant any harm . . ."

"'Course not," said Nanny, soothingly.

". . . many's the time I've seen 'em look up at the Box. They always felt the better for it if they saw him . . . and then poor Mr. Pounder was strangulated. I looked around and there was his hat, just like that . . ."

"It's terrible when that happens," said Nanny Ogg. "What's your name, dear?"

"Mrs. Plinge," sniffed Mrs. Plinge. "It came right down in front of me. I'd have recognized it anywhere . . ."

"I think it would be a good idea if we took you home, Mrs. Plinge," said Granny.

"Oh, dear! I've got all these ladies and gentlemen to see to! And anyway it's dangerous going home this time of night . . . Walter walks me home but he's got to stay late tonight . . . oh dear . . ."

"Have another good blow," said Nanny. "Find a bit that isn't too soggy."

There was a series of sharp pops. Granny Weatherwax had interlocked her fingers and extended her hands at arm's length, so that her knuckles cracked.

"Dangerous, eh?" she said. "Well, we can't see you all upset like this. I'll walk you home and Mrs. Ogg will see to things here."

". . . only I've got to attend to the Boxes . . . I've got all these drinks to serve . . . could've sworn I had them a moment ago . . ."

"Mrs. Ogg knows all about drinks," said Granny, glaring at her friend.

"There's nothing I don't know about drinks," agreed Nanny, shamelessly emptying the last glass. "Especially these."

". . . and what about our Walter? He'll worry himself silly . . ."

"Walter's your son?" said Granny. "Wears a beret?"

The old woman nodded.

"Only I always comes back for him if he's working late . . ." she began.

"You come back for him . . . but *he* sees you home?" said Granny.

"It's . . . he's . . . he's . . ." Mrs. Plinge rallied. "He's a good boy," she said defiantly.

"I'm sure he is, Mrs. Plinge," said Granny.

She carefully lifted the little white bonnet off Mrs. Plinge's head and handed it to Nanny, who put it on, and also took the little white apron. That was the good thing about black. You could be nearly anything, wearing black. Mother Superior or Madam, it was really just a matter of the style. It just depended on the details.

There was a click. Box Eight had bolted itself. And then there was the very faint scrape of a chair being wedged under the door handle.

Granny smiled, and took Mrs. Plinge's arm. "I'll be back as soon as I can," she said.

Nanny nodded, and watched them go.

There was a little cupboard at the end of the corridor. It contained a stool, Mrs. Plinge's knitting, and a small but very well stocked bar. There were also, on a polished mahogany plank, a number of bells on big coiled springs.

Several of them were bouncing up and down angrily.

Nanny poured herself a gin and gin with a dash of gin and inspected the rows of bottles with considerable interest.

Another bell started to ring.

There was a huge jar of stuffed olives. Nanny helped herself to a handful and blew the dust off a bottle of port.

A bell fell off its spring.

Somewhere out in the corridor a door opened and a young man's voice bellowed, "Where are those drinks, woman!"

Nanny tried the port.

Nanny Ogg was used to the idea of domestic service. As a girl, she'd been a maid at Lancre Castle, where the king was inclined to press his intentions and anything else he could get hold of. Young Gytha Ogg had already lost her innocence* but she had some

---

*Without regret, since she hadn't found any use for it.

clear ideas about unwelcome intentions, and when he jumped out at her in the scullery she had technically committed treason with a large leg of lamb swung in both hands. That had ended her life below stairs and put a lengthy crimp in the king's activities above them.

The brief experience had given her certain views which weren't anything so definite as political but were very firmly Oggish. And Mrs. Plinge had looked as if she didn't get very much to eat and not a lot of time to sleep, either. Her hands had been thin and red. Nanny had a lot of time for the Plinges of the world.

Did port go with sherry? Oh, well, no harm in trying . . .

All the bells were ringing now. It must be coming up to the interval.

She methodically unscrewed the top off a jar of cocktail onions, and thoughtfully crunched a couple.

Then, as other people started to poke their heads around the doors and make angry demands, she went to the champagne shelf and took down a couple of magnums. She gave them a damn good shake, tucked one under each arm with a thumb on the corks, and stepped out into the corridor.

Nanny's philosophy of life was to do what seemed like a good idea at the time, and do it as hard as possible. It had never let her down.

The curtains closed. The audience was still on its feet, applauding.

"What happens now?" whispered Agnes to the next gypsy.

He pulled off his bandanna. "Well, dear, we generally nip out to— Oh, no, they're going for a curtain call!"

The curtains opened again. The light caught Christine, who curtsied and waved and sparkled.

Her fellow gypsy nudged Agnes. "Look at Dame Timpani," he said. "There's a nose in a sling if ever I saw one."

Agnes stared at the prima donna.

"She's smiling," she said.

"So does a tiger, dear."

The curtains shut once more, with a finality that said the stage manager was going to strike the set and would scream at someone if they dared to touch those ropes again . . .

Agnes ran off with the others. There wasn't too much to do in the next act. She'd tried to memorize the plot earlier—although other members of the chorus had done their best to dissuade her, on the basis that you could either sing them or understand them, but not both.

Nevertheless, Agnes was conscientious.

". . . so Peccadillo (ten.), the son of Duke Tagliatella (bass), has secretly disguised himself as a swineherd to woo Quizella, not knowing that Doctor Bufola (bar.) has sold the elixir to Ludi the servant, without realizing he is really the maid Iodine (sop.) dressed up as a boy because Count Artaud (bar.) claims that . . ."

A deputy stage manager pulled her out of the way and waved at someone in the wings.

"Lose the countryside, Ron."

There was a series of whistles from offstage, answered by another from above.

The backcloth rose. From the gloom above, the sandbag counterweights began to descend.

". . . then Artaud reveals, er, that Zibeline must marry Fideli, I mean Fiabe, not knowing, er, that the family fortunes . . ."

The sandbags came down. On one side of the stage, at least. On the other side, Agnes was interrupted in her impossible task by the screaming, and looked around into the upside-down and not at all well features of the late Dr. Undershaft.

Nanny skipped through a handy door, shut it behind her, and leaned on it. After a few moments the sound of running feet clattered past.

Well, that had been fun.

She removed the lace bonnet and apron and, because there was a basic honesty in Nanny, she tucked them in a pocket to give back to Mrs. Plinge later. Then she pulled out a flat, round black shape and banged it against her arm. The point shot out. After a few adjustments her official hat was almost as good as new.

She looked around. A certain absence of light and carpeting, together with a very presence of dust, suggested that this was a part of the place the public weren't supposed to see.

Oh, damn. She supposed she had better find another door. Of course, that'd mean she'd have to leave Greebo, wherever he was, but he'd turn up. He always did when he wanted feeding.

There was a flight of steps leading down. She followed them to a corridor which was slightly better lit and ambled along it for quite a way. And then all she had to do was follow the screams.

She emerged among the flats and jumbled props backstage.

No one bothered about her. The appearance of a small, amiable old lady was not about to cause comment at this point.

People were running backward and forward, shouting. More impressionable people were just standing in one place and screaming. A large lady was sprawled over two chairs having hysterics, while some distracted stagehands tried to fan her with a script.

Nanny Ogg was not certain whether something important had happened or whether this was just a continuation of opera by other means.

"I should loosen her corsets, if I was you," she said as she ambled past.

"Good heavens, madam, there's enough panic in here as it is!"

Nanny moved on to an interesting crowd of gypsies, noblemen and stagehands.

Witches are curious by definition and inquisitive by nature. She moved in.

"Let me through. I'm a nosy person," she said, employing both elbows. It worked, as this sort of approach generally does.

There was a dead person lying on the floor. Nanny had seen death in a wide variety of guises, and certainly knew strangulation when it presented itself. It wasn't the nicest end, although it could be quite colorful.

"Oh dear," she said. "Poor man. What happened to him?"

"Mr. Bucket says he must have got caught up in the—" someone began.

"He didn't get caught in anything! This is the Ghost's work!" said someone else. "He could still be up there!"

All eyes turned upward.

"Mr. Salzella's sent some stagehands to flush him out."

"Have they got flaming torches?" said Nanny.

Several of them looked at her as if wondering, for the first time, who she was.

"What?"

"Got to have flaming torches when you're tracking down evil monsters," said Nanny. "Well-known fact."

There was a moment while this sunk in, and then:

"That's true."

"She's right, you know."

"Well-known fact, dear."

"Did they have flaming torches?"

"Don't think so. Just ordinary lanterns."

"Oh, they're no good," said Nanny. "That's for smugglers, lanterns. For evil monsters you need flaming—"

"Excuse me, boys and girls!"

The stage manager had stood on a box.

"Now," he said, a little pale around the face, "I know you're all familiar with the phrase 'the show must go on' . . ."

There was a chorus of groans from the chorus.

"It's very hard to sing a jolly song about eating

hedgehogs when you're waiting for an *accident* to happen to you," shouted a gypsy king.

"Funny thing, if we're talking about songs about hedgehogs, I myself—" Nanny began, but no one was paying her any attention.

"Now, we don't actually know what happened—"

"Really? Shall we guess?" said a gypsy.

"—but we have men up in the fly loft now—"

"Oh? In case of more *accidents*?"

"—and Mr. Bucket has authorized me to say that there will be an additional two dollars' bonus tonight in recognition of your bravely agreeing to *continue with the show*—"

"Money? After a shock like this? Money? He thinks he can offer us a couple of dollars and we'll agree to stay on this cursed stage?"

"Shame!"

"Heartless!"

"Unthinkable!"

"Should be at least four!"

"Right! Right!"

"For shame, my friends! To talk about a few dollars when there is a dead man lying there . . . Have you no respect for his memory?"

"Exactly! A few dollars *is* disrespectful. Five dollars or nothing!"

Nanny Ogg nodded to herself, and wandered off and found a sufficiently big piece of cloth to cover the late Dr. Undershaft.

Nanny rather liked the theatrical world. It was its own kind of magic. That was why Esme disliked it, she reckoned. It was the magic of illusions and misdirection and foolery, and that was fine by Nanny

Ogg, because you couldn't be married three times without a little fooling. But it was just close enough to Granny's own kind of magic to make Granny uneasy. Which meant she couldn't leave it alone. It was like scratching an itch.

People didn't take any notice of little old ladies who looked as though they fitted in, and Nanny Ogg could fit in faster than a dead chicken in a maggot factory.

Besides, Nanny had one additional little talent, which was a mind like a buzz saw behind a face like an elderly apple.

Someone was crying.

A strange figure was kneeling beside the late chorus master. It looked like a puppet with the strings cut.

"Can you give me a hand with this sheet, mister?" said Nanny quietly.

The face looked up. Two watery eyes, running with tears, blinked at Nanny. "He won't wake up!"

Nanny mentally changed gear. "That's right, luv," she said. "You're Walter, ain't you?"

"He was always very good to me and our mum! He never gave me a kick!"

It was obvious to Nanny that there was no help here. She knelt down and began to do her best with the departed.

"Miss they say it were the Ghost miss! It weren't the Ghost miss! He'd never do a thing like that! He was always good to me and our mum!"

Nanny changed gear again. You had to slow down a bit for Walter Plinge.

"My mum'd know what to do!"

"Yes, well . . . she's gone home early, Walter."

Walter's waxy face started to contort into an expression of terminal horror.

"She mustn't walk home without Walter to look after her!" he shouted.

"I bet she always says that," said Nanny. "I bet she always makes sure her Walter's with her when she goes home. But I expect that right now she'd want her Walter to just get on with things so's she can be proud of him. Show's not half over yet."

" 'S dangerous for our mum!"

Nanny patted his hand and absentmindedly wiped her own hand on her dress.

"That's a good boy," she said. "Now, I've got to go off—"

"The Ghost wouldn't harm no one!"

"Yes, Walter, only I've got to go but I'll find someone to help you and you must put poor Dr. Undershaft somewhere safe until after the show. Understand? And I'm Mrs. Ogg."

Walter gawped at her, and then nodded sharply.

"Good boy."

Nanny left him still looking at the body and headed farther backstage.

A young man hurrying past found that he'd suddenly acquired an Ogg.

" 'Scuse me, young man," said Nanny, still holding his arm, "but d'you know anyone around here called Agnes? Agnes Nitt?"

"Can't say I do, ma'am. What does she do?" He made to hurry on as politely as possible, but Nanny's grip was steel.

"She sings a bit. Big girl. Voice with double joints in it. Wears black."

"You don't mean Perdita?"

"Perdita? Oh, yes. That'd be her all right."

"I think she's seeing to Christine. They're in Mr. Salzella's office."

"Would Christine be the thin girl in white?"

"Yes, ma'am."

"And I expect you're going to show me where this Mr. Salzella's office is?"

"Er, am I— Er, yes. It's just along the stage there, first door on the right."

"What a good boy to help an old lady," said Nanny. Her grip increased to a few ounces short of cutting off circulation. "And wouldn't it be a good idea if you helped young Walter back there do something respectful for the poor dead man?"

"Back where?"

Nanny turned around. The late Dr. Undershaft had gone nowhere, but Walter had vanished.

"Poor chap was a bit upset, I shouldn't wonder," said Nanny. "Only to be expected. So . . . how about if you got another strapping young lad to help you out instead?"

"Er . . . yes."

"What a good boy," Nanny repeated.

It was mid-evening. Granny and Mrs. Plinge pushed their way through the crowds toward the Shades, a part of the city that was as thronged as a rookery, fragrant as a cesspit, and vice versa.

"So," said Granny, as they entered the network of

fetid alleys, "your boy Walter usually sees you home, does he?"

"He's a good boy, Mistress Weatherwax," said Mrs. Plinge defensively.

"I'm sure you're grateful for a strong lad to lean on," said Granny.

Mrs. Plinge looked up. Looking into Granny's eyes was like looking into a mirror. What you saw looking back at you was yourself, and there was no hiding place.

"They torment him so," she mumbled. "They poke at him and hide his broom. They're not bad boys round here, but they will torment him."

"He brings his broom home, does he?"

"He looks after his things," said Mrs. Plinge. "I've always brought him up to look after his things and not be a trouble. But they will poke the poor soul and call him such names . . ."

The alleyway opened into a yard, like a well between the high buildings. Washing lines crisscrossed the rectangle of moonlit sky.

"I'm just in here," said Mrs. Plinge. "Much obliged to you."

"How does Walter get home without you?" said Granny.

"Oh, there's plenty of places to sleep in the Opera House. He knows that if I don't come for him he's to stop there for the night. He does what he's told, Mistress Weatherwax. He's never any trouble."

"I never said he was."

Mrs. Plinge fumbled in her purse, as much to escape Granny's stare as to look for the key.

"I expect your Walter sees most of what goes on in the Opera House," said Granny, taking one of Mrs. Plinge's wrists in her hand. "I wonder what your Walter . . . saw?"

The pulse jumped at the same time as the thieves did. Shadows unfolded themselves. There was the scrape of metal.

A low voice said, "There's two of you, ladies, and there's six of us. There's no use in screaming."

"Oh, deary deary me," said Granny.

Mrs. Plinge dropped to her knees. "Oh, please don't hurt us, kind sirs, we are harmless old ladies! Haven't you got mothers?"

Granny rolled her eyes. Damn, damn and blast. She was a good witch. That was her role in life. That was the burden she had to bear. Good and Evil were quite superfluous when you'd grown up with a highly developed sense of Right and Wrong. She hoped, oh she hoped, that young though these were, they were dyed-in-the-wool criminals . . .

"I 'ad a mother once," said the nearest thief. "Only I think I must of et 'er . . ."

Ah. Top marks. Granny raised both hands to her hat to draw out two long hat pins . . .

A tile slid off the roof, and splashed into a puddle. They looked up.

A caped figure was visible for a moment against the moonlight. It thrust out a sword at arm's length. Then it dropped, landing lightly in front of one astonished man.

The sword whirled.

The first thief spun and thrust at the shadowy

shape in front of him, which turned out to be another thief, whose arm jerked up and dragged its own knife along the rib cage of the thief beside him.

The masked figure danced among the gang, his sword almost leaving trails in the air. It occurred to Granny later that it never actually made contact, but then, it never needed to—when six are against one in a mêlée in the shadows, and especially if those six aren't used to a target that is harder to hit than a wasp, and even more so if they got all their ideas of knife fighting from other amateurs, then there's six chances in seven that they'll stab a crony and about one chance in twelve that they'll nick their own earlobe.

The two that remained uninjured after ten seconds looked at one another, turned, and ran.

And then it was over.

The surviving vertical figure bowed low in front of Granny Weatherwax. "Ah. *Bella* Donna!"

There was a swirl of black cloak and red silk, and it too was gone. For a moment soft footsteps could be heard skimming over the cobbles.

Granny's hand was still halfway to her hat.

"Well I never!" she said.

She looked down. Various bodies were groaning or making soft bubbling noises.

"Deary deary me," she said. Then she pulled herself together.

"I reckon we're going to need some nice hot water and some bits of bandage, and a good sharp needle for the stitching, Mrs. Plinge," she said. "We can't let these poor men bleed to death now, can we, even if they do try to rob old ladies . . ."

Mrs. Plinge looked horrified.

"We've got to be charitable, Mrs. Plinge," Granny insisted.

"I'll pump up the fire and tear up a sheet," said Mrs. Plinge. "Don't know if I can find a needle . . ."

"Oh, I 'spect I've got a needle," said Granny, extracting one from the brim of her hat.

She knelt down by a fallen thief. "It's rather rusty and blunt," she added, "but we shall have to do the best we can."

The needle gleamed in the moonlight. His round, frightened eyes focused on it, and then on Granny's face. He whimpered. His shoulder blades tried to dig him into the cobbles.

It was perhaps as well that no one else could see Granny's face in the shadows.

"Let's do some good," she said.

Salzella threw his hands in the air. "Supposing he'd come down in the middle of the act?" he said.

"All right, all *right*," said Bucket, who was sitting behind his desk as a man might hide behind a bunker. "I agree. After the show we call in the Watch. No two ways about it. We shall just have to ask them to be discreet."

"Discreet? Have you ever met a Watchman?" said Salzella.

"Not that they'll find anything. He'll have been over the rooftops and away, you may depend upon it. Whoever he is. Poor Dr. Undershaft. He was always so highly strung."

"Never more so than tonight," said Salzella.

"That was tasteless!"

Salzella leaned over the desk. "Tasteless or not, the company are theater people. Superstitious. One little thing like someone being murdered onstage and they go all to pieces."

"He wasn't murdered onstage, he was murdered offstage. And we can't be *sure* it was murder! He'd been very . . . depressed, lately."

Agnes had been shocked, but it hadn't been shock at Dr. Undershaft's death. She'd been astonished at her own reaction. It had been startling and unpleasant to see the man, but even worse to see herself actually being *interested* in what was happening—in the way people reacted, in the way they moved, in the things they said. It had been as if she'd stood outside herself, watching the whole thing.

Christine, on the other hand, had just folded up. So had Dame Timpani. Far more people had fussed over Christine than around the prima donna, despite the fact that Dame Timpani had come around and fainted again quite pointedly several times and had eventually been forced to go for hysterics. No one had assumed for a minute that Agnes couldn't cope.

Christine had been carried into Salzella's back-stage office and put on a couch. Agnes had to fetch a bowl of water and a cloth and was wiping her forehead, for there are some people who are destined to be carried to comfortable couches and some people whose only fate is fetching a bowl of cold water.

"Curtain goes up again in two minutes," said Salzella. "I'd better go and round up the orchestra. They'll all be in the Stab In The Back over the road. The swine can get through half a pint before the applause has died away."

"Are they capable of playing?"

"They never have been, so I don't see why they should start now," said Salzella. "They're *musicians*, Bucket. The only way a dead body would upset them is if it fell in their beer, and even then they'd play if you offered them Dead Body Money."

Bucket walked over to the recumbent Christine. "How is she?"

"She keeps mumbling a bit—" Agnes began.

"Cup of tea? Tea? Cup of tea, anyone? Nothing nicer than a cup of tea, well, I tell a lie, but I see the couch is occupied, just my little joke, no offense meant, anyone for a nice cup of tea?"

Agnes looked around in horror.

"Well, *I* could certainly do with one," said Bucket, with false joviality.

"How about you, miss?" Nanny winked at Agnes.

"Er . . . no, thank you . . . do you *work* here?" said Agnes.

"I'm just helping out for Mrs. Plinge, who has been taken poorly," said Nanny, giving her another wink. "I'm Mrs. Ogg. Don't mind me."

This seemed to satisfy Bucket, if only because random tea distributors represented the most minor of threats at this point.

"It's more like *Grand Guignol* than opera out there tonight," said Nanny. She nudged Bucket. "'S foreign for 'blood all over the stage,'" she said helpfully.

"Really."

"Yep. It means . . . Big Gignol."

Music started in the distance.

"That's the overture to Act Two," said Bucket. "Well, if Christine is still unwell, then . . ." He looked desperately at Agnes. Well, at a time like this people would understand.

Agnes's chest swelled further with pride. "Yes, Mr. Bucket?"

"Perhaps we could find you a white—"

Christine, her eyes still shut, raised her wrist to her forehead and groaned.

"Oh, dear, what happened?"

Bucket knelt down instantly. "Are you all right? You had a nasty shock! Do you think you could go on for the sake of your art and people not asking for their money back?"

She gave him a brave smile. Unnecessarily brave, it seemed to Agnes.

"I can't disappoint the dear public!" she said.

"*Jolly* good!" said Bucket. "I should hurry on out there, then. Perdita will help you—won't you, Perdita?"

"Yes. Of course."

"And you'll be in the chorus for the duet," said Bucket. "*Nearby* in the chorus."

Agnes sighed. "Yes, I know. Come on, Christine."

"Dear Perdita . . ." said Christine.

Nanny watched them go. Then she said, "I'll have that cup if you've finished with it."

"Oh. Yes. Yes, it was very nice," said Bucket.

"Er . . . I had a bit of an accident up at the Boxes," said Nanny.

Bucket clutched at his chest. "How many died?"

"Oh, no one died, no one died. They got a bit damp because I spilled some champagne."

Bucket sagged with relief. "Oh, I wouldn't worry about that," he said.

"When I say spilled . . . I mean, it went on happening . . ."

He waved her away. "It cleans up well off the carpet," he said.

"Does it stain ceilings?"

"Mrs. . . . ?"

"Ogg."

"Please just go away."

Nanny nodded, gathered up the teacups and wandered out of the office. If no one questioned an old lady with a tray of tea, they certainly weren't bothered about one behind a pile of washing-up. Washing-up is a badge of membership anywhere.

As far as Nanny Ogg was concerned, washing-up was also something that happened to other people, but she felt that it might be a good idea to stay in character. She found an alcove with a pump and a sink in it, rolled up her sleeves, and set to work.

Someone tapped her on the shoulder.

"You shouldn't do that, you know," said a voice. "That's very unlucky."

She glanced around at a stagehand.

"What, washing-up causes seven years' bad luck?" she said.

"You were whistling."

"Well? I always whistle when I'm thinkin'."

"You shouldn't whistle onstage, I meant."

"It's unlucky?"

"I suppose you could say that. We use whistle codes when we're shifting the scenery. Having a sack of sandbags land on you *could* be unlucky, I suppose."

Nanny glanced up. His gaze followed hers. Just here the ceiling was about two feet away.

"It's just safest not to whistle," the boy mumbled.

"I'll remember that," said Nanny. "No whistlin'. Interestin'. We do live and learn, don't we?"

The curtain went up on Act Two. Nanny watched from the wings.

The interesting thing was the way in which people contrived to keep one hand higher than their necks in case of *accidents*. There seemed to be far more salutes and waves and dramatic gestures than were strictly called for in the opera.

She watched the duet between Iodine and Bufola, possibly the first in the history of the opera where both singers kept their eyes turned resolutely upward.

Nanny enjoyed music, as well. If music were the food of love, she was game for a sonata and chips at any time. But it was clear that the sparkle had gone out of things tonight.

She shook her head.

A figure moved through the shadows behind her, and reached out. She turned, and looked at a fearsome face.

"Oh, hello, Esme. How did you get in?"

"You've still got the tickets so I had to talk to the man on the door. But he'll be right as rain in a minute or two. What's been happening?"

"Well . . . the Duke's sung a long song to say that he must be going, and the Count has sung a song saying how nice it is in the springtime, and a dead body's fallen out of the ceiling."

"That goes on a lot in opera, does it?"

"Shouldn't think so."

"Ah. In the theater, I've noticed, if you watch dead bodies long enough you can see them move."

"Doubt if this one'll move. Strangled. Someone's murdering opera people. I bin chatting to the ballet girls."

"Indeed?"

"It's this Ghost they're all talking about."

"Hmm. Wears one of those black opera suits and a white mask?"

"How did you know that?"

Granny looked smug.

"I mean, I can't imagine who'd want to murder opera people . . ." Nanny thought of the expression on Dame Timpani's face. "Except p'raps other opera people. And p'raps the musicians. And some of the audience, p'raps."

"I don't believe in ghosts," said Granny firmly.

"Oh, Esme! You *know* I've got a dozen of 'em in my house!"

"Oh, I believe in *ghosts*," said Granny. "Sad things hangin' around goin' woogy woogy woogy . . . but I don't believe they kill people or use swords." She walked away a little. "There's too many ghosts here already."

Nanny kept quiet. It was best to do so when Granny was listening without using her ears.

"Gytha?"

"Yes, Esme?"

"What does 'Bella Donna' mean?"

"It's the nobby name for Deadly Nightshade, Esme."

"I thought so. Huh! The cheek of it!"

"Only, in opera, it means Beautiful Woman."

"Really? Oh." Granny's hand reached up and patted the iron-hard bun of her hair. "Foolishness!"

. . . he'd moved like music, like someone dancing to a rhythm inside his head. And his face for a moment in the moonlight was the skull of an angel . . .

The duet got another standing ovation.

Agnes faded gently back into the chorus. She had to do little else during the remainder of the act except dance, or at least move as rhythmically as she could, with the rest of the chorus during the Gypsy Fair, and listen to the Duke singing a song about how lovely the countryside was in summer. With an arm extended dramatically above his head.

She kept peering into the wings.

If Nanny Ogg was here then the other one would be around somewhere. She wished she'd never written those wretched letters home. Well . . . they wouldn't drag her back, no matter what they tried . . .

The remainder of the opera passed without anyone dying, except where the score required them to do so at some length. There was a minor upset when a member of the chorus was almost brained by a sandbag dislodged from a gantry by the stagehands stationed there to prevent accidents.

There was more applause at the end. Christine got most of it.

And then the curtains closed.

And opened and closed a few times as Christine took her bows.

Agnes considered she took one more bow than the

applause really justified. Perdita, looking out through her eyes, said: Of course she did.

And then they closed the curtains for the last time. The audience went home.

From the wings, and up in the flies, the stagehands whistled their commands. Parts of the world vanished into the aerial darkness. Someone went around and put out most of the lights. Rising like a birthday cake, the chandelier was winched into its loft so that the candles could be snuffed. Then there were the footsteps of the men leaving the loft . . .

Within twenty minutes of the last hand clap of applause the auditorium was empty and dark, except for just a few lights.

There was the clank of a bucket.

Walter Plinge walked onto the stage, if such a word could be employed for his mode of progress. He moved like a puppet on elastic strings, so that it seemed only coincidentally that his feet touched the ground.

Very slowly, and very conscientiously, he began to mop the stage.

After a few minutes a shadow detached itself from the curtains and walked over to him. Walter looked down.

"Hello Mister Pussy Cat," he said.

Greebo rubbed against his legs. Cats have an instinct for anyone daft enough to give them food, and Walter certainly was well qualified.

"I shall go and find you some milk shall I Mister Cat?"

Greebo purred like a thunderstorm.

Walking his strange walk, advancing only by averages, Walter disappeared into the wings.

There were two dark figures sitting in the balcony.

"Sad," said Nanny.

"He's got a good job in the warm and his mother keeps an eye on him," said Granny. "A lot of people fare worse."

"Not a big future for him, though," said Nanny. "Not when you think about it."

"There was a couple of cold potatoes and half a herring for their supper," said Granny. "Hardly a stick of furniture, too."

"Shame."

"Mind you, she's a little bit richer now," Granny conceded. "Especially if she sells all those knives and boots," she added to herself.

"It's a cruel world for old ladies," said Nanny, matriarch of a vast extended tribe and undisputed tyrant of half the Ramtops.

"Especially one as terrified as Mrs. Plinge," said Granny.

"Well, I'd be frightened, too, if I was old and had Walter to think about."

"I ain't talking about that, Gytha. I know about fear."

"That's true," said Nanny. "Most of the people you meet are full of fear."

"Mrs. Plinge is living in fear," said Granny, appearing not to hear this. "Her mind is flat with it. She can't hardly think for the terror. I could feel it coming off of her like mist."

"Why? Because of the Ghost?"

"I don't know yet. Not all of it, anyway. But I *will* find out."

Nanny fished in the recesses of her clothing.

"Fancy a drink?" she said. There was a muffled *clink* from somewhere in her petticoats. "I got champagne, brandy and port. Also some nibbles and biscuits."

"Gytha Ogg, I believe you are a thief," said Granny.

"I ain't!" said Nanny, and added, with that grasp of advanced morality that comes naturally to a witch: "Just because I occasionally technic'ly steal something, that doesn't make me a thief. I don't *think* thief."

"Let's get back to Mrs. Palm's."

"All right," said Nanny. "But can we get something to eat first? I don't mind the cooking, but the grub there is a bit of an all-day breakfast, if you know what I mean . . ."

There was a sound from the stage as they stood up. Walter had returned, followed by a slightly fatter Greebo. Oblivious to the watchers, he continued to mop the stage.

"First thing tomorrow," said Granny, "we'll go and see Mr. Goatberger the Almanack man again. I've had time to think about what to do next. And then we're going to sort this out."

She glared at the innocent figure washing the stage and said, under her breath: "What is it you know, Walter Plinge? What is it you've seen?"

* * *

"Wasn't it *amazing*?!" said Christine, sitting up in bed. Her nightdress, Agnes had noted, was white. And extremely lacy.

"Yes, indeed," said Agnes.

"Five curtain calls!! Mr. Bucket says that's more than anyone's ever had since Dame Gigli!! I'm sure I won't be able to *sleep* for the excitement!!"

"So you just drink up that lovely hot milk drink I've done for us," said Agnes. "It took me ages to carry the saucepan up those stairs."

"And the flowers!!" said Christine, ignoring the mug Agnes had placed beside her. "They started arriving right after the performance, Mr. Bucket said!! He said—"

There was a soft knock at the door.

Christine adjusted her dress.

"Come!!"

The door opened and Walter Plinge shuffled in, hidden under the bouquets of flowers.

After a few steps he stumbled on his own feet, plunged forward, and dropped them. Then he stared at the two girls in mute embarrassment, turned suddenly, and walked into the door.

Christine giggled.

"Sorry mu-miss," said Walter.

"Thank you, Walter," said Agnes.

The door closed.

"Isn't he strange?! Have you seen the way he stares at me?! Do you think you could find some water for these, Perdita?!"

"Certainly, Christine. It's only seven flights of stairs."

"And as a reward I shall drink this lovely drink you have made for me!! Has it got spices in it?"

"Oh, yes. Spices," said Agnes.

"It's not like one of those potions your witches cook up, is it?!"

"Er, no," said Agnes. After all, everyone in Lancre used *fresh* herbs. "Er . . . there's not going to be anything like enough vases for them all, even if I use the guzunder . . ."

"The what?!"

"The . . . you know. It's goes-under . . . the bed. Guzunder."

"You're so *funny*!!"

"There won't be, anyway," said Agnes, blushing hotly. Behind her eyes, Perdita committed murder.

"Then put in all the ones from the earls and knights and I shall see to the others tomorrow!" said Christine, picking up the drink.

Agnes picked up the kettle and started toward the door.

"Perdita, dear?" said Christine, the mug halfway to her lips.

Agnes turned.

"It did seem to me you were singing the *teensiest* bit loud, dear! I'm sure it must have been a little difficult for everyone to hear me."

"Sorry, Christine," said Agnes.

She walked down in darkness. Tonight there was a candle burning in a niche on every second landing. Without them the stairs would have been merely dark; *with* them, shadows crept and leapt at every corner.

She reached the pump in the little alcove by the stage manager's office, and filled the kettle.

Out on the stage, someone began to sing.

It was Peccadillo's part of a duet of three hours earlier, but sung without music and in a tenor voice of such tone and purity that the kettle dropped out of Agnes's hand and spilled cold water over her feet.

She listened for a while, and then realized that she was singing the soprano part under her breath.

The song came to an end. She could hear, far off, the hollow sound of footsteps retreating in the distance.

She ran to the door to the stage, paused a moment, and then opened it and went forward and out onto the huge dim emptiness. The candles left burning were as much illumination as stars on a clear night. There was no one there.

She walked into the center of the stage, and stopped, and caught her breath at the shock.

She could *feel* the auditorium in front of her, the huge empty space making the sound that velvet would make if it could snore.

It wasn't silence. A stage is never silent. It was the noise produced by a million other sounds that have never quite died away—the thunder of applause, the overtures, the arias. They poured down . . . fragments of tunes, lost chords, snatches of song.

She stepped back, and trod on someone's foot.

Agnes spun around. "André, there's no—"

Someone crouched back. "Sorry miss!"

Agnes breathed out. "Walter?"

"Sorry miss!"

"It's all right! You just startled me."

"Didn't see you miss!"

Walter was holding something. To Agnes's amazement, the darker shape in the darkness was a cat, flopped over Walter's arms like an old rug and purring happily. It was like seeing someone poking their arm into a mincing machine to find out what was jamming it.

"That's *Greebo*, isn't it?"

"He's a happy cat! He's full of milk!"

"Walter, why're you in the middle of the stage in the dark when everyone's gone home?"

"What were *you* doing miss?"

It was the first time she'd heard Walter ask a question. And he's sort of a janitor, after all, she told herself. He's allowed to go anywhere.

"I . . . got lost," she said, ashamed at the lie. "I . . . I'll be going up to my room now. Er. Did you hear someone singing?"

"All the time miss!"

"I meant just now."

"Just now I'm talking to you miss!"

"Oh . . ."

"G'night miss!"

She walked through the soft warm gloom to the backstage door, resisting at every step the urge to look round. She collected the kettle and hurried up the stairs.

Behind her, on the stage, Walter carefully lowered Greebo to the floor, took off his beret, and removed something white and papery from inside it.

"What shall we listen to, Mister Cat? I know, we shall listen to the overture to *Die Flederleiv* by J. Q. Bubbla, cond. Vochua Doinov."

Greebo gave him the fat-cheeked look of a cat prepared to put up with practically anything for food.

And Walter sat down beside him and listened to the music coming out of the walls.

When Agnes got back to the room Christine was already fast asleep, snoring the snore of those in herbal heaven. The mug lay by the bed.

It wasn't a *bad* thing to do, Agnes reassured herself. Christine probably needed a good night's sleep. It was practically a kindly act.

She turned her attention to the flowers. There were quite a lot of roses and orchids. Most of them had cards attached. Many aristocratic men apparently appreciated good singing or, at least, good singing that appeared to come from a face like Christine's.

Agnes arranged the flowers Lancre fashion, which was to hold the pot with one hand and the bouquet in the other and forcibly bring the two into conjunction.

The last bunch was the smallest, and wrapped in red paper. There was no card. In fact, there were no flowers.

Someone had merely wrapped up half a dozen blackened and spindly rose stems and then, for some reason, sprayed them with scent. It was musky and rather pleasant, but a bad joke all the same. She threw them in the bin with the rubbish, blew out the candle, and sat down to wait.

She wasn't certain for whom. Or what.

After a minute or two she was aware that there was a glow coming from the waste bin. It was the barest fluorescence, like a sick glowworm, but it was there.

She crawled across the floor and peered in.

There were rosebuds on the dead sticks, transparent as glass, visible only by the glimmer on the edge of each petal. They flickered like marsh lights.

Agnes lifted them out carefully and fumbled in the darkness for the empty mug. It wasn't the best of vases, but it would have to do. Then she sat and watched the ghostly flowers until . . .

. . . someone coughed. She jerked her head up, aware that she'd fallen asleep."

"Madam?"

"Sir?!"

The voice was melodious. It suggested that, at any minute, it might break into song.

"Attend. Tomorrow you must sing the part of Laura in *Il Truccatore*. We have much to do. One night is barely enough. The aria in Act One will occupy much of our time."

There was a brief passage of violin music.

"Your performance tonight was . . . good. But there are areas that we must build upon. Attend."

"Did *you* send the roses?!"

"You like the roses? They bloom only in darkness."

"Who *are* you?! Was it you I heard singing just now!?"

There was silence for a moment.

"Yes."

Then:

"Let us examine the role of Laura in *Il Truccatore*— 'The Master of Disguise', also sometimes vulgarly known as 'The Man with a Thousand Faces' . . ."

* * *

When the witches arrived at Goatberger's offices next morning they found a very large troll sitting on the stairs. It had a club across its knees and held up a shovel-sized hand to prevent them going any farther.

"No one's allowed in," it said. "Mr. Goatberger is in a meetin'."

"How long is this meetin' going to be?" said Granny.

"Mr. Goatberger is a very elongated meeter."

Granny gave the troll an appraising stare. "You been in publishin' long?" she said.

"Since dis mornin'," said the troll proudly.

"Mr. Goatberger gave you the job?"

"Yup. Come up Quarry Lane and picked me special for . . ."—the troll's brow creased as it tried to remember the unfamiliar words—". . . the fast track inna fast-movin' worlda publishin'."

"And what exactly is your job?"

"'Ead 'itter."

"'Scuse me," said Nanny, pushing forward. "I'd know that strata anywhere. You're from Copperhead in Lancre, ain't you?"

"So what?"

"We're from Lancre, too."

"Yeah?"

"This is Granny Weatherwax, you know."

The troll gave her a disbelieving grin, and then its brow corrugated again, and then it looked at Granny. She nodded.

"The one you boys call *Aaoograha hoa*, you know?" said Nanny. "'She Who Must Be Avoided'?"

The troll looked at its club as if seriously considering the possibility of beating itself to death.

Granny patted it on the lichen-encrusted shoulder. "What's your name, lad?"

"Carborundum, miss," it mumbled. One of its legs began to tremble.

"Well, I'm sure you're going to make a good life for yourself here in the big city," said Granny.

"Yes, why don't you go and start now?" said Nanny.

The troll gave her a grateful look and fled, without even bothering to open the door.

"Do they really call me that?" said Granny.

"Er. Yes," said Nanny, kicking herself. "It's a mark of respect, of course."

"Oh."

"Er . . ."

"I've always done my best to get along with trolls, you know that."

"Oh, yes."

"How about the dwarfs?" said Granny, as someone might who had found a hitherto unsuspected boil and couldn't resist poking it. "Have they got a name for me, too?"

"Let's go and see Mr. Goatberger, shall we?" said Nanny brightly.

"*Gytha!*"

"Er . . . well . . . I think it's *K'ez'rek d'b'duz*," said Nanny.

"What does that mean?"

"Er . . . 'Go Around the Other Side of the Mountain'," said Nanny.

"Oh."

Granny was uncharacteristically silent as they made their way up the stairs.

Nanny didn't bother to knock. She opened the

door and said, "Coo–ee, Mr. Goatberger! It's us again, just like you said. Oh, I shouldn't try to get out of the window like that—you're three flights up and that bag of money is a bit dangerous if you're climbing around."

The man edged around the room so that his desk was between him and the witches.

"Wasn't there a troll downstairs?" he said.

"It's decided to break out of publishing," said Nanny. She sat down and gave him a big smile. "I 'spect you've got some money for us."

Mr. Goatberger realized that he was trapped. His face contorted into a series of twisted expressions as he experimented with some replies. Then he smiled as widely as Nanny and sat down opposite her.

"Of course, things are very difficult at the moment," he said. "In fact I can't recall a worse time," he added, with considerable honesty.

He looked at Granny's face. His grin stayed where it was but the rest of his face began to edge away.

"People just don't seem to be buying books," he said. "And the cost of the etchings, well, it's wicked."

"Everyone I knows buys the Almanack," said Granny. "I reckon everyone in Lancre buys your Almanack. Everyone in the whole Ramtops buys the Almanack, even the dwarfs. That's a lot of half dollars. And Gytha's book seems to be doing very well."

"Well, of course, I'm glad it's so popular, but what with distribution, paying the peddlers, the wear and tear on—"

"Your Almanack will last a household all winter,

with care," said Granny. "Providing no one's ill and the paper's nice and thin."

"My son Jason buys *two* copies," said Nanny. "Of course, he's got a big family. The privy door never stops swinging—"

"Yes but, you see, the point is . . . I don't actually have to pay you *anything*," said Mr. Goatberger, trying to ignore this. His smile had the face all to itself now. "You paid *me* to print it, and I gave you your money back. In fact I think our accounts department made a slight error in your favor, but I won't—"

His voice trailed away.

Granny Weatherwax was unfolding a sheet of paper. "These predictions for next year . . ." she said.

"Where'd you get that?"

"I borrowed it. You can have it back if you like—"

"Well, what about them?"

"They're wrong."

"What do you mean, they're wrong? They're *predictions*!"

"I don't see there being a rain of curry in Klatch next May. You don't get curry that early."

"You know about the predictions business?" said Goatberger. "You? I've been printing predictions for years."

"I don't do clever stuff for years ahead, like you do," Granny admitted. "But I'm pretty accurate if you want a thirty-second one."

"Indeed? What's going to happen in thirty seconds?"

Granny told him.

Goatberger roared with laughter. "Oh, yes, that's a good one, you should be writing them for us!" he said. "Oh, my word. Nothing like being ambitious, eh? That's better than the spontaneous combustion of the Bishop of Quirm, and that didn't even happen! In thirty seconds, eh?"

"No."

"No?"

"Twenty-one seconds now," said Granny.

Mr. Bucket had arrived at the Opera House early to see if anyone had died so far today.

He made it as far as his office without a single body dropping out of the shadows.

He really hadn't expected it to be like this. He'd *liked* opera. It had all seemed so *artistic*. He'd watched hundreds of operas and practically no one had died, except once during the ballet scene in *La Triviata* when a ballerina had rather over-enthusiastically been flung into the lap of an elderly gentleman in the front row of the Stalls. She hadn't been hurt, but the old man had died in one incredibly happy instant.

Someone knocked at the door.

Mr. Bucket opened it about a quarter of an inch. "Who's dead?" he said.

"N—no one Mr. Bucket! I've got your letters!"

"Oh, it's you, Walter. Thank you."

He took the bundle and shut the door.

There were bills. There were always bills. The Opera House practically runs itself, they'd told him. Well, yes, but it practically ran on money. He rummaged through the let—

There was an envelope with the Opera House crest on it.

He looked at it like a man looks at a very fierce dog on a very thin leash.

It did nothing except lie there and look as gummed as an envelope can be.

Finally he disembowelled it with the paper knife and then flung it down on the desk again, as if it would bite.

When it did not do so he reached out hesitantly and withdrew the folded letter. It read as follows:

My dear Bucket

> *I should be most grateful if Christine sings the role of Laura tonight. I assure you she is more than capable.*
>
> *The second violinist is a little slow, I feel, and the second act last night was frankly extremely wooden. This really is not good enough.*
>
> *May I extend my own welcome to Señor Basilica. I congratulate you on his arrival.*
>
> *Wishing you the very best,*
> *The Opera Ghost*

"Mr. Salzella!"

Salzella was eventually located. He read the note. "You do not intend to accede to this?" he said.

"She *does* sing superbly, Salzella."

"You mean the Nitt girl?"

"Well . . . yes . . . you know what I mean."

"But this is nothing less than blackmail!"

"Is it? He's not actually threatening anything."

"You let her . . . I mean them, of course . . . you let them sing last night, and much good it did poor Dr. Undershaft."

"What do you advise, then?"

There was another series of disjointed knocks on the door.

"Come in, Walter," said Bucket and Salzella together.

Walter jerked in, holding the coal scuttle.

"I've been to see Commander Vimes of the city Watch," said Salzella. "He said he'll have some of his best men here tonight. Undercover."

"I thought you said they were all incompetent."

Salzella shrugged. "We've got to do this properly. Did you know Dr. Undershaft was strangled before he was hung?"

"Hanged," said Bucket, without thinking. "Men are hanged. It's dead meat that's hung."

"Indeed?" said Salzella. "I appreciate the information. Well, poor old Undershaft was strangled, apparently. And then he was hung."

"Really, Salzella, you do have a misplaced sense—"

"I've finished now Mr. Bucket!"

"Yes, thank you, Walter. You may go."

"Yes Mr. Bucket!"

Walter closed the door behind him, very conscientiously.

"I'm afraid it's working here," said Salzella. "If you don't find some way of dealing with . . . are you all right, Mr. Bucket?"

"What?" Bucket, who'd been staring at the closed door, shook his head. "Oh. Yes. Er. Walter . . ."

"What about him?"

"He's . . . all right, is he?"

"Oh, he's got his . . . funny little ways. He's harmless enough, if that's what you mean. Some of the stagehands and musicians are a bit cruel to him . . . you know, sending him out for a tin of invisible paint or a bag of nail holes and so on. He believes what he's told. Why?"

"Oh . . . I just wondered. Silly, really."

"I suppose he is, technically."

"No, I meant—Oh, it doesn't matter . . ."

Granny Weatherwax and Nanny Ogg left Goatberger's office and walked demurely down the street. At least, Granny walked demurely. Nanny leaned somewhat.

Every thirty seconds she'd say, "How much was that again?"

"Three thousand, two hundred and seventy dollars and eighty-seven pence," said Granny. She was looking thoughtful.

"I thought it was nice of him to look in all the ashtrays for all the odd coppers he could round up," said Nanny. "Those he could reach, anyway. How much was that again?"

"Three thousand, two hundred and seventy dollars and eighty-seven pence."

"I've never had seventy dollars before," said Nanny.

"I didn't say just seventy dollars, I said—"

"Yes, I know. But I'm working my way up to it gradual. I'll say this about money. It really chafes."

"I don't know why you have to keep your purse in your knicker leg," said Granny.

"It's the last place anybody would look." Nanny sighed. "How much did you say it was?"

"Three thousand, two hundred and seventy dollars and eighty-seven pence."

"I'm going to need a bigger tin."

"You're going to need a bigger chimney."

"I could certainly do with a bigger knicker leg." She nudged Granny. "You're going to have to be polite to me now I'm rich," she said.

"Yes, indeed," said Granny, with a faraway look in her eyes. "Don't think I'm not considering that."

She stopped. Nanny walked into her, with a tinkle of lingerie.

The frontage of the Opera House loomed over them.

"We've got to get back in there," Granny said. "And into Box Eight."

"Crowbar," said Nanny, firmly. "A No. 3 claw end should do it."

"We're not your Nev," said Granny. "Anyway, breaking in wouldn't be the same thing. We've got to have a *right* to be there."

"Cleaners," said Nanny. "We could be cleaners, and . . . no, 's not right me being a cleaner now, in my position."

"No, we can't have that, with you in your position."

Granny glanced down at Nanny as a coach pulled up outside the Opera House. "O' course," she said, artfulness dripping off her voice like toffee, "we could always *buy* Box Eight."

"Wouldn't work," said Nanny. People were hurrying down the steps with the cuff-adjusting, sticky looks of welcoming committees everywhere. "They're scared of selling it."

"Why not?" said Granny. "There's people dying and the opera goes on. That means someone's prepared to sell his own grandmother if he'd make enough money."

"It'd cost a fortune, anyway," said Nanny.

She looked at Granny's triumphant expression and groaned. "Oh, Esme! I was going to save that money for me old age!" She thought for a moment. "Anyway, it *still* wouldn't work. I mean, look at us, we don't look like the right kind of people . . ."

Enrico Basilica got out of the coach.

"But we *know* the right kind of people," said Granny.

"Oh, Esme!"

The shop bell tinkled in a refined tone, as if it were embarrassed to do something as vulgar as ring. It would have much preferred to give a polite cough.

This was Ankh-Morpork's most prestigious dress shop, and one way of telling was the apparent absence of anything so crass as merchandise. The occasional carefully placed piece of expensive material merely hinted at the possibilities available.

This was not a shop where things were bought. This was an emporium where you had a cup of coffee and a chat. Possibly, as a result of that muted conversation, four or five yards of exquisite fabric would change ownership in some ethereal way, and yet nothing so crass as *trade* would have taken place.

"Shop!" yelled Nanny.

A lady appeared from behind a curtain and observed the visitors, quite possibly with her nose.

"Have you come to the right entrance?" she said. Madame Dawning had been brought up to be polite to servants and tradespeople, even when they were as scruffy as these two old crows.

"My friend here wants a new dress," said the dumpier of the two. "One of the nobby ones with a train and a padded bum."

"In black," said the thin one.

"And we wants all the trimmings," said the dumpy one. "Little handbag onna string, pair of glasses onna stick, the whole thing."

"I think perhaps that might be a *leetle* more than you're thinking of spending," said Madame Dawning.

"How much is a leetle?" said the dumpy one.

"I mean that this is rather a *select* dress shop."

"That's why we're here. We don't want rubbish. My name's Nanny Ogg and this here is . . . Lady Esmerelda Weatherwax."

Madame Dawning regarded Lady Esmerelda quizzically. There was no doubt that the woman had a certain bearing. And she stared like a duchess.

"From Lancre," said Nanny Ogg. "And she could have a conservatory if she liked, but she doesn't want one."

"Er . . ." Madame Dawning decided to play along for a while. "What style were you considering?"

"Something nobby," said Nanny Ogg.

"I perhaps would like a *leetle* more guidance than that—"

"Perhaps you could show us some things," said Lady Esmerelda, sitting down. "It's for the opera."

"Oh, you patronize the opera?"

"Lady Esmerelda patronizes *everything*," said Nanny Ogg stoutly.

Madame Dawning had a manner peculiar to her class and upbringing. She'd been raised to see the world in a certain way. When it didn't act in that certain way she wobbled a bit but, like a gyroscope, eventually recovered and went on spinning just as if it had. If civilization were to collapse totally and the survivors were reduced to eating cockroaches, Madame Dawning would still use a napkin and look down on people who ate their cockroaches the wrong way around.

"I will, er, show you some examples," she said. "Excuse me *one* moment."

She scuttled into the long workrooms behind the shop, where there was considerably less gilt, and leaned against the wall and summoned her chief seamstress.

"Mildred, there are two *very* strange—"

She stopped. They'd *followed* her!

They were wandering down the aisle between the rows of dressmakers, nodding at people and inspecting some of the dresses on the dummies.

She hurried back. "I'm *sure* you'd prefer—"

"How much is this one?" said Lady Esmerelda, fingering a creation intended for the Dowager Duchess of Quirm.

"I am *afraid* that one is not for sale—"

"How much would it be if it was for sale?"

"Three hundred dollars, I believe," said Madame Dawning.

"Five hundred seems about right," said Lady Esmerelda.

"Does it?" said Nanny Ogg. "Oh, it does, does it?"

The dress was black. At least, in theory it was black. It was black in the same way that a starling's wing is black. It was black silk, with jet beads and sequins. It was black on holiday.

"It looks about my size. We'll take it. Pay the woman, Gytha."

Madame's gyroscope precessed rapidly. "Take it? Now? Five hundred dollars? Pay? Pay *now*? *Cash*?"

"See to it, Gytha."

"Oh, all *right*."

Nanny Ogg turned away modestly and raised her skirt. There was a series of rustlings and elasticated twangings, and then she turned around, holding a bag.

She counted out fifty rather warm ten-dollar pieces into Madame Dawning's unprotesting hand.

"And now we'll go back into the shop and have a poke around for the other stuff," said Lady Esmerelda. "I fancy ostrich feathers myself. And one of those big cloaks the ladies wear. And one of those fans edged with lace."

"Why don't we get some great big diamonds while we're about it?" said Nanny Ogg sharply.

"Good idea."

Madame Dawning could hear them bickering as they ambled away up the aisle.

She looked down at the money in her hand.

She knew about old money, which was somehow

hallowed by the fact that people had hung on to it for years, and she knew about new money, which seemed to be being made by all these upstarts that were flooding into the city these days. But under her powdered bosom she was an Ankh-Morpork shop-keeper, and knew that the best kind of money was the sort that was in her hand rather than someone else's. The best kind of money was mine, not yours.

Besides, she was also enough of a snob to confuse rudeness with good breeding. In the same way that the really rich can never be mad (they're eccentric), so they can also never be rude (they're outspoken and forthright).

She hurried after Lady Esmerelda and her rather strange friend. Salt of the earth, she told herself.

She was in time to overhear a mysterious conversation.

"I'm being punished, ain't I, Esme?"

"Can't imagine what you're talking about, Gytha."

"Just 'cos I had my little moment."

"I really don't follow you. Anyway, you said you were at your wits' end with thinking what you'd do with the money."

"Yes, but I'd have quite liked to have been at my wits' end on a big comfy *chase longyou* somewhere with lots of big strong men buyin' me chocolates and pressin' their favors on me."

"Money don't buy happiness, Gytha."

"I only wanted to rent it for a few weeks."

Agnes rose late, the music still ringing in her ears, and dressed in a dream. But she hung a bed sheet over the mirror first, just in case.

There were half a dozen of the chorus dancers in the canteen, sharing a stick of celery and giggling.

And there was André. He was eating something absentmindedly while staring at a sheet of music. Occasionally he'd wave his spoon in the air with a faraway look on his face, and then put it down and make a few notes.

In mid-beat he caught sight of Agnes, and grinned. "Hello. You look tired."

"Er . . . yes."

"You've missed all the excitement."

"Have I?"

"The Watch have been here, talking to everyone and asking lots of questions and writing things down very slowly."

"What sort of questions?"

"Well, knowing the Watch, probably 'Was it you what did it, then?' They're rather slow thinkers."

"Oh dear. Does that mean tonight's performance is canceled?"

André laughed. He had a rather pleasant laugh. "I don't think Mr. Bucket could possibly cancel it!" he said. "Even if people *are* dropping likes flies out of the flies."

"Why not?"

"People have been queuing for tickets!"

"Why?"

He told her.

"That's disgusting!" said Agnes. "You mean they're coming because it might be dangerous?"

"Human nature, I'm afraid. Of course, some of them want to hear Enrico Basilica. And . . . well . . .

Christine seems popular . . ." He gave her a sorrow-
ful look.

"I don't mind, honestly," lied Agnes. "Um . . . how
long have you worked here, André?"

"Er . . . only a few months. I . . . used to teach
music to the Seriph's children in Klatch."

"Um . . . what do you think about the Ghost?"

He shrugged. "Just some kind of madman, I suppose."

"Um . . . do you know if he sings? I mean, is *good*
at singing?"

"I heard that he sends little critiques to the manager. Some of the girls say they've heard someone
singing in the night, but they're always saying silly
things."

"Um . . . are there any secret passages here?"

He looked at her with his head on one side.
"Who've you been talking to?"

"Sorry?"

"The girls say there are. Of course, *they* say they
see the Ghost all the time. And sometimes in two
places at once."

"Why should they see him more?"

"Perhaps he just likes looking at young ladies.
They're always practicing in odd corners. Besides,
they're all half-crazed with hunger anyway."

"Aren't you *interested* in the Ghost? People have
been killed!"

"Well, people are saying it might have been Dr.
Undershaft."

"But he *was* killed!"

"He might have hanged himself. He'd been very

depressed lately. And he'd always been a bit strange. Nervy. It's going to be a bit difficult without him, though. Here, I've brought you a stack of old programs. Some of the notes may help, since you haven't been in the opera long."

Agnes stared at them, unseeing.

People were disappearing and the first thought that everyone had was that it was going to be inconvenient without them.

The show must go on. Everyone said that. People said it all the time. Often they smiled when they said it, but they were serious all the same, under the smile. No one ever said *why*. But yesterday, when the chorus had been arguing about the money, everyone knew that they weren't actually going to refuse to sing. It was all a game.

The show went on. She'd heard all the stories. She'd heard about shows continuing while fire raged around the city, while a dragon was roosting on the roof, while there was rioting in the streets outside. Scenery collapsed? The show went on. Leading tenor died? Then appeal to the audience for any student of music who knew the part, and give him his big chance while his predecessor's body cooled gently in the wings. Why? It was only a performance, for heaven's sake. It wasn't like something important. But . . . the show goes on. Everyone took this so much for granted that they didn't even think about it anymore, as though there were fog in their heads.

On the other hand . . . someone was teaching her to sing at night. A mysterious person sang songs on the stage when everyone had gone home. She tried to think of that voice belonging to someone who killed people. It didn't work. Maybe she'd caught some of the fog and didn't *want* it to work. What sort of person could have that feel for music and kill people?

She'd been idly turning the pages of an old program and a name caught her eye.

She quickly shuffled through the others beneath. There it was again. Not in every performance, and never in a major role, but it was there. Generally it played an innkeeper or a servant.

"Walter Plinge?" she said. "*Walter?* But . . . *he* doesn't sing, does he?"

She held up a program and pointed.

"What? Oh, no!" André laughed. "Good heavens . . . it's a . . . a kind of convenient name, I suppose. Sometimes someone has to sing a very minor part . . . perhaps a singer is in a role that they'd rather not be remembered in . . . well, here, they just go down on the program as Walter Plinge. Lots of theaters have a useful name like that. Like A. N. Other. It's convenient for everyone."

"But . . . *Walter Plinge?*"

"Well, I suppose it started as a joke. I mean, can you imagine Walter Plinge onstage?" André grinned. "In that little beret he wears?"

"What does he think about it?"

"I don't think he minds. It's hard to tell, isn't it?"

There was a crash from the direction of the kitchen, although it was really more of a crashendo— the long-drawn-out clatter that begins when a pile of plates begins to slip, continues when someone tries to grab at them, develops a desperate counter-theme when the person realizes they don't have three hands, and ends with the *roinroinroin* of the one miraculously intact plate spinning around and around on the floor.

They heard an irate female voice.

"Walter Plinge!"

"Sorry Mrs. Clamp!"

"Damn thing keeps holding onto the edge of the pan! Let go, you wretched insect—"

There was the sound of crockery being swept up, and then a rubbery noise that could approximately be described as a *spoing*.

"*Now* where's it gone?"

"Don't know Mrs. Clamp!"

"And what's that cat doing in here?"

André turned back to Agnes and flashed her a sad smile. "It is a little cruel, I suppose," he said. "The poor chap is a bit daft."

"I'm not at all sure," said Agnes, "that I've met anyone here who isn't."

He grinned again. "I know," he said.

"I mean, everyone acts as if it's only the music that matters! The plots don't make sense! Half the stories rely on people not recognizing their servants or wives because they've got a tiny mask on! Large ladies play the part of consumptive girls! No one can act properly! No wonder everyone accepts me singing for Christine—that's practically *normal* compared to opera! It's an operatic kind of idea! There should be a sign on the door saying 'Leave your common sense here'! If it wasn't for the music the whole thing would be ridiculous!"

She realized he was looking at her with an opera face.

"Of course, that's it, isn't it. It *is* the show that matters, isn't it?" she said. "It's *all* show."

"It's not meant to be real," said André. "It's not like theater. No one's saying, 'You've got to pretend this is a big battlefield and that guy in the cardboard crown is really a king.' The plot's only there to fill in time before the next song."

He leaned forward and took her hand. "This must be wretched for you," he said.

No male had ever touched Agnes before, except perhaps to push her over and steal her sweets.

She pulled her hand away.

"I, er, better go and practice," she said, feeling the blush start.

"You really picked up the role of Iodine very well," said André.

"I, er, have a private tutor," said Agnes.

"Then he's really studied opera, that's all I can say."

"I . . . think he has."

"Esme?"

"Yes, Gytha?"

"It's not that I'm complaining or anything . . ."

"Yes?"

". . . but why isn't it *me* who's being the posh opera patronizer?"

"Because you're as common as muck, Gytha."

"Oh. Right." Nanny subjected this statement to some thought and couldn't see any point of inaccuracy that would sway a jury. "Fair enough."

"It's not as though *I* like this."

"Shall I do madam's feet?" said the manicurist.

She stared at Granny's boots and wondered if it might be necessary to use a hammer.

"I got to admit, it's a nice hair style," said Nanny.

"Madam has *marvelous* hair," said the hairdresser. "What is the secret?"

"You've got to make sure there's no newts in the water," said Granny. She looked at her reflection in the mirror over the washbasin, and went to look away . . . and then sneaked another glance. Her lips pursed. "Hmm," she said.

At the other end, the manicurist had succeeded in getting Granny's boots and socks off. Much to her amazement there was revealed, instead of the corned and bunioned monstrosities she'd been expecting, a pair of perfect feet. She didn't know where to start because there was nowhere to begin, but this manicure was costing twenty dollars and in those circumstances you damn well find something to do.

Nanny sat beside their pile of packages and tried to work everything out on a scrap of paper. She didn't have Granny's gift for numbers. They tended to writhe under her gaze and add themselves up wrong.

"Esme? I reckon we've spent . . . probably more'n a thousand dollars so far, and that's not including hirin' the coach, and we haven't paid Mrs. Palm for the room."

"You said nothing was too much trouble to help a Lancre girl," said Granny.

But I didn't say nothing was too much money, thought Nanny, and then scolded herself for thinking like that. But she was definitely feeling a little lighter in the underwear regions.

There seemed to be a general consensus among

the artisans of beauty that they'd done what they could. Granny swiveled the chair around.

"What do you think?" she said.

Nanny Ogg stared. She'd seen many strange things in her life, some of them twice. She'd seen elves and walking stones and the shoeing of a unicorn. She'd had a farmhouse dropped on her head. But she'd never seen Granny Weatherwax in rouge.

All her normal expletives of shock and surprise fused instantly, and she found herself resorting to an ancient curse belonging to her grandmother.

"Well, I'll be *mogadored*!" she said.

"Madam has extremely good skin," said the cosmetics lady.

"I know," said Granny. "Can't seem to do anything about it."

"I'll be *mogadored*!" said Nanny again.

"Powder and paint," said Granny. "Huh. Just another kind of mask. Oh, well." She gave the hairdresser a dreadful smile. "How much do we owe you?" she said.

"Er . . . thirty dollars?" said the hairdresser. "That is . . ."

"Give the w . . . man thirty dollars and another twenty to make up for his trouble," said Granny, clutching at her head.

"Fifty dollars? You could buy a *shop* for—"

"Gytha!"

"Oh, all *right*. 'Scuse me, I'm just going to the bank."

She turned away demurely, raised the hem of her skirt—

—twangtwingtwongtwang—

—and turned back with a handful of coins.

"There you go, my good wo . . . sir," she said sourly.

There was a coach waiting outside. It was the best Granny had been able to hire with Nanny's money. A footman held open the door as Nanny helped her friend aboard.

"We'll go straight to Mrs. Palm's so's I can change," said Granny as they pulled away. "And then to the Opera House. We ain't got much time."

"Are you all right?"

"Never felt better." Granny patted her hair. "Gytha Ogg, you wouldn't be a witch if you couldn't jump to conclusions, right?"

Nanny nodded. "Oh, yes." There was no shame in it. Sometimes there wasn't time to do anything else but take a flying leap. Sometimes you had to trust to experience and intuition and general awareness and take a running jump. Nanny herself could clear quite a tall conclusion from a standing start.

"So I've no doubt at all that there's some kind of idea floating around in your mind about this Ghost . . ."

"Well . . . sort of an idea, yes . . ."

"A name, perhaps?"

Nanny shifted uncomfortably, and not only because of the money bags under her skirt.

"I got to admit something crossed my mind. A kind of . . . feeling. I mean, you never can tell . . ."

Granny nodded. "Yes. It's all neat, isn't it? It's a lie."

"You said last night you saw the whole thing!"

"It's still a lie. Like the lie about masks."

"What lie about masks?"

"The way people say they hide faces."

"They *do* hide faces," said Nanny Ogg.

"Only the one on the outside."

No one took much notice of Agnes. The stage was being set for the new performance tonight. The orchestra was rehearsing. The ballerinas had been herded into their practice room. In various other rooms people were singing at cross-purposes. But no one seemed to want her to do anything.

I'm just a wandering voice, she thought.

She climbed the stairs to her room and sat on the bed. The curtains were still drawn and, in the gloom, the strange roses glowed. She had rescued them from the bin because they were beautiful, but, in a way, she'd have been happier if they weren't there. Then she could have believed she'd imagined the whole thing.

There was no sound from Christine's room. Telling herself that it was really *her* room *anyway*, and Christine had just been allowed to borrow it, Agnes went in.

It was a mess. Christine had got up, got dressed—either that or a thorough but overenthusiastic burglar had gone through every drawer in the place—and gone. The bouquets that Agnes had put into whatever receptacles she could find last night were where she had left them. The others were where she had left them, too, and they were already dying.

She caught herself wondering where she could find some jars and pots for them, and hated herself for it. It was as bad as saying "poot!" You might as well paint WELCOME on yourself and lie down on the doorstep of the universe. It was no fun at all, having a wonderful personality. Oh . . . and good hair.

And then she went and found pots for them anyway.

The mirror dominated the room. It seemed to grow a little larger each time she looked at it.

All right. She had to know, didn't she?

Heart pounding, she felt around the edges of it. There was a little raised area that might have looked like part of the frame, but as her fingers moved across it there was a "click" and the mirror swung inward a fraction of an inch. When she pushed at it, it moved.

She breathed out. And stepped in.

"It's disgusting!" said Salzella. "It's pandering to the most depraved taste!"

Mr. Bucket shrugged. "It's not as though we're putting 'Good Chance of Seeing Someone Throttled on Stage' on the posters," he said. "But news has got around. People like . . . drama."

"You mean the Watch didn't want us to shut down?"

"No. They just said we should mount guards like last night and they'd take steps."

"Steps to the nearest place of safety, no doubt."

"I don't like it any more than you do, but it's gone too far. We need the Watch now. Anyway, there'd be a riot if we closed. Ankh-Morpork has always enjoyed . . . excitement. We're completely sold out. The show must go on."

"Oh, yes," said Salzella nastily. "Would you like me to slit a few throats in the second act? Just so no one feels disappointed?"

"Of course not," said Bucket. "We don't want any deaths. But . . ."

The "but" hung in the air like the late Dr. Undershaft.

Salzella threw up his hands.

"Anyway, I believe we are past the worst," said Mr. Bucket.

"I hope so," said Salzella.

"Where's Señor Basilica?" said Bucket.

"Mrs. Plinge is showing him his dressing room."

"Mrs. Plinge hasn't been murdered?"

"No, no one has been found dead so far today," said Salzella.

"That *is* good news."

"Yes, and it must be, oh, at least ten past twelve," said Salzella with an irony that Bucket quite failed to notice. "I will go and fetch him up so that we can have lunch, shall I? It must be a good half an hour since he had a snack."

Bucket nodded. After the director had gone he surreptitiously checked his desk drawers again. There was no letter. Perhaps it *was* over . . . Perhaps it was true what they were saying about the late doctor.

Someone knocked at the door, four times. Only one person could achieve four knocks without any rhythm whatsoever.

"Come in, Walter."

Walter Plinge stumbled into the room. "There's a lady!" he said. "She's to see Mr. Bucket!"

Nanny Ogg poked her head around the door. "Coo-ee," she said. "It's only me."

"It's . . . Mrs. Ogg, isn't it?" said Mr. Bucket.

There was something slightly worrying about the woman. He didn't recall her name on the list of employees. On the other hand, she was clearly around the place, she wasn't dead, and she made a decent cup of tea, so was it his worry if she wasn't getting paid?

"Good gracious, I'm not the *lady*," said Nanny Ogg. "I'm as common as muck, me, on the highest authority. No, *she's* waiting down in the foyer. I thought I'd better nip around here and warn you."

"Warn me? Warn me about what? I don't have any other appointments this morning. Who is this lady?"

"Have you ever heard of Lady Esmerelda Weatherwax?"

"No. Should I?"

"Famous patron of the opera. Conservatories all over the place," said Nanny. "Pots of money, too."

"Really? But I'm due to—"

Bucket looked out of the window. There was a coach and four horses outside. It had so much rococo ornamentation on it that it was surprising it ever managed to move.

"Well, I—" he began again. "It is really very incon—"

"She ain't the sort of person who likes to be kept waiting," said Nanny, with absolute honesty. And then, because Granny had been getting on her nerves all morning and the initial embarrassment at Mrs.

Palm's still rankled and there was a streak of mischief in Nanny a mile wide, she added, "They say she was a famous courtesan in her younger days. They say she didn't like to be kept waiting then, either. Retired now, of course. So they say."

"You know, I've visited most of the major opera houses and I've never heard the name," mused Bucket.

"Ah, I heard she likes to keep her donations secret," said Nanny.

Mr. Bucket's mental compass once again swung around to point due Money.

"You'd better show her up," he said. "I could perhaps give her a few minutes—"

"No one ever gave Lady Esmerelda less than half an hour," said Nanny, and gave Bucket a wink. "I'll go and fetch her, shall I?"

She bustled away, towing Walter behind her.

Mr. Bucket stared after her. Then, after a moment's thought, he got up and checked the set of his mustache in the mirror over the fireplace.

He heard the door open and turned with his finest smile in place.

It faded only slightly at the sight of Salzella, ushering the impressive bulk of Basilica in front of him. The little manager and interpreter fussed along beside him, like a tugboat.

"Ah, Señor Basilica," said Bucket. "I trust the dressing rooms are to your satisfaction?"

Basilica gave him a blank smile while the interpreter spoke in Brindisian, and then replied.

"Señor Basilica says they are fine but the larder isn't big enough," he said.

"Haha," said Bucket, and then stopped when no one else laughed.

"In fact," he said hurriedly, "Señor Basilica will I'm sure be very happy to hear that our kitchens have made a special effort to—"

There was *another* knock at the door. He hurried across and opened it.

Granny Weatherwax stood there, but not for long. She pushed him aside and swept into the room.

There was a choking noise from Enrico Basilica.

"Which one of you is Bucket?" she demanded.

"Er . . . me . . ."

Granny removed a glove and extended her hand. "So sorry," she said. "Ai am not used to important people opening their own doors. Ai am Esmerelda Weatherwax."

"How charming. I've heard so much about you," lied Bucket. "Pray let me introduce you. No doubt you know Señor Basilica?"

"Of course," said Granny, looking Henry Slugg in the eye. "I'm sure Señor Basilica recalls the many happy times we've had in other opera houses whose names I can't quite remember at the moment."

Henry grimaced a smile, and said something to the interpreter.

"That is astonishing," said the interpreter. "Señor Basilica has just said how fondly he recalls meeting you many times before at opera houses that have just slipped his mind at present."

Henry kissed Granny's hand, and looked up at her with pleading in his eyes.

My word, thought Bucket, that look he's giving her . . . I wonder if they ever—

"Oh, uh, and this is Mr. Salzella, our director of music," he said, remembering himself.

"Honored," said Salzella, giving Granny a firm handshake and looking her squarely in the eye. She nodded.

"And what's the first thing you'd take out of a burning house, Mr. Salzella?" she inquired.

He smiled politely. "What would you like me to take, madam?"

She nodded thoughtfully and let go of his hand.

"May I get you a drink?" said Bucket.

"A small sherry," said Granny.

Salzella sidled up to Bucket as he was pouring the drink. "Who the hell is she?"

"Apparently she's rolling in money," whispered Bucket. "And very keen on opera."

"Never heard of her."

"Well, Señor Basilica has, and that's good enough for me. Make yourself pleasant to them, will you, while I try to sort out lunch."

He pulled open the door and tripped over Nanny Ogg.

"Sorry!" said Nanny, standing up and giving him a cheerful grin. "These doorknobs are a bugger to polish, aren't they?"

"Er, Mrs.—"

"Ogg."

"—Ogg, could you run along to the kitchens and tell Mrs. Clamp there will be another one for lunch, please."

"Right you are."

Nanny bustled away. Bucket nodded approvingly. What a reliable old lady, he thought.

* * *

It wasn't exactly a *secret*. When the room had been divided a space had been left between the walls. At the far end it opened onto a staircase, a perfectly ordinary staircase, which even had some grubby daylight via a dirt-encrusted window.

Agnes was vaguely disappointed. She had expected, well, a *real* secret passage, perhaps with a few torches flickering secretly in rather valuable secret wrought-iron holders. But the staircase had just been walled off from the rest of the place at some time. It wasn't secret—it had merely been forgotten.

There were cobwebs in the corners. The cocoons of extinct flies hung down from the ceiling. The air smelled of long-dead birds.

But there was a clear track through the dust. Someone had used the stairs several times.

She hesitated between up and down, and headed up. That was no great journey—after one more flight it ended at a trapdoor that wasn't even bolted.

She pushed at it, and then blinked in the unaccustomed light. Wind caught at her hair. A pigeon stared at her, and flew away as she poked her head into the fresh air.

The door had opened out onto the Opera House's roof, just one more item in a forest of skylights and air shafts.

She went back inside and headed downward. And became aware, as she did so, of the voices . . .

The old stairs hadn't been *totally* forgotten. Someone had at least seen their usefulness as an air shaft. Voices filtered up. There were scales, distant music, snatches of conversation. As she went down she passed through layers of noise, like a very carefully made sundae of sound.

Greebo sat on top of the kitchen cupboard and watched the performance with interest.

"Use the ladle, why don't you?" said a scene shifter.

"It won't reach! Walter!"

"Yes Mrs. Clamp?"

"Give me that broom!"

"Yes Mrs. Clamp!"

Greebo looked up at the high ceiling, to which was affixed a sort of thin, ten-pointed star.

In the middle of it was a pair of very frightened eyes.

"'Plunge it into boiling water,'" said Mrs. Clamp, "that's what it said in the cookbook. It never said 'Watch out, it'll grip the sides of the pot and spring straight up in the air—'"

She flailed around with the broom handle. The squid shrank back.

"And that pasta's all gone wrong," she muttered. "I've had it grilling for hours and it's still hard as nails, the wretched stuff."

"Coo—ee, it's only me," said Nanny Ogg, poking her head around the door, and such was the all-embracing nature of her personality that even those who didn't know who she was took this on trust. "Having a bit of trouble, are you?"

She surveyed the scene, including the ceiling. There was a smell of burning pasta in the air.

"Ah," she said. "This'd be the special lunch for Senior Basilica, would it?"

"It was *meant* to be," said the cook, still making ineffectual swipes. "Blasted thing won't come down, though."

Other pots were simmering on the long iron range. Nanny nodded toward them. "What's everyone else having?" she said.

"Mutton and clootie dumplings, with slumpie," said the cook.

"Ah. Good, honest food," said Nanny, speaking of wall-to-wall suet oiled with lard.

"And there's supposed to be Jammy Devils for pudding and I've been so tied up with this wretched thing I haven't even made a start!"

Nanny carefully took the broom out of the cook's hands. "Tell you what," she said, "you make enough dumplings and slumpie for five people, and I'll help by knocking up a quick pudding, how about that?"

"Well, that's a very handsome offer, Mrs.—"

"Ogg."

"The jam's in the jar by—"

"Oh, I won't bother about jam," said Nanny. She looked at the spice rack, grinned, and then stepped behind a table for modesty—

—twingtwangtwongtwang—

—"Got any chocolate?" she said, producing a slim volume. "I've got a recipe right here that might be fun . . ."

She licked her thumb and opened the book at page 53. Chocolate Delight with Special Secret Sauce.

Yes, thought Nanny, that *would* be fun.

If people wanted to go around teaching people lessons, other people should remember that those people knew a thing or two about people.

* * *

Scraps of conversation floated out of the walls as Agnes wound her secret way down the forgotten stairs.

It was . . . thrilling.

No one was saying anything important. There were no convenient guilty secrets. There were just the sounds of people getting through the day. But they were *secret* sounds.

It was wrong to listen, of course.

Agnes had been brought up in the knowledge that a lot of things were wrong. It was wrong to listen at doors, to look people directly in the eye, to talk out of turn, to answer back, to *put yourself forward* . . .

But behind the walls she could be the Perdita she'd always wanted to be. Perdita didn't care about anything. Perdita got things done. Perdita could wear anything she wanted. Perdita X Nitt, mistress of the darkness, magdalen of cool, could listen in to other people's lives. And never, ever have to have a wonderful personality.

Agnes knew she should go back up to her room. Whatever lay in the increasingly shadowy depths was probably something she ought not to find.

Perdita continued downward. Agnes went along for the ride.

The pre-luncheon drinks were going quite well, Mr. Bucket thought. Everyone was making polite conversation and absolutely no one had been killed up to the present moment.

And it had been very gratifying to see the tears of gratitude in Señor Basilica's eyes when he was told that the cook was preparing a special Brindisian meal, just for him. He'd seemed quite overcome.

It was reassuring that he knew Lady Esmerelda. There was something about the woman that left Mr. Bucket terribly perplexed. He was finding it a little difficult to converse with her. As a conversational gambit, "Hello, I understand you have a lot of money, can I have some please?" lacked, he felt, a certain subtlety.

"So, er, madam," he ventured, "what brings you to our, er, city?"

"I thought perhaps I could come and spend some money," said Granny. "Got rather a lot of it, you know. Keep havin' to change banks 'cos they get filled up."

Somewhere in Bucket's tortured brain, part of his mind went "whoopee" and clicked its heels.

"I'm sure if there's anything I can do—" he murmured.

"As a matter of fact, there is," said Granny. "I was thinking of—"

A gong banged.

"Ah," said Mr. Bucket. "Luncheon is served."

He extended his arm to Granny, who gave it an odd look before remembering who she was and taking it.

There was a small exclusive dining room off his office. It contained a table set for five and, looking rather fetching in a waitress's lacy bonnet, Nanny Ogg.

She bobbed a curtsy.

Enrico Basilica made a tiny strangling noise at the back of his throat.

"'Scuse me, there's been a bit of a problem," said Nanny.

"Who's dead?" said Bucket.

"Oh, no one's dead," said Nanny. "It's the dinner, it's still alive and hangin' on to the ceiling. And the pasta's all gone black, see. I said to Mrs. Clamp, I said, it may be foreign but I don't reckon it should be crunchy—"

"This is terrible! What a way to treat an honored guest!" said Bucket. He turned to the interpreter. "Please assure Señor Basilica that we will send out for fresh pasta straight away. What were we having, Mrs. Ogg?"

"Roast mutton with clootie dumplings," said Nanny.

Behind the face of Señor Basilica the throat of Henry Slugg made another little growling sound.

"And there's some nice slumpie with a knob of butter," Nanny went on.

Bucket looked around, puzzled. "Is there a dog somewhere in here?" he said.

"Well, I for one don't believe in pandering to singers," said Granny Weatherwax. "Fancy food, indeed! I never heard the like! Why not give him mutton with the rest of us?"

"Oh, Lady Esmerelda, that's hardly a way to treat—" Bucket began.

Enrico's elbow nudged his interpreter, with the special nudge of a man who could see clootie dumplings vanishing into the long grass if he weren't careful. He rumbled out a very pointed sentence.

"Señor Basilica says he would be more than happy

to taste the indigenous food of Ankh-Morpork," said the interpreter.

"No, we really can't—" Bucket tried again.

"In fact Señor Basilica *insists* that he tries the indigenous food of Ankh-Morpork," said the interpreter.

"'S'right. Si," said Basilica.

"Good," said Granny. "And give him some beer while you're about it." She gave the tenor's stomach a playful poke, losing her finger down to the second joint. "Why, in a day or two I expect you could practically turn him into a native!"

The wooden stairs gave way to stone.

Perdita said: He'll have a vast cave somewhere under the Opera House. There will be hundreds of candles, casting an exciting yet romantic light over the, yes, the lake, and there will be a dinner table shining with crystal glass and silverware, and of course he will have, yes, a huge organ—

Agnes blushed hotly in the darkness.

—on which, that is to say, he will play in a virtuoso style many operatic classics.

Agnes said: It'll be damp. There will be rats.

"Another clootie dumpling, Senior?" said Nanny Ogg.

"Mmfmmfmmf!"

"Take two while you're about it."

It was an education watching Enrico Basilica eat. It wasn't as though he gobbled his food, but he did eat continuously, like a man who intends to go on doing it all day on industrial lines, his napkin tucked neatly into his collar. The fork was loaded while the current consignment was being thoroughly masticated, so that the actual time between mouthfuls was as small as possible. Even Nanny, no stranger to a metabolism going for the burn, was impressed. Enrico Basilica ate like a man freed at last from the tyranny of tomatoes with everything.

"I'll order another mint-sauce tanker, shall I?" she said.

Mr. Bucket turned to Granny Weatherwax. "You were saying that you might be inclined to patronize our Opera House," he murmured.

"Oh, yes," said Granny. "Is Señor Basilica going to sing tonight?"

"Mmfmmf."

"I hope so," muttered Salzella. "That or explode."

"Then I shall definitely want to be there," said Granny. "A little more lamb here, my good woman."

"Yes ma'am," said Nanny Ogg, making a face at the back of Granny's head.

"Er . . . seats for tonight, in fact, are—" Bucket began.

"A Box would do me," said Granny. "I'm not fussy."

"In fact, even the Boxes are—"

"How about Box Eight? I've heard as Box Eight is always empty."

Bucket's knife rattled on his plate. "Er, Box Eight, Box Eight, you see, we don't . . ."

"I was thinking of donating a little something," said Granny.

"But Box Eight, you see, although technically unsold, is . . ."

"Two thousand dollars was what I had in mind,"

said Granny. "Oh, dear me, your waitress has let her dumplings go all over the place. It's so difficult to get reliable and *polite* staff these days, ain't it . . . ?"

Salzella and Bucket stared at one another across the table.

Then Bucket said, "Excuse me, my lady, I must just have a brief discussion with my director of music."

The two men hurried to the far end of the room, where they began to argue in whispers.

"Two thousand dollars!" hissed Nanny, watching them.

"It might not be enough," said Granny. "They're both looking very red in the face."

"Yes, but *two thousand dollars*!"

"It's only money."

"Yes, but it's only my money, not only your money," Nanny pointed out.

"We witches have always held everything in common, you know that," said Granny.

"Well, *yes*," said Nanny, and once again cut to the heart of the sociopolitical debate. "It's easy to hold everything in common when no one's got anything."

"Why, Gytha Ogg," said Granny, "I thought you despised riches!"

"Right, so I'd like to get the chance to despise them up close."

"But I knows you, Gytha Ogg. Money'd spoil you."

"I'd just like the chance to prove that it wouldn't, that's all I'm saying."

"Hush, they're coming back—"

Mr. Bucket approached, smiled uneasily, and sat down. "Er," he began, "it has to be Box Eight, does it? Only we could perhaps persuade someone in one of the other—"

"Wouldn't hear of it," said Granny. "I've heard that there's no one ever seen in Box Eight."

"Er . . . haha . . . it's laughable, I know, but there are some old theatrical traditions associated with Box Eight, absolute rubbish of course, but . . ."

He left the "but" hanging there hopefully. It froze in the face of Granny's stare.

"You see, it's haunted," he mumbled.

"Oh lawks," said Nanny Ogg, vaguely remembering to stay in character. "Another vat of slumpie, Senior Basilica? And how about another quart of beer?"

"Mmfmmf," said the tenor encouragingly, taking time out from his eating to point a fork at his empty mug.

Granny went on staring.

"Excuse me," said Bucket again.

He and Salzella went into another huddle, out of which came sounds like "But *two thousand dollars*! That's a lot of shoes!"

Bucket surfaced again. His face was gray. Granny's stare could do that to people.

"Er . . . because of the danger, er, which of course doesn't exist, haha, we . . . that is, the management . . . feel it incumbent on us to insist, that is, politely request, that if you do enter Box Eight you do so in company with a . . . man."

He ducked slightly.

"A man?" said Granny.

"For protection," said Bucket in a little voice.

"Although who'd protect *him* we really couldn't say," said Salzella under his breath.

"We thought perhaps one of the staff . . ." Bucket mumbled.

"Ai am quate capable of finding my own man should the need arise," said Granny, in a voice with snow on it.

Bucket's polite reply died in his throat when he saw, just behind Lady Esmerelda, Mrs. Ogg grinning like a full moon.

"Anyone for pudding?" she said.

She held a big bowl on a tray. There seemed to be a haze over it.

"My word," he said, "that looks delicious!"

Enrico Basilica looked over the top of his food with the expression of a man who has had the amazing privilege of going to heaven while still alive.

"Mmmf!"

It *was* damp. And, with the demise of Mr. Pounder, there were indeed rats.

The stone looked old, too. Of course, all stone was old, Agnes told herself, but this had grown old as masonry. Ankh-Morpork had been here for thousands of years. Where other cities were built on clay or rock or loam, Ankh-Morpork was built on Ankh-Morpork. People constructed new buildings on the remains of earlier ones, knocking out a few doorways here and there to turn ancient bedrooms into cellars.

The stairs petered out on damp flagstones, in almost total darkness.

Perdita thought it looked romantic and gothic.

Agnes thought it looked gloomy.

If someone used this place they'd need lights,

wouldn't they? And a fumbling search confirmed it. She found a candle and some matches tucked into a niche in the wall.

That was sobering for Agnes and Perdita together. Someone used this prosaic book of matches with a picture of a grinning troll on the cover, and this piece of perfectly ordinary candle. Perdita would have preferred a flaming torch. Agnes didn't know *what* she would have preferred. It was just that, if a mysterious person came and sang in the walls, and moved around the place like a ghost, and possibly killed people . . . well, you'd prefer a bit more style than a box of matches with a picture of a grinning troll on it. That was the sort of thing a *murderer* would use.

She lit the candle and, in two minds about it all, went on into the dark.

Chocolate Delight with Special Secret Sauce was a great success and heading down the little red lane as though hot-wired.

"More, Mr. Salzella?" said Bucket. "This really is first-class stuff, isn't it? I must congratulate Mrs. Clamp."

"There is a certain piquancy, I must say," said the director of music. "How about you, Señor Basilica?"

"Mmmf."

"Lady Esmerelda?"

"I don't mind if I do," said Granny, passing her plate across.

"I'm sure I detect a hint of cinnamon," said the interpreter, a brown ring around his mouth.

"Indeed, and possibly just a trace of nutmeg," said Mr. Bucket.

"I thought . . . cardamom?" said Salzella.

"Creamy yet spicy," said Bucket. His eyes unfocused slightly. "And curiously . . . warming."

Granny stopped chewing, and looked down suspiciously at her plate.

Then she sniffed at her spoon.

"Is it, er . . . is it just me, or is it a trifle . . . *warm* in here?" said Bucket.

Salzella had gripped the arms of his chair. His forehead glistened. "Do you think we could open a window?" he said. "I feel a little . . . strange."

"Yes, by all means," said Bucket.

Salzella half-rose, and then a preoccupied expression suffused his features. He sat down suddenly.

"No, I rather believe I'll just sit quietly for a moment," he said.

"Oh, dear," said the interpreter. There was a hint of vapor around his collar.

Basilica tapped him politely on the shoulder, grunted hopefully, and made pass-it-here motions in the direction of the half-finished dish of chocolate pudding.

"Mmmf?" he said.

"Oh, *dear*," said the interpreter.

Mr. Bucket ran a finger around his collar. Sweat was beginning to roll down his face.

Basilica gave up on his stricken colleague and reached across in a businesslike way to hook the dish with his fork.

"Er . . . yes," said Bucket, trying to keep his eyes away from Granny.

"Yes . . . indeed," said Salzella, his voice coming from a long way away.

"Oh, *dear*," said the interpreter, his eyes watering. "Ai! Meu Deus! Dio Mio! O Goden! D'zuk f't! Aagorahaa!"

Señor Basilica upended the rest of the Special Secret Sauce onto his plate and carefully scraped out the dish with his spoon, holding it upside-down to reach the last little bit.

"The weather has been a little . . . cool of late," Bucket managed. "Very *cold*, in fact."

Enrico held the sauce dish up to the light and regarded it critically in case there was any drop hiding in a corner.

"Snow, ice, frost . . . that sort of thing," said Salzella. "Yes, indeed! Coldness of all descriptions, in fact."

"Yes! Yes!" said Bucket gratefully. "And at a time like this I think it is very important to try to remember the names of, say, any number of boring and hopefully chilly things!"

"Wind, glaciers, icicles—"

"Not icicles!"

"Oh," said the interpreter, and slumped forward into his plate. His head hit a spoon, which cartwheeled into the air and bounced off Enrico's head.

Salzella started to whistle under his breath and pound the arm of his chair.

Bucket blinked. In front of him was the water jug. The *cold* water jug. He reached out . . .

"Oh, oh, *oh*, dear me, what can I say, I seem to have spilled it all over myself," he said, through the rising clouds of steam. "What a butterfingers I am, to be sure. I shall ring for Mrs. Ogg to bring us another one."

"Yes, indeed," said Salzella. "And perhaps you would care to do it soon? I am also feeling very . . . accident-prone."

Basilica, still chewing, lifted his interpreter's head off the table and carefully tipped the man's unfinished pudding into his own plate.

"In fact, in fact, in fact," said Salzella, "I think I shall just . . . have a brisk . . . have a nice cold . . . if you would excuse me a minute . . ."

He pushed back his chair and fled the room in a kind of crouching gait.

Mr. Bucket glistened. "I'll just, I'll just, I'll just . . . be back quite shortly," he said, and scurried away.

There was silence, broken only by the scrape of Señor Basilica's spoon and a sizzling noise from the interpreter.

Then the tenor belched baritone. "Whoops, pardon my Klatchian," he said. "Oh . . . *damn*."

He appeared to notice the depleted table for the first time. He shrugged, and smiled hopefully at Granny. "Is there a cheese board, do you think?" he said.

The door flew open and Nanny Ogg burst in, holding a bucket of water in both hands.

"All right, all right, that's—" she began, and then stopped.

Granny dabbed primly at the corners of her mouth with her napkin. "I'm sorry, Mrs. Ogg?" she said.

Nanny looked at the empty dish in front of Basilica.

"Or perhaps some fruit?" said the tenor. "A few nuts?"

"How much has he had?" she whispered.

"Best part of half," said Granny. "But I don't reckon it's having any effect on account of not touching the sides."

Nanny turned her attention to Granny's plate. "How about you?" she said.

"Two helpings," said Granny. "With *extra* sauce, Gytha Ogg, may you be forgiven."

Nanny looked at her with something like admiration in her eyes. "You ain't even sweating!" she said.

Granny picked up her water glass and held it at arm's length.

After a few seconds, the water began to boil.

"All right, you're getting really good, I've got to admit it," said Nanny. "I reckon I should have to get up real early to put one over on you."

"I reckon you should never go to sleep," said Granny.

"Sorry, Esme."

Señor Basilica, at a loss to follow the conversation, realized with reluctance that the meal was probably over.

"Absolutely superb," he said. "I just *loved* that pudding, Mrs. Ogg."

"I should just jolly well expect you did, Henry Slugg," said Nanny.

Henry carefully removed a clean handkerchief from his pocket, put it over his face, and leaned back in his chair. The first snore occurred a few seconds later.

"He's easy to have around, isn't he?" said Nanny. "Eat, sleep and sing. You certainly know where you are with him. I've found Greebo, by the way. He's still following Walter Plinge around." Her expression became a little defiant. "Say what you like, young Walter's all right by me if Greebo likes him."

Granny sighed. "Gytha, Greebo would like Norris the Eyeball-Eating Maniac of Quirm if he knew how to put food in a bowl."

And now she was lost. She'd done her best not to be. As Agnes had walked through each dank room she'd thoughtfully taken note of details. She'd carefully remembered right and left turns. And yet she was lost.

Here and there were steps down to lower cellars, but the water-level was so high that it was lapping at the first step. And it stank. The candle burned with a greenish-blue edge to the flame.

Somewhere, said Perdita, there *was* the secret room. If there wasn't a huge and glittering secret cavern, what on earth was life for? There *had* to be a secret room. A room, full of . . . giant candles, and enormous stalagmites . . .

But it certainly isn't *here*, said Agnes.

She felt a complete idiot. She'd gone through the mirror looking for . . . well, she wasn't quite prepared to admit what she might have been looking for, but whatever it was it certainly wasn't this.

She'd have to shout for help.

Of course, someone might *hear*, but that was always a risk when you shouted for help.

She coughed.

"Er . . . hello?"

The water gurgled.

"Er . . . help? Is there anyone there?"

A rat ran over her foot.

Oh, *yes*, she thought bitterly with Perdita's part of her brain, if *Christine* had come down here there probably *would* have been some great glistening cave and delicious danger. The world saved up rats and smelly cellars for Agnes, because she had such a wonderful personality.

"Um . . . anyone?"

More rats scuttled across the floor. There was a faint squeaking from the side passages.

"Hello?"

She was lost in some cellars with a candle getting shorter by the second. The air was foul, the flagstones were slippery, no one knew where she was, she could die down here, she could be—

Eyes glowed in the darkness.

One was green-yellow, the other pearly white.

A light appeared behind them.

Something was coming along the passageway, casting long shadows.

Rats tumbled over themselves in their panic to get away . . .

Agnes tried to press herself into the stone.

"Hello Miss Perdita X Nitt!"

A familiar shape juddered out of the darkness, just behind Greebo. It was all knees and elbows; it carried a sack over one shoulder and held a lantern in its other hand. Something fled from the darkness. The terror leached out of it . . .

"You don't want to be down here Miss Nitt with all the rats!"

"Walter!"

"Got to do Mister Pounder's job now the poor

man is passed away! I am a person of all jobs! No peas for the wicked! But Mister Greebo just hits them with his paws and they're off to rat heaven in a jiff!"

"Walter!" repeated Agnes, out of sheer relief.

"Come for an explore have you? These ole tunnels goes all the way to the river! You have to keep your wits about you not to get lost down here! Want to come back with me?"

It was impossible to be frightened of Walter Plinge. Walter attracted a number of emotions, but terror wasn't among them.

"Er . . . yes," said Agnes. "I got lost. Sorry."

Greebo sat down and started to wash himself in what Agnes considered to be a supercilious way. If a cat could snigger, he would be sniggering.

"Now I've got a full sack I have to take it to Mister Gimlet's shop!" announced Walter, turning around and loping out of the cellar without bothering to see if she was following him. "We get a ha'penny each which is not to be sneezed at! The dwarfs think a rat is a good meal which only goes to show it would be a strange world if we were all alike!"

It seemed a ridiculously short journey to the foot of some different stairs, which had a well-used look to them.

"Have you ever seen the Ghost, Walter?" said Agnes, as Walter put his foot on the first step.

He didn't turn around. "It is wrong to tell lies!"

"Er . . . yes, so I believe. So . . . when did you last see the Ghost?"

"I last saw the Ghost in the big room in the ballet school!"

"Really? What did he do?"

Walter paused for a moment, and then the words came out all together. "He ran off!"

He stamped up the stairs in a way that suggested very emphatically that the exchange was over.

Greebo sneered at Agnes and followed him.

The stairs went up just one flight and came out through a trapdoor backstage. She had been lost only a door or two from the real world.

No one noticed her emerge. But then no one noticed her at all. They just assumed that she'd be around when she was needed.

Walter Plinge had already loped off, in something of a hurry.

Agnes hesitated. They probably wouldn't even notice she wasn't there, right up to the point when Christine opened her mouth . . .

He hadn't wanted to answer, but Walter Plinge spoke when spoken to and she had a feeling that he wasn't able to lie. Telling lies would be being bad.

She'd never seen the ballet school. It wasn't far backstage, but it was a world of its own. The dancers issued from it every day like so many very thin and twittering sheep under the control of elderly women who looked as though they breakfasted on pickled limes. It was only after she'd timidly asked a few questions of the stagehands that she'd realized that the girls had joined the ballet because they *wanted* to.

She *had* seen the dancers' dressing room, where thirty girls washed and changed in a space rather smaller than Bucket's office. It bore the same relationship to ballet as compost did to roses.

She looked around again. Still no one had paid any attention to her.

She headed for the school. It was up a few steps, along a fetid corridor lined with notice boards and smelling of ancient grease. A couple of girls fluttered past. You never saw just one: they went around in groups, like mayflies. She pushed open the door and stepped into the school.

Reflections of reflections of reflections . . .

There were mirrors on every wall.

A few girls, practicing on the bars that lined the room, looked up as she entered.

Mirrors . . .

Out in the passage she leaned against the wall and got her breath back. She'd *never* liked mirrors. They always seemed to be laughing at her. But didn't they say it was the mark of a witch, not liking to get between two mirrors? It sucked out your soul, or something. A witch would never get between two mirrors if she could help it . . .

But, of course, she *very definitely* wasn't a witch. So she took a deep breath, and went back into the room.

Images of herself stretched away in every direction.

She managed a few steps, then wheeled around and groped for the doorway again, watched by the surprised dancers.

Lack of sleep, she told herself. And general over-excitement. Anyway, she didn't *need* to go right into the room, now that she knew who the Ghost was.

It was so *obvious*. The Ghost didn't require any mysterious nonexistent caves when all he needed to do was hide where everyone could see him.

* * *

Mr. Bucket knocked at the door of Salzella's office. A muffled voice said, "Come in."

There was no one in the office, but there was another closed door in the far wall. Bucket knocked again, and then rattled the door handle.

"I'm in the bath," said Salzella.

"Are you decent?"

"I'm fully clothed, if that's what you mean. Is there a pail of ice out there?"

"Was it you who ordered it?" said Bucket guiltily.

"Yes!"

"Only I, er, I had it taken to my office so I could stick my feet in it . . ."

"Your *feet*?"

"Yes. Er . . . I went for a brisk run around the city, don't know why, just felt like it . . ."

"Well?"

"My boots caught fire on the second lap."

There was a sloshing noise and some sotto voce grumbling and then the door swung open, revealing Salzella in a purple dressing gown.

"Has Señor Basilica been safely tethered?" he said, dripping on the floor.

"He's going through the music with Herr Trubelmacher."

"And he's . . . all right?"

"He sent along to the kitchen for a snack."

Salzella shook his head. "Astonishing."

"And they've put the interpreter in a cupboard. They don't seem to be able to get him unfolded."

Bucket sat down carefully. He was wearing carpet slippers.

"And—" Salzella prompted.

"And what?"

"Where did that *dreadful* woman go?"

"Mrs. Ogg is showing her around. Well, what else could I do? Two thousand dollars, remember!"

"I am endeavoring to forget," said Salzella. "I promise never to talk about that lunch ever again, if you don't either."

"What lunch?" said Bucket innocently.

"Well done."

"She does seem to have an amazing effect though, doesn't she . . ."

"I don't know who you are talking about."

"I mean, it's not hard to see how she made her money . . ."

"Good heavens, man, she's got a face like a hatchet!"

"They say that Queen Ezeriel of Klatch had a squint, but that didn't stop her having fourteen husbands, and that was only the official score. Besides, she's knocking on a bit . . ."

"I thought she'd been dead for two hundred years!"

"I'm talking about Lady Esmerelda."

"So am I."

"At least try to be civil to her at the soirée before the performance tonight."

"I'll try."

"The two thousand might be only the start, I hope. Every time I open a drawer there are more bills! We seem to owe money to everyone!"

"Opera *is* expensive."

"You're telling me. Whenever I try to make a start on the books, something dreadful happens. Do you think I might just have a few hours without something awful happening?"

"In an opera house?"

The voice was muffled by the half-dismantled mechanism of the organ.

"All right—give me middle C."

A hairy finger pressed a key. It made a thudding noise and somewhere in the mechanism something else went *woing.*

"Blast, it's come off the peg . . . hold on . . . try again . . ."

The note rang out sweet and clear.

"*O-kay,*" said the voice of the man hidden in the exposed entrails of the organ. "Wait until I tighten the peg . . ."

Agnes stepped closer. The hulking figure seated at the organ turned around and gave her a friendly grin, which was much wider than the average grin. Its owner was covered in red hair and, while short-changed in the leg department, had obviously been first in the queue when the arm counter opened. And had also been given a special free offer of lip.

"André?" said Agnes weakly.

The organist extracted himself from the mechanism. He was holding a complicated wooden bar with springs on it. "Oh, hello," he said.

"Er . . . who is this?" said Agnes, backing away from the primeval organist.

"Oh, this is the Librarian. I don't think he *has* a name. He's the Librarian at Unseen University but, much more importantly, he's their organist and it turns out our organ is a Johnson,* just like theirs. He's given us some spare parts—"

"*Ook.*"

"Sorry, *lent* us some spare parts."

"He plays the organ?"

"In an amazingly prehensile way, yes."

Agnes relaxed. The creature didn't seem about to attack.

"Oh," she said. "Well . . . I suppose it's natural, because sometimes barrel-organ men came to our village and they often had a dear little mon—"

There was a crashing chord. The orangutan raised its other hand and waved a finger politely in front of Agnes's face.

"He doesn't like being called a monkey," said André. "And he likes you."

"How can you tell?"

"He doesn't usually go in for warnings."

She stepped back quickly and grabbed the boy's arm. "Can I have a word with you?" she said.

"We've got only a few hours and I'd really like to get this—"

"It's *important*."

He followed her into the wings. Behind them,

---

*Bergholt Stuttley ("Bloody Stupid") Johnson was Ankh-Morpork's most famous, or rather most notorious, inventor. He was renowned for never letting his number blindness, his lack of any skill whatsoever or his complete failure to grasp the essence of a problem stand in the way of his cheerful progress as the first Counter-Renaissance man. Shortly after building the famous Collapsed Tower of Quirm he turned his attention to the world of music, particularly large organs and mechanical orchestras. Examples of his handiwork still occasionally come to light in sales, auctions, and quite frequently, wreckage.

the Librarian tapped a few keys on the half-repaired keyboard and then ducked underneath.

"I know who the Ghost is," whispered Agnes.

André stared at her. Then he pulled her farther into the shadows. "The Ghost isn't *anybody*," he said softly. "Don't be silly. It's just the Ghost."

"I mean he's someone else when he takes his mask off."

"Who?"

"Should I tell Mr. Bucket and Mr. Salzella?"

"*Who?* Tell them about *who?*"

"Walter Plinge."

He stared at her again.

"If you laugh I'll . . . I'll kick you," said Agnes.

"But Walter isn't even—"

"I didn't believe it either but he said he saw the Ghost in the ballet school and there's mirrors all over the walls and he'd be quite tall if he stood up properly and he roams around in the cellars—"

"Oh, come *on* . . ."

"The other night I thought I heard him singing on the stage when everyone else had gone."

"You saw him?"

"It was dark."

"Oh, well . . ." André began dismissively.

"But afterward I'm *certain* I heard him talking to the cat. Talking normally, I mean. I mean like a normal person, I mean. And you've got to admit . . . he is strange. Isn't he just the sort of person who'd want to wear a mask to hide who he is?" She sagged. "Look, I can see you don't want to listen—"

"No! No, I think . . . well . . ."

"I just thought I'd feel better if I told someone."

André smiled in the gloom. "I wouldn't mention it to anyone else, though."

Agnes looked down at her feet. "I suppose it does sound a bit far-fetched . . ."

André laid a hand on her arm. Perdita felt Agnes draw herself back. "*Do* you feel better?" he said.

"I . . . don't know . . . I mean . . . I don't know . . . I mean, I just can't imagine him hurting anyone . . . I feel so stupid . . ."

"Everyone's on edge. Don't worry about it."

"I'd . . . hate you to think I was being silly—"

"I'll keep an eye on Walter, if you like." He smiled at her. "But I'd better get on with things," he added. He gave her another smile, as fast and brief as summer lightning.

"Thank y—"

He was already walking back to the organ.

This shop was a gentlemen's outfitters.

"It's not for me," said Nanny Ogg. "It's for a friend. He's six foot tall, very broad shoulders."

"Inside leg?"

"Oh, yes."

She looked around the store. Might as well go all the way. It was her money, after all.

"And a black coat, long black tights, shoes with them shiny buckles, one of those top hats, a big cloak with a red silk lining, a bow tie, a really posh black cane with a very nobby silver knob on it . . . and . . . a black eye patch."

"An eye patch?"

"Yes. Maybe with sequins or something on it, since it's the opera."

The tailor stared at Nanny. "This is a little irregular," he said. "Why can't the gentleman come in himself?"

"He ain't quite a gentleman yet."

"But, madam, I meant that we have to get the size right."

Nanny Ogg looked around the shop. "Tell you what," she said, "you sell me something that looks about right and we'll adjust him to fit. 'Scuse me . . ."

She turned away demurely—

—twingtwangtwong—

—and turned back, smoothing down her dress and holding a leather bag.

"How much'll it be?" she said.

The tailor looked blankly at the bag. "I'm afraid we won't be able to have all that ready until at least next Wednesday," he said.

Nanny Ogg sighed. She felt she was becoming familiar with one of the most fundamental laws of physics. Time equaled money. Therefore, money equaled time.

"I was sort of hoping to get it all a bit quicker than that," she said, jingling the bag up and down.

The tailor looked down his nose at her. "We are craftsmen, madam. How long did you think it should take?"

"How about ten minutes?"

Twelve minutes later she left the shop with a large packet under one arm, a hat box under the other, and an ebony cane between her teeth.

Granny was waiting outside. "Got it all?"

"Ess."

"I'll take the eye patch, shall I?"

"We've got to get a third witch," said Nanny, trying to rearrange the parcels. "Young Agnes has got good strong arms."

"You know if we was to drag her out of there by the scruff of her neck we'd never hear the last of it," said Granny. "She'll be a witch when she wants to be."

They headed for the Opera House's stage door.

"Afternoon, Les," said Nanny cheerfully as they entered. "Stopped itching now, has it?"

"Marvelous bit of ointment that was you gave me, Mrs. Ogg," said the stage doorkeeper, his mustache bending into something that might have been a smile.

"Mrs. Les keeping well? How's her sister's leg?"

"Doing very well, Mrs. Ogg, thank you for asking."

"This is just Esme Weatherwax who's helping me with some stuff," said Nanny.

The doorkeeper nodded. It was clear that any friend of Mrs. Ogg was a friend of his. "No trouble at all, Mrs. Ogg."

As they passed through into the dusty network of corridors Granny reflected, not for the first time, that Nanny had a magic all of her own.

Nanny didn't so much enter places as insinuate herself; she had unconsciously taken a natural talent for liking people and developed it into an occult science. Granny Weatherwax did not doubt that her friend already knew the names, family histories, birthdays and favorite topics of conversation of half the people here, and probably also the vital wedge that would cause them to open up. It might be talking about their children, or a potion for their bad feet, or one of Nanny's really filthy stories, but Nanny would be *in* and after twenty-four hours they'd have known her all their lives. And they'd tell her things. *Of their own free will.* Nanny Got On with people. Nanny could get a statue to cry on her shoulder and say what it really thought about pigeons.

It was a knack. Granny had never had the patience to acquire it. Just occasionally, she wondered whether it might have been a good idea.

"Curtain up in an hour and a half," said Nanny. "I promised Giselle I'd give her a hand . . ."

"Who's Giselle?"

"She does makeup."

"You don't know how to do makeup!"

"I distempered our privy, didn't I?" said Nanny. "And I paint faces on eggs for the kiddies every Soul Cake Tuesday."

"Got to do anything else, have you?" said Granny sarcastically. "Open the curtains? Fill in for a ballet dancer who's been taken poorly?"

"I did say I'd help with the drinks at the swarray," said Nanny, letting the irony slide off like water on a red-hot stove. "Well, a lot of the staff have buggered off 'cos of the Ghost. It's in the big foyer in half an hour. I expect you ought to be there, being a patronizer."

"What's a swarray?" said Granny suspiciously.

"It's a sort of posh party before the opera."

"What do I have to do?"

"Drink sherry and make polite conversation," said

Nanny. "Or conversation, anyway. I saw the grub being done for it. They've even got little cubes of cheese on sticks stuck in a grapefruit, and you don't get much posher than that."

"Gytha Ogg, you ain't done any . . . *special* dishes, have you?"

"No, Esme," said Nanny Ogg meekly.

"Only you've got an imp of mischief in you."

"Been far too busy for anything like that," said Nanny.

Granny nodded. "Then we'd better find Greebo," she said.

"You sure about this, Esme?" said Nanny.

"We might have a lot to do tonight," said Granny. "Maybe we could do with an extra pair of hands."

"Paws."

"At the moment, yes."

It *was* Walter. Agnes knew it. It wasn't knowledge in her mind, exactly. It was practically something she breathed. She felt it as a tree feels the sun.

It all fitted. He could go anywhere, and no one took any notice of Walter Plinge. In a way he was invisible, because he was always there. And, if you were someone like Walter Plinge, wouldn't you long to be someone as debonair and dashing as the Ghost?

If you were someone like Agnes Nitt, wouldn't you long to be someone as dark and mysterious as Perdita X Dream?

The traitor thought was there before she could choke it off. She added hurriedly: But I've never killed anyone.

Because that's what I'd have to believe, isn't it? If he's the Ghost, then he's killed people.

All the same . . . he does look odd, and he talks as if the words are trying to escape . . .

A hand touched her shoulder. She spun round.

"It's only me!" said Christine.

". . . Oh."

"Don't you think this is a *marvelous* dress!?"

"What?"

"This dress, silly!!"

Agnes looked her up and down. "Oh. Yes. Very nice," she said, disinterest lying on her voice like rain on a midnight pavement.

"You don't sound very impressed!! Really, Perdita, there's no need to be *jealous*!!"

"I'm not jealous, I was thinking . . ."

She'd only seen the Ghost for a moment, but he certainly hadn't *moved* like Walter. Walter walked as though his body were being dragged along by his head. But the certainty was as hard as marble now.

"Well, you don't seem very impressed, I must say!!"

"I'm wondering if Walter Plinge is the Ghost," said Agnes, and immediately cursed herself, or at least pooted. She felt embarrassed enough about André's reaction.

Christine's eyes widened. "But he's a clown!!"

"He walks odd and he talks odd," said Agnes, "but if he stood up straight—"

Christine laughed. Agnes felt herself getting angry. "And he practically *told* me he was!"

"You believed him, did you?!" Christine made a

little tutting sound that Agnes considered quite offensive. "Really, you girls believe the strangest things!!"

"What do you mean, *we* girls?"

"Oh, *you* know! The dancers are always saying they've seen the Ghost all over the place—"

"Good grief! Do you think I'm some sort of impressionable idiot? *Think* for a minute before answering!"

"Well, of course I don't, but—"

"Huh!"

Agnes strode off into the wings, concerned more with effect than direction. The background noise of the stage faded behind her as she stepped into the scenery store. It didn't lead anywhere except to a pair of big double doors opening to the world outside. It was full of bits of castles, balconies and romantic prison cells, stacked any old how.

Christine hurried up behind her.

"I really didn't mean . . . look, not *Walter* . . . he's just a very odd odd-job man!"

"He does all kinds of jobs! No one ever knows where he is—they all just assume he's around!"

"All right, but you don't have to get so worked up—"

There was the faintest of sounds behind them.

They turned.

The Ghost bowed.

"Who's a good boy, then? Nanny's got a bowl of fish eggs for a good boy," said Nanny, trying to see under the big dresser in the kitchen.

"Fish eggs?" said Granny, coldly.

"I borrowed them from the stuff they've done for the swarray," said Nanny.

"Borrowed?" said Granny.

"That's right. Come along, Greebo, who's a good boy then?"

"Borrowed. You mean . . . when the cat's finished with them, you're going to give them back?"

"It's only a manner of speaking, Esme," said Nanny in a hurt little voice. "It's not the same as stealing if you don't *mean* it. Come along, boy, here's some lovely fish eggs for you . . ."

Greebo pulled himself farther into the shadows.

There was a little sigh from Christine and she folded up into a faint. But she managed, Agnes noticed sourly, to collapse in a way that probably didn't hurt when she hit the ground and which showed off her dress to the best effect. It was beginning to dawn on Agnes that Christine was remarkably clever in some specialized ways.

She looked back at the mask.

"It's all right," she said, her voice sounding hoarse even to her. "I know why you're doing it. I really do."

No expression could cross that ivory face, but the eyes flickered.

Agnes swallowed. The Perdita part of her wanted to give in right now, because that would be more exciting, but she stood her ground.

"You want to be something else and you're stuck with what you are," said Agnes. "I know all about that. *You're* lucky. All *you* have to do is put on a mask. At least you're the right shape. But why did you have to go and kill people? Why? Mr. Pounder couldn't have done you any harm! But . . . he poked around in odd places, didn't he, and he . . . found something?"

The Ghost nodded slightly, and then held out his ebony cane. He grasped both ends and pulled, so that a long thin sword slid out.

"I know who you are!" Agnes burst out, as he stepped forward. "I . . . I could probably help you! It might not have been your fault!" She backed away. "*I* haven't done anything to you! You don't have to be afraid of me!"

She backed away farther as the figure advanced. The eyes, in the dark hollows of the mask, glinted like tiny jewels.

"I'm your *friend*, don't you see? Please, Walter! *Walter!*"

There was, far off, an answering sound that seemed as loud as thunder and as impossible, in the circumstances, as a chocolate kettle.

It was the clank of a bucket handle.

"What's the matter Miss Perdita Nitt?"

The Ghost hesitated.

There was the sound of footsteps. Irregular footsteps.

The Ghost lowered the sword, opened a door in a piece of scenery painted to represent a castle wall, bowed ironically and slipped away.

Walter rounded a corner.

He was an unlikely knight errant. For one thing, he had on evening dress obviously designed for someone of a different shape. He was still wearing his beret. He also wore an apron and was carrying a mop and bucket. But no heroic lance-wielding rescuer ever galloped over a drawbridge more happily. He was practically surrounded by a golden glow.

". . . Walter?"

"What's the matter with Miss Christine?"

"She . . . er . . . she fainted," said Agnes. "Er. Probably . . . yes, probably the excitement. With the opera. Tonight. Yes. Probably. The excitement. Because of the opera tonight."

Walter gave her a slightly worried look. "Yes," he said, and added patiently, "I know where there's a medicine box shall I get it?"

Christine groaned and fluttered her eyelashes. "Where am I?"

Perdita gritted Agnes's teeth. *Where am I?* That didn't sound the sort of thing someone said when they woke up from a faint; it sounded more like the sort of thing they said because they'd heard it was the sort of thing people said.

"You fainted," she said. She looked hard at Walter. "Why were you in here, Walter?"

"Got to mop out the stagehands' privy Miss Nitt. Always having trouble I've been working on it for months!"

"But you're wearing evening dress!"

"Yes then I got to be a waiter afterward because we're short-handed and there's no one else to be a waiter when they have drinks and sausages on poles before the opera."

No one could have moved that fast. True, Walter and the Ghost hadn't both been in the room at the same time, but she'd heard his voice. No one could have had time to duck around behind the piles of flats and turn up at the opposite side of the room in seconds, unless they were some sort of wizard. Some of the girls *did* say the Ghost could almost seem to be in two places at once. Perhaps there were other secret places like the old staircase. Perhaps he—

She stopped herself. Walter Plinge wasn't the Ghost, then. There was no sense in trying to find some excitable explanation to prove wrong right.

She'd told Christine. Well, Christine was giving her just a slightly bemused look as Walter helped her up. And she'd told André, but he hadn't seemed to believe her so probably that was all right.

Which meant that the Ghost was . . .

. . . someone else.

She'd been so *certain*.

"You'll enjoy it, mother. You really will."

"'Tain't for the likes of us, Henry. I don't see why Mr. Morecombe couldn't give you tickets to see Nellie Stamp at the music hall. Now that's what I call music. Proper tunes you can understand."

"Songs like 'She Sits Among the Cabbages and Leeks' are not very cultural, mother."

Two figures wandered through the crowds heading for the Opera House. This was their conversation.

"'S a good laugh, though. And you don't have to hire suits. Seems daft to me, havin' to wear a special suit just to listen to music."

"It enhances the experience," said young Henry, who had read this somewhere.

"I mean, how does the music know?" said his mother. "Now, Nellie Stamp—"

"Come *along*, mother."

It was going to be one of those evenings, he knew it.

Henry Lawsy did his best. And, given the starting point, it wasn't a bad best. He was a clerk in the firm of Morecombe, Slant & Honeyplace, a somewhat old-fashioned legal partnership. One reason for its less-than-modern approach was the fact that Messrs. Morecombe and Honeyplace were vampires and Mr. Slant was a zombie. The three partners were, therefore, technically dead, although this did not prevent them putting in a proper day's work—normally during the night, in the case of Mr. Morecombe and Mr. Honeyplace.

From Henry's point of view the hours were good and the job was not onerous, but he chafed somewhat about his promotion prospects because clearly dead men's shoes were being fully occupied by dead men. He'd decided that the only way to succeed was to better himself by Improving His Mind, which he tried to do at every opportunity. It is probably a full description of Henry Lawsy's mind that if you had given him a book called *How to Improve Your Mind in Five Minutes*, he would have read it with a stopwatch. His progress through life was hampered by his tremendous sense of his own ignorance, a disability which affects all too few people.

Mr. Morecombe had given him two opera tickets as a reward for sorting out a particularly problematical tort. He'd invited his mother because she represented 100 percent of all the women he knew.

People tended to shake Henry's hand cautiously, in case it came off.

He'd bought a book about the opera and read it carefully, because he'd heard that it was absolutely unheard-of to go to an opera without knowing what it was about, and the chance of finding out while you were actually watching it was remote. The book's reassuring weight was in his pocket right now. All he needed to complete the evening was a less embarrassing parent.

"Can we get some peanuts before we go in?" said his mother.

"Mother, they don't sell peanuts at the opera."

"No peanuts? What're you supposed to do if you don't like the songs?"

Greebo's suspicious eyes were two glows in the gloom.

"Poke him with a broom handle," suggested Granny.

"No," said Nanny. "With someone like Greebo you have to use a little bit of kindness."

Granny closed her eyes and waved a hand.

There was a yowl from under the kitchen's dresser and a sound of frantic scrabbling. Then, his claws scoring tracks in the floor, Greebo came out backward, fighting all the way.

"Mind you, a lot of cruelty does the trick as well," Nanny conceded. "You've never been much of a cat person, have you, Esme?"

Greebo would have hissed at Granny, except that even his cat brain was just bright enough to realize this was not the best move he could make.

"Give him his fish eggs," Granny said. "He might as well have them now as later."

Greebo inspected the dish. Oh, this was all right, then. They wanted to give him food.

Granny nodded at Nanny Ogg. They held out their hands, palm up.

Greebo was halfway through the caviar when he felt It happening.

"Wrrroowlllll—" he wailed, and then the voice went deeper as his chest expanded, and rose physically as his back legs lengthened under him.

His ears flattened against his head, and then crept down the sides.

"—lllllwwaaaa—"

"The jacket's a forty-four-inch chest," said Nanny. Granny nodded.

"—aaaaooooo—"

His face flattened. His whiskers spread out. Greebo's nose developed a life of its own.

"—ooooooss . . . sshit!"

"He certainly gets the hang of it quicker these days," said Nanny.

"You put some clothes on right now, my lad," said Granny, who had shut her eyes.

Not that this made much difference, she had to admit later. Greebo fully clothed still managed to communicate the nakedness beneath. The insouciant mustache, the long sideburns and the tousled black hair combined with the well-developed muscles to give the impression of the more louche kind of buccaneer or a romantic poet who'd given up on the opium and tried red meat instead. He had a scar running across his face, and a black patch now where it crossed the eye. When he smiled, he exuded an easy air of undistilled, excitingly dangerous lasciviousness. He could swagger while asleep. Greebo could, in fact, commit sexual harassment simply by sitting very quietly in the next room.

Except as far as the witches were concerned. To Granny a cat was a damn cat whatever shape it was, and Nanny Ogg always thought of him as Mister Fluffy.

She adjusted the bow tie and stood back critically. "What do you think?" she said.

"He looks like an assassin, but he'll do," said Granny.

"Oh, what a nasty thing to say!"

Greebo waved his arms experimentally and fumbled with the ebony cane. Fingers took a bit of getting used to, but cat reflexes learned fast.

Nanny waved a finger playfully under his nose. He took a half hearted swipe at it.

"Now you just stay with Granny and do what she tells you like a good boy," she said.

"Yess, Nan–ny," said Greebo reluctantly. He managed to grip the stick properly.

"And no fighting."

"No, Nan–ny."

"And no leaving bits of people on the doormat."

"No, Nan–ny."

"We'll have no trouble like we did with those robbers last month."

"No, Nan–ny."

He looked depressed. Humans had no *fun*. Incredible complications surrounded the most basic activities.

"And no turning back into a cat again until we say."

"Yess, Nan–ny."

"Play your cards right and there could be a kipper in this for you."

"Yess, Nan–ny."

"What're we going to call him?" said Granny. "He can't just be Greebo, which I've always said was a damn silly name for a cat."

"Well, he looks aristocratic—" Nanny began.

"He looks like a beautiful brainless bully," Granny corrected her.

"Aristocratic," repeated Nanny.

"Same thing."

"We can't call him Greebo, anyway."

"We'll think of something."

Salzella leaned disconsolately against the marble banister of the foyer's grand staircase and stared gloomily into his drink.

It had always seemed to him that one of the major flaws in the whole business of opera was the audience. They were quite unsuitable. The only ones worse than the ones who didn't know anything at all about music, and whose idea of a sensible observation was "I liked that bit near the end when her voice went wobbly," were the ones who thought they did . . .

"Want a drink do you Mister Salzella? There's lots you know!"

Walter Plinge ambled by, his black suit making him look like a very good class of scarecrow.

"Plinge, you just say 'Drink, sir?'" said the director of music. "And please take off that ridiculous beret."

"My mum made it for me!"

"I'm sure she did, but—"

Bucket sidled up to him. "I thought I told you to keep Señor Basilica away from the canapés!" he hissed.

"I'm sorry, I couldn't find a big enough crowbar," said Salzella, waving away Walter and his beret. "Anyway, isn't he supposed to be communing with his muse in his dressing room? The curtain goes up in twenty minutes!"

"He says he sings better on a full stomach."

"Then we're in for a big treat tonight."

Bucket turned and surveyed the scene. "It's going well, anyway," he said.

"I suppose so."

"The Watch are here, you know. In secret. They're mingling."

"Ah . . . let me guess . . ."

Salzella looked around at the crowds. There was, indeed, a very short man in a suit intended for a rather larger man; this was especially the case with the opera cloak, which actually trailed on the floor behind him to give the overall impression of a superhero who had spent too much time around the Kryptonite. He was wearing a deformed fur hat and trying surreptitiously to smoke a cigarette.

"You mean that little man with the words 'Watchman in Disguise' flashing on and off just above his head?"

"Where? I didn't see that!"

Salzella sighed. "It's Corporal Nobby Nobbs," he said wearily. "The only known person to require an identity card to prove his species. I've watched him mingle with three large sherries."

"He's not the only one, though," said Mr. Bucket. "They're taking this seriously."

"Oh, yes," said Salzella. "If we look over there, for example, we see Sergeant Detritus, who is a troll, and who is wearing what in the circumstances is actually a rather well-fitting suit. It is therefore, I feel, something of a pity he has neglected to remove his helmet. And these, you understand, the Watch has chosen for their ability to blend."

"Well, they'll certainly be useful if the Ghost strikes again," said Bucket, hopelessly.

"The Ghost would have to—" Salzella stopped. He blinked. "Oh, good grief," he whispered. "What *has* she found?"

Bucket turned. "That's Lady Esmerelda . . . oh."

Greebo strolled in alongside her with the gentle swagger that makes women thoughtful and men's knuckles go white. The buzz of conversation was momentarily hushed, and then rose again to a slightly shriller buzz.

"I'm impressed," said Salzella.

"He certainly doesn't look like a *gentleman*," said Bucket. "Look at the color of that eye!" He set his face into what he hoped was a smile, and bowed.

"Lady Esmerelda!" he said. "How pleasant to see you again! Won't you introduce us to your . . . guest?"

"This is Lord Gribeau," said Granny. "Mr. Bucket, the owner, and Mr. Salzella, who seems to run the place."

"Haha," said Salzella.

Gribeau snarled, revealing longer incisors than any that Bucket had seen outside a zoo. And Bucket had never seen such a greenish-yellow eye. The pupil was all wrong . . .

"Ahaha . . ." he said. "And may I order you something?"

"He'll have milk," said Granny firmly.

"I expect he has to keep up his strength," said Salzella.

Granny spun around. Her expression would have etched steel.

"Anyone for a drink?" said Nanny Ogg, appearing out of nowhere with a tray and adroitly stepping between them like a very small peacekeeping force. "Got a bit of everything here . . ."

"Including a glass of milk, I see," said Bucket.

Salzella looked from one witch to the other. "That's remarkably foresighted of you," he said.

"Well, you never know," said Nanny.

Gribeau took the glass in both hands and lapped at it with his tongue. Then he looked at Salzella.

"What yourrr lookin aat? Neverrr seein mil—uk drun beforr?"

"Never quite . . . like that, I must admit."

Nanny winked at Granny Weatherwax as she turned to scurry away.

Granny caught her arm. "Remember," she whispered, "when we go into the Box . . . you keep an eye on Mrs. Plinge. Mrs. Plinge knows something. I ain't sure what's going to happen. But it is going to happen."

"Right," said Nanny. She bustled off, muttering under her breath, "Oh, yes . . . do this, do that—"

"Drink here, please, ma'am."

Nanny looked down. "Good grief," she said. "What are you?"

The apparition in the fur hat winked at her. "I'm the Count de Nobbs," it said, "and this here," it added, indicating a mobile wall, "is the Count de Tritus."

Nanny glanced at the troll. "Another Count? I'm sure there's unaccountably more Counts here than I can count. And what can I get you, officers?" she said.

"Officers? Us?" said the Count de Nobbs. "What makes you think we're Watchmen?"

"He's got a helmet on," Nanny pointed out. "Also, he's got his badge pinned to his coat."

"I *told* you to put it away!" Nobby hissed. He looked at Nanny and smiled uneasily. "Milit'ry chic," he said. "It's just a fashion accessory. Actually, we are gentlemen of means and have nothing to do with the city Watch whatsoever."

"Well, *gentlemen*, would you like some wine?"

"Not while we on duty, t'anks," said the troll.

"Oh, yes, thank you very much, Count de Tritus," said Nobby bitterly. "Oh, yes, very undercover, that is! Why don't you just wave your truncheon around where everyone can see it?"

"Well, if you t'ink it'd help—"

"Put it *away*!"

The Count de Tritus's eyebrows met with the effort of thought. "Dat was irony, den, was it? To a superior officer?"

"Can't be a superior officer, can you, 'cos we ain't Watchmen. Look, Commander Vimes *explained* it three times . . ."

Nanny Ogg tactfully moved away. It was bad enough watching them blow their cover without sucking at it as well.

This was a new world, all right. She was used to a life where the men wore the bright clothes and the women wore black. It made it a lot easier to decide what to put on in the mornings. But inside the Opera House the rules of clothing were all in reverse, just like the laws of common sense. Here the women dressed like frosted peacocks and the men looked like penguins.

So . . . there were coppers here. Nanny Ogg was basically a law-abiding person when she had no reason to break the law, and therefore had that kind of person's attitude to law-enforcement officers, which was one of deep and permanent distrust.

There was their approach to theft, for example. Nanny had a witch's view of theft, which was a lot more complicated than the attitude adopted by the law and, if it came to it, people who owned property worth stealing. They tended to wield the huge blunt ax of the law in circumstances that required the delicate scalpel of common sense.

No, thought Nanny. Policemen with their great big boots were not required here on a night like this. It would be a good idea to put a thumbtack under the ponderous feet of Justice.

She ducked behind a gilt statue and fumbled in the recesses of her clothing while people nearby looked around in puzzlement at the erratic twanging of elastic. She was sure she had one around somewhere—she'd packed it in case of emergencies . . .

There was the clink of a small bottle. Ah, yes.

A moment later Nanny Ogg emerged decorously with two small glasses on her tray, and headed purposefully for the Watchmen.

"Fruit drink, officers?" she said. "Oh, silly me, what am I saying, I didn't mean officers. Homemade fruit drink?"

Detritus sniffed suspiciously, immediately clearing his sinuses. "What's in it?" he said.

"Apples," said Nanny Ogg promptly. "Well . . . mainly apples."

Under her hand, a couple of spilt drops finished eating their way through the metal of the tray and dropped onto the carpet, where they smoked.

The auditorium buzzed with the sound of opera-goers settling down and Mrs. Lawsy trying to find her shoes.

"You really shouldn't have taken them off, mother."

"My feet are giving me gyp."

"Did you bring your knitting?"

"I think I must've left it in the Ladies."

"Oh, *mother*."

Henry Lawsy marked his place in his book and raised his runny eyes heavenward, and blinked. Right above him—a long way above him—was a glittering circle of light.

His mother followed his gaze. "What's that, then?"

"I think it's a chandelier, mother."

"It's a pretty big one. What's holding it up?"

"I'm sure they've got special ropes and things, mother."

"Looks a bit dangerous, to my mind."

"I'm sure it's absolutely safe, mother."

"What do you know about chandeliers?"

"I'm sure people wouldn't come into the Opera House if there was any chance of a chandelier dropping on their heads, mother," said Henry, trying to read his book.

Il Truccatore, The Master of Disguise. Il Truccatore (ten.), a mysterious nobleman, causes scandal in the city when he woos high-born ladies while disguised as their husbands. However, Laura (sop.), the new bride of Capriccio (bar.), refuses to give in to his blandishments—

Henry put a bookmark in the book, took a smaller book from his pocket, and carefully looked up "blandishments." He was moving in a world he wasn't quite sure of; embarrassment lay waiting at every turn, and he wasn't going to get caught out over a word. Henry lived his life in permanent dread of Being Asked Questions Later.

—and with the help of his servant Wingie (ten.) he adopts a subterfuge—

The dictionary came out again for a moment.

—culminating—

And again.

—in the scene at the famous Masked Ball at the Duke's Palace. But Il Truccatore has not reckoned with his old adversary the Count de—

"Adversary" . . . Henry sighed, and reached for his pocket.

Curtain up in five minutes . . .

Salzella reviewed his troops. They consisted of scene builders and painters and all those other employees who could be spared for the evening. At the end of the line, about fifty percent of Walter Plinge had managed to stand to attention.

"Now, you all know your positions," said Salzella. "And if you see anything, anything at all, you are to let me know at once. Do you understand?"

"Mr. Salzella!"

"Yes, Walter?"

"We mustn't interrupt the opera Mr. Salzella!"

Salzella shook his head. "People will understand, I'm sure—"

"Show must go on Mr. Salzella!"

"Walter, you will do what you're told!"

Someone raised a hand. "He's got a point, though, Mr. Salzella . . ."

Salzella rolled his eyes. "Just catch the Ghost," he said. "If we can do it without a lot of shouting, that's good. Of course I don't want to stop the show." He saw them relax.

A deep chord rolled out over the stage.

"What the hell was that?"

Salzella strode behind the stage and was met by André, looking excited.

"What's going on?"

"We repaired it, Mr. Salzella! Only . . . well, he doesn't want to give up the seat . . ."

The Librarian nodded at the director of music. Salzella knew the orangutan, and among the things he knew was that, if the Librarian wanted to sit somewhere, then that was where he sat. But he was a first-class organist, Salzella had to admit. His lunch-time recitals in the Great Hall of Unseen University were extremely popular, especially since the University's organ had every single sound-effect that Bloody Stupid Johnson's inverted genius had been able to contrive. No one would have believed, before a pair of simian hands had worked on the project, that something like Doinov's romantic *Prelude in G* could be rescored for Whoopee Cushion and Squashed Rabbits.

"There's the overtures," said André, "and the ballroom scene . . ."

"At least get him a bow-tie," said Salzella.

"No one can see him, Mr. Salzella, and he hasn't really got much of a neck . . ."

"We *do* have standards, André."

"Yes, Mr. Salzella."

"Since you seem to have been relieved of employment this evening, then perhaps you could help us apprehend the Ghost."

"Certainly, Mr. Salzella."

"Fetch him a tie, then, and come with me."

A little later, left to himself, the Librarian opened his copy of the score and placed it carefully on the stand.

He reached down under the seat and pulled out a large brown paper bag of peanuts. He wasn't entirely sure why André, having talked him into playing the organ this evening, had told the other man that it was because he, the Librarian, wouldn't budge. In fact, he'd got some interesting cataloguing to do and had been looking forward to it. Instead, he seemed to be here for the night, although a pound of shelled peanuts *was* handsome pay by any ape's standards. The human mind was a deep and abiding mystery and the Librarian was glad he didn't have one anymore.

He inspected the bow tie. As André had foreseen, it presented certain problems to someone who'd been behind the door when the necks were handed out.

Granny Weatherwax stopped in front of Box Eight and looked around. Mrs. Plinge wasn't visible. She unlocked the door with what was probably the most expensive key in the world.

"And you behave yourself," she said.

"Ye–ess, Gran–ny," moaned Greebo.

"No going to the lavatory in the corners."

"No, Gran-ny."

Granny glared at her escort. Even in a bow tie, even with his fine mustaches waxed, he was still a cat. You just couldn't trust them to do anything except turn up for meals.

The inside of the Box was rich red plush, picked out with gilt decoration. It was like a soft little private room.

There were a couple of fat pillars on either side, supporting part of the weight of the balcony above. She looked over the edge and noted the drop to the Stalls below. Of course, someone could probably climb in from one of the adjacent Boxes, but that'd be in full view of the audience and would be bound to cause some comment. She peeked under the seats. She stood on a chair and felt around the ceiling, which had gilt stars on it. She inspected the carpet minutely.

She smiled at what she saw. She'd been prepared to bet that she knew how the Ghost got in, and now she was certain.

Greebo spat on his hand and tried ineffectually to groom his hair.

"You sit quiet and eat your fish eggs," said Granny.

"Ye–ess, Gran–ny."

"And watch the opera, it's good for you."

"Ye–ess, Gran–ny."

"Evenin', Mrs. Plinge!" said Nanny cheerfully. "Ain't this excitin'? The buzz of the audience, the air of expectation, the blokes in the orchestra findin' somewhere to hide the bottles and tryin' to remember how to play . . . all the exhilaration an' drama of the operatic experience waitin' to unfold . . ."

"Oh, hello, Mrs. Ogg," said Mrs. Plinge. She was polishing glasses in her tiny bar.

"Certainly very packed," said Nanny. She looked sidelong at the old woman.* "Every seat sold, I heard."

This didn't achieve the expected reaction.

"Shall I give you a hand cleaning out Box Eight?" she went on.

---

*It was central to Nanny Ogg's soul that she never considered herself an old woman, while of course availing herself of every advantage that other people's perceptions of her as such would bring.

"Oh, I cleaned it out last week," said Mrs. Plinge. She held a glass up to the light.

"Yes, but I heard her ladyship is very particular," said Nanny. "Very picky about things."

"What ladyship?"

"Mr. Bucket has sold Box Eight, see," said Nanny.

She heard a faint tinkle of glass. *Ah.*

Mrs. Plinge appeared at the doorway of her nook. "But he can't do that!"

"It's his Opera House," said Nanny, watching Mrs. Plinge carefully. "I suppose he thinks he can."

"It's the *Ghost's* Box!"

Operagoers were appearing along the corridor.

"I shouldn't think he'd mind just for one night," said Nanny Ogg. "The show must go on, eh? Are you all right, Mrs. Plinge?"

"I think I'd just better go and—" she began, stepping forward.

"No, you have a good sit down and a rest," said Nanny, pressing her back with gentle but irresistible force.

"But I should go and—"

"*And what*, Mrs. Plinge?" said Nanny.

The old woman went pale. Granny Weatherwax could be nasty, but then nastiness was always in the window: you were aware that it might turn up on the menu. Sharpness from Nanny Ogg, though, was like being bitten by a big friendly dog. It was all the worse for being unexpected.

"I daresay you wanted to go and have a word with somebody, did you, Mrs. Plinge?" said Nanny softly. "Someone who might be a little shocked to find his

Box full, perhaps? I reckon I could put a name to that someone, Mrs. Plinge. Now, if—"

The old woman's hand came up holding a bottle of champagne and then came down hard in an effort to launch the SS *Gytha Ogg* onto the seas of unconsciousness. The bottle bounced.

Then Mrs. Plinge leapt past and scuttled away, her polished little black boots twinkling.

Nanny Ogg caught the door frame and swayed a little while blue and purple fireworks went off behind her eyes. But there was dwarf in the Ogg ancestry, and that meant a skull you could go mining with.

She stared muzzily at the bottle. "Year of the Insulted Goat," she mumbled. "'S a good year."

Then consciousness gained the upper hand.

She grinned as she galloped after the retreating figure. In Mrs. Plinge's place she'd have done exactly the same thing, except a good deal harder.

Agnes waited with the others for the curtain to go up. She was one of the crowd of fifty or so townspeople who would hear Enrico Basilica sing of his success as a master of disguise, it being a vital part of the entire process that, while the chorus would listen to expositions of the plot, and even sing along, they would suffer an instant lapse of memory afterward so that later unmaskings would come as a surprise.

For some reason, without any word being spoken, as many people as possible seemed to have acquired very broad-brimmed hats. Those who hadn't were taking every opportunity to glance upward.

Beyond the curtain, Herr Trubelmacher launched the overture.

Enrico, who had been chewing a chicken leg, carefully put the bone on a plate and nodded. The waiting stagehand dashed off.

The opera had begun.

Mrs. Plinge reached the bottom of the grand staircase and hung on to the banister, panting.

The opera had started. There was no one around. And no sounds of pursuit, either.

She straightened up, and tried to get her breath back.

"Coo–ee, Mrs. Plinge!"

Nanny Ogg, waving the champagne bottle like a club, was already traveling at speed when she hit the first turn in the banister, but she leaned like a professional and kept her balance as she went into the straight, and then tilted again for the next curve . . .

. . . which left only the big gilt statue at the bottom. It is the fate of all banisters worth sliding down that there is something nasty waiting at the far end. But Nanny Ogg's response was superb. She swung a leg over as she hurtled downward and pushed herself off, her nailed boots leaving grooves in the marble as she spun to a halt in front of the old woman.

Mrs. Plinge was lifted off her feet and carried into the shadows behind another statue.

"You don't want to try and outrun me, Mrs. Plinge," Nanny whispered, as she clamped a hand firmly over Mrs. Plinge's mouth. "You just want to wait here *quietly* with me. And don't go thinking I'm nice. I'm only nice compared to Esme, but so is practic'ly everyone . . ."

"Mmf!"

With one hand tightly around Mrs. Plinge's arm and another over her mouth, Nanny peered round the statue. She could hear the singing, far off.

Nothing else happened. After a while, she started to fret. Perhaps he'd taken fright. Perhaps Mrs. Plinge had left him some sort of signal. Perhaps he'd decided that the world was currently too dangerous for Ghosts, although Nanny doubted he could ever decide that . . .

At this rate the first act would be over before—

A door opened somewhere. A lanky figure in a black suit and a ridiculous beret crossed the foyer and went up the stairs. At the top, they saw it turn in the direction of the Boxes and disappear.

"Y'see," said Nanny, trying to get the stiffness out of her limbs, "the thing about Esme is, she's stupid . . ."

"Mmf?"

". . . so she thinks that the most obvious way, d'y'see, for the Ghost to get in and out of the Box is through the door. If you can't find a secret panel, she reckons, it's because it ain't there. A secret panel that ain't there is the best kind there is, the reason bein', no bugger can find it. That's where you people all think too operatic, see? You're all cooped up in this place, listening to daft plots what don't make sense, and I reckon it does something to your minds. People can't find a trapdoor so they say, oh, deary me, what a hidden trapdoor it must be. Whereas a normal person, e.g., me and Esme, we'd say: Maybe there ain't one, then. And the best way for the Ghost to get around the place without being seen is for him to be seen and not noticed. Especially if he's got keys. People don't notice Walter. They looks the other way."

She gently released her grip. "Now, I don't blame you, Mrs. Plinge, 'cos I'd do the same for one of mine, but you'd have done better to trust Esme right at the start. She'll help you if she can."

Nanny let Mrs. Plinge go, but kept a grip on the champagne bottle, just in case.

"What if she can't?" said Mrs. Plinge bitterly.

"You think Walter did those murders?"

"He's a good boy!"

"I'm sure that's the same as a 'no,' isn't it?"

"They'll put him in prison!"

"If he done them murders, Esme won't let that happen," said Nanny.

Something sank into Mrs. Plinge's not very alert mind. "What do you mean, she won't let that happen?" she said.

"I mean," said Nanny, "that if you throw yourself on Esme's mercy, you better be damn sure you deserve to bounce."

"Oh, Mrs. Ogg!"

"Now, don't you worry about anything," said Nanny, perhaps a little late under the circumstances. It occurred to her that the immediate future might be a little bit easier on everyone if Mrs. Plinge got some well-earned rest. She fumbled in her clothing and produced a bottle, half-full of some cloudy orange liquid. "I'll just give you a sip of a little something to calm your nerves . . ."

"What is it?"

"It's a sort of tonic," said Nanny. She flicked the cork out with her thumb; on the ceiling above her, the paint crinkled. "It's made from apples. Well . . . mainly apples . . ."

Walter Plinge stopped outside Box Eight and looked around.

Then he removed his beret and pulled out the mask. The beret went into his pocket.

He straightened up, and it looked very much as though Walter Plinge with the mask on was several inches taller.

He took a key from his pocket and unlocked the door, and the figure that stepped into the Box did not move like Walter Plinge. It moved as though every nerve and muscle were under full and athletic control.

The sounds of the opera filled the Box. The walls had been lined with red velvet and were hung with curtains. The chairs were high and well padded.

The Ghost slipped into one of them and settled down.

A figure leaned forward out of the other chair and said, "You carrn't havve my fisssh eggs!"

The Ghost leapt up. The door clicked behind him.

Granny stepped out from the curtains.

"Well, well, we meet again," she said.

He backed away to the edge of the Box.

"I shouldn't think you could jump," said Granny. "It's a long way down." She focused her best stare on the white mask. "And now, Mister Ghost—"

He sprang back onto the edge of the Box, saluted Granny flamboyantly, and leapt upward.

Granny blinked.

Up until now the Stare had always worked . . .

"Too damn *dark*," she muttered. "Greebo!"

The bowl of caviar flew out of his nervous fingers and caused a Fortean experience somewhere in the Stalls.

"Yess, Gran–ny!"

"Catch him! And there could be a kipper in it for you!"

Greebo snarled happily. This was more like it. Opera had begun to pall for him the moment he realized that no one was going to pour a bucket of cold water over the singers. He understood chasing things.

Besides, he liked to play with his friends.

Agnes saw the movement out of the corner of her eye. A figure had jumped out of one of the Boxes and was climbing up to the balcony. Then another figure clambered after it, scrambling over the gilt cherubs.

Singers faltered in mid-note. There was no mistaking the leading figure. It was the Ghost.

The Librarian was aware that the orchestra had stopped playing. Somewhere on the other side of the backcloth the singers had stopped, too. There was a buzz of excited conversation and one or two cries.

The hairs all over his body began to prickle. Senses designed to protect his species in the depths of the rain forest had adjusted nicely to the conditions of a big city, which was merely drier and had more carnivores.

He picked up the discarded bow tie and, with great deliberation, tied it around his forehead so that he looked like a really formal Kamikaze warrior. Then he threw away the opera score and stared blankly into space for a moment. He knew instinctively that some situations required musical accompaniment.

This organ lacked what he considered the most basic of facilities, such as the Thunder pedal, a 128-foot Earthquake pipe and a complete keyboard of animal noises, but he was certain there was something exciting that could be done in the bass register.

He stretched out his arms and cracked his knuckles. This took some time.

And then he began to play.

The Ghost danced along the edge of the balcony, scattering hats and opera glasses. The audience watched in astonishment, and then began to clap. They couldn't quite see how it fitted into the plot of the opera—but this *was* an opera, after all.

He reached the center of the balcony, trotted a little way up the aisle, and then turned and ran down again at speed. He reached the edge, jumped, jumped again, soared out into the auditorium . . .

. . . and landed on the chandelier, which jingled and began to sway gently.

The audience stood up and applauded as he climbed through the jangling tiers toward the central cable.

Then another shape clambered over the edge of

the balcony and loped along in pursuit. This was a stockier figure than the first man, one-eyed, broad in the shoulders and tapering at the waist; he looked evil in an interesting kind of way, like a pirate who really understood the words "Jolly Roger." He didn't even take a run but, when he reached the closest part to the chandelier, simply launched himself into space.

It was clear that he wasn't going to make it.

And then it wasn't clear how he did.

Those watching through opera glasses swore later that the man thrust out an arm which merely seemed to graze the chandelier and yet was then somehow able to swivel his entire body in mid-air.

A couple of people swore even harder that, just as the man reached out, his fingernails appeared to grow by several inches.

The huge glass mountain swung ponderously on its rope and, as it reached the end of the swing, Greebo swung out farther, like a trapeze artist. There was an appreciative "oo" from the audience.

He twisted again. The chandelier hesitated for a moment at the extremity of its arc, and then swept back again.

As it jangled and creaked over the Stalls the hanging figure swung upward, let go and did a backward somersault that dropped him in the middle of the crystals. Candles and prisms were scattered over the seats below.

And then, with the audience clapping and cheering, he scrambled up the rope after the fleeing Ghost.

Henry Lawsy tried to move his arm, but a fallen crystal had stapled the sleeve of his coat to his arm rest.

It was a quandary. He was pretty sure this wasn't supposed to happen, but he wasn't *certain*.

Around him he could hear people hissing questions.

"Was that part of the plot?"

"I'm sure it must have been."

"Oh, yes. Yes. It certainly was," said someone farther down the row, authoritatively. "Yes. Yes. The famous chase scene. Indeed. Oh, yes. They did it in Quirm, you know."

"Oh . . . yes. Yes, of course. I'm sure I heard about it . . ."

"I thought it was bloody good," said Mrs. Lawsy.

"Mother!"

"About time something interesting happened. You should've told me. I'd've put my glasses on."

Nanny Ogg pounded up the back stairs toward the fly loft.

"Something's gone wrong!" she muttered under her breath as she took the stairs two at a time. "She reckons she's only got to stare at 'em and they're toffee in her hands, and then who has to sort it out afterward, eh? Go on, guess . . ."

The ancient wooden door at the top of the stairs gave way to Nanny Ogg's boot with Nanny Ogg's momentum behind it, and cracked open onto a big, shadowy space. It was full of running figures. Legs flickered in the light of lanterns. People were shouting.

A figure ran straight toward her.

Nanny sprang into a crouch, both thumbs on the

cork of the badly shaken champagne bottle she held cradled under one arm.

"This is a magnum," she said, "and I'm not afraid to drink it!"

The figure stopped. "Oh, it's you, Mrs. Ogg . . ."

Nanny's infallible memory for personal details threw up a card. "Peter, isn't it?" she said, relaxing. "The one with the bad feet?"

"That's right, Mrs. Ogg."

"The powder I give you is working, is it?"

"They're a lot better now, Mrs. Ogg—"

"So what's been happening?"

"Mr. Salzella caught the Ghost!"

"Really?"

Now that Nanny's eyes had managed to discern some order in the chaos, she could see a cluster of people in the middle of the floor, around the chandelier.

Salzella was sitting on the planking. His collar was torn and a sleeve had been ripped off his jacket, but he had a triumphant look in his eyes.

He waved something in the air.

It was white. It looked like a piece of a skull.

"It was Plinge!" he said. "I tell you, it was Walter Plinge! Why are you all standing around? Get after him!"

"Walter?" said one of the men, doubtfully.

"Yes, *Walter*!"

Another man hurried up, waving his lantern.

"I saw the Ghost heading up to the roof! And there was some big one-eyed bastard going after him like a scalded cat!"

That's wrong, thought Nanny. *Something wrong here.*

"To the roof!" shouted Salzella.

"Hadn't we better get the flaming torches first?"

"Flaming torches are not compulsory!"

"Pitchforks and scythes?"

"That's only for vampires!"

"How about just *one* torch?"

"Get up there now! Understand?"

The curtains closed. There was a smattering of applause which was barely audible above the chatter from the audience.

The chorus turned to one another. "Was that supposed to happen?"

Dust rained down. Stagehands were scampering across the gantries far above. Shouts echoed among the ropes and dusty backdrops. A stagehand ran across the stage, holding a flaming torch.

"Here, what's going on?" said a tenor.

"They've got the Ghost! He's heading for the roof! It's Walter *Plinge*!"

"What, Walter?"

"*Our* Walter Plinge?"

"Yes!"

The stagehand ran on in a trail of sparks, leaving the yeast of rumor to ferment in the ready dough that was the chorus.

"Walter? Surely not!"

"Weeelll . . . he's a bit odd, isn't he . . . ?"

"But only this morning he said to me, 'It's a nice day Mr. Sidney!' Just like that. Normal as anything. Well . . . normal for Walter . . ."

"As a matter of fact, it's always worried me, the

way his eyes move as though they don't talk to each other—"

"And he's always around the place!"

"Yes, but he's the odd-job man—"

"No argument about that!"

"It's not Walter," said Agnes.

They looked at her.

"That's who he said they're chasing, dear."

"I don't know who they're chasing, but Walter's not the Ghost. Fancy anyone thinking Walter's the Ghost!" said Agnes, hotly. "He wouldn't hurt a fly! Anyway, I've seen—"

"He's always struck me as a bit slimy, though."

"And they say he goes down into the cellars a lot. What for, I ask myself? Let's face it. Fair's fair. He's crazy."

"He doesn't act crazy!" said Agnes.

"Well, he always looks as though he's about to, you must admit. I'm going to see what's happening. Anyone coming?"

Agnes gave up. It was a horrible thing to learn, but there are times when evidence gets trampled and the hunt is on.

A hatch flew open. The Ghost clambered out, looked down, and slammed the hatch shut. There was a yowl from below.

Then he danced across the leads until he reached the gargoyle-encrusted parapet, black and silver in the moonlight. The wind caught at his cloak as he ran along the very edge of the roof and dropped down again near another door.

And a gargoyle was suddenly no longer a gargoyle,

but a figure that reached down suddenly and twitched off his mask.

It was like cutting strings.

"Good evening, Walter," said Granny, as he sagged to his knees.

"Hello Missus Weatherwax!"

"Mistress," Granny corrected him. "Now stand up."

There was a growl farther along the roof, and then a thump. Bits of trapdoor rose for a moment against the moonlight.

"It's nice up here, ain't it?" said Granny. "There's fresh air and stars. I thought: up or down? But there's only rats down below."

In another swift movement she grabbed Walter's chin and tilted it, just as Greebo pulled himself onto the roof with prolonged murder in his heart.

"How does your mind work, Walter Plinge? If your house was on fire, what's the first thing you'd try to take out?"

Greebo stalked along the rooftop, growling. He liked rooftops in general, and some of his fondest memories involved them, but a trapdoor had just been slammed on his head and he was looking for anything he could disembowel.

Then he recognized the shape of Walter Plinge as someone who had given him food. And, standing right next to him, the much more unwelcome shape of Granny Weatherwax, who had once caught him digging in her garden and had kicked him in the cucumbers.

Walter said something. Greebo didn't take much notice of it.

Granny Weatherwax said: "Well done. A good answer. Greebo!"

Greebo nudged Walter heavily in the back.

"Want milluk right noaow! Purr, purr!"

Granny thrust the mask at the cat. In the distance people were running up stairs and shouting.

"You put this on! And you stay down real low, Walter Plinge. One man in a mask is pretty much like another, after all. And when they chase you, Greebo . . . give them a run for their money. Do it right and there could be—"

"Yurr, I knoaow," said Greebo despondently, taking the mask. It was turning out to be a long and busy evening for a kipper.

Someone poked their head out of the stricken trapdoor. The light glinted off Greebo's mask . . . and it had to be said, even by Granny, that he made a good Ghost. For one thing, his morphogenic field was trying to reassert itself. His claws could no longer even remotely be thought of as fingernails.

He spat at the pursuit as they poured up the steps, arched his back dramatically on the very edge of the roof, and stepped off.

One story down he thrust out an arm, caught a windowsill, and landed on the head of a gargoyle, which said "Oh, fank oo ver' mush" in a reproachful voice.

The pursuers looked down at him. Some of them *had* managed to get hold of flaming torches, because sometimes convention is too strong to be lightly denied.

Greebo snarled defiance and dropped again, springing from sill to drain pipe to balcony and pausing every now and again for another dramatic pose and another snarl at the pursuers.

"We'd better get after him, Corporal de Nobbs," said one of them, who was staggering along behind.

"We'd better get after him by carefully going back down the stairs, you mean. 'Cos somethin' I drank don't want to stay drunk. Much more runnin' and I'll be droppin' a custard, I'm tellin' you."

The other members of the posse also seemed to be reaching the conclusion that there was no extended future in chasing a man down the sheer wall of a building. As one mob they turned and, shouting and waving their torches in the air, headed back to the stairs.

The parting crowd revealed Nanny Ogg, holding a pitchfork in one hand and a torch in the other and thrusting them both in the air while muttering, "Rhubarb, rhubarb."

Granny walked over and tapped her on the shoulder. "They've gone, Gytha."

"Rhuba— Oh, hello, Esme," said Nanny, lowering the implements of righteous retribution. "I was just tagging along to see it didn't get out of hand. Was that Greebo I saw just then?"

"Yes."

"Awww, bless him," said Nanny. "He looked a bit bothered, though. I hope he doesn't happen to anybody."

"Where's your broomstick?" said Granny.

"It's in the cleaners' cupboard backstage."

"Then I'll borrow it and keep an eye on things," said Granny.

"Hey, he's *my* cat, I ought to be looking after him—" Nanny began.

Granny stepped aside, revealing a huddled shape sitting hugging its knees. "You look after Walter Plinge," she said. "It's something you'd be better at than me."

"Hello Mrs. Ogg!" said Walter, mournfully.

Nanny looked at him for a moment.

"So he is the—?"

"Yes."

"You mean he really did do the mur—?"

"What do *you* think?" said Granny.

"Well, if it comes to it, I think he didn't," said Nanny. "Can I have a word in your ear, Esme? I don't reckon I should say this in front of young Walter."

The witches bent their heads together. There was a brief whispered conversation.

"Everything is simple when you know the answer," said Granny. "I'll be back soon."

She hurried off. Nanny heard her shoes clattering on the stairs.

Nanny looked down at Walter again, and held out her hand. "Up you get, Walter."

"Yes Mrs. Ogg!"

"I expect we'd better find somewhere for you to lie low, eh?"

"I know a hidden place Mrs. Ogg!"

"You do, do you?"

Walter lurched across the roof toward another trapdoor, and pointed to it proudly.

"That?" said Nanny. "That doesn't look very hidden to me, Walter."

Walter gave it a puzzled look, and then grinned in the way a scientist might after he'd solved a particularly difficult equation. "It's hidden where everyone can see it Mrs. Ogg!"

Nanny gave him a sharp look, but there was nothing but a slightly glazed innocence in Walter's eyes.

He lifted up the trapdoor and pointed politely downward. "You go down the ladder first so I will not see your drawers!"

"Very . . . kind of you," said Nanny. It was the first time anyone had ever said anything like that to her.

The man waited patiently until she had reached the bottom of the ladder, and then climbed laboriously down after her.

"This is just an old staircase, isn't it?" said Nanny, prodding at the darkness with her torch.

"Yes! It goes all the way down! Except at the bottom where it goes all the way up!"

"Anyone else know about it?"

"The Ghost Mrs. Ogg!" said Walter, climbing down.

"Oh, yes," said Nanny slowly. "And where's the Ghost now, Walter?"

"He ran away!"

She held up the torch. There was still nothing to be read in Walter's expression. "What does the Ghost do here, Walter?"

"He watches over the Opera!"

"That's very kind of him, I'm sure."

Nanny started downward, and as the shadows danced around her she heard Walter say: "You know she asked me a very silly question Mrs. Ogg! It was a silly question any fool knows the answer!"

"Oh, yes," said Nanny, peering at the walls. "About houses on fire, I expect . . ."

"Yes! What would I take out of our house if it was on fire!"

"I expect you were a good boy and said you'd take your mum," said Nanny.

"No! My mum would take herself!"

Nanny ran her hands over the nearest wall. Doors had been nailed shut when the staircase had been abandoned. Someone walking up and down here, with a keen pair of ears, could hear a lot of things . . .

"What would you take out then, Walter?" she said.

"The fire!"

Nanny stared unseeing at the wall, and then her face slowly broke into a grin.

"You're daft, Walter Plinge," she said.

"Daft as a broom Mrs. Ogg!" said Walter cheerfully.

But you ain't insane, she thought. You're daft but you're sane. That's what Esme would say. And there's worser things.

Greebo pounded along Broadway. He was suddenly not feeling very well. Muscles were twitching in odd ways. A tingling at the base of his spine indicated that his tail wanted to grow, and his ears definitely wanted to creep up the sides of his head, which is always embarrassing when it happens in company.

In this case the company was about a hundred yards behind and apparently intent on moving his ears quite a long way from their current position, embarrassment or not.

It was gaining, too. Greebo normally had a famous turn of speed, but not when his knees were trying to reverse direction every few seconds.

His normal plan when pursued was to jump onto the water-butt behind Nanny Ogg's cottage and rake the pursuer across the nose with his claws when it came around the corner. Since this would now involve a five-hundred-mile dash, an alternative had to be sought.

There was a coach waiting outside one of the houses. He lurched over to it, pulled himself up, grabbed the reins and briefly turned his attention to the driver.

"Get orfff."

Greebo's teeth shone in the moonlight. The coachman, with great presence of mind and urgent absence of body, somersaulted backward into the night.

The horses reared, and tried to break into a gallop from a standing start. Animals are less capable of being fooled than are humans; they knew that what they had behind them was a very large cat, and the fact that it was man-shaped didn't make them any happier.

The coach lumbered off. Greebo looked over his twitching shoulder at the torchlit crowd and waved a paw derisively. The effect pleased him so much that he clambered onto the roof of the swaying coach and continued to jeer.

It is a catlike attribute to spit defiance at the enemy from a place of safety. In the circumstances it would have been better if catlike attributes had included the ability to steer.

A wheel hit the parapet of the Brass Bridge and scraped along it, the iron rim kicking up sparks. The shock knocked Greebo from his perch in mid-gesture. He landed on his feet in the middle of the road, while the terrified horses continued on with the coach rocking dangerously from side to side.

The pursuers stopped.

"What's he doing now?"

"He's just standing there."

"There's only one of him and there's lots of us, right? We could easily overpower him."

"Good idea. On the count of three, we'll all rush him, right? One . . . two . . . three . . ." Pause. "You didn't run."

"Well, nor did you."

"Yes, but I was the one saying 'one, two, three.'"

"Remember what he did to Mr. Pounder!"

"Yes, well, I never liked the man all that much . . ."

Greebo snarled. Ticklish things were happening to his body. He threw his head back and roared.

"Look, at worst he'd only be able to get one or two of us—"

"Oh, that's good, is it?"

"Here, why's he twisting around like that?"

"Maybe he hurt himself falling off the coach—"

"Let's get him!"

The mob closed in. Greebo, struggling against a morphogenic field swinging wildly between species, punched the first man in the face with a hand and clawed the shirt off another man with something more like a giant paw.

"Oh, shiiiooooo—"

Twenty hands grabbed him. And then, in the mêlée

and the darkness, twenty hands were holding just cloth and emptiness. Vengeful boots connected with nothing more than air. Clubs that had been swung at a snarling face whirled through empty space and returned to hit their owner on the ear.

"—ooooaaawwwwl!"

Quite unnoticed in the scrum, a flat-eared bullet of gray fur shot out from between the scuffling legs.

The kicking and punching stopped only when it became apparent that all the mob was attacking was itself. And, since the IQ of a mob is the IQ of its most stupid member divided by the number of mobsters, it was never very clear to anyone what had happened. Obviously they'd closed in on the Ghost, and he certainly couldn't have escaped. All that was left was a mask and some torn clothing. So, the mob reasoned, he must have ended up in the river. And good riddance, too.

Happy in the knowledge of a job well done, they adjourned to the nearest pub.

This left Sergeant Count de Tritus and Corporal the Count de Nobby Nobbs, who lurched to the middle of the bridge and regarded the few scraps of cloth.

"Commander Vimes isn't . . . isn't . . . isn't goin' to like dis," said Detritus. "You know he likes prisoners to be alive."

"Yeah, but this one would've been hung anyway," said Nobby, who was trying to stand upright. "This way was just a bit more . . . democratic. A great saving in terms of rope, not to mention wear and tear on locks and keys."

Detritus scratched his head. "Shouldn't there be some blood?" he ventured.

Nobby gave him a sour look. "He couldn't've got away," he said. "So don't go asking questions like that."

"Only, if humans is hit hard enough, they leaks all over der place," said Detritus.

Nobby sighed. That was the caliber of people you got in the Watch these days. They had to make a mystery of things. In days gone by, when it had been just the old gang and an unofficial policy of *lazy fair*, they'd have said a heartfelt "Well done, lads" to the vigilantes and turned in early. But now old Vimes had been promoted to Commander he seemed to be enrolling people who asked questions all the time. It was even affecting Detritus, considered by other trolls to be as dim as a dead glowworm.

Detritus reached down and picked up an eye patch.

"What d'you think, then?" said Nobby scornfully. "You think he turned into a bat and flew away?"

"Ha! I do not t'ink that 'cos it is in . . . consist . . . ent with modern policing," said Detritus.

"Well, *I* think," said Nobby, "that when you have ruled out the impossible, what is left, however improbable, ain't worth hanging around on a cold night wonderin' about when you could be getting on the outside of a big drink. Come on. I want to try a leg of the elephant that bit me."

"Was dat irony?"

"That was metaphor."

Detritus, uneasy in what was technically his mind, prodded at the torn pieces of clothing.

Something brushed against his leg. It was a cat. It had tattered ears, one good eye, and a face like a fist with fur on it.

"Hello, little cat," said Detritus.

The cat stretched and grinned. "Gerrt lorssst, coppuurrrr . . ."

Detritus blinked. There are no such things as troll cats, and Detritus had never seen a cat before he'd arrived in Ankh-Morpork and discovered that they were very, very hard to eat. And he'd never heard of them talking. On the other hand, he was very much aware of his reputation as the most stupid person in the city, and he wasn't going to draw attention to a talking cat if it were going to turn out that everybody except him knew that they talked all the time.

In the gutter, a few feet away, there was something white. He picked it up carefully. It looked like the mask the Ghost had worn.

This was probably a Clue.

He waved it urgently. "Hey, Nobby—"

"Thank you." Something dipped through the darkness, snatched the mask from the troll's hand, and soared into the night.

Corporal Nobbs turned around. "Yes?" he said.

"Er . . . how big are birds? Normally?"

"Oh, blimey, I dunno. Some are small, some are big. Who cares?"

Detritus sucked his finger. "Oh, no reason," he said. "I am far too smart to be taken in by perfec'ly normal t'ings."

Something squelched underfoot.

"It's pretty damp down here, Walter," said Nanny.

And the air was stale and heavy and seemed to be squeezing the light from the torch. There was a dark edge to the flame.

"Not far now Mrs. Ogg!"

Keys jingled in the darkness, and some hinges creaked.

"I found this Mrs. Ogg! It's the Ghost's secret cave!"

"Secret cave, eh?"

"You got to shut your eyes! You got to shut your eyes!" said Walter urgently.

Nanny did so, but to her shame kept a grip on the torch, just in case. She said: "And is the Ghost in there, Walter?"

"No!"

There was the rattle of a matchbox and some scuffling, and then—

"You can open them now Mrs. Ogg!"

Nanny did so.

Color and light blurred and then swam into focus, first in her eyes and then, eventually, in her brain. "Oh, my," she murmured. "Oh, my, my . . ."

There were candles, the big flat ones used to illuminate the stage, floating in shallow bowls. The light they gave was soft, and it rippled over the room like the soul of water.

It glinted off the beak of a huge swan. It glittered in the eye of a vast, sagging dragon.

Nanny Ogg turned slowly. Her experience of opera had not been a lengthy one but witches pick things up quickly, and *there* was the winged helmet worn by Hildabrun in *The Ring of the Nibelungingung*, and *here* was the striped pole from *The Barber of Pseudopolis*, and *there* was the pantomime horse with the humorous trapdoor from *The Enchanted Piccolo*, and here . . .

. . . here was opera, all piled in a heap. Once the eye had taken it all in, it had time to notice the peeling paint and rotting plaster and the general air of gentle moldering. The decrepit props and threadbare costumes had been dumped in here because people didn't want them anywhere else.

But someone *did* want them here. After the eye had seen the ruin, then there was time for it to see the little patches of recent repair, the careful areas of fresh paint.

There was something like a desk in the tiny area of floor not occupied by the props. And then Nanny realized that it had a keyboard and a stool, and there were neat piles of paper on top of it.

Walter was watching her with a big, proud grin.

Nanny ambled over to the thing. "It's a harmonium, ain't it? A tiny organ?"

"That's right Mrs. Ogg!"

Nanny picked up one of the sheaves of paper. Her lips moved as she read the meticulous copperplate writing.

"An opera about *cats*?" she said. "Never heard of an opera about *cats* . . ."

She thought for a moment, and then added to herself: But why not? It's a damn good idea. The lives of cats are just like operas, when you come to think about it.

She leafed through the other piles. "*Guys and Trolls? Hubward Side Story? Miserable Les?* Who's he? *Seven Dwarfs for Seven Other Dwarfs?* What're all these, Walter?"

She sat down on the stool and pressed a few of the cracked yellow keys, which moved with an audible creak. There were a couple of large pedals under the harmonium. You pedaled these and that worked the bellows and these spongy keys produced something which was to organ music what "poot" was to cursing.

So this was where Wal . . . where the Ghost sat, thought Nanny, down under the stage, among the discarded wreckage of old performances; down under the huge windowless room where, night after night, music and songs and rampant emotion echoed back and forth and never escaped or entirely died away. The Ghost worked down here, with a mind as open as a well, and it filled up with opera. Opera went in at the ears, and something else came out of the mind.

Nanny pumped the pedals a few times. Air hissed from inefficient seams. She tried a few notes. They were reedy. But, she considered, sometimes the old lie was true, and size really did not matter. It really was what you did with it that counted.

Walter watched her expectantly.

She took down another wad of paper and peered at the first page. But Walter leaned over and snatched at the script.

"That one's not finished Mrs. Ogg!"

The Opera House was still in uproar. Half the audience had gone outside and the other half was hanging around in case further interesting events were going to transpire. The orchestra was in a huddle in the pit, preparing its request for a special Being Upset By A Ghost Allowance. The curtains were closed. Some of the chorus had stayed onstage; others had hurried off to take part in the chase. The air had the excited electric feel it gets when normal civilized life is temporarily short-circuited.

Agnes bounced frantically from rumor to rumor. The Ghost had been caught, and it was Walter Plinge. The Ghost had been caught *by* Walter Plinge. The Ghost had been caught by someone else. The Ghost had escaped. The Ghost was dead.

There were arguments breaking out everywhere.

"I still can't believe it was Walter! I mean, good grief . . . Walter?"

"What about the show? We can't just stop! You *never* stop the show, not even if someone dies!"

"Oh, we have stopped when people died . . ."

"Yes, but only as long as it took to get the body offstage!"

Agnes stepped back into the wings, and trod on something. "Sorry," she said automatically.

"It was only my foot," said Granny Weatherwax. "So . . . how is life in the big city, Agnes Nitt?"

Agnes turned. "Oh . . . hello, Granny . . ." she mumbled. "And I'm not Agnes here, thank you," she added, a shade more defiantly.

"It's a good job, is it, bein' someone else's voice?"

"I'm doing what I want to do," said Agnes. She drew herself up to her full width. "And you can't stop me!"

"But you ain't part of it, are you?" said Granny conversationally. "You try, but you always find yourself watchin' yourself watchin' people, eh? Never quite believin' anything? Thinkin' the wrong thoughts?"

"Shut up!"

"Ah. Thought so."

"I have no intention of becoming a witch, thank you very much!"

"Now, don't go getting upset just because you know it's going to happen. A witch you're going to be because a witch you are, and if you turn your back on him now then I don't know what's going to happen to Walter Plinge."

"He's not dead?"

"No."

Agnes hesitated. "I *knew* he was the Ghost," she began. "But then I saw he couldn't be."

"Ah," said Granny. "Believed the evidence of your own eyes, did you? In a place like this?"

"One of the stagehands just told me they chased him up onto the roof and then down into the street and beat him to death!"

"Oh, well," said Granny, "you'll never get anywhere if you believe what you *hear*. What do you *know*?"

"What do you mean, what do I know?"

"Don't try cleverness on me, miss."

Agnes looked at Granny's expression, and knew when to fold. "I know he's the Ghost," she said.

"Right."

"But I can see that he isn't."

"Yes?"

"And I know . . . I'm pretty *sure* he doesn't mean any harm."

"Good. Well done. Walter might not know his right from his left, but he does know his right from his wrong." Granny rubbed her hands together. "Well, we're already home and looking for a clean towel, eh?"

"What? You haven't solved anything!"

"'Course we have. We know that it wasn't Walter what done the murders, so now we just have to find out who it was. Easy."

"Where's Walter now?"

"Nanny's got him somewhere."

"She's all by herself?"

"I told you, she's got Walter."

"I meant . . . well, he's a bit strange."

"Only where it shows."

Agnes sighed, and started to say that it wasn't her problem. And realized it was useless even to try. The knowledge sat like a smug intruder in her mind. Whatever it was, it was her problem.

"All right," she said. "I'll help you if I can, because I'm here. But afterward . . . that's *it*! Afterward, you'll leave me alone. Promise?"

"Certainly."

"Well . . . all right, then . . ." Agnes stopped. "Oh, no," she said. "That was too easy. I don't trust you."

"Don't trust me?" said Granny. "You're saying you don't trust me?"

"Yes. I don't. You'll find a way to wriggle around it."

"I never wriggle," said Granny. "It's Nanny Ogg who thinks we ought to have a third witch. I reckon life's difficult enough without some girl cluttering up the place just because she thinks she looks good in a pointy hat."

There was a pause. Then Agnes said, "I'm not falling for *that* one, either. It's where you say I'm too stupid to be a witch and I say, oh no I'm not, and you end up winning again. I'd rather be someone else's voice than some old witch with no friends and having everyone frightened of me and being nothing more than just a bit cleverer than other people and not doing any *real* magic at all . . ."

Granny put her head on one side.

"Seems to me you're so sharp you might cut yourself," she said.

"All right. When it's all over, I'll let you go your own way. I won't stop you. Now show me the way to Mr. Bucket's office . . ."

Nanny smiled her jolly-wrinkled-old-apple smile. "Now, you just hand it over, Walter," she said. "No harm in letting me see it, is there? Not old Nanny."

"Can't see it till it's finished!"

"Well, now," said Nanny, hating herself for dropping the atom bomb, "I'm sure your mam wouldn't want to hear that you've been a bad boy, would she?"

Expressions floated over Walter's waxen features as he struggled with several ideas at once. Finally, without a word, he thrust the bundle at her, his arms trembling with tension.

"There's a *good* boy," said Nanny.

She glanced at the first few pages, and then moved them nearer to the light. "Hmm."

She treadled the harmonium for a while and played a few notes with her left hand. They represented most of the musical notes she knew how to read. It was a very simple little theme, such as might be picked out on the keyboard with one finger. "Hey . . ."

Her lips moved as she read the narrative.

"Well now, Walter," she said, "isn't this a sort of opera about a ghost who lives in an opera house?" She turned a page. "Very smart and debonair, he is. He's got a secret cave, I see . . ."

She played another short riff. "Catchy music, too."

She read on, occasionally saying things like "Well, well" and "Lawks." Every now and again she'd give Walter an appraising look.

"I wonder why the Ghost wrote this, Walter?" she said, after a while. "Quiet sort of chap, ain't he? Put it all into his music."

Walter stared at his feet. "There's going to be a lot of trouble Mrs. Ogg."

"Oh, me and Granny will sort it all out," said Nanny.

"It's wrong to tell lies," said Walter.

"Probably," said Nanny, who'd never let it worry her up to now.

"It wouldn't be right for our mum to lose her job Mrs. Ogg."

"It wouldn't be right, no."

The feeling drifted over Nanny that Walter was trying to put across some sort of message. "Er . . . what sort of lies would it be wrong to tell, Walter?"

Walter's eyes bulged. "Lies . . . about things you see Mrs. Ogg! Even if you did see them!"

Nanny thought it was probably time to present the Oggish point of view. "It's all right to tell lies if you don't *think* lies," she said.

"He said our mum would lose her job and I'd be locked up if I said Mrs. Ogg!"

"Did he? Which 'he' was he?"

"The Ghost Mrs. Ogg!"

"I reckon Granny ought to have a good look at you, Walter," said Nanny. "I reckon your mind's all tangled up like a ball of string what's been dropped."

She pedaled the harmonium thoughtfully. "Was it the Ghost that wrote all this music, Walter?"

"It's wrong to tell lies about the room with the sacks in it Mrs. Ogg!"

Ah, thought Nanny. "That'd be down here, would it?"

"He said I wasn't to tell anyone!"

"Who did?"

"The Ghost Mrs. Ogg!"

"But you're—" Nanny began, and then tried another way. "Ah, but I ain't anyone," she said. "Anyway, if you was to go to this room with the sacks and I was to follow you, that wouldn't be telling anyone, would it? It wouldn't be your fault if some ole woman followed you, would it?"

Walter's face was an agony of indecision but, erratic though his thinking might have been, it was no match for Nanny Ogg's meretricious duplicity. He was up against a mind that regarded truth as a reference point but certainly not as a shackle. Nanny Ogg could think her way through a corkscrew in a tornado without touching the sides.

"Anyway, it's all right if it's me," she added for good measure. "In fact, he prob'ly meant to say 'except for Mrs. Ogg,' only he forgot."

Slowly, Walter reached out and picked up a candle. Without saying a word he walked out of the door and into the damp darkness of the cellars.

Nanny Ogg followed him, her boots making squelching noises in the mud.

It didn't seem like much of a distance. As far as Nanny could work out they were no longer under the Opera House, but it was hard to be sure. Their shadows danced around them and they walked through other rooms, even more dark and dripping than the ones they'd been in. Walter stopped in front of a pile of timber that glistened with rot, and pulled a few of the spongy planks aside.

There were some sacks neatly piled.

Nanny kicked one, and it broke.

In the flickering candlelight all that she could really see were sparkles of light as the cascade poured out, but there was no mistaking the gentle metallic scraping of lots of money. Lots and lots of money. Enough money to suggest very clearly that it belonged to either a thief or a publisher, and there didn't seem to be any books around.

"What's this, Walter?"

"It's the Ghost's money Mrs. Ogg!"

There was a square hole in the opposite corner of the room. Water glinted a few inches below. Beside the hole were half a dozen containers of various sorts—old biscuit tins, broken bowls and the like. There was a stick, or possibly a dead shrub, in each one.

"And those, Walter? What are those?"

"Rose bushes Mrs. Ogg!"

"Down here? But nothing could gr—"

Nanny stopped.

She squelched over to the pots. They'd been filled with muck scraped from the floor. The dead stems glistened with slime.

Nothing could grow down here, of course. There was no light. Everything that grew needed something else to feed on. And . . . she moved the candle closer, and sniffed the fragrance. Yes. It was subtle, but it was there. Roses in darkness.

"Well, my word, Walter Plinge," she said. "Always one for the surprises, you are."

Books were piled on Mr. Bucket's desk.

"What you're doing is *wrong*, Granny Weatherwax," said Agnes from the doorway.

Granny glanced up. "Wrong as living other people's lives for them?" she said. " 'S'matter of fact, there's something even worse than that, which is living other people's lives for yourself. That kind of wrong?"

Agnes said nothing. Granny Weatherwax couldn't *know*.

Granny turned back to the books. "Anyway, this only *looks* wrong. Appearances is deceivin'. You just pay attention to watching the corridor, madam."

She riffled through the bits of torn envelope and scribbled notes that seemed to be the Opera House's equivalent of proper accounts. It was a mess. In fact, it was more than a mess. It was far too much of a mess to be a real mess, because a real mess has occasional bits of coherence, bits of what might be called random order. Rather, it was the kind of erratic mess that suggested that someone had set out to be messy.

Take the account books. They were full of tiny rows and columns, but someone hadn't thought it worthwhile to invest in lined paper and had handwriting that wandered a bit. There were forty rows on the left-hand side but only thirty-six by the time they reached the other side of the page. It was hard to spot because of the way your eyes watered.

"What are you doing?" said Agnes, tearing her gaze away from the corridor.

"Amazin'," said Granny. "Some things is entered

twice! And I reckon there's a page here where some-one's added the month and taken away the time of day!"

"I thought you didn't like books," said Agnes.

"I don't," said Granny, turning a page. "They can look you right in the face and still lie. How many fiddle players are there in the band?"

"I think there are nine violinists in the orchestra."

The correction appeared to pass unnoticed.

"Well, there's a thing," said Granny, without moving her head. "Seems that twelve of 'em are drawing wages, but three of 'em is over the page, so you mightn't notice." She looked up and rubbed her hands happily. "Unless you've got a good memory, that is."

She ran a skinny finger down another erratic col-umn. "What's a flying ratchet?"

"I don't know!"

"Says here 'Repairs to flying ratchet, new springs for rotation cog assembly, and making good. Hun-dred and sixty dollars and sixty-three pence.' Hah!"

She licked her finger and tried another page.

"Even Nanny ain't this bad at numbers," she said. "To be this bad at numbers you've got to be good. Hah! No wonder this place never makes any money. You might as well try to fill a sieve."

Agnes darted into the room. "There's someone coming!"

Granny got up and blew out the lamp. "You get behind the curtains," she commanded.

"What're *you* going to do?"

"Oh . . . I'll just have to make myself inconspic-uous . . ."

Agnes hurried across to the big window and turned to look at Granny, who was standing by the fireplace.

The old witch faded. She didn't disappear. She merely slid into the background.

An arm gradually became part of the mantelpiece. A fold of her dress was a piece of shadow. An elbow became the top of the chair behind her. Her face became one with a vase of faded flowers.

She was still there, like the old woman in the puzzle picture they sometimes printed in the Almanack, where you could see the old woman *or* the young girl but not both at once, because one was made of the shadows of the other. Granny Weatherwax was standing by the fireplace, but you could see her only if you knew she was there.

Agnes blinked. And there were just the shadows, the chair and the fire.

The door opened. She ducked behind the curtains, feeling as conspicuous as a strawberry in a stew, certain that the sound of her heart would give her away.

The door shut, carefully, with barely a click. Footsteps crossed the floor. A wooden scraping noise might have been a chair being moved slightly.

A scratch and a hiss were the sound of a match, striking. A clink was the glass of the lamp, being lifted . . .

All noise ceased.

Agnes crouched, every muscle suddenly screaming with the strain. The lamp hadn't been lit—she'd have seen the light around the curtain.

Someone out there was making no noise.

Someone out there was suddenly suspicious.

A floorboard squeaked verrrry slowwwly, as some-one shifted their weight.

She felt as if she was going to scream, or burst with the effort of silence. The handle of the window behind her, a mere point of pressure a moment ago, was trying seriously to become part of her life. Her mouth was so dry that she knew it'd creak like a hinge if she dared to swallow.

It couldn't be anyone who had a right to be here. People who had a right to be in places walked around noisily.

The handle was getting really *personal*.

Try to think of something else . . .

The curtain moved. Someone was standing on the other side of it.

If her throat weren't so arid she might be able to scream.

She could *feel* the presence through the cloth. Any moment now, someone was going to twitch the cur-tain aside.

She leapt, or as close to a leap as was feasible—it was a kind of vertical lumber, billowing the curtain aside, colliding with a slim body behind it, and ending on the floor in a tangle of limbs and ripping velvet.

She gulped air, and pressed down on the squirm-ing bundle below her.

"I'll scream!" she said. "And if I do your eardrums will come down your nose!"

The writhing stopped.

"*Perdifa?*" said a muffled voice.

Above her, the curtain rail sagged at one end and the brass rings, one at a time, spun toward the floor.

* * *

Nanny went back to the sacks. Each one bulged with round hard shapes that clinked gently under her questing finger.

"This is a lot of money, Walter," she said carefully.

"Yes Mrs. Ogg!"

Nanny lost track of money fairly easily, although this didn't mean the subject didn't interest her: it was just that, beyond a certain point, it became dream-like. All she could be sure of was that the amount in front of her would make *anyone's* drawers drop.

"I suppose," she said, "that if I was to ask you how it'd got here, you'd say it was the Ghost, yes? Like the roses?"

"Yes Mrs. Ogg!"

She gave him a worried look. "You'll be all right down here, will you?" she said. "You'll sit quiet? I reckon I need to talk to some people."

"Where's my mum Mrs. Ogg?"

"She's having a nice sleep, Walter."

Walter seemed satisfied with this.

"You'll sit quiet in your . . . in that room, will you?"

"Yes Mrs. Ogg!"

"There's a good boy."

She glanced at the money bags again. Money was trouble.

Agnes sat back.

André raised himself on his elbows and pulled the curtain off his face. "What the hell were you doing there?" he said.

"I was—What do you mean, what was *I* doing there? *You* were creeping around!"

"You were hiding behind the curtain!" said André,

getting to his feet and fumbling for the matches again. "Next time you blow out a lamp, remember it'll still be warm."

"*We* were . . . on important business . . ."

The lamp glowed. André turned. "We?" he said.

Agnes nodded, and looked across at Granny. The witch hadn't moved, although it took a deliberate effort of will to focus on her among the shapes and shadows.

André picked up the lamp and stepped forward.

The shadows shifted.

"Well?" he said.

Agnes strode across the room and waved a hand in the air. There was the chair back, there was the vase, there was . . . nothing else.

"But she was there!"

"A ghost, eh?" said André sarcastically.

Agnes backed away.

There is something about the light of a lamp held lower than someone's face. The shadows are wrong. They fall in unfortunate places. Teeth seem more prominent. Agnes came to realize that she was alone in a room in suspicious circumstances with a man whose face suddenly looked a lot more unpleasant than it had before.

"I suggest," he said, "that you get back to the stage right now, yes? That would be the very best thing you could do. And don't meddle in things that don't concern you. You've done too much as it is."

The fear hadn't drained out of Agnes, but it had found a space in which to metamorphose into anger.

"I don't have to put up with that! For all I know, *you* might be the Ghost!"

"Really? *I* was told that Walter Plinge was the Ghost," said André. "How many people did you tell? And now it turns out that he's dead . . ."

"No, he's not!"

It was out before she could stop it. She'd said it merely to wipe the sneer off his face. This happened. But the expression that replaced it was no improvement.

A floorboard creaked.

They both turned.

There was a hat stand in the corner, next to a bookcase. There were a few coats and scarves hanging from it. It was surely only the way that the shadows fell that made it look, from this angle, like an old woman. Or . . .

"Damn floors," said Granny, fading into the foreground. She stepped away from the coats.

As Agnes said, later: it wasn't as though she'd been invisible. She'd simply become part of the scenery until she put herself forward again; she was there, but not *there*. She didn't stand out at all. She was as unnoticeable as the very best of butlers.

"How did you get in?" said André. "I looked all round the room!"

"Seein' is believin'," said Granny, calmly. "Of course, the trouble is that believin' is also seein', and there's been too much of that round here lately. Now, I *know* you ain't the Ghost . . . so what are you, to be sneaking around in places where you shouldn't be?"

"I could ask you the same quest—"

"Me? I'm a witch, and *I'm pretty good at it.*"

"She's, er, from Lancre. Where I come from," Agnes mumbled, trying to look at her feet.

"Oh? Not the one who wrote the book?" said André. "I've heard people talking about—"

"No! I'm much worse than her, understand?"

"She is," mumbled Agnes.

André gave Granny a long look, like a man weighing up his chances. He must have decided that they were bobbing along the ceiling.

"I . . . hang around in dark places looking for trouble," he said.

"Really? There's a nasty name for people like that," snapped Granny.

"Yes," said André. "It's 'policeman.'"

Nanny Ogg climbed out of the cellars, rubbing her chin thoughtfully. Musicians and singers were still milling around, uncertain about what was going to happen next. The Ghost had had the decency to be chased and killed during the interval. In theory that meant there was no reason why there shouldn't be a third act, as soon as Herr Trubelmacher had scoured the nearby pubs and dragged the orchestra back. The show must go on.

Yes, she thought, it has to go on. It's like the buildup to a thunderstorm . . . no . . . it's more like making love. Yes. That was a far more Oggish metaphor. You put everything you've got into it, so sooner or later there's a point where it's got to go on, because you can't imagine stopping. The stage manager could dock a couple of dollars from their wages and they'd still go on, and everyone knew it. And they would still go on.

She reached a ladder and climbed slowly into the flies.

She hadn't been certain. She needed to be certain now.

The fly loft was empty. She walked carefully along the catwalk until she was over the auditorium. The buzz of the audience came through the ceiling beneath her, slightly muffled.

Light shone up at the point where the thick cable for the chandelier disappeared into the hole. She stepped out over the creaking trapdoor and peered down.

Terrific heat almost frizzled her hair. A few yards below her hundreds of candles were burning.

"Dreadful if that lot fell down," she said quietly. "I 'spect this place'd go up like a haystack . . ."

She let her gaze travel up and up the cable to the point, at just about waist-height, where it was half-cut through. You'd never see it, if you weren't expecting to find it.

Then her gaze dropped again, and moved across the gloomy, dusty floor until it found something half-hidden in the dust.

Behind her, a shadow among the shadows rose to its feet, balanced itself carefully, and started to run.

"I knows about policemen," said Granny. "They've got big helmets and big feet and you can see them a mile off. There's a couple lurching around backstage. Anyone can see *they're* policemen. You don't look like one." She turned the badge over and over in her hands. "I ain't happy with the idea of *secret* policemen," she said. "Why do you need secret policemen?"

"Because," said André, "sometimes you have secret criminals."

Granny almost smiled. "That's a fact," she said. She peered at the small engraving on the back of the badge. "Says here 'Cable Street Particulars' . . ."

"There aren't many of us," said André. "We've only just started. Commander Vimes said that, since we can't do anything about the Thieves' Guild and the Assassins' Guild, we'd better look for other crimes. Hidden crimes. That need Watchmen with . . . different skills. And I can play the piano quite well . . ."

"What kind of skills have that troll and that dwarf got?" said Granny. "Seems to me the only thing they're really good at is standing around looking obvious and stupi—Hah! Yes . . ."

"Right. And they didn't even need much training," said André. "Commander Vimes says they're the most obvious policemen anyone could think of. Incidentally, Corporal Nobbs has got some papers to prove he's a human being."

"Forged?"

"I don't think so."

Granny Weatherwax put her head on one side. "If your house was on fire, what's the first thing you'd take out of it?"

"Oh, Granny—" Agnes began.

"Hmm. Who set fire to it?" said André.

"You're a policeman, right enough." Granny handed him his badge. "You come to arrest poor Walter?" she said.

"I know he didn't murder Dr. Undershaft. I was watching him. He was trying to unblock the privies all afternoon—"

"I've had proof that Walter *isn't* the Ghost," said Agnes.

"I was almost sure it was Salzella," said André. "I know he creeps off to the cellars sometimes and I'm sure he's stealing money. But the Ghost has been seen when Salzella is perfectly visible. So now I think—"

"Think? Think?" said Granny. "Someone thinking around here at last? How'd you recognize the Ghost, Mister Policeman?"

"Well . . . he's got a mask on . . ."

"Really? Now say it again, and *listen* to what you say. Good grief! You can *recognize* him because he's got a *mask* on? You recognize him *because* you don't know who he is? Life isn't neat! Whoever said there's only one Ghost?"

The figure ran through the shadows of the fly loft, cloak billowing around it. Nanny Ogg was outlined against the light, peering down.

She said, without turning her head: "Hello, Mr. Ghost. Come back for your saw, have you?"

Then she darted around behind the cable until she faced the shadow. "Millions of people knows I'm up here! You wouldn't hurt a little old lady, would you? Oh, dear . . . me poor old heart!"

She keeled over backward, hitting the floor hard enough to make the cable swing.

The figure hesitated. Then it took a length of thin rope from a pocket and advanced cautiously toward the fallen witch. It knelt down, wound an end of the rope around each hand, and leaned forward.

Nanny's knee came up sharply.

"Feels a lot better now, mister," she said, as he reared backward.

She scrambled up again and grabbed the saw.

"Come back to finish it, eh?" she said, waving the implement in the air. "Wonder how you'd blame *that* on Walter! Make you happy, would it, the whole place burning down?"

The figure, moving awkwardly, backed away as she advanced. Then it turned, lurched along the wobbling catwalk and disappeared into the gloom.

Nanny pounded after him and saw the figure climbing down a ladder. She looked around quickly, grabbed a rope to slide after him, and heard a pulley somewhere above start to clatter.

She descended, skirts billowing around her. When she was about halfway down, a bunch of sandbags went upward past her in a hurry.

As she rattled onward she saw, between her boots, someone struggling with the trapdoor to the cellars.

She landed a few feet away, still holding the rope.

"Mr. Salzella?"

Nanny stuck two fingers in her mouth and let out a whistle that could have melted earwax.

She let go of the rope.

Salzella glanced up at her as he raised the trapdoor, and then saw the shape dropping out of the roof.

One hundred and eighty pounds of sandbag hit the door, slamming it shut.

"Watch out!" said Nanny, cheerfully.

Bucket waited nervously in the wings. Unnecessarily nervously, of course. The Ghost was dead. There couldn't be anything to worry about. People said they'd *seen* him killed, although they were, Bucket had to admit, a bit hazy on the actual details.

Nothing to worry about.

Not a thing.

Nothing whatsoever in any way.

Everything was absolutely nothing to worry about in any way.

He ran a finger around the inside of his collar. It hadn't been such a bad life in wholesale cheese. The most you had to worry about was one of poor old Reg Plenty's trouser buttons in the Farmhouse Nutty and the time young Weevins minced his thumb in the stirring machine and it was only by luck they happened to be doing strawberry yogurt at the time—

A figure loomed up beside him. He clutched at a curtain for support and then turned to see, with relief, the majestic and reassuring stomach of Enrico Basilica. The tenor looked magnificent in a huge cockerel costume, complete with giant beak, wattles and comb.

"Ah, señor," Bucket burbled. "Very impressive, may I say."

"Si," said a muffled voice from somewhere behind the beak, as other members of the company hurried past onto the stage.

"May I say how sorry I am about all that business earlier. I can assure you that it doesn't happen every night, ahahah . . ."

"Si?"

"Probably just high spirits, ahaha . . ."

The beak turned toward him. Bucket backed away.

"Si!"

". . . yes . . . well, I'm glad you're so understanding . . ."

Temperamental, he thought, as the tenor strode

onto the stage and the overture to Act Three drifted to its close. They're like that, the real *artistes*. Nerves stretched like rubber bands, I expect. It's just like waiting for the cheese, really. You can get really edgy waiting to see whether you've got half a ton of best blue-vein or just a vat full of pig food. It's probably like that when you've got an aria working its way up—

"Where'd he go? Where'd he go?"

"What? Oh . . . Mrs. Ogg . . ."

The old woman waved a saw in front of his face. It was not, in Mr. Bucket's current state of mental tension, a helpful gesture.

He was suddenly surrounded by other figures, equally conducive to multiple exclamation marks.

'Perdita? Why aren't you onstage . . . oh, Lady Esmerelda, I didn't see you there, of course if you want to come backstage you only have to—"

"Where's Salzella?" said André.

Bucket looked around vaguely. "He was here a few minutes ago . . . That is," he said, pulling himself together, "*Mr.* Salzella is probably attending to his duties somewhere which, young man, is more than I can say for—"

"I demand you stop the show *now*," said André.

"Oh, you do, do you? And by what authority, may I ask?"

"He's been sawing through the rope!" said Nanny.

André pulled out a badge. "This!"

Bucket looked closely. " 'Ankh-Morpork Guild of Musicians member 1244'?"

André glared at him, then at the badge, and started to pat his pockets urgently. "No! Blast, I know I had the other one a moment ago . . . Look, you've got to clear the theater, we've got to search it, and that means—"

"Don't stop the show," said Granny.

"I won't stop the show," said Bucket.

" 'Cos I reckon he'd like to see the show stopped. The show must go on, eh? Isn't that what you believe? Could he have got out of the building?"

"I sent Corporal Nobbs to the stage door and Sergeant Detritus is in the foyer," said André. "When it comes to standing in doorways, they're among the best."

"Excuse me, what's happening?" said Bucket.

"He could be anywhere!" said Agnes. "There're hundreds of hiding places!"

"Who?" said Bucket.

"How about these cellars everyone talks about?" said Granny.

"Where?"

"There's only one entrance," said André. "He's not stupid."

"He can't get into the cellars," said Nanny. "He ran off! Probably in a cupboard somewhere by now!"

"No, he'll stay where there's crowds," said Granny. "That's what I'd do."

"What?" said Bucket.

"Could he have got into the audience from here?" said Nanny.

"Who?" said Bucket.

Granny jerked a thumb toward the stage. "He's somewhere on there. I can *feel* him."

"Then we'll wait until he comes off!"

"Eighty people coming offstage all at once?" said

Agnes. "Don't you know what it's *like* when the curtain goes down?"

"And we don't want to stop the show," Granny mused.

"No, we don't want to stop the show," said Bucket, grasping at a familiar idea as it swept by on a tide of incomprehensibility. "Or give people their money back in any fashion whatsoever. What are we talking about, does anyone know?"

"The show must go on . . ." murmured Granny Weatherwax, still staring out of the wings. "Things have to end right. This is an opera house. They should end . . . operatically . . ."

Nanny Ogg hopped up and down excitedly. "Oo, I know what you're thinking, Esme!" she squeaked. "Oo, yes! Can we? Just so's I can say I done it! Eh? Can we? Go on! Let's!"

Henry Lawsy peered closely at his opera notes. He had not, of course, fully understood the events of the first two acts, but knew that this was perfectly okay because one would have to be quite naïve to expect good sense as well as good songs. Anyway, it would all be explained in the last act, which was the Masked Ball in the Duke's Palace. It would almost certainly turn out that the woman one of the men had been rather daringly courting would be his own wife, but so cunningly disguised by a very small mask that her husband wouldn't have spotted that she wore the same clothes and had the same hairstyle. Someone's serving man would turn out to be someone else's daughter in disguise; someone would die of something that didn't prevent them from singing about it for several minutes; and the plot would be resolved by some coincidences which, in real life, would be as likely as a cardboard hammer.

He didn't know any of this for a fact. He was making a calculated guess.

In the meantime Act Three opened with the traditional ballet, this time apparently a country dance by the Maidens of the Court.

Henry was aware of muffled laughter around him.

This was because, if you ran an eye at head-height along the row of ballerinas as they tripped, arm in arm, onto the stage, there was an apparent gap.

This was only filled if the gaze went downward a foot or two, to a small fat ballerina in a huge grin, an overstretched tutu, long white drawers and . . . boots.

Henry stared. They were *big* boots. They moved back and forth at an astonishing speed. The satin slippers of the other dancers twinkled as they drifted across the floor, but the boots flashed and clattered like a tap dancer afraid of falling into the sink.

The pirouettes were novel, too. While the other dancers whirled like snowflakes, the little fat one spun like a top and moved across the floor like one, too, bits of her anatomy trying to achieve local orbit.

Around Henry members of the audience were whispering to one another.

"Oh yes," he heard someone declare, "they tried this in Pseudopolis . . ."

His mother nudged him. "This supposed to happen?"

"Er . . . I don't think so . . ."

"'S bloody good, though! A good laugh!"

As the fat ballerina collided with a donkey in evening dress she staggered and grabbed at his mask, which came off . . .

Herr Trubelmacher, the conductor, froze in horror and astonishment. Around him the orchestra rattled to a standstill, except for the tuba player—

—oom-BAH-oom-BAH-oom-BAH—

—who had memorized his score years ago and never took much interest in current affairs.

Two figures rose up right in front of Trubelmacher. A hand grabbed his baton.

"Sorry, sir," said André, "but the show must go on, yes?" He handed the stick to the other figure.

"There you are," he said. "And *don't let them stop.*"

"Ook!"

The Librarian carefully lifted Herr Trubelmacher aside with one hand, licked the baton thoughtfully, and then focused his gaze on the tuba player.

—oom-BAH-oom-BAHhhh . . . oom . . . om . . .

The tuba player tapped a trombonist on the shoulder.

"Hey, Frank, there's a monkey where old troublemaker should be—"

"Shutupshutupshutup!"

Satisfied, the orangutan raised his arms.

The orchestra looked up. And then looked up a bit more. No conductor in musical history, not even the one who once fried and ate the piccolo player's liver on a cymbal for one wrong note too many, not even the one who skewered three troublesome violinists on his baton, not even the one who made really *hurtful* sarcastic remarks in a loud voice, was ever the focus of such reverential attention.

Onstage, Nanny Ogg took advantage of the hush to pull the head off a frog.

"Madam!"

"Sorry, thought you might be someone else . . ."

The long arms dropped. The orchestra, in one huge muddled chord, slammed back into life.

The dancers, after a moment's confusion during which Nanny Ogg took the opportunity to decapitate a clown and a phoenix, tried to continue.

The chorus watched in bemusement.

Christine felt a tap on her shoulder, and turned to see Agnes. "Perdita! Where have you been!?" she hissed. "It's nearly time for my duet with Enrico!"

"You've got to help!" hissed Agnes. But down in her soul Perdita said: Enrico, eh? It's Señor Basilica to everyone else . . .

"Help you what!?" said Christine.

"Take everyone's masks off!"

Christine's forehead wrinkled beautifully. "That's not supposed to happen until the end of the opera, is it?"

"Er . . . it's all been changed!" said Agnes urgently. She turned to a nobleman in a zebra mask and tugged it desperately. The singer underneath glared at her.

"Sorry!" she whispered. "I thought you were someone else!"

"We're not supposed to take them off until the end!"

"It's been changed!"

"Has it? No one told me!"

A short-necked giraffe next to him leaned sideways. "What's that?"

"The big unmasking scene is now, apparently!"

"No one told *me*!"

"Yes, but when does anyone ever tell us anything? *We're* only the chorus . . . here, why is old Trouble-maker wearing a monkey mask . . . ?"

Nanny Ogg pirouetted past, cannoned into an elephant in evening dress and beheaded him by the trunk. She whispered: "We're looking for the Ghost, see?"

"But . . . the Ghost is dead, isn't he?"

"Hard things to kill, ghosts," said Nanny.

The whisper spread outward from that point. There is nothing like a chorus for rumor. People who would not believe a High Priest if he said the sky was blue, and was able to produce signed affidavits to this effect from his white-haired old mother and three Vestal virgins, would trust just about anything whispered darkly behind their hand by a complete stranger in a pub.

A cockatoo spun around and pulled the mask off a parrot . . .

Bucket sobbed. This was worse than the day the buttermilk exploded. This was worse than the flash heatwave that had led a whole warehouseful of Lancre Extra Strong to riot.

The opera had turned into a *pantomime*.

The audience was *laughing*.

About the only character still with a mask on was Señor Basilica, who was watching the struggling chorus with as much aloof amazement as his own mask could convey—and this, amazingly enough, was quite a lot.

"Oh, no . . ." moaned Bucket. "We'll never live it

down! He'll never come back! It'll be all over the opera circuit and no one will ever want to come here ever again!"

"Ever again wha'?" mumbled a voice behind him.

Bucket turned. "Oh, Señor Basilica," he said. "Didn't see you there . . . I was just thinking, I do hope you don't think this is typical!"

Señor Basilica stared through him, swaying slightly from side to side. He was wearing a torn shirt.

"Summon . . ." he said.

"I'm sorry?"

"Summon . . . summon hit me onna head," said the tenor. "Wanna glassa water pliss . . ."

"But you're . . . just about . . . to . . . sing . . . aren't you?" said Bucket. He grabbed the stunned man by the collar to pull him closer, but this simply meant that he dragged himself off the floor, bringing his shoes about level with Basilica's knees. "Tell me . . . you're out there . . . on the stage . . . please!!!"

Even in his stunned state, Enrico Basilica a.k.a. Henry Slugg recognized what might be called the essential dichotomy of the statement. He stuck to what he knew.

"Summon bashed me inna corridor . . ." he volunteered.

"That's not you out there?"

Basilica blinked heavily. "'M not me?"

"You're going to sing the famous duet in a moment!!!"

Another thought staggered through Basilica's abused skull. "'M I?" he said "'S good . . .'ll look forwa' to that. Ne'er had a chance to hear me befo' . . ."

He gave a happy little sigh and fell full-length backward.

Bucket leaned against a pillar for support. Then his brow furrowed and, in the best traditions of the extended double take, he stared at the fallen tenor and counted to one on his fingers. Then he turned toward the stage and counted to two.

He could feel a fourth exclamation mark coming on any time now.

The Enrico Basilica onstage turned his mask this way and that. Stage right, Bucket was whispering to a group of stagehands. Stage left, André the secret pianist was waiting. A large troll loomed next to him.

The fat red singer walked to center stage as the prelude to the duet began. The audience settled down again. Fun and games among the chorus was all very well—it might even be in the plot—but this was what they'd paid for. This was what it was all about.

Agnes stared at him as Christine walked toward him. Now she could see he wasn't right. Oh, he was fat, in a pillow-up-your-shirt sort of way, but he didn't move like Basilica. Basilica moved lightly on his feet, as fat men often do, giving the effect of a barely tethered balloon.

She glanced at Nanny, who was also watching him carefully. She couldn't see Granny Weatherwax anywhere. That probably meant she was really close.

The expectancy of the audience dragged at them all. Ears opened like petals. The fourth wall of the stage, the big black sucking darkness outside, was a well of silence begging to be filled up.

Christine was walking toward him quite unconcerned. Christine would walk into a dragon's mouth if it had a sign on it saying "Totally harmless, I promise you" . . . at least, if it was printed in large, easy-to-understand letters.

No one seemed to want to *do* anything.

It *was* a famous duet. And a beautiful one. Agnes ought to know. She'd been singing it all last night.

Christine took the false Basilica's hand and, as the opening bars of the duet began, opened her mouth—

"Stop right there!"

Agnes put everything she could into it. The chandelier tinkled.

The orchestra went silent in a skid of wheezes and twangs.

In a fading of chords and a dying of echoes, the show stopped.

Walter Plinge sat in the candlelit gloom under the stage, his hands resting on his lap. It was not often that Walter Plinge had nothing to do, but, when he did have nothing to do, he did nothing.

He liked it down here. It was familiar. The sounds of the opera filtered through. They were muffled, but that didn't matter. Walter knew all the words, every note of music, every step of every dance. He needed the actual performances only in the same way that a clock needs its tiny little escapement mechanism; it kept him ticking nicely.

Mrs. Plinge had taught him to read using the old programs. That's how he knew he was part of it all. But he knew that anyway. He'd cut what teeth he had on a helmet with horns on it. The first bed he could remember was the very same trampoline used by Dame Gigli in the infamous Bouncing Gigli incident.

Walter Plinge lived opera. He breathed its songs, painted its scenery, lit its fires, washed its floors and shined its shoes. Opera filled up places in Walter Plinge that might otherwise have been empty.

And now the show had stopped.

But all the energy, all the raw pent-up emotion that is dammed up behind a show—all the screaming, the fears, the hopes, the desires—flew on, like a body hurled from the wreckage.

The terrible momentum smashed into Walter Plinge like a tidal wave hitting a teacup.

It propelled him out of his chair and flung him against the crumbling scenery.

He slid down and rolled into a twitching heap on the floor, clapping his hands over his ears to shut out the sudden, unnatural silence.

A shape stepped out of the shadows.

Granny Weatherwax had never heard of psychiatry and would have had no truck with it even if she had. There are some arts too black even for a witch. She practiced headology—practiced, in fact, until she was very good at it. And though there may be some superficial similarities between a psychiatrist and a headologist, there is a huge practical difference. A psychiatrist, dealing with a man who fears he is being followed by a large and terrible monster, will endeavor to convince him that monsters don't exist. Granny Weatherwax would simply give him a chair to stand on and a very heavy stick.

"Stand up, Walter Plinge," she said.

Walter stood up, staring straight ahead of him.

"It's stopped! It's stopped! It's *bad luck* to stop the show!" he said hoarsely.

"Someone better start it again," said Granny.

"You can't stop the show! It's the *show*!"

"Yes. Someone better start it again, Walter Plinge."

Walter didn't appear to notice her. He pawed aimlessly through his stack of music and ran his hands through the drifts of old programs. One hand touched the keyboard of the harmonium and played a few neurotic notes.

"Wrong to stop. Show must go on . . ."

"Mr. Salzella is trying to stop the show, isn't he, Walter?"

Walter's head shot up. He stared straight ahead of him.

"You haven't seen anything, Walter Plinge!" he said, in a voice so like Salzella's that even Granny raised an eyebrow. "And if you tell lies, you will be locked up and I'll see to it that there's big trouble for your mother!"

Granny nodded.

"He found out about the Ghost, didn't he?" she said. "The Ghost who comes out when he has a mask on . . . doesn't he, Walter Plinge? And the man thought: I can use that. And when it's time for the Ghost to be caught . . . well, there *is* a Ghost that can be caught. And the *best* thing is that everyone will believe it. They'll feel bad about themselves, maybe, but they'll believe it. Even Walter Plinge won't be certain, 'cos his mind's all tangled up."

Granny took a deep breath. "It's tangled, but it *ain't* twisted." There was a sigh. "Well, matters will have to resolve themselves. There's nothing else for it."

She removed her hat and fished around in the point. "I don't mind tellin' you this, Walter," she said, "because you won't understand and you won't remember. There was a wicked ole witch once called Black Aliss. She was an unholy terror. There's never been one worse or more powerful. Until now. Because I could spit in her eye and steal her teeth, see. Because she didn't know Right from Wrong, so she got all twisted up and that was the end of her.

"The trouble is, you see, that if you *do* know Right from Wrong you can't choose Wrong. You just can't do it and live. So . . . if I was a bad witch I could make Mister Salzella's muscles turn against his bones and break them where he stood . . . if I was bad. I could do things inside his head, change the shape he thinks he is, and he'd be down on what'd been his knees and *begging* to be turned into a frog . . . if I was bad. I could leave him with a mind like a scrambled egg, listening to colors and hearing smells . . . if I was bad. Oh, yes." There was another sigh, deeper and more heartfelt. "But I can't do none of that stuff. That wouldn't be Right."

She gave a deprecating little chuckle. And if Nanny Ogg had been listening, she would have resolved as follows: that no maddened cackle from Black Aliss of infamous memory, no evil little giggle from some crazed vampyre whose morals were worse than his spelling, no side-splitting guffaw from the most inventive torturer, was quite so unnerving as a happy little chuckle from a Granny Weatherwax about to do what's best.

From the point of her hat Granny withdrew a

paper-thin mask. It was a simple face—smooth, white, basic. There were semicircular holes for the eyes. It was neither happy nor sad.

She turned it over in her hands. Walter seemed to stop breathing.

"Simple thing, ain't it?" said Granny. "Looks beautiful, but it's really just a simple bit of stuff, just like any other mask. Wizards could poke at this for a year and still say there was nothing magic about it, eh? Which just shows how much *they* know, Walter Plinge."

She tossed it to him. He caught it hungrily and pulled it over his face.

Then he stood up in one flowing movement, moving like a dancer.

"I don't know what you are when you're behind the mask," said Granny, "but 'ghost' is just another word for 'spirit' and 'spirit' is just another word for 'soul.' Off you go, Walter Plinge."

The masked figure did not move.

"I meant . . . off you go, Ghost. The show *must* go on."

The mask nodded, and darted away.

Granny slapped her hands together like the crack of doom.

"Right! Let's do some good!" she said, to the universe at large.

Everyone was looking at her.

This was a moment in time, a little point between the past and future, when a second could stretch out and out . . .

Agnes felt the blush begin. It was heading for her face like the revenge of the volcano god. When it got there, she knew, it would be all over for her.

You'll apologize, Perdita jeered.

"Shut up!" shouted Agnes.

She strode forward before the echo had had time to come back from the farther ends of the auditorium, and wrenched at the red mask.

The entire chorus came in on cue. This was opera, after all. The show had stopped, but opera continued . . .

"*Salzella!*"

He grabbed Agnes, clamping his hand over her mouth. His other hand flew to his belt and drew his sword.

It wasn't a stage prop. The blade hissed through the air as he spun to face the chorus.

"Oh *dear* oh *dear* oh *dear*," he said. "How extremely *operatic* of me. And now, I fear, I shall have to take this poor girl hostage. It's the appropriate thing to do, isn't it?"

He looked around triumphantly. The audience watched in fascinated silence.

"Isn't anyone going to say 'You won't get away with this'?" he said.

"You won't get away with this," said André, from the wings.

"You have the place surrounded, I have no doubt?" said Salzella brightly.

"Yes, we have the place surrounded."

Christine screamed and fainted.

Salzella smiled even more brightly.

"Ah, now *there's* someone operatic!" he said. "But,

you see, I *am* going to get away with it, because I *don't* think operatically. Myself and this young lady here are going to go down to the cellars where I may, possibly, leave her unharmed. I doubt very much that you have the cellars surrounded. Even I don't know everywhere they go, and believe me my knowledge is really rather extensive—"

He paused. Agnes tried to break free, but his grip tightened around her neck.

"By now," he said, "someone should have said: 'But *why*, Salzella?' Honestly, do I have to do *everything* around here?"

Bucket realized he had his mouth open. "That's what I was *going* to say!" he said.

"Ah, good. Well, in that case, I should say something like: Because I wanted to. Because I rather like money, you see. But more than that"—he took a deep breath—"I really hate opera. I don't want to get needlessly excited about this, but opera, I am afraid, really is dreadful. And I have had *enough*. So, while I have the stage, let me tell you what a wretched, self-adoring, totally unrealistic, worthless art form it is, what a terrible waste of fine music, what a—"

There was a whirr off on one side of the stage. The skirts of costumes began to flap. Dust flew up.

André looked around. Beside him, the wind machine had started up. The handle was turning by itself.

Salzella turned to see what everyone was staring at.

The Ghost had dropped lightly onto the stage. His opera cloak billowed around him . . . operatically.

He bowed slightly, and drew his sword.

"But you're dea—" Salzella began. "Oh, *yes*! A ghost of a Ghost! Totally unbelievable and an offense against common sense, in the best operatic tradition! This was really too much to hope for!"

He thrust Agnes away, and nodded happily.

"That's what opera does to a man," he said. "It rots the brain, you see, and I doubt whether he had too much of that to begin with. It drives people mad. Mad, d'you hear me, mad!! Ahem. They act irrationally. Don't you think I've watched you, over the years? It's like a hothouse for insanity!! D'you hear me? Insanity!!"

He and the Ghost began to circle one another.

"You don't know what it has been like, I assure you, being the only sane man in this madhouse!! You believe *anything*!! You'd prefer to believe a ghost can be in two places at once than that there might simply be two people!! Even Pounder thought he could blackmail me!! Poking around in places that he shouldn't!! Well, of course, I *had* to kill him for his own good. This place sends even rat catchers mad!! And Undershaft . . . well, why couldn't he have forgotten his glasses like he usually did, eh?"

He lashed out with his sword. The Ghost parried.

"And now I'll fight your Ghost," he said, moving forward in a flurry of strokes, "and you'll notice that our Ghost here doesn't actually know how to fence . . . because he only knows stage fencing, you see . . . where the whole point, of course, is simply to hit the other fellow's sword with a suitably impressive metallic noise . . . so that you can die very dramatically merely because he's carefully thrust his sword under your armpit . . ."

The Ghost was forced to retreat under the on-slaught, until he fell backward over the unconscious body of Christine.

"See?" said Salzella. "That's what comes of be-lieving in opera!!!"

He reached down quickly and tugged the mask off Walter Plinge's face.

"Really, Walter!!! You *are* a bad boy!!!!"

"Sorry Mr. Salzella!"

"Look how everyone's staring!!!!"

"Sorry Mr. Salzella!"

The mask crumpled in Salzella's fingers. He let the fragments tumble to the floor. Then he pulled Walter to his feet.

"See, company? *This* is your luck!!! *This* is your Ghost!!! Without his mask he's just an idiot who can hardly tie his shoelaces!!! Ahahaha!!!! Ahem. It's all your fault, Walter Plinge . . ."

"Yes Mr. Salzella!"

"*No.*"

Salzella looked around.

A voice said, *"No one would believe Walter Plinge. Even Walter Plinge gets confused about the things Walter Plinge sees. Even his mother was afraid he might have murdered people. People could accept just about anything of a Walter Plinge."*

There was a steady tapping noise.

The trapdoor opened beside Salzella.

A pointy hat appeared slowly, followed by the rest of Granny Weatherwax, with her arms folded. She glared at Salzella as the floor clicked into place. Her foot stopped tapping on the boards.

"Well, well," he said. "Lady Esmerelda, eh?"

"I'm stoppin' bein' a lady, Mr. Salzella."

He glanced up at the pointy hat. "So you are a witch instead?"

"Yes, indeed."

"A bad witch, no doubt?"

"Worse."

"But *this*," said Salzella, "is a sword. Everyone knows witches can't magic iron and steel. Get out of my way!!!"

The sword hissed down.

Granny thrust out her hand. There was a blur of flesh and steel and . . .

. . . she held the sword, by the blade.

"Tell you what, Mr. Salzella," she said, levelly, "it *ought* to be Walter Plinge who finishes this, eh? It's him you harmed, apart from the ones you murdered, o' course. You didn't need to do that. But you wore a mask, didn't you? There's a kind of magic in masks. Masks conceal one face, but they reveal another. The one that only comes out in darkness. I bet you could do just what you *liked*, behind a mask . . . ?"

Salzella blinked at her. He pulled on his sword, tugged hard on a sharp blade held in an unprotected hand.

There was a groan from several members of the chorus. Granny grinned. Her knuckles whitened as she redoubled her grip.

She turned her head toward Walter Plinge. "Put your mask on, Walter."

Everyone looked down at the crumpled cardboard on the stage.

"Don't have one anymore Mistress Weatherwax!"

Granny followed his gaze. "Oh deary, deary me,"

she said. "Well, I can see we shall have to do something about that. Look at me, Walter."

He did as he was told. Granny's eyes half-closed. "You . . . trust *Perdita*, don't you, Walter?"

"Yes Mistress Weatherwax!"

"That's good, because she's got a new mask for you, Walter Plinge. A magic one. It's just like your old one, d'you see, only you wear it under your skin and you don't have to take it off and no one but you will ever need to know it's there. Got it, Perdita?"

"But I—" Agnes began.

"*Got it?*"

"Er . . . oh, yes. Here it is. Yes. I've got it in my hand." She waved an empty hand vaguely.

"You're holding it the wrong way up, my girl!"

"Oh. Sorry."

"Well? Give it to him, then."

"Er. Yes."

Agnes advanced on Walter.

"Now you take it, Walter," said Granny, still gripping the sword.

"Yes Mistress Weatherwax . . ."

He reached out toward Agnes. As he did so, she was sure that, just for a moment, there was a faint pressure on her fingertips.

"*Well?* Put it on!"

Walter looked uncertain.

"You do *believe* there's a mask there, don't you, Walter?" Granny demanded. "Perdita's sensible and *she* knows an invisible mask when she sees one."

He nodded, slowly, and raised his hands to his face.

And Agnes was sure that he'd somehow come into focus. Almost certainly nothing had happened that could be measured with any kind of instrument, any more than you could weigh an idea or sell good fortune by the yard. But Walter stood up, smiling faintly.

"Good," said Granny. She stared at Salzella.

"I reckon you two should fight again," she said. "But it can't be said I'm unfair. I expect *you've* got a Ghost mask somewhere? Mrs. Ogg saw you waving it, see. And she's not as gormless as she looks—"

"Thank you," said a fat ballerina.

"—so she thought, how could people still say afterward that they'd seen the Ghost? 'Cos that's how you recognize the Ghost, by his mask. So there's *two* masks."

Under her gaze, telling himself that he could resist any time he wanted to, Salzella reached into his jacket and produced his own mask.

"Put it on, then." She let go of the sword. "Then who *you* are can fight who *he* is."

Down in the pit, the percussionist stared as his sticks rose and began a drum roll.

"Are you doing that, Gytha?" said Granny Weatherwax.

"I thought *you* were."

"It's opera, then. The show must go on."

Walter Plinge raised his sword. The masked Salzella glanced from him to Granny, and then lunged.

The swords met.

It was, Agnes realized, stage-fighting. The swords clashed and rattled as the fighters danced back and forth across the stage. Walter wasn't trying to hit Salzella. Every thrust was parried. Every opportunity to strike back, as the director of music grew more angry, was ignored.

"This isn't fighting!" Salzella shouted, standing back. "This is—"

Walter thrust.

Salzella staggered away, until he cannoned into Nanny Ogg. He lurched sideways. Then he staggered forward, dropped onto one knee, got unsteadily to his feet again, and staggered into the center of the stage.

"Whatever happens," he gasped, wrenching off his mask, "it can't be worse than a season of opera!!!! I don't mind where I'm going so long as there are no fat men pretending to be thin boys, and no huge long songs which everyone says are so beautiful just because they don't understand what the hell they're actually about!!!! Ah—Ah-argh . . ."

He slumped to the floor.

"But Walter didn't—" Agnes began.

"Shut up," said Nanny Ogg, out of the corner of her mouth.

"But he *hasn't*—" Bucket began.

"Incidentally, *another* thing I can't stand about opera," said Salzella, rising to his feet and reeling crabwise toward the curtains, "are the plots. They make no sense!! And no one ever says so!!! And the quality of the acting? It's nonexistent!! Everyone stands around watching the person who's singing. Ye gods, it's going to be a relief to put that behind . . . ah . . . argh . . ."

He slumped to the floor.

"Is that it?" said Nanny.

"Shouldn't think so," said Granny Weatherwax.

"As for the people who attend opera," said Salzella, struggling upright again and staggering sideways, "I think I just possibly hate them even worse!!! They're so *ignorant*!!! There's hardly a one of them out there who knows the first thing about music!!! They go on about *tunes*!!! They spend all day endeavoring to be sensible human beings, and then they walk in here and they leave their intelligence on a nail by the door—"

"Then why didn't you just leave?" snapped Agnes. "If you'd stolen all this money why didn't you just go away somewhere, if you hated it so much?"

Salzella stared at her while swaying back and forth. His mouth opened and shut once or twice, as if he were trying out unfamiliar words.

"Leave?" he managed. "*Leave?* Leave the *opera*? . . . Argh argh argh . . ."

He hit the floor again.

André prodded the fallen director. "Is he dead yet?" he said.

"How can he be dead?" said Agnes. "Good grief, can't anyone see that—?"

"You know what *really* gets me down," said Salzella, rising to his knees, "is the way that in opera everyone takes such a *long*!!!!! . . . time!!!!! . . . to!!!!! . . . argh . . . argh . . . argh . . ."

He keeled over.

The company waited for a while. The audience held its collective breath.

Nanny Ogg poked him with a boot. "Yep, that's about it. Looks like he's gone down for the last curtain call," she said.

"But Walter *didn't* stab him!" said Agnes. "Why

won't anyone listen? Look, the sword isn't even sticking in him! It's just tucked between his body and his arm, for heaven's sake!"

"Yes," said Nanny. "I s'pose, really, it's a shame he dint notice that." She scratched at her shoulder. "Here, these ballet dresses really tickle . . ."

"But he's dead!"

"Got a bit overexcited, perhaps," said Nanny, fidgeting with a strap.

"Overexcited?"

"Frantic. You know these artistic types. Well, you are one, of course."

"He's *really* dead?" said Bucket.

"Seems to be," said Granny. "One of the best operatic deaths ever, I wouldn't mind betting."

"That's terrible!!" Bucket grabbed the former Salzella by the collar and hauled him upright. "Where's my money? Come on, out with it, tell me what you've done with my money!!! I don't *hear* you!!!! He's not saying anything!!!"

"That's on account of being dead," said Granny. "Not talkative, the deceased. As a rule."

"Well, you're a witch!!! Can't you do that thing with the cards and the glasses?"

"Well, yes . . . we could have a poker game," said Nanny. "Good idea."

"The money is in the cellars," said Granny. "Walter'll show you."

Walter Plinge clicked his heels. "Certainly," he said. "I would be glad to."

Bucket stared. It was Walter Plinge's voice and it was coming out of Walter Plinge's face, but both face and voice were different. Subtly different. The voice had lost the uncertain, frightened edge. The lopsided look had gone from the face.

"Good grief," Bucket murmured, and let go of Salzella's coat. There was a thump.

"And since you're going to be needing a new director of music," said Granny, "you could do worse than look to Walter here."

"*Walter?*"

"He knows everything there is to know about opera," said Granny. "And everything about the Opera House, too."

"You should see the music he's written—" said Nanny.

"Walter? Musical director?" said Bucket.

"—stuff you can really hum—"

"Yes, I think you might be surprised," said Granny.

"—there's one with lots of sailors dancin' around singin' about how there's no women—"

"This *is* Walter, isn't it?"

"—and then some bloke called Les who's miserable all the time—"

"Oh, this is Walter," said Granny. "The same person."

"—and there's one, hah, with all cats all leapin' around all singin', that was fun," Nanny burbled. "Can't imagine how he thought up that one—"

Bucket scratched his chin. He was feeling light-headed enough as it was.

"And he's trustworthy," said Granny. "And he's *honest.* And he knows all about the Opera House, as I said. And . . . where everything is . . ."

That was enough for Mr. Bucket. "Want to be director of music, Walter?" he said.

"Thank you, Mr. Bucket," said Walter Plinge. "I should like that very much. But what about cleaning the privies?"

"Sorry?"

"I won't have to stop doing them, will I? I've just got them working right."

"Oh? Right. Really?" Mr. Bucket's eyes crossed for a moment. "Well, fine. You can sing while you're doing it, if you like," he added generously. "And I won't even cut your pay! I'll . . . I'll raise it! Six . . . no, *seven* shiny dollars!"

Walter rubbed his face thoughtfully. "Mr. Bucket . . ."

"Yes, Walter?"

"I think . . . you paid Mr. Salzella forty shiny dollars . . ."

Bucket turned to Granny. "Is he some kind of monster?"

"You just listen to the stuff he's been writin'," said Nanny. "Amazin' songs, not even in foreign. Will you just look at this stuff . . .'scuse me . . ."

She turned her back on the audience—

—twingtwangtwong—

—and twirled round again with a wad of music paper in her hands.

"I know good music when I sees it," she said, handing it to Bucket and pointing excitedly at extracts. "It's got blobs and curly bits all over it, see?"

"*You* have been writing this music?" said Bucket to Walter. "Which is unaccountably warm?"

"Indeed, Mr. Bucket."

"In *my* time?"

"There's a lovely song here," said Nanny, " 'Don't

cry for me, Genua.' It's very sad. That reminds me, I'd better go and see if Mrs. Plinge has come rou . . . has woken up. I may have overdone it a bit on the scumble.' She ambled off, twitching at bits of her costume, and nudged a fascinated ballerina. "This balleting doesn't half make you sweat, don't you find?"

"Excuse me, there's something I didn't quite believe," said André. He took Salzella's sword and tested the blade carefully.

"Ow!" he shouted.

"Sharp, is it?" said Agnes.

"Yes!" André sucked his thumb. "She caught it in her *hand*."

"She's a witch," said Agnes.

"But it was steel! I thought no one could magic steel! Everyone *knows* that."

"I wouldn't be too impressed if I was you," said Agnes sourly. "It was probably just some kind of trick . . ."

André turned to Granny. "Your hand isn't even scratched! How did . . . you . . ."

Her stare held him in its sapphire vice for a moment. When he turned away he looked vaguely puzzled, like a man who can't remember where he's just put something down.

"I hope he didn't hurt Christine," he mumbled. "Why isn't anyone seeing to her?"

"Probably because she makes sure she screams and faints before anything happens," said Perdita, through Agnes.

André set off across the stage. Agnes trailed after him. A couple of dancers were kneeling down next to Christine.

"It'd be terrible if anything happened to her," said André.

"Oh . . . yes."

"Everyone says she's showing such promise . . ."

Walter stepped up beside him. "Yes. We should get her somewhere," he said. His voice was clipped and precise.

Agnes felt the bottom start to drop out of her world. "Yes, but . . . *you* know it was me doing the singing."

"Oh, yes . . . yes, of course . . ." said André, awkwardly. "But . . . well . . . this is opera . . . you know . . ."

Walter took her hand.

"But it was *me* you taught!" she said desperately.

"Then you were *very* good," said Walter. "I suspect she will never be quite that good, even with many months of my tuition. But, Perdita, have you ever heard of the words 'star quality'?"

"Is it the same as *talent*?" snapped Agnes.

"It is rarer."

She stared at him. His face, however it was controlled now, was quite handsome in the glare of the footlights.

She pulled her hand free. "I liked you better when you were Walter Plinge," she said.

Agnes turned away, and felt Granny Weatherwax's gaze on her. She was sure it was a mocking gaze.

"Er . . . we ought to get Christine into Mr. Bucket's office," André said.

This seemed to break some sort of spell.

"Yes, indeed!!!" said Bucket. "And we can't leave Mr. Salzella corpsing onstage, either. You two, you'd better take him backstage. The rest of you . . . well, it was nearly over anyway . . . er . . . that's it. The . . . opera is over . . ."

"Walter Plinge!"

Nanny Ogg entered, supporting Mrs. Plinge. Walter's mother fixed him with a beady gaze. "Have you been a bad boy?"

Mr. Bucket walked over to her and patted her hand. "I think you'd better come along to my office, too," he said. He handed the sheaf of music to André, who opened it at random.

André gave it a glance, and then stared. "Hey . . . this is *good*," he said.

"Is it?"

André looked at another page. "Good heavens!"

"What? What?" said Bucket.

"I've just never . . . I mean, even I can see . . . tum-ti TUM tum-tum . . . yes . . . Mr. Bucket, you do know this isn't opera? There's music and . . . yes . . . danc-ing and singing all right, but it's not opera. Not opera at all. A long way from opera."

"How far? You don't mean . . ." Bucket hesitated, savoring the idea, "you don't mean that it's just pos-sible that you put music *in* and you get money *out*?"

André hummed a few bars. "This could very well be the case, Mr. Bucket."

Bucket beamed. He put one arm around André and the other around Walter. "Good!!!!!" he said. "This calls for a very lar . . . for a medium-sized drink!!!!!"

One by one, or in groups, the singers and dancers left the stage. And the witches and Agnes were left alone.

"Is that *it*?" said Agnes.

"Not quite yet," said Granny.

Someone staggered onto the stage. A kindly hand had bandaged Enrico Basilica's head, and presumably another kindly hand had given him the plate of spaghetti he was holding. Mild concussion still seemed to have him in its grip. He blinked at the witches and then spoke like a man who'd lost his hold on immediate events and so was clinging hard to more ancient considerations.

"Summon give me some 'ghetti," he said.

"That's nice," said Nanny.

"Hah! 'Ghetti is fine for them as likes it . . . but not me! Hah! Yes!" He turned and peered muzzily at the darkness of the audience.

"You know what I'm goin' to do? You know what I'm goin' to do now? I'm sayin' goodbye to Enrico Basilica! Oh yes! He's chewed his last tentacle! I'm goin' to go right out now and have eight pints of Turbot's Really Odd. Yes! And probably a sausage ina bun! And then I'm goin' down to the music hall to hear Nellie Stamp sing 'A Winkle's No Use if You Don't Have a Pin'—and if I sing again here it's goin' to be under the proud old name of Henry Slugg, do you hear—?"

There was a shriek from somewhere in the audience. "Henry Slugg?"

"Er . . . yes?"

"I *thought* it was you! You've grown a beard and stuffed a haystack down your trousers but, I thought, under that little mask, that's my Henry, that was!"

Henry Slugg shaded his eyes from the footlights' glare.

". . . Angeline?"

"Oh, no!" said Agnes, wearily. "This sort of thing *does not* happen."

"Happens in the theater all the time," said Nanny Ogg.

"It certainly does," said Granny. "It's only a mercy he doesn't have a long-lost twin brother."

There was the sound of much scuffling in the audience. Someone was climbing along a row, dragging someone else.

"Mother!" came a voice from the gloom. "What do you think you are doing?"

"You just come with me, young Henry!"

"Mother, we can't go up on the stage . . . !"

Henry Slugg frisbeed the plate into the wings, clambered down from the stage and heaved himself over the edge of the orchestra pit, assisted by a couple of violinists.

They met at the first row of seats. Agnes could just hear their voices.

"I *meant* to come back. You know that!"

"I wanted to wait but, what with one thing and another . . . especially one thing. Come here, young Henry . . ."

"Mother, *what* is happening?"

"Son . . . you know I always said your father was Mr. Lawsy the eel juggler?"

"Yes, of—"

"Please, both of you, come back to my dressing room! I can see we've got such a lot to talk about."

"Oh, yes. A lot . . ."

Agnes watched them go. The audience, who could spot opera even if it wasn't being sung, applauded.

"All right," she said. "And *now* is it the end?"

"Nearly," said Granny.

"Did you do something to everyone's heads?"

"No, but I felt like smacking a few," said Nanny.

"But no one said 'thank you' or anything!"

"Often the case," said Granny.

"Too busy thinking about the next performance," said Nanny. "The show must go on," she added.

"That's . . . that's madness!"

"It's opera. I noticed that even Mr. Bucket's caught it, too," said Nanny. "And that young André has been rescued from being a policeman, if I'm any judge."

"But what about *me*?"

"Oh, them as *makes* the endings don't *get* them," said Granny. She brushed an invisible speck of dust off her shoulder.

"I expect we'd better be gettin' along, Gytha," she said, turning her back on Agnes. "Early start tomorrow."

Nanny walked forward, shading her eyes as she stared out into the dark maw of the auditorium.

"The audience haven't gone, you know," she said. "They're still sitting out there."

Granny joined her, and peered into the gloom. "I can't imagine why," she said. "He did *say* the opera's over . . ."

They turned and looked at Agnes, who was standing in the center of the stage and glowering at nothing.

"Feeling a bit angry?" said Nanny. "Only to be expected."

"Yes!"

"Feeling that everything's happened for other people and not for you?"

"*Yes!*"

"But," said Granny Weatherwax, "look at it like this: what's Christine got to look forward to? She'll just become a singer. Stuck in a little world. Oh, maybe she'll be good enough to get a little fame, but one day the voice'll crack and that's the end of her life. *You* have got a choice. You can either be on the stage, just a performer, just going through the lines . . . or you can be outside it, and know how the script works, where the scenery hangs, and where the trapdoors are. Isn't that better?"

"*No!*"

The infuriating thing about Nanny Ogg and Granny Weatherwax, Agnes thought later, was the way they sometimes acted in tandem, without exchanging a word. Of course, there were plenty of other things—the way they never thought that meddling was meddling if *they* did it; the way they automatically assumed that everyone else's business was their own; the way they went through life in a straight line; the way, in fact, that they arrived in any situation and immediately started to change it. Compared to that, acting on unspoken agreement was a mere minor annoyance, but it was here and up close.

They walked toward her, and each laid a hand on her shoulder.

"Feeling *angry*?" said Granny.

"*Yes!*"

"I should let it out then, if I was you," said Nanny.

Agnes shut her eyes, clenched her fists, opened her mouth and screamed.

It started low. Plaster dust drifted down from the

ceiling. The prisms on the chandelier chimed gently as they shook.

It rose, passing quickly through the mysterious pitch at fourteen cycles per second where the human spirit begins to feel distinctly uncomfortable about the universe and the place in it of the bowels. Small items around the Opera House vibrated off shelves and smashed on the floor.

The note climbed, rang like a bell, climbed again. In the Pit, all the violin strings snapped, one by one.

As the tone rose, the crystal prisms shook in the chandelier. In the bar, champagne corks fired a salvo. Ice jingled and shattered in its bucket. A line of wine-glasses joined in the chorus, blurred around the rims, and then exploded like hazardous thistle down with attitude.

There were harmonics and echoes that caused strange effects. In the dressing rooms the No. 3 greasepaint melted. Mirrors cracked, filling the ballet school with a million fractured images.

Dust rose, insects fell. In the stones of the Opera House tiny particles of quartz danced briefly . . .

Then there was silence, broken by the occasional thud and tinkle.

Nanny grinned.

"Ah," she said, "*Now* the opera's over."

Salzella opened his eyes.

The stage was empty, and dark, and nevertheless brilliantly lit. That is, a huge shadowless light was streaming from some unseen source and yet, apart from Salzella himself, there was nothing for it to illuminate.

Footsteps sounded in the distance. Their owner took some time to arrive, but when he stepped into the liquid air around Salzella he seemed to burst into flame.

He wore red: a red suit with red lace, a red cloak, red shoes with ruby buckles, and a broad-brimmed red hat with a huge red feather. He even walked with a long red stick, bedecked with red ribbons. But for someone who had taken such meticulous trouble with his costume, he'd been remiss in the matter of his mask. It was a crude one of a skull, such as might be bought in any theatrical shop—Salzella could even see the string.

"Where did everyone go?" Salzella demanded. Unpleasant recent memories were beginning to bubble up in his mind. He couldn't quite recall them clearly at the moment, but the taste of them was bad.

The figure said nothing.

"Where's the orchestra? What happened to the audience?"

There was a barely perceptible shrug from the tall red figure.

Salzella began to notice other details. What he had thought was the stage seemed slightly gritty underfoot. The ceiling above him was a long way away, perhaps as far away as anything could be, and was filled with cold, hard points of light.

"I asked you a question!"

THREE QUESTIONS, IN FACT.

The words turned up on the inside of Salzella's ears with no suggestion that they had had to travel like normal sound.

"You didn't answer me!"

SOME THINGS YOU HAVE TO WORK OUT FOR YOUR-
SELF, AND THIS IS ONE OF THEM, BELIEVE ME.

"Who *are* you? You're not a member of the cast, I
know that! Take off that mask!"

AS YOU WISH. I DO LIKE TO GET INTO THE SPIRIT
OF THE THING.

The figure removed its mask.

"And now take off that other mask!" said Salzella,
as the frozen fingers of dread rose through him.

Death touched a secret spring on the stick. A blade
shot out, so thin that it was transparent, its edge
glittering blue as air molecules were sliced into their
component atoms.

AH, he said, raising the scythe. THERE I THINK
YOU HAVE ME.

It was dark in the cellars, but Nanny Ogg had walked
alone in the strange caverns under Lancre and
through the nighttime forests with Granny Weatherwax. Darkness held no fears for an Ogg.

She struck a match.

"Greebo?"

People had been tramping to and fro for hours.
The darkness wasn't private anymore. It had taken
quite a lot of people to carry all the money, for a
start. Up until the end of the opera, there *had* been
something mysterious about these cellars. Now they
were just . . . well . . . damp underground rooms.
Something that had lived here had moved on.

Her foot rattled a piece of pottery.

She grunted as she went down on one knee. Spilled
mud and shards of broken pot littered the floor. Here

and there, unrooted and snapped, were some un-heeded pieces of dead twig.

Only some kind of fool would have stuck bits of wood in pots of mud far underground and expected anything to happen.

Nanny picked one up and sniffed it tentatively. It smelled of mud. And nothing else.

She'd have liked to have known how it had been done. Just professional interest, of course. And she knew she never would, now. Walter was a busy man now, up in the light. And, for something to begin, other things had to end.

"We all wears a mask of one sort or another," she said to the damp air. "No sense in upsetting things now, eh . . ."

The coach didn't leave until seven o'clock in the morning. By Lancre standards that was practically midday. The witches got there early.

"I was hoping to shop for a few souvenirs," said Nanny, stamping her feet on the cobbles to keep warm. "For the kiddies."

"No time," said Granny Weatherwax.

"Not that it would have made any difference on account of me not having any money to buy 'em with," Nanny went on.

"Not my fault if you fritter your money away," said Granny.

"I don't recall having a single chance to frit."

"Money's only useful for the things it can do."

"Well, yes. I could've done with having some new boots, for a start."

Nanny jiggled up and down a bit, and whistled around her tooth.

"Nice of Mrs. Palm to let us stay there gratis," she said.

"Yes."

"O' course, I helped out playin' the piano and tellin' jokes."

"An added bonus," said Granny, nodding.

"An' of course there was all those little nibbles I prepared. With the Special Party Dip."

"Yes indeed," said Granny, poker-faced. "Mrs. Palm was saying only this morning that she's thinking of retiring next year."

Nanny looked up and down the street again.

"I 'spect young Agnes'll be turning up any minute now," she said.

"I really couldn't say," said Granny haughtily.

"Not as though there's much for her here, after all."

Granny sniffed. "That's up to her, I'm sure."

"Everyone was very impressed, I reckon, when you caught that sword in your hand . . ."

Granny sighed. "Hah! Yes, I expect they were. They didn't think clearly, did they? People're just lazy. They never think: maybe she had something in her hand, a bit of metal or something. They don't think for a minute it was just a trick. They don't think there's always a perfectly good explanation if you look for it. They probably think it was some kind of magic."

"Yeah, but . . . you *didn't* have anything in your hand, did you?"

"That's not the point. I *might* have done." Granny

looked up and down the square. "Besides, you can't magic iron."

"That's very true. Not iron. Now, someone like ole Black Aliss, they could make their skin tougher than steel . . . but that's just an ole legend, I expect . . ."

"She could do it all right," said Granny. "But you can't go round messin' with cause and effect. That's what sent her mad, come the finish. She thought she could put herself outside of things like cause and effect. Well, you can't. You grab a sharp sword by the blade, you get hurt. World'd be a terrible place if people forgot that."

"*You* weren't hurt."

"Not my fault. I didn't have time."

Nanny blew on her hands. "One good thing, though," she said. "It's a blessing the chandelier never came down. I was worried about that soon as I saw it. Looks too dramatic for its own good, I thought. First thing I'd smash, if I was a loony."

"Yes."

"Haven't been able to find Greebo since last night."

"Good."

"He always turns up, though."

"Unfortunately."

There was a clatter as the coach swung around the corner.

It stopped.

Then the coachman tugged on the reins and it did a U-turn and disappeared again.

"Esme?" said Nanny, after a while.

"Yes?"

"There's a man and two horses peering at us around the corner." She raised her voice. "Come on,

I know you're there! Seven o'clock, this coach is supposed to leave! Did you get the tickets, Esme?"

"Me?"

"Ah," said Nanny uncertainly. "So . . . we haven't got eighty dollars for the tickets, then?"

"What've you got stuffed up your elastic?" said Granny as the coach advanced cautiously.

"Nothin' that is legal tender for travelin' purposes, I fear."

"Then . . . no, we can't afford tickets."

Nanny sighed. "Oh, well, I'll just have to use charm."

"It's going to be a long walk," said Granny.

The coach pulled up. Nanny looked up at the driver, and smiled innocently. "Good morning, my good sir!"

He gave her a slightly frightened but mainly suspicious look. "Is it?"

"We are desirous of traveling to Lancre but unfortunately we find ourselves a bit embarrassed in the knicker department."

"You are?"

"But we are witches and could prob'ly pay for our travel by, e.g., curing any embarrassing little ailments you may have."

The coachman frowned. "I ain't carrying you for nothing, old crone. And I haven't got any embarrassing little ailments!"

Granny stepped forward.

"How many would you like?" she said.

Rain rolled over the plains. It wasn't an impressive Ramtops thunderstorm but a lazy, persistent, low-cloud rain, like a fat fog. It had been following them all day.

The witches had the coach to themselves. Several people had opened the door while it had been waiting to leave, but for some reason had suddenly decided that today's travel plans didn't include a coach ride.

"Making good time," said Nanny, opening the curtains and peering out of the window.

"I expect the driver's in a hurry."

"Yes, I 'spect he is."

"Shut the window, though. It's getting wet in here."

"Righty-ho."

Nanny grabbed the strap and then suddenly poked her head out into the rain.

"Stop! Stop! Tell the man to stop!"

The coach slewed to a halt in a sheet of mud.

Nanny threw open the door. "I don't know, trying to walk home, and in this weather, too! You'll catch your death!"

Rain and fog rolled in through the open doorway. Then a bedraggled shape pulled itself over the sill and slunk under the seats, leaving small puddles behind it.

"Tryin' to be independent," said Nanny. "Bless 'im."

The coach got under way again. Granny stared out at the endless darkening fields and the relentless drizzle, and saw another figure toiling along in the mud by the road that would, eventually, reach Lancre. As the coach swept past, it drenched the walker in thin slurry.

"Yes, indeed. Being independent's a fine ambition," she said, drawing the curtains.

* * *

The trees were bare when Granny Weatherwax got back to her cottage.

Twigs and seeds had blown in under the door. Soot had fallen down the chimney. Her home, always somewhat organic, had grown a little closer to its roots in the clay.

There were things to do, so she did them. There were leaves to be swept, and the woodpile to be built up under the eaves. The wind sock behind the beehives, tattered by autumn storms, needed to be darned. Hay had to be got in for the goats. Apples had to be stored in the loft. The walls could do with another coat of whitewash.

But there was something that had to be done first. It'd make the other jobs a bit more difficult, but there was no help for that. You couldn't magic iron. And you couldn't grab a sword without being hurt. If that wasn't true, the world'd be all over the place.

Granny made herself some tea, and then boiled up the kettle again. She took a handful of herbs out of a box on the dresser, and dropped them in a bowl with the steaming water. She took a length of clean bandage out of a drawer and set it carefully on the table beside the bowl. She threaded an extremely sharp needle and laid needle and thread beside the bandage. She scooped a fingerful of greenish ointment out of a small tin, and smeared it on a square of lint.

That seemed to be it.

She sat down, and rested her arm on the table, palm-up.

"Well," she said, to no one in particular, "I reckon I've got time now."

* * *

The privy had to be moved. It was a job Granny preferred to do for herself. There was something incredibly satisfying in digging a very deep hole. It was *uncomplicated*. You knew where you were with a hole in the ground. Dirt didn't get strange ideas, or believe that people were honest because they had a steady gaze and a firm handshake. It just lay there, waiting for you to move it. And, after you'd done it, you could sit there in the lovely warm knowledge that it'd be months before you had to do it again.

It was while she was at the bottom of the hole that a shadow fell across it.

"Afternoon, Perdita," she said without looking up.

She lifted another shovelful to head-height and flung it over the edge.

"Come home for a visit, have you?" she said.

She rammed the shovel into the clay at the bottom of the hole again, winced, and forced it down with her foot.

"Thought you were doing very well in the opera," she went on. "'Course, I'm not an expert in these things. Good to see young people seeking their fortune in the big city, though."

She looked up with a bright, friendly smile.

"I see you've lost a bit of weight, too." Innocence hung from her words like loops of toffee.

"I've been . . . taking exercise," said Agnes.

"Exercise is a fine thing, certainly," said Granny, getting back to her digging. "Though they do say you can have too much of it. When are you going back?"

"I . . . haven't decided."

"Weeelll, it doesn't pay to be always planning.

Don't tie yourself down the whole time, I've always said that. Staying with your ma, are you?"

"Yes," said Agnes.

"Ah? Only Magrat's old cottage is still empty. You'd be doing everyone a favor if you aired it out a bit. You know . . . as long as you're here."

Agnes said nothing. She couldn't think of anything to say.

"Funny ole thing," said Granny, hacking around a particularly troublesome tree root. "I wouldn't tell everyone, but I was only thinking the other day, about when I was younger and called myself Endemonidia . . ."

"You *did*? When?"

Granny rubbed her forehead with her bandaged hand, leaving a clay-red smudge.

"Oh, for about three, four hours," she said. "Some names don't have the stayin' power. Never pick yourself a name you can't scrub the floor in."

She threw her shovel out of the hole. "Give me a hand up, will you?"

Agnes did so. Granny brushed the dirt and leaf mold off her apron and tried to stamp the clay off her boots.

"Time for a cup of tea, eh?" she said. "My, you *are* looking well. It's the fresh air. Too much stuffy air in that Opera House, I thought."

Agnes tried in vain to detect anything in Granny Weatherwax's eyes other than transparent honesty and goodwill.

"Yes. I thought so, too," she said. "Er . . . you've hurt your hand?"

"It'll heal. A lot of things do."

She shouldered her shovel and headed toward the cottage; and then, halfway up the path, turned and looked back.

"This is just me askin', you understand, in a kind neighborly way, takin' an interest sort of thing, wouldn't be human if I didn't—"

Agnes sighed. "Yes?"

". . . you got much to do with your evenin's these days?"

There was just enough rebellion left in Agnes to put a sarcastic edge on her voice. "Oh? Are you offering to teach me something?"

"Teach? No," said Granny. "Ain't got the patience for teaching. But I might let you learn."

"When shall we three meet again?"

"We haven't met *once*, yet."

"O' course we have. I've person'ly known you for at least—"

"I mean we *Three* haven't *Met*. You know . . . officially . . ."

"All right . . . When shall we three meet?"

"We're already here."

"All right. When shall—?"

"Just shut up and get out the marshmallows. Agnes, give Nanny the marshmallows."

"Yes, Granny."

"And mind you don't burn mine."

Granny sat back. It was a clear night, although clouds mounting toward the hub promised snow soon. A few sparks flew up toward the stars. She looked around proudly.

"Isn't this *nice*," she said.

NEW YORK TIMES BESTSELLING AUTHOR
Terry Pratchett
The Discworld® Novels

SNUFF
978-0-06-221886-5
For Sam Vimes, commander of the City Watch, a vacation in the country is anything but relaxing when a dead body turns up.

UNSEEN ACADEMICALS
978-0-06-116172-8
The wizards at Ankh-Morpork's Unseen University must somehow win a football match—*without* using magic.

MAKING MONEY
978-0-06-116165-0
You have to spend money to make money . . . or the other way around.

THUD!
978-0-06-081531-8
It's a game of Trolls and Dwarfs where the player must take both sides to win.

GOING POSTAL
978-0-06-050293-5
Suddenly, condemned arch-swindler Moist von Lipwig found himself with a noose around his neck and dropping through a trapdoor into . . . a *government job?*

MONSTROUS REGIMENT
978-0-06-001316-5
A sharp, stinging, and hilarious send-up of war and all its glory—and the courageous women who fight it!

Don't miss the next book by your favorite author.
Sign up for AuthorTracker by visiting www.AuthorTracker.com

TP 1013

Available wherever books are sold, or call 1-800-331-3761 to order.

NEW YORK TIMES BESTSELLING AUTHOR

Terry Pratchett

The Discworld® Novels

"Discworld takes the classic fantasy universe through its logical, and comic, evolution."

Cleveland Plain Dealer

NIGHT WATCH	978-0-06-000131-7
THE FIFTH ELEPHANT	978-0-06-102040-7
THIEF OF TIME	978-0-06-103132-8
THE TRUTH	978-0-380-81319-8
MEN AT ARMS	978-0-06-223740-8
SOUL MUSIC	978-0-06-223741-5
INTERESTING TIMES	978-0-06-227629-2
MASKERADE	978-0-06-227552-3
FEET OF CLAY	978-0-06-227551-6
HOGFATHER	978-0-06-227628-5
JINGO	978-0-06-105906-3
THE LAST CONTINENT	978-0-06-105907-0
CARPE JUGULUM	978-0-06-102039-1

www.terrypratchettbooks.com

TPA 1013

Don't miss the next book by your favorite author.
Sign up for AuthorTracker by visiting www.AuthorTracker.com

Available wherever books are sold, or call 1-800-331-3761 to order.